PAWS

TO

PROPHECIES

A NOVEL

JJ FRISK

In memory of

AEZ 1976-2021

…and all the rest who could not find the strength to
hold on.

We Love you.

Contents

Prologue by Delux

I was just sitting in my apartment minding my business after DJing an amazing sold-out New Year's Eve party the night before. The snow was coming down hard outside as Ruka, my blind five-year-old Pitbull and I, were staying bundled up with the heat on in our high-rise apartment complex downtown. The phone rang with a woman's voice and police sounds in the background. We were disconnected before I could answer all her questions, and soon a van pulled up under the building. Wait, wait, wait.... No. It all started with a trip to Trinidad and a punch in the face from a supermodel.

I was living in Miami Beach back in the day when it was cool. I was delivering model portfolios to agents who were looking for beautiful people, and I wasn't one of them. My boss, Rob, had a Rottweiler named Terminator who loved to go on walks with me, yet disliked everyone else but Rob and I. From this, Rob knew I loved animals, so one day he asked me if I wanted to take care of a friend's ferrets. We will call this friend Tess. Tess was leaving the United States, to go get married in her home country of South Africa, and she could not take her beloved ferrets with her. Georgie and Porgy were their names, and one of them wanted to bite me.

I kept Georgie and Porgy for two weeks, and they were the worst things I ever had (and I used to have a pet snapping turtle). The one that was always trying to bite me with razor sharp teeth, would hide under the oven while it was on, or squeeze its rat-like body under the back door and escape to the stairs that took you down to the door to the outside world.

My friend Ed offered to take the ferrets from me and put them at his casting office where for sure some model would take them. No model took the ferrets the week Ed was expected to be in Orlando, so he was forced to take the ferrets with him. While in the hotel in

Orlando, the ferrets escaped and were missing for Ed's entire stay. It wasn't until Ed was two hours into his return trip home to Miami, when the hotel called him and said they had found the ferrets. Ed turned around and only received one of them when he got there. The one that likes to bite, bit his way to freedom, but was found, 30 minutes after Ed left, so he turned around, only to return with a new origin story for his furry friends.

A few days went by, and a model walked into Ed's office and saw the ferrets and fell in love. She not only took the ferrets, she took the new story with her, then she took a bunch of photos of them with a film camera. She developed those photos, found the best ones, and then she carried those photos with her to every casting she went to as she left them at home.

I moved away from South Beach, back to Minnesota where I am from, with my new dog, Ruka, that I was randomly gifted after the ferrets were out of my hands. Tess went back to South Africa, but decided not to get married, and she later flew back to Miami looking for more modeling work, and her ferrets. The modeling work was there, but I was not. Her ferrets were gone forever.

Until one day Tess had a casting for a commercial and went to it only to see there was a long line of girls trying to get the same role. She wrote her name on a list and sat against the wall with another model who was holding photographs in her hand.

"Excuse me, but can I see those pictures?"

"Sure," the young model said.

"Nice ferrets."

"Thank you. They are my babies."

"Where did you get them? Who gave them to you?"

"I got them from Ed over at Unique Casting on 17th street."

"You didn't get them from a bald military looking guy?"

"No, Ed gave them to me. He's a big, tall guy, dark hair."

This model then proceeded to tell Tess all about how the ferrets came with this horror story from Orlando, and this casting director guy named Ed. No where in the story was me, the random guy who'd promised some random model who was leaving the country that I would take care of her ferrets. Tess wanted revenge, but I was nowhere to be found.

I was in Minneapolis with my dog planning a trip to Trinidad to DJ a big party at some big thing that was opening on the tiny island. My connections in Miami got me the gig there, so I gave my parents my dog to watch, and I flew to Miami to meet my friends and then go to Trinidad. When I got to Miami, my friend never showed up to pick me up. He never returned my calls when I arrived, or the rest of the day as I looked for a couch to crash on at a friend's house, seeing as he was not picking up.

I was now stuck in Miami. Two days went by of me sleeping on a friend's couch, when she told me her boyfriend was coming back so I had to go. I called my old boss, Rob, and he had our friend Scotty pick me up, who had a room for me. Scotty had a girl in the front seat of his truck when he arrived, so I jumped in the back of the truck bed with my bag, and off we went. We arrived at his 3-bedroom house that he shared with a roommate, who was not this beautiful blonde in the front seat, leaving one bedroom and a couch neither the blonde, nor I, could fit on because we were both six feet tall, and the couch was 4'-11". Her name was Tess and we were both clueless that we had met in the past.

We both seemed like decent people, so we shared the bedroom and both of us slept with our clothes on, sharing stories of my DJ life back home in Minnesota, and her wanting to quit the modeling industry and go to Costa Rica. The next morning, we all had breakfast, Tess went for a coffee and a cigarette, and we decided we would drive down to South Beach and see Rob later. Later, all four of us were walking down the sidewalk as I was trying to use my cellphone to get ahold of my still missing friend who had me fly here for nothing. I was still trying to call my friend when all of a sudden, I got punched in the face by Tess who, reflected her fist off my jaw, into my hand holding my phone, knocking it to the ground, breaking it into pieces.

"You mother fucker!" Tess screamed out, now being held back by both Rob and Scotty.

"You gave away my ferrets, you mother fucker."

We all paused and assessed what was happening. After calming Tess down, we all got a good laugh and thought to ourselves, what are the odds? I spent five days with Tess, hanging out with our mutual friends and I felt I truly experienced what it's like to just let go, and live in the moment. Two months later, Tess completely surprised me by showing up in Minnesota on January 1st at 7pm in a 1977 Dodge Lazydaze mobile home. She showed up, because she heard a rumor I wanted to move back to South Beach. She wanted to drive to Costa Rica, so she decided to be a friend and pick me up and move me before she carried on to Costa Rica in her new, yet very old and beat-up RV. This is that story.

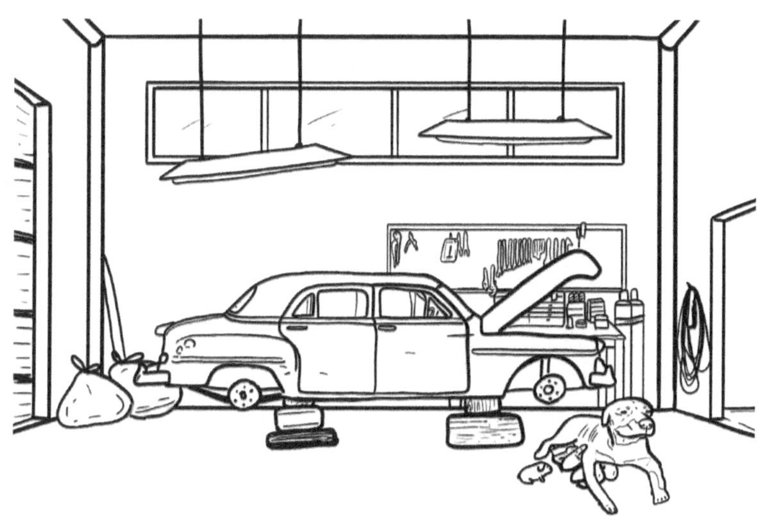

CHAPTER 1

'DOG'

"OK, I must remember, I must remember. What just happened?"

I died.

I was running toward a group of men who were holding guns. I surprised the group with something Senior Chief had made for them. That was the end of them... and me.

"Senior Chief!" I remembered.

He was my old handler.

"Military. I was in the Military," I thought.

Music. Senior Chief loved music.

I sat there behind the darkness of my eyelids, trying to recollect as much of my past life as I could. "The more you can remember, the better your chances are of making wise, or wiser, decisions here," I remembered. I was trying to remember.

Here I was again. I am God, ready to do this world we're all in some service. This creation, although perfect, was full of opinions and perspectives of how some think it's not as perfect as it should be.

Things in this creation feel a little backwards right now, so you can call me 'Dog'. I manifested myself here, because... Well... Some of us need a little help getting through the journey that we all chose to take here, including me.

Lately... I'd been saving people that the world still needs, or I was getting rid of the ones it doesn't. Either way, it was never an easy task. I never did my deeds alone though, I remember that. Some lifetimes, I knew what I was doing. I knew I had a set mission. Other lifetimes, I had no clue, and I had to figure it all out.

This time, it felt like I had to figure it all out. Something felt... different than the last few times I was here. It was a common feeling I remembered having every time I arrived here in a new body with my same old spirit.

Things can feel funny in a body.

I didn't know yet, but my instincts were telling me... I think... Shoot, I forgot. I hate overthinking. Wait, how do I know I overthink? Do I overthink? I don't know... I wondered as I was where I was.

Anyways... What could I remember about Dog? Huh... Not much as I tried to dig deep into my consciousness. "What is life, if we have all the answers anyways, right?" I thought out loud.

Today, I found myself with another set of pups. From the looks of my mom and all these pups around me, I was a Rottweiler. Where was my dad? I can always tell if I can see my dad. I could hardly see... so I tried my nose to see what I could smell... It was too soon to tell. Usually, Dad was around here somewhere when I showed up in a new life form, but this time, it appeared that I was on my own for now.

It was me, my mom, plus eight other pups that treated me like I didn't exist.

"Is this a dream, or is this real?" I thought for a second.

I got a back paw to the face from another pup that threw my head back.

"Yeah, this is real."

As the pups climbed all around me, pushing me out of the way, I realized quickly I was gonna have to fight to get the food I needed from our mom, but I didn't feel like fighting. My belly felt weird for some reason when I tried to move around. I was pushed around every time Momma laid down to rest and give us food. I didn't know how she got any rest with nine of us bouncing all over her.

The door opened to the small room we were being held in and a large man appeared. His energy was dark. He counted us and said something about money, when a little girl appeared from behind him.

"Can I keep one, Daddy?" she asked him, looking up at him with her big brown eyes.

"Go to your room!" he shouted as he pushed her back and closed the door.

Momma had jumped up when the door opened, and the big man showed himself. I noticed her tail didn't wag when he appeared, and she was a bit apprehensive when he left. I've been a dog a few hundred times now. I may be a puppy, but I remember this behavior in humans.

From how it felt when the Big Man and the Little Girl came into the room, my mission had something to do with these two, I was guessing.

Momma laid back down in the farthest corner, looking toward the door that big man came out of. All my siblings rushed for a nipple. The only one left, was the one that didn't work. Instead of biting and clawing at it like the rest did, I just held my momma with my head and body and ate when someone was finished.

Days went by rather quickly in that closed-up room full of the family's dirty clothes. Next thing you know, we were all too big to be in the small room together. We were moved to a bigger room where the adults parked their cars, and the little girl had her toys she played with outside. It smelled like cars in that room, even though there was a big door that opened up to let in the hot humid air from outside. One car never moved and was held up in the air with metal stands. It was always cooler under that broken down car I felt.

People began to come by and look at us puppies. Big Man would instantly turn friendly when people were around.

Another big man came over with his son and my dad on a leash. Mom went crazy when she saw him. You could tell she missed my dad. Dad went crazy when he saw her, too, and all of us. Dad was jumping and pulling on the leash trying to get close to us. My dad was a big guy. Even standing next to the big men and this little boy, my dad was huge.

"Gimme the first born," the owner of my dad said.

The little boy was handed the biggest of us all.

"What about that one?" the big guy asked pointing at me.

"He's got a hole in his belly. Something's wrong with that one," Big Man said.

The little boy and the big guy left with my dad and a puppy.

"Don't trust any man!" my dad barked out to me, looking directly into my eyes, while being pulled away by the big guy.

I sat there in silence watching my dad walk away barking that he missed my mom and he would find a way for them to be together again.

In the next days, more random people began showing up at the house looking for puppies. One at a time, they would look at all of us. They would try to pick some of us up if we allowed it. Some pups bonded with the people that chose them right away, and other pups were just taken because they were liked. The strangers would give Big Man money and leave with one of my brothers or sisters before I could even get to know them.

Life was happening quick for all of us. What was going to happen to me?

The pups that were left continued to step on me and push me away when I tried to eat. Even though there were now more free nipples that worked, my siblings continued to push me away, mumbling words I could not understand.

Momma would always keep one nipple of food for me. When the rest of the pups were asleep, she would let me in, and I would get my fill of milk. Momma licked my head while I ate and tell me I was something special, that I was different then all her other pups.

One morning, the little girl opened the door to our room to sneak in and pet us all. Her touch was soft like my mother's tongue, but I didn't feel the thing I usually feel when I found my mission bond. I was confused by this non-attachment I was feeling with the world around me.

The little girl heard Big Man coming. She put the pups down and ran out of the room as fast as she could. I could see she was living in fear. This was not good, I noticed, especially for a lonely little girl. I never saw her with other kids. She didn't seem to have any friends, only her dolls and the stuffed animals she played with.

One by one, as the pups went away in exchange for money, nobody picked me because of the hole in my belly. Destiny of staying with this little girl was happening I thought.

Eventually the little girl did more than just pet my head, she picked me up for the first time. She always picked up the others but never me. Especially the biggest of us all, but he went first with the little boy with dark energy. Both the little girl and momma were sad every time one of us left with a stranger. Big Man was in control, and everyone knew it. He was always telling the little girl to go away when she came into the room with us.

Soon, all the pups were gone and it came down to just me. All my siblings were picked, and the phone stopped ringing of potential people who had found Big Man's advertisement of dogs for sale. Big Man lightened up a little with the help of his wife, nagging him to let the little girl get close to me because nobody was gonna buy me with my hole.

They would let the little girl and I play together with her dolls, but it didn't last long. The dolls had a smell to them so strange that I couldn't resist. I had to taste one and when I did, I tore the head off accidentally, and the little girl began to cry.

I felt the power of Big Man when he got home that night. He was mad I was not sold yet. He was mad he didn't have enough money to fix his car. He was mad the little girl got close with me and wanted to keep me when he didn't. Not to mention, he was mad that I kept peeing in the house. Nobody took me outside to pee, so I peed when and where I had to. My peeing made Big Man angry and after that, he beat me, and I was forever scared to pee in the house again, but it kept happening. I couldn't control my pee urges even if I tried.

Everyone in that house lived on eggshells, including me. Was Big Man my mission? Was I here to be the best dog I could be for him? Did he need saving like some of the rest of the lives I lived?

I could see his flaws, but he was so comfortable in his savage ways I didn't know where to start. I felt he knew no other way than to be the way he was. There was a saying I remembered: you can't teach an old dog, a new trick. Big Man was definitely an "old dog."

I tried not to pee in the house, but it would just come out at times when I didn't expect it. The little girl would try to hide it for me, or even clean it up, but she was young, and her attempts only made the situation worse. With the smell of my festering pee in the carpets and rugs, Big Man was bound to smell it sooner or later.

"It smells like piss down here," Big Man said, kicking the toys of the little girl around the room.

While kicking her toys, he found an old pile of my poo behind her doll house. The little girl called it the wood pile, but that was not wood. I mean, there might have been a couple wood chips in that, "wood pile," but it was poo.

Big man shoved my face in it. Then he dragged me across the floor to where I had peed. The floor was still wet from pee, and I had poo in my face, so when he smeared my face into the pee, he smeared poo across more of the floor making him even more angry.

His grip was hard and tight around my neck, pinching my skin. I peed again while he held me down. I was shocked he was treating me like that. He had no idea, I might have been a dog, but I had a bigger spirit inside of me.

His actions made me hate him, and I decided I would do whatever was in my power to save this little girl from the outbursts caused by himself. Even if I had to bite him, I would.

While Big Man worked during the day, I studied the little girl's every move. I wanted to learn everything I could about her. So far, she hated her bare feet on the grass or getting them wet. She hated every vegetable except green beans and corn, and at six years of age, she was addicted to sugar and allergic to almost everything around her.

Her neighbor would come over. It was the bad energy kid who took the first-born pup. He was a little shit of a boy, holding the same dark energy as Big Man. I noticed the little boy would like to have his way with the little girl when they were alone. He treated her like she was always doing something wrong, so she was afraid to tell anyone what was happening to her. The little boy was sweet around her parents, but a devil behind closed doors. I would try to bite this little kid every chance I got but I always failed for he was too quick for me, pushing me away.

Big Man and his wife called me the Lil Fucker, but I knew bad energy when I felt it, and these guys were bad. Big man liked my attitude, but he still treated me like shit, and wanted to beat every mistake I made, out of me.

I knew I had to wait until I was bigger to bite Big Man, but nothing held me back from biting this little boy.

Now with my siblings all gone, I get all of mom's milk if she lets me, and there was plenty of water to drink between the toilet and the shower floor that was in the garage.

I heard a strange cry and walked over to the bathroom. I caught the neighbor boy outside the door with the little girl inside. He had walked in on her. "Accidentally" he said, but he didn't leave her alone when she asked him to leave. He touched her. She asked him to stop, but he touched her again.

Something took control of me, and I ran into the bathroom. By the time I got there, it was too late. He had made her legs bleed.

"Just put a Band-Aid on it," he told her, pulling up his shorts.

I couldn't figure out how he made her bleed. The smell in the room was off. Something triggered me and I went for his leg. I went behind him and bit him in the back of his skinny leg. My puppy teeth tore his flesh wide open, and I could instantly taste and smell his blood. The boy screamed. He tried to swing at me, but I moved away just in time.

"A Band-Aid ain't gonna fix that one, kid," I told him as he ran home crying.

Big Man beat me when he came home. His wife told him what I had done, and he hit me in front of the little girl. Then Big Man left and went down the street to check on the little boy. When he came back, he beat me again.

"Put another add in the paper. He's gotta go. He bites people, yet he's the biggest pussy, pissing on himself scared all the time," Big Man yelled out to his wife, making the little girl cry.

I wanted to bite Big Man, but he was big. I could smell my dad on him when he returned to beat me the second time. The neighborhood bully lived with my dad. How do I get this little girl out of this situation? I thought.

Three days passed. I peed again in the house that morning. I got beat, when a strange truck pulled into our driveway. I wasn't tall enough to see out of the window, but whoever it was, made my mom go nuts. She wanted to bust through the fence and fuck shit up. This alerted my dad who was over at his house barking up a storm. It all had me asking, "What was going on over here?" My parents never barked like this.

Two truck doors shut outside. I could hear some muttered voices between my mom's inhales before she went back to her insane barking.

The little girl came and grabbed me. "I love you, Feisty," she said holding me tight. Not as tight as Big Man would when he was mad, but the same kind of uncomfortable tightness. The little girl's hugs were almost too much for me at times.

Big Man suddenly burst into the room and grabbed me away from her, sending her into tears.

"Come on, you little fuck. You cost me a whole paycheck with that bite. You're outta here."

"Daddy, no!" she yelled back looking into my eyes before he turned me away from her, squeezing me in his arms.

This made me pee.

"Ah, you little shit," Big Man said squeezing me tighter before he brought me outside.

He brought me out the front door. I never go out the front door. I could see my mom behind the fence, off to the side of the house. She was angry, yelling, not to take her boy, not to take her last child.

I got nervous and I started to pee again as Big Man walked me out to the strangers. I peed on his arm and his legs with the long strides he takes.

"Ah, little fucker," he laughed his fake people laugh. He's a bit nervous, this one," Big Man said.

"Yeah, around you, asshole," I said, but nobody was listening. Not even Mom.

"Hi, little guy," this random guy with tattoos said to me.

I lifted my leg and pee'd some more as Big Man put me down on the ground.

"Please don't beat me," my eyes said, but all he saw was me peeing on myself.

I was embarrassed as I laid there on the ground, not sure if I should stand up. I was hoping my mom would jump the fence and help me figure this out, but she was helpless and weak after her puppies, and Big Man cutting back on her food, to feed us.

"We have to see if our Pit likes him. She can be a bit of a bitch dog around Rottweilers. She's not gonna jump the fence, is she?" the guy asked Big Man, pointing towards my mom.

"No, she's fine," he replied.
"Daddy," the little girl said as she opened the front door trying to hold back her tears.

I looked at my sad, little friend. I looked at this random guy and his girlfriend outside, who were now holding the leash of a muscle-faced monster of a dog they took out of the back of the truck. My mom went nuts behind her fence when this pit bull showed up.

"I'm here on business, ma'am, don't mind us," the muscled-out pit bull shouted out.

I looked this monster in her eyes as she sniffed the ground pulling herself towards me. Her eyes were different. She was coming right towards me. Time slowed down as she got closer and closer.
The sound of my dad's barking in the distance, and my mom yelling behind me faded away. All I could hear was this monster's nose sniffing the ground.

"There you are," she said, sniffing me. "Remember me?"

I peed again.

"What the heck, kid?" she said to me, pulling back.

"I hate Rottweilers, and right now you just made a very bad first impression," she said.

"If you could understand me, he's not the one, but I approve. We'll have to toughen him up though... a lot!" she told the couple who called themselves "Babe."

"I'm tough. I bit a kid in the leg," I told her.

"You're tough for responding to me with accountability, but not for biting someone. Anyone can do that."

"I did it to save that little girl."

"Well, we're here to save you," she told me.

"But I have to save this little girl here."

"It sounds like you did that already by biting someone in the leg as you said you did."

"Ahh sweet," the tattooed guy said. "Ruka's sitting with him, verses trying to rip him apart."

"You were gonna rip me apart?" I asked the monster as I peed a little more watching the Babe Guy walking towards me.

"I bite things too," she told me.

"My name's Ruka," the pit bull said to me. "Welcome to the family, kid."

"Don't worry little guy, you're gonna be ok," the Babe Guy said, picking me up.

This couple handed Big Man a few twenties then put me into the front seat of their pickup truck, while tying Ruka up in the back.

"Here we go, little guy," the Babe Guy said, starting the truck up, and we drove away as I sat on the lady's lap.

Who are these people that call themselves Babe, and where are they taking me? I wanted to fight back but I cowered down and kept my head low. The man driving had an energy about him I was unsure of so I didn't make eye contact. The woman, held me soft but I was unsure of her as well. I thought to myself, should I bite my way out of this?

TOE-JAM

CHAPTER 2

TOE JAM BACK LOT

The Babes and Ruka took me. Paid for me actually. He calls her Babe, and she calls him Babe.

As we pulled away from my house, the sound of my mom's barks faded away over the sound of the engine that was propelling me into an unknown future.

"Who are these people?" I wondered as we drove away. "Why am I being taken away from my mission of helping that little girl? Did I already help her?"

I wondered if I ever wondered these things before when I was reincarnated back into this mysterious game of life. All these questions... I usually remembered so much more. Did all my lives start out this way? I swear, I remembered it being easier than this. "Why can't I remember more?"

I felt there was something blocking me as I looked up at the woman holding me.

"What should we call him?" she asked looking down at me, then up out the window.

"Tess, you want ice cream? We should stop for ice cream. You like ice cream?" Babe asked, looking down at me.

"Delux! Watch the road!" the woman yelled as we swerved a bit.

During the long drive out of the country, before we got to the city, the Babes decided to name me Buddha. They liked my calmness. But I was scared not calm.

Tess, was the lady's name. She held me and was petting me on my head as the other Babe, Delux, drove us. Her hands were so soft like the little girl's hands.

When Delux Babe touched me, I could feel the heaviness of his hand, yet he was soft, and his touch distracted me from thinking about back home. His touch was the opposite of how Big Man touched me, but I still felt scared in their presence, and there was no instant bond like I saw with my siblings with other humans or how I thought it should be.

I felt we were now very far away from where my little friend was. I hope she stayed safe.

The truck stopped somewhere with a lot of cars and people walking around us.

"Buddha, we'll be right back. You wait here," they told me rolling the windows down a bit and leaving me inside the truck.

"You too, Ruka. Stay put and keep an eye on Buddha here," they tell her outside in the back.

The Babes' smell disappeared into the people around us, and when they came back a bit later, they had bags of stuff that smelled dangerous. In my eight weeks with Big Man, I had learned this smell. Although it smells delicious, it leads to beatings if I get too close, so I moved to the floor by Tess Babe's feet. It was the farthest I could go.

"He seems so scared," Delux Babe said.

"It's okay, Buddha, you're going to be safe with us," Tess said touching my head.

"Yeah, buddy. We're gonna make you into a big strong dog," Delux said, looking into my eyes with a smile.

"Trust no man," my dad's voice rang out in my head.

"We need you to be strong and brave, because you're gonna protect us while we drive to Costa Rica," Tess said to me scratching the top of my head.

The truck came to a stop a bit later.

"Is this Costa Rica?" I wondered.

Tess Babe got out of the truck and unlocked a big metal gate and rolled it back to open it up. Then Delux drove us into a big lot that was surrounded by twelve-foot-high walls, and a giant, metal gate.

"I'll just put the key back where I found it, and nobody will ever know we borrowed the truck, eh Buddha?" Delux said bending down and hiding the key in the floor while petting my head.

"Welcome home, my boy," he said to me, smiling.

Tess came and took me out of the truck while Delux brought the bags of deliciously dangerous smells into a large building.

"You need to go potty?" Tess asked me, putting me down on the ground.

I froze. As soon as my paws touched the rocky surface, I could feel an energy run into me up from the ground. It was daytime, but this place seemed dark, and it scared me. The sun was out heating up this half parking lot, half dead grass zone, outside of a warehouse building, with a large garage door. I only saw this kind of place on a TV crime show. It was bright out, but I could feel a darkness here as I looked around. The Babes obviously didn't feel it. Neither did Ruka, or she just didn't care.

Delux came back and let Ruka out of the back of the truck and she walked right to me.

"Welcome home, kid. This place is temporary so don't get too attached to it," she said sniffing around and taking a pee not too far from me.

"Ruka, this place scares me," I told her as I laid close to the ground and looked around me.

There was an old doghouse in the corner with a large rope hanging from the only tree in the lot. Delux picked me up and took me over to that area. Seeing the rope in the tree freaked me out. I wiggled my way out of his hands, and when I hit the ground, I ran back to the truck to hide under it.

"What's up, kid?" Ruka asked me.

"I feel something over there in that corner, stronger than over here. I feel it into my bones like something is there and it wants to hurt me. Something with that rope in the tree."

"Congratulations, kid. You can feel stuff. It's normal for dogs. That weird feeling is everywhere, you'll find out. Some places and people are stronger than others, but it's all with a purpose. As a dog, you need to control and navigate those feelings. Do you remember any of them?" Ruka asked me, coming under the truck with me.

"I'm not sure what I can remember. Any memory I have fades the second it comes to me," I told Ruka.

"Wow, look at Ruka, she's like an instant momma for him. That's so cute," Tess told Delux.

My leg lifted itself into the air as Ruka got close to me.

"What's up with your leg?" Ruka asked me.

"I feel something in my belly. It makes my pee come out more than average my mom would tell me. Moving my leg helps with the pressure when I lay down but when my leg comes down, pee comes out. What's up with your eyes?" I asked her, looking into the cloudy marbles in her face.

"So you're like a pee pump, and your leg is the lever," she said laughing to herself. "I am blind, kid. I can't see a thing, but I know where you are," she said looking right at me.

Delux came down to grab me, and his hands coming at me reminded me of Big Man, and I pee'd all over myself again.

"Ahh, Buddha, it's ok buddy, come here," Delux said compassionately, grabbing a hold of me as soft as I think he could. "Let's clean you up, buddy."

I squirmed around trying to get out of Delux's grip, but I could feel his hold on me only got tighter, so I relaxed. "How could Ruka see my leg lift if she's blind?" I wondered as I was carried away.

Delux set me down to turn on the hose and as the water came out, so was I. I ran away from the water before it had a chance to hit the ground. Big Man used to push me under water when he cleaned the pee off me. I wanted nothing to do with water, even if it came from Delux's soft hands.

This place inside the tall fence was a big open space. The scary old doghouse was in the far corner, with old rusty cars in the other. There was a small patch of grass and weeds trying to survive between both decrepit areas, both were scary. The rest of the place was an open concrete lot with a few large, bus style RV's parked side to side. In the corner that Delux had taken me to, was the water hose, and in front of me in the other corner, the direction where I was attempting my escape, was an old, smaller RV that looked like it had an explosion happened to it. I ran under that.

"Why was I running?" I thought to myself.

Before I could make another thought, Tess grabbed me by the back of my neck and softly pulled me from under the RV.

"Buddha, you're covered in pee, and now dirt. We have to clean you up, buddy," she said walking me over to the hose again.

"Babe, I'll hold him," she said holding me out in her arms while I was looking deep into Delux's eyes holding a water hose.

"You're holding him like Lion King."

"He's full of piss, you wanna hold him?"

"I already got the hose," Delux said, softy misting Tess with his finger over the hose making her squirm around.

I could feel Delux's energy. He was about love and kindness, but he was also holding a water hose. I could tell Delux had a bit of a dark side as he washed me softly while Tess held me. Something said not to trust him, or her, or both.

They had to wet my face because I peed on it twice now. They washed it nicely, but I felt something strange from them. I didn't feel like I was drowning while under the hose. Water didn't go into my ears. They both rubbed me down softly and then took turns drying me in the biggest, softest towel which was the best part.

Big Man used to just let me drip dry in the corner after spraying me with the hose for several minutes. These two Babes were treating me nice considering I'd peed on them too.

"How you doing kid?" Ruka asked me after Delux put me down and went inside the warehouse.

"I'm scared," I told her as I lay down outside.

"Scared of what? There's nothing to be afraid of here. Delux and Tess are good souls, and they only have the best intentions for us."

"This place feels scary."

"I felt scared when we first arrived here, too, but you'll learn, the world itself can be a scary place if you choose to look at it that way. Besides the crackheads outside the fence, there's nothing to worry about once we're inside here," Ruka said looking around the lot.

"And when people see us together outside these gates... They're going to go the other way, so there's nothing to fear."

"How did your eyes get like that?" I asked looking at them.

"Over time, I lost my vision, and my eyes are slowly fading away, but I can still see."

"How do you see if you're blind?"
"I use my other senses. As long as things don't move around too much, I remember where they are."

"It's a big world out here no"? I ask looking around the giant lot we had all to ourselves.

"Yes, but Delux sees for me, and he keeps me safe and happy. He'll do the same for you if you let him."

"But he took me away from a little girl who needs my help. She's home alone and is being abused by an older boy. These Babes seem fine so I must help her."

"What do you mean, he is abusing her?"

I didn't want to say. The memories of it were horrible. Hearing her tiny little voice scream for him to stop when he didn't. Watching his lack of care after he hurt her and made her bleed.

"He forced himself on her and made her bleed. Then a force inside me drove me to bite him."

"Maybe that was your mission and you completed it. After that bite, I'm sure that little monster of a kid will think twice next time."

"Maybe... But I miss her. And my mom."

"That's natural, kid. Nothing lasts forever in this life. The quicker you learn that, the happier you'll be for all those around you in the present moment."

"That sounds like something my mom would say."

"I'm not a fan of Rottweilers, but your mom sounds like she is wise. I too was taken from my mom. I was able to see her often, but not as much as I liked. And life, my friend... Life is full of many missions with ups and downs. Yours, are just beginning."

"Who wants some food?" Delux yelled from the warehouse.

"Oh, dinner time is here, you'll want to come for this," Ruka tells me running into the warehouse. "I bet it's gonna be great, let's go!"

I sat there thinking about what Ruka had said. My mission with the little girl did not feel over, but maybe it was. How many missions would I have? I remembered just having one at a time with every lifetime I manifested in, but at this point, I didn't know.

"You have to believe." My mom's voice came strongly into my head. "Now go eat. I love you," she said fading away.

I ran out from the under the RV and into the large warehouse door where the smell of food filled my nose.

"Holy shit, he's coming in hot," Delux said laughing at my entrance.

The inside of this building was wide open with things of all sorts spread out everywhere. There was a truck from the 1940's being worked on, a mint condition Corvette from the 1980's parked there, and a boat that sat on a trailer. There was just as much graffiti inside the place, as the outside. Every painting sprayed on a wall was beautiful and detailed. There was a large, raised music stage, and a music carpet on the ground, full of instruments and wires.

I could smell the smell of a Rottweiler on this fake green plastic grass that made up the area of drums, guitars, and speakers, but the other Rottweiler was nowhere to be found.

Before I could observe any more, a chill came up my spine and I forced myself to run for cover. I didn't know where to go. There were so many things everywhere. I could feel a presence of something coming over me, and it freaked me out. The food enticed me, but I was instantly afraid for my life. I peed a little as I ran under a couch that was next to a pool table.

Tess's arm reached under the couch and grabbed ahold of me, gently pulling me out. I peed some more.

"Ahh, Buddha, come here. It's okay. You don't have to be so scared," Tess said, picking me up.

"I wonder why he is such a little scaredy cat?" Delux asked, roughly rubbing the top of my head. "You are so freaking cute," he added looking into my eyes.

"Maybe put him in front of his food, and he'll see we're here to love him," Delux told Tess.

She brought me over to my very own bowl of food. I never got food in a bowl before. It was always just thrown on the floor, and I had to find all the tiny pieces before my starving mother did. This food looked and smelled delicious.

"Dig in, Buddha," Ruka told me between chewing and swallowing her own food from her own bowl.

"It's ok, Buddha, eat your food," Tess said softly.

I tasted it. The food was delicious. I got food all over my face while I spun in circles around my bowl eating every tiny scrap. My stubby tail went side to side faster and faster with every bite I took in. It felt so tasty to lick my lips after I was done and still taste the smells that I used to get hit over by Big Man if I got too close.

I remembered a time when Big Man hit me because I got a little too curious to what he was eating. Tonight, I had my very own bowl. I finished eating and went over to the couch, where Ruka was laying, licking her paws.

"How was your food kid?" she asked me.

"It was great. Do you always get food like that?"

"Pretty much. I think tonight was a little extra because you're here now, but Delux treats me good all the time, and Tess, she's nice."

"Now what do we do?"

"We chill. Take a look around if you like. Go familiarize yourself with the place because this is gonna be your home for a bit."

"For a bit? Then what?"

"The Babes are fixing that RV outside, to drive it to Costa Rica."
"This isn't Costa Rica?"

"No. This is Overtown. One of the toughest places in Miami. This is where you're going to learn what it takes to be a dog, that can protect us on the trip to Costa Rica."

I sniffed around the floor finding smells that took me to every corner inside the warehouse. I noticed I lost my fears after having a full belly of food, so I explored the warehouse. Every corner felt different. One corner had a scary looking bathroom that seemed out of order because of its condition. The toilet was cracked. There was a hole in the ceiling above the sink, and there was red candle wax on the floor under the hole, looking like blood has dripped out of it. I got outta there quick.

The other far corner had a makeshift bedroom tucked away in it. There were fake wall panels surrounding a bunk bed and a small table. A few pieces of clothes were on the floor from someone who smelled like they live here but hadn't been there in a while. There was a giant clown face painted on the wall with a giant silver foam ball between the makeshift bedroom and the scary bathroom.

In the middle of the warehouse against the wall, was the large, raised sound stage that was next to a useable bathroom covered in everything small, made in the early 1990's. The shower was on one side of a wall, with the toilet and sink on the other. A tall row of lockers made up a privacy wall blocking the bathroom from the rest of the warehouse.

I thought I remembered the 90's. I was a service dog in the military during a different lifetime of mine, I think. I belonged to some guy named Chief or Senior, I didn't remember.

I looked at a toy solider that was glued to the wall, and I had a flashback. I was a small German Shepard working with a bunch of guys who called themselves crazy, and everyone else called them SEALs. I remember being in the jungle, looking for the worst kind of human this world can produce, then blowing them up on command. I was successful, but I was killed in action a lot. They made a statue out of me, I think.

I then reincarnated as another service dog, only to be put down early because my "team" memories didn't leave me, and I bit too many people when I was supposed to be kind and friendly. I had trauma from past creations. Some say to be like God, is to recognize our mistakes, and to fix them. I'm not god, I'm a dog, I told myself feeling strange as I said it.

Some souls repeat cycles, I shred them to pieces, or blow them up.

"What am I doing here with these hippies and that piece of shit RV outside?"

I could hear the Babes playing pool. Still looking at the toy soldier on the wall, I remembered my old, team guys would always play pool, and the sounds of the balls cracking against each other, brought me right back to those days.

Why was I remembering those old military days? What did I need to remember about them? I wondered. Maybe it was just an old toy I was giving too much attention to I thought as I walked out of the bathroom.

"Relax, Delux. You're not in the military anymore," Tess said after he hit a ball intensely.

I ran over to the pool table ready to see my old buddies. Old memories filled my empty, wondering mind, only to quickly vanish as I approached the pool table. I made my way around a chair that was designed to dry hair, only to see the Babes, and not Senior Chief with his crew of misfits.

Usually when an old memory thing happens, that old memory triggers my new purpose in this life. What is my purpose? What is my purpose? I tried to focus.

"I said, you're not in the military anymore. Stop being so perfect," Tess repeated.

"You beat me so many times, it's my turn now," Delux told Tess.

I could see Delux Babe's eyes and head just over the edge of the pool table looking intensely at a shot. He hit a ball, and made it into the pocket.

"That's another game. One more and we're tied."

Tess took out her knife, and notched part of a broken pool cue. "Na... two more and you tied me."

"What? You're up by two?"

"Yep."

Tess watched Delux walk around the table pulling the balls out of the pockets, while Ruka laid on the floor licking her paws.

From the looks of it, the Babes and Ruka had things figured out. They had a huge warehouse full of cars, fake bedrooms, a boat, and a pool table. Not to mention a shark cage, two band stages, and a tool shop... Oh, and the old RV parked outside with the walls ripped off.

I walked over to the entrance of the warehouse and laid down thinking about my current situation. The Babes continued to play a few more games of pool while my food kicked in and sent me into a nap. I awoke with Ruka sniffing me.

"It's time to go, kid, follow me," Ruka told me as I woke up from a dream of being back in the jungle with Senior Chief. I could see him and his team, but none of their faces.

"Buddha," Tess said from behind me, putting her soft hands on my head, bringing be back to my reality. "It's time for bed, buddy," she said picking me up and then putting me back down.

Ruka and the Babes walked outside the warehouse and shut the door. I was confused. There were two bedrooms inside the warehouse, why were we all going outside?

Ruka jumped into the old RV with missing walls and windows that was parked outside.

"Up here, Buddha," Ruka told me from inside the RV.

I was scared outside in the big open lot. I could feel a sense of evil or darkness in the calm night air around us. The feeling of fear took over my entire body. It was hard to control. Even when I tried taking control of my emotions, I could still feel a presence of something unknown around us. Even though the Babes were behind me, and I seemed safe, I made a run for it.

I thought about going under the RV where I know it was safe, but it was dark under there now. I decided at the last minute to jump into the RV where Ruka was, but my legs didn't have the muscle or the coordination to help me succeed, and I smashed chest-first into the doorstep, falling backwards onto my bum.

"Almost, little guy," Delux said, picking me up.

I could feel something in his hands. It was a feeling I was unsure of. I peed.

"Woah, dude. What the heck? There's no need to be scared and pee, I was just gonna put you in the RV."

My pee landed on the inside step of the RV. It was a lot.

"Maybe take him out to the grass first and see if he pees again," Tess said.

"Ruka!" Delux called out while carrying me over to the part of the warehouse lot I didn't like.

Ruka jumped out of the RV and followed us.

"Buddha, now is the time for your last pee or poo break before bed. If you gotta go, go now ok," Ruka said.

I was eight weeks old, I knew when it was time to pee and poo I thought. I just didn't want to do it here, where the energy or something was weird.

While Ruka peed, I stood there for a second, then ran back to the RV and went under it.

"I guess you don't have to go," Ruka said, coming back and jumping into the RV. "We sleep inside, kid," Ruka said, looking down out the door. "There's no peeing or pooping inside here though, got it?" she told me backing up.

Delux called out to me a few times, but I was too scared to come out from under the RV, so he had to crouch down and pull me out.

"Buddha, what's your deal? It's ok, you're safe here," Delux said while pulling me out.

I peed again. On myself... again...

"Buddha, you are, a little pisser," Delux said.

"Tess, can you help me wash him again?"

"Well, at least he won't have to go through the night," she noted.

I got a light bath, and a nice towel-off session with Tess's soft hands behind an even softer towel. I should pee on myself all the time, I thought. I liked this towel thing.

I was carried over and placed inside the RV on the top step. It was messy inside. Were they building this thing, or destroying it? I wondered too sacred to ask.

Ruka had her spot already in the middle. There was a large pillow for her that fit perfectly between the two front seats on the floor.

The front of the RV was the only thing clean and organized. The back of the RV was all torn apart. If I got too close to a hole in the back floor, I would for sure fall out, so I stayed up front and tried to fit myself onto Ruka's pillow with her.

"Welcome to your new home, kid, but this is my spot. You will need to find your own spot somewhere else."

"Where should I go?"

"You're small now, but you're going to grow into a big dog, so pick your spot wisely. May I suggest the floor, because that's the only place you're going to fit later in life."

"Is this RV going to be our home?" I asked.

"Yep, so get comfy."

"It's so small," I said looking around.

"Says the smallest thing in here," Ruka said getting comfy on her pillow.

The Babes went up top above the front seats. There was a human-size bed up there that they both got into after petting us on our heads.

After looking around the RV, I decided on the driver's seat. I crawled on top of Ruka to reach the top of it.

"Hey, kid. I'm not a step."

"Sorry, Ruka. I'm just trying to get up here. Here we go." I struggled. I had never been in a driver's seat before. I liked the idea of the steering wheel next to me. It made me feel safe.

"Good night, doggies," the Babes told us, as they shut off the last remaining light for them to see.

All was silent.

After the sound of Ruka taking a deep breath and exhaling out, and the Babes settling into each other in the top bunk, the stillness of the night took over. Even though we were close to the city, the night was quiet with only the sound of the occasional mosquito coming under your ear. With no windows in the back, mosquitoes were to be expected.

"Ruka, what is this thing?"

"What thing?"

"This open box we're in."

"This is the RV. It's your new home, Buddha. You'll need to learn how and when to protect this thing and us, from anything not like us."

"Why me?"

"Because I can't see, and you were an ad in a paper."

"What?"

"Because I cannot see the world around us, you were chosen. The Babes were about to buy some other dog from a store when some little girl walked in and said she wanted what Delux was holding. He gave the little girl the puppy, and then we went to your mom's house, and found you instead. You were not wanted by your people, and I didn't want to kill you when we arrived so it's probably destiny. I absolutely hate Rottweilers, so you're welcome."

I didn't know what to say.

"It seemed like your first eight weeks at that place were tough."

"Why do you say that?" I wondered as I had flashbacks of playing with my little friend and her dolls.

"I could tell by how you were glued to the ground when we first met you."

"Why do you hate Rottweilers so much?"

"I'm a Pitt Bull. We don't need a reason. But for the record, you guys have a smell to you I don't like. It drives me nuts."

"How did you end up here with the Babes?"

"I've been with Delux for years now. He rescued me from an abusive man like you, here in Florida. We stayed here in Miami a bit, then left for Minnesota where I was introduced to snow, which is terrible by the way," Ruka said licking her paw. "Then after some time in Minnesota, one night Tess showed up with this RV."

"Why?"

"She wants to drive to Costa Rica and on her way, she came to surprise Delux, and she took us back to Miami, but Delux and her fell in love on the way down, so now they're together fixing this RV, to drive to Costa Rica."

"Do they know each other well?"

"No. Not really... They..."

Ruka's story made me fall asleep. I started dreaming about my mom before awakening to the sunlight coming into the back of the windowless RV. I had to pee.

"Ruka, I gotta pee," I said getting off the front seat landing on her head. " Sorry about that. Hey, I gotta pee. I gotta pee. How do I get out of this box?" I said spinning in circles trying to hold it in.

"You gotta make some noise and wake up the Babes, but I think they're already awake."

I looked up to where I saw them tuck themselves away last night, and they were both looking down at me.

"Good day, Buddha!" Tess said to me smiling.

"It looks like he has to pee," Delux said.

"We should let him out," Tess said while leaning down out of the bed to open the side door.

I couldn't make it up into the RV, but I was sure I could jump out of it. I went for it, only to quickly realize I was very top heavy, and I landed on my face then did a summersault. "I meant to do that," I said while taking two steps forward and bending my hips down to let out my pee.

"Wow, he really had to go. Ruka, outside," Delux said.

Ruka got up and jumped out the RV as the Babes jumped down out of bed.

"You will need to learn to pee over here kid. We don't pee where we live, ok?"

"I really had to go."

"It's because you didn't go last night, you just pee'd on yourself," Ruka said walking over to the grassy part of the lot.

I was still peeing on the concrete by the front door. The sun felt warm on my back for 7am.

The Babes got out of the RV and went into the warehouse to do their morning business and start breakfast. Something about this warehouse creeped me out, even in the morning.

Is this what missing mom feels like? I wondered. I'd never felt more lost in such a big open space. Actually, now that I thought about it, I'd never been in a big open space…

Delux Babe grabbed me by my sides and lifted me into the air with ease.

"Buddha. You had to go pee-pee, huh buddy? We don't pee here, we pee over here," Delux said carrying me towards Ruka. "You did drink a lot of water last night," he tells me holding me in one hand while scratching my head with the other, looking into my eyes. "Do you gotta go caca?" he asked me, softly putting me down after walking me out to the rocky grass.

I looked around. No matter what I saw, nothing felt right out here.

"Buddha, this is where you poop," Ruka tells me. "It's okay. There is nothing to be afraid of."

"How'd it go?" Tess asked.

"He's scared shitless. I put him down out there, and he just runs back under the RV the second you put him down. I don't get it. I've never seen a puppy act like this. I thought they would be more playful."

The sun was hot out there on my back, and thinking about caca as Delux called it, I wasn't feeling it. I was fine. Ruka sniffed me out from under the RV.

"Come on, let's go inside, they'll feed us again, and you will probably want to poo after that."

The thought of food again overruled everything, so I followed Ruka inside the warehouse. Ruka laid down in the middle of the room and began licking her paws.

"You love to have clean feet, don't you?" I asked her.

"Yes, and actually, there's something about the flavor of the ground in your mouth before a bowl of food. The flavors go well together. You should try it."

I laid down and tried to lick my paws. I'd never tried to lick my paws before. I started with the front paws and had no issues. Ruka was right. My paws were tasty.

"Ruka. Are our paws the same? Do they taste the same? Can I taste yours?"

"You can lick my back paw here," Ruka said stretching out her leg to me.

I crawled closer to her paw. Her paws smelled good. So good, I licked the one she had extended.

"Ah cute. Babe, come look at the dogs," Tess said spying on us.
"Buddha, I can feel your fear. You can relax here, there's nothing to be afraid of," Ruka told me after I heard the sound of Tess's voice.

"I feel weird inside, Ruka. My belly has a feeling in it, and it makes me irritated."

"It's probably you just missing your mom and your old life, and that's normal. This is something that all dogs go through."

"They say I have a hole in my belly."

"A hole? Let me see."

Ruka came over and sniffed my stomach.

"Ugh, you smell so weird for a dog," Ruka said sniffing. "I don't sense anything wrong, but I'm no doctor."

I wanted to understand. My belly rolled… Was that a sign? I was distracted by the word "food" and Ruka getting up. The Babes said that word last night then gave me a great meal. Today, it smelled the same.

As I stood up, I felt it move. My dinner from last night was pushing out of me. I looked out the door at the rocky grass from across the parking lot. It was far. It was hot out there. I looked at the Babes. They were putting down the food bowls with their backs to us. Ruka walked her way to the kitchen, and I shot off to the farthest corner in the warehouse and did what Delux called a caca. I wanted to get as far away as I could, so I chose to go the empty bedroom I'd found earlier.

Before I had a chance to sniff out the perfect spot, I emptied myself in a short trail while sniffing the ground. I noticed earlier, Ruka poos in a pile. Mine, was in a trail.

I hurried back over to the door. Wait, what? Why am I running outside?

"Buddha, come eat. Food!" Delux yelled out.

I ran under the RV. Once I got there, I was left with more confusion. "What is going on with me?" I wondered out loud.

I never had this much trouble figuring out this thing called life. Why was I so scared?

My previous lives started flashing thought my head. I always seemed to come back as a military style dog, dying in the line of duty for the sake of someone's greater good.

There's broken glass, piles of bricks… I'm running, I'm jumping, I'm biting people, or I'm blowing them up. I saw Big Man punishing me for going potty in the house in my mind.

While sitting under the RV, I sank back into the reality of where I was at. I just pooped in the warehouse because I was afraid to go outside… A voice came over me. You're a dog, and you're here to heal, and forgive."

"Buddha, come on buddy, heel," Delux yelled outside the warehouse door.

Next thing you know, he was next to the RV, pulling me out from under it with Ruka. He must have known I was not going to come. "Come on, goofball, come eat your food." He walked me inside the warehouse holding me in one arm and petting my head like a sadistic dictator.

"Where was he?" Tess asked.

"Under the RV again. I think that's his favorite spot."

"Here, eat your food, buddy," Delux said, setting me down next to a bowl with delicious smelling food.

Their intentions seemed good, but I didn't want to trust them. They just picked me from an ad I thought as I ate my food. They paid Big Man money he will probably just use to buy beer and cigarettes. They took me away from the mission I was born into keeping a little girl safe. They took me away from my mom. My dad… I ate my breakfast.

Delux found my poo in the warehouse after it stunk up the place. He picked it up with a plastic bag and took me outside with it. He put the poo in the rocky grass and set me down next to it. "You go caca here, Buddha. Caca. Caca," he repeated, pointing at the poo. I looked at it and ran back under the RV the first chance I had.

"There's water inside if you need it," Delux said, going back inside the warehouse leaving me be.

"Don't worry, kid, you'll figure it out. Everything's new for you, but your mission here is simple, Buddha. Hang out here with the Babes and I. Bark at people you don't feel good about. And relax, kid. That's it."

"What about all the rest of the time?" I asked.

"I just told you, relax, kid. See that street cone over there. We chew on it. See that rope thing laying by the back tire. We chew on that. This bone here, we chew on this, and we can play tag with each other."

"What's tag?"

"I nip you, and you chase me. Then you nip me, and I chase you."

"How will you find me if you can't see?"

"I'll worry about that. Just don't let me catch you," Ruka said jumping playfully toward me and then rolling on her back.

"Now what?"

"You get me."

I jumped on top of Ruka. Mouth open, puppy teeth out. "Arrrrgh!" I growled out to match the noises she was making. I felt right away, I like Ruka. She is old like my mom, but playful. She let me jump and climb all over her, releasing all the anxiety I had inside of me. I was able to let go a bit and it made me feel free. I felt like a real dog with Ruka around me. Maybe I could get used to this.

CHAPTER 3

THREE MONTHS OLD

I awoke from the nicest nap on the front seat of the RV. I wasn't sure what it meant, but I was now three months old they say. Here I was, living with these hippy kids and a blind dog. I've been with the Babes and Ruka now for a whole month.

I'm still a kid according to Ruka. I've learned that me and Ruka's job is to play as much as possible. Bark at anyone who comes to the big metal gate, and then get back to playing. There's been a few times where someone came past the gate that opens to our space. Ruka would bark and run in that direction when she heard them, so I barked and followed her. Soon, I understood. If anyone is by the gate outside, we bark, and let them know we are here by trying to bite them through the fence and punch at it with our paws, letting them know, they are not welcome. I mean, that's what Ruka seems to be doing as I bark behind her.

"Damn Ruka, you're brave," I told her.

"Bad energy is bad energy." She said after barking and chasing someone away from the gate.

Ruka was a good teacher. I was walking around with more confidence these days than when I first got here.

Delux would walk me outside the fence and get a lot of attention with the two of us on leashes.

The police came over one day to our gate while the Babes were painting some art they thought they could try selling later on the road. The police offered to buy me from the Babes, but they said no and closed the gate on them. Even though I still wasn't listening very well, wouldn't play with the Babes, or bring the ball back like Ruka did, they turned down the offer of $500 cash on the spot for me.

"They probably robbed some drug dealer and that was their money," Tess said.

Ruka truly was blind as a bat. When we played, I could easily get away from her, running in circles around her, zigging, and zagging. If I got too close, she let me know she was the boss and read my moves before I made them and grabbed ahold of me. My moves were still like a puppy and all sloppy, but I was soaking up her strategy with every lunge she made toward me.

I would like to say I had stopped with my random turd droppings inside the warehouse, but something inside me, just made me do it. Last night I shat on the green carpet that sat under the rock band's equipment. The Babes were worried because after they cleaned it up, it still looked like I shat there. The Babes moved the band's speaker to cover the new stain I left, but when the band came to practice, they moved their speaker and discovered the poo stain. I was trying my best to go outside, but as a dog, we have instincts that sometimes can't be explained, and I think I actually wanted to poo on their stage grass. Their music was terrible. They were good at being terrible. I did like the drummer's insane style, but the other two guys just yelled into the mics while playing the guitar.

Delux had all of his DJ gear set up inside the warehouse on the main stage that was raised up. He was able to connect to the speakers that their friend's band would use. He was always taking breaks between working on the RV to practice his mixing, and the music would be thumping. Rob's band would come to practice and Delux would DJ with them at times, scratching his hip hop music with their soulful, trippy live sounds. Their sound was mellow compared to the metal band.

When the Babes were not taking breaks with Rob and his band, they were pounding away on the RV, or walking several blocks away to a hardware store that was selling them all of their supplies. The Babes would walk back with huge sheets of plywood and 2x4's balanced on their heads.

Delux carried a huge power converter back with him one day that they ordered from the hardware store. The Babes took us with them that day. The sun was setting, and the air was not as humid as it can be.

"Babe, look at that construction site with all that wood. We should just take a few of their pieces… It's not like we need a lot?"

"You think so? Right now, or come back later?" Tess asked.

"Ha ha, just kidding, but glad to know you're willing to and I could see you instantly thought of a plan, didn't you?"

"Ah yeah, we could easily get that shit. It's cheaper than that hardware store. I feel like they're raping us."

"True that. This fucking thing was expensive and it's heavy," Delux said putting it down and taking a break.

"You want me to carry it?" Tess asked.

"No, I got it, I just needed to turn it. One side is heavier than the other."

When they returned from a hardware store run, they were usually too tired to work after that, but today, they walked over to the corner store to get "other" supplies they needed. At the corner store, they would get chips and a drink, plus four small bags of herbs they liked to smoke when they were taking their work breaks. We walked to that store almost daily with the babes.

One day we walked to the corner store and a boy was on a bicycle who came racing past us super close, startling us.

"What the heck was that?" Ruka asked me.

"Some little kid on a bike who just came to a stop," I answered.

"Hey, what are you doing here?" the kid asked Delux.

"We're walking to the store to get some snacks. What're you doing here?"

"When I tell my daddy some white folks are here, he's gonna shoot you."

"Really?" Delux said shocked.

"Tell him we live right over there," Delux said to the child who was reaching for something in his waistband.

Delux picked up on the actions of the child and held us all back, including Tess. The little boy turned around and threw a full pack of fireworks at us. There was popping and explosions going crazy all around.

"Ruka!" I bit and snapped at the fireworks exploding in the air around us.

It gave me flashbacks of the military. I wanted to run and bite that kid who just threw firecrackers at us, but Delux held me back. Senior Chief would have let me get him. Those noises lead to injury or death I remembered. I hate fireworks.

We made it to the corner store and this time, the Babes met the owner of the store. The babes were buying a lot of herbs from her, so she wanted to meet the Babes. When she did, she was very afraid of me and Ruka. Both Ruka and I behaved ourselves in her establishment by just laying on the floor. I found the floor to be the coolest spot on that hot afternoon after walking all the way there. The babes got their herbs and we walked home with no more little brats or their dads ready to mess with us. Ruka was right. This is a tough neighborhood.

Life in the warehouse was nothing but fun 99% of the time. One night after dinner, I was playing with Ruka and running around inside the warehouse trying to get away from her as she tried to bite my legs. I ran into the bathroom the Babes used to hide. It was full of small trinkets from the 80's and 90's glued to every inch of every wall. I found a small ball that was a bit loose on the lower part of the wall. Ruka recently broke her ball with her strong jaw, so I figured I would bring her this one to play with. The ball was sorta attached to the wall, but I was easily able to get it off with a simple tug. As I turned around, excited to bring Ruka the ball, the ball went to the back of my mouth. I tried to push it forward with my tongue, but it slipped deeper into my throat and then, I swallowed it.

I ran over to Ruka, and she started to wrestle with me.

"Ruka, I have something for you, but I swallowed it," I told her as she gently bit my back leg and lifted my rear end in the air.

"Oh yeah? You're always eating everything of mine, aren't you? My bone. My cone. The corner of my pillow, which the Babes still have not seen yet." She attacked me playfully sounding like a jungle tiger.

The Babes finished cleaning up the kitchen and sat on the floor to watch Ruka and I play. It took Delux less than a few seconds after sitting down to think something was wrong with me. I didn't want to get in trouble for taking the ball, but I was fine where it was. I remember tearing up and swallowing some of Big Man's things when I was back with Mom, and he didn't like that one bit.

"What if the Babes really like this ball?" I wondered. I jumped back on top of Ruka playing rough with her.

"Babe! Something's wrong with Buddha. Look at him. He's choking!" Delux said in a panic.

"What do you mean? He's fine. He's not choking. They're playing," she replied.

I was fine, besides the small ball in me. Did Delux know…?

Ruka grabbed me and put me on my back. "You okay, kid?" Ruka asked, biting my ear.

"Yeah, I am fine. I mean, I have a small ball inside of me, but I'm fine." I got up and jumped at her to try and tackle her back.

"No, Babe, for real, something's wrong with Buddha," Delux said in a panic again and grabbed me.

"Babe. He's playing, he's fine. Look at him," she said.

Delux held me. I could feel he was very concerned for me, but how did he know? I showed no signs of anything being wrong. He looked into my eyes, and I looked back into his. I could see he was just as confused as I was, as I breathed heavily into his face. I was hiding the fact that I had just swallowed a ball pretty well, so he put me down.

"What the fuck. I swear I saw him choking on something. I'm… I'm losing my mind," Delux said, confused.

"I'll try and help you get the ball out," Ruka said, putting her leg on my chest, pushing on me.

"Babe… For real… I just saw Buddha choking in my mind or something, but look, in reality, he's fine. Fuck. Am I going crazy?" Delux sat there baffled. "I'm so confused. What I just saw felt so real," he said.

Delux paused. He realized looking at me, I was actually fine. I wasn't choking, I was playing with Ruka. "What the fuck?" he asked, as Ruka pushed me down again. I growled and jumped up on top of her after escaping her grip.
"Relax, Babe, he's fine. Look at him play," Tess said, touching his arm.

Ruka and I continued to wrestle on the green carpet. "For a monster of a dog, you are gentle, Ruka," I whispered in her ear as I bit onto it.

"Gentle, huh?" Ruka said in her growl back to me. Ruka threw a solid paw to my belly, then suddenly, I couldn't breathe. "How gentle was that?"

Her paw hitting my belly pushed the ball up a bit back into my throat, but now it was stuck in my throat, and I couldn't breathe. I sat down and opened my mouth.

Nothing.
I pushed with my lungs, nothing.
I shook my head around and nothing.
I let out a faint noise that Delux was able to hear.

"Buddha!" he yelled out, grabbing my mouth with one hand and sticking his fingers down my throat with the other, pulling the ball out.

I don't think he even thought about it, he knew I was choking before I was choking and he responded perfectly. Tess sat there in disbelief.

"Babe, how did you know he was choking, or going to choke, before he was choking?"

"I don't know, I just saw it like a movie in my head as we sat down next to them and then that shit happened exactly as I saw it. I'm so confused," Delux said.

Delux sat there holding me, questioning what had just happened.

"Ruka, can Delux see the future?" I asked.

"I don't know about seeing the future, but Delux sees something. I'm blind so I don't know what it is, but he's watching something, or something's watching him," Ruka said.

"Well, there's your ball," I told her.

I was confused how Delux saw the future. I think we all were, but I didn't care at the moment. I had discovered that playing with Ruka was a lot of fun and I wanted more of it. Delux got up and threw the ball in the trash. I got up and jumped back on top of Ruka who was already lying on her back waiting for me to get her.

Life in the hands of the Babes was easy. Eat. Play. Sleep. Drink. Find shade, play some more. Eat, play some more, and then sleep again.

While the Babes' hands were busy building the RV with a power drill and an old school hand saw, Ruka and I would trade off chewing up a city street cone that Delux brought home from a walk to the corner store.

I loved our walks outside of the warehouse walls. I would pull Delux around on a lowrider bicycle he found in the warehouse. If any of the crackheads on the street saw us, they would cross to the other side and not make eye contact, yet still keep an eye on us. The crackheads around the area had dark souls. All except one. Delux would let him stay outside the gate, and that crackhead would tell the other crack heads to leave.

It was a good thought being friends with a crackhead, but it didn't work out long. While we were all away on a walk to the hardware store, someone broke in and stole an exhaust fan the Babes had bought for the RV.

"Fuck! If this happens while you're here, bite these fools," Delux told me once they found out what was missing and who most likely took it.

I just wanted to play with Ruka.

The Babes worked every morning on the RV, and took a break when it got hot, which was usually right after breakfast. Delux would try to get me to play fetch with him while he was outside with us, but I didn't care to run in the sun or fetch a ball. He figured out quick I don't like the sun, so he tried the fetch game inside the warehouse, and I still didn't bother to try. There was more to me than playing games I felt, unless Ruka was involved. I'm here to save, not play games, I contemplated with myself.

If Delux bounced the ball when he threw it, Ruka would find it just by its sound and smell, then she'd rush it back to him and drop the ball at his feet.

"Ruka, why do you play this game with Delux?"

"Why not? What else are we gonna do?"

I couldn't see the reasoning behind fetch at all. When nobody was around to watch, I began to make sounds that left the Babes questioning what was failing in the warehouse. I was getting bigger and, to be honest, my body grew faster than what my mind knew what to do with. I struggled to lay down smoothly, Ruka would tell me.

I had no style or grace for a dog named Buddha. I would lay down far away from everyone once I was over my fears of the warehouse. I would do my typical three spins in a circle, sniff out just the right spot in that circle, then flop myself down onto that spot. My hips were big and clunky. They didn't allow me much grace in my movements and my body would make a "doof" noise when hitting the floor. Because I didn't care to hang out close with the Babes, I did my "doofing" off in the warehouse by myself. The babes would always ask what the noise was, but they never saw it was me. They just stuck to their cutting sheets of plywood with a hand saw, or their constant pool game breaks.

We no longer had to go to the corner store, the corner store lady was coming to us now. She brought her brother with her, who was a huge guy. Ruka and I could feel they were both very afraid of us as we walked around our open lot.

"You feel that, Ruka?"

"Yeah, I feel it."

"What should we do?"

"Let's stay chill, and if anything pops off, just be ready."

Delux told us to hang back in the RV by putting us in there and shutting the door so we couldn't get out and keep the fear level of the guests on max.

Us locked away in the RV made the store lady and her brother a bit calmer. I noticed while in the RV, if you just breathed on the side door handle, the door would easily open. I breathed, and just like that, the door opened. "Come on, Ruka, let's go!" I shouted as I ran out.

"You know, for not liking to hang out with the Babes, you sure like to cause a lot of trouble to be around them."

"Who said I want I hang out with them? Outside is way better than in the RV. We're in here all night, so let's go," I shouted in excitement.

We both jumped out and made our way into the warehouse where the Babes were playing pool with the corner store lady and her brother. The guests were scared to see us out, but after a bit of coaxing from both of the Babes, we were allowed to stay and hang out around them, as long as we didn't bother them. Ruka and I were on our best behavior even though I just broke us out of the RV.

"Look at that, Buddha, you got us out of the RV and hanging out with the Babes. Maybe your mission is to be with the Babes?"

I did my typical three spin move, hit the deck, and let out a deep breath.

(Doof)

"I don't know, Ruka. I just wanted to be outside."

It was hot that day, and I was excited to lay down on the cool concrete floor inside the warehouse. It was always the coolest place to lay down.

"Buddha, what the heck, man? You okay?" Delux asked walking over from the pool table.

"What happened?" Tess wondered.

I wondered too as I looked at them. I was fine.

"Ruka, what's going on with the Babes?" I asked as they approached me.

"I think they're concerned."

"Concerned for what?"

"Buddha, you okay"? Delux asked as Tess walked up from behind.

"What'd I do?" I asked to deaf human ears as my leg started to raise.

"He's gonna pee, let's just leave him."

"Babe, he's making that 'doof' noise we've been hearing. It's his head and body hitting the concrete," Delux said in disbelief and concern.

"Buddha? This noise is you? Can you lay down a little softer?" Tess asked.

"We've been hearing that 'doof' noise for a long time now. If it's been his head this whole time, geez, he's gonna have brain damage," Delux said to our guests.

"Buddha, you gotta be careful, buddy, there's only so many hits to the head one can take before you don't come back to your normal self," Delux said petting my head.

"What did he mean by that?" I asked Ruka.

"It means you're gonna be dumb if you keep whacking your head on the floor like that."

"I was hit harder by Big Man. This concrete floor don't phase me," I said stretching out.

After a few games of pool and a large exchange of herbs, the guests left the babes to their afternoon, which consisted mostly of smoking the herbs while painting pictures and getting messy. I didn't like their smoke.

"Before Tess came around, Delux never smoked weed at all. I like when he does," Ruka told me.

"Really? Why do you like weed so much Ruka?"

"It helps me cope with not being able to see like I used to. I now see all kinds of things that make no sense in my mind compared to what I used to remember. The herb smoke helps calm it all down so I can get some real rest. When Delux blows smoke around me, I try to inhale as much as I can."

"Yeah, I see that. I don't like it."

"It's not for everyone," Ruka told me.

Tess finally got a modeling gig so they could help pay for all of the work they've been doing on the RV. She left us the entire day, and she didn't return until late that evening. When she arrived back home, her hair was bright red, when her hair was usually soft blonde. She was upset. We'd never seen Tess upset like this.

"How am I going to work again now? They cut my hair so short, and now it's fucking red, and burnt! These fucking idiots."

"Ahh, Babe," Delux said, trying to help.

"They first dyed my hair white, took some photos, then turned me this fucking red color, and took other photos."

I let out a bark because I didn't like to hear Tess angry.

"For a couple grand, I'm left like this? Tess questioned angrily, looking into a mirror that was bent against the wall making everything look short and fat when you looked into it. "I want you to cut my hair," she turned and said to Delux.

"What?"

"Yes. Right now. Cut my hair."

"I've never cut hair before!"

"After what I see on my head, you can't fuck it up. I trust you."

"Babe, look at my head, I can fuck it up. You shouldn't trust me."

I looked at Delux. He had a hairline like a M when he did have hair, so I could see why he shaved his head. I looked at both Tess and Delux's heads. It was hard to compare Tess's head shape with her thick hair that stuck out like an afro. I imagined them both bald like Delux, and I laughed going to find Ruka.

Delux grabbed a pair of scissors and went to work cutting off chunks of hair. When he was finished, Tess still looked the same.

"I bet he is too timid to cut too much off at once," Ruka told me.

Tess grabbed the scissors from Delux and cut off some more hair as to how she wanted it, and then Delux did some finishing touches, just because.

"It looks likeTess has a helmet for hair now," I told Ruka.

"Ugh, this is bullshit!" Tess let out, looking in the mirror.

I could see and feel Delux's energy change when Tess was upset. He became on guard, or hyper aware, when Tess was raising her voice and shouting about her hair. I wondered why he changed like that?

Three months passed at the warehouse, and after a lot of pounding, cutting, drilling, sealing, running wires, fixing water lines, pumps, installing a converter, and making sure all the inside and outside lights worked, the Babes had this RV looking good. Ruka said I was doing good too now, by listening and paying a bit more attention to the world around me without being such an idiot.

The Babes took me to the doctor to fix the hole in my belly and to stop the fat from pushing out. I was in pain after the surgery, but I felt so much better with it fixed. Nobody told me they'd be taking my balls at the same time they were doing this surgery though. I was so disappointed as I fought with the plastic cone they stuck around my neck. I felt I was becoming a beast of a dog when someone told Delux a rumor that taking my balls would calm me down a bit, so... I was gonna make sure I did the opposite. I decided that I wasn't gonna fetch, I was not gonna calm down. I was not going to come when called and I would not sit. I would go into the RV, and that was it.

For two weeks I had to run around with a stupid lamp shade on my head making everything difficult. I would hit everything I walked past, even when I felt I was far enough away from it all. The cone made more noise than I did, yet I could not be trusted with it off. I would instantly go for my balls that were no longer there.

"Ruka, you know what it's like to have to scratch your balls when you can't because A: They are not there, and B: I have to wear this stupid cone."

"I don't have balls Buddha, so I have no idea."

The Babes decided to change my name to Doofus because of the noise I made when laying down. Apparently, it was a perfect "doof" noise, according to Delux. What could I do? I was getting bigger, and the lamp shade thing I had to wear didn't help.

Once my surgery healed and the lamp shade came off, the Babes took Ruka and me to a fancy art fair in the neighborhood. Tess seemed a bit off this night.

I was not sure if she was still upset about her hair, or if it was something else that was making her feel sick in her belly.

Some guy at the event came up to us and said, looking at the size of my paws and nose, I would grow up to be a small dog. He then offered to buy me from them, but the Babes both told him to fuck off. Usually, the Babes were nice. Something was up with them tonight, but I couldn't put a paw on it. The art party was lame, so we left.

Our warehouse was in the middle of a run-down industrial neighborhood full of crackheads who lined up outside an empty lot with old, freezer coolers on their sides. They were there to get something injected into their butts on Father's Day. The babes videotaped the whole thing from inside our fence.

"Who's providing the drugs so thirty guys can all get injected for free?" Delux asked.

"They're using the same needle over and over again with every person."

"Look at the line down the street. How do they all know to come here?"

Ruka and I sat next to the babes looking out a hole in the fence at the activities across the street.

"It's a big evil world out there Buddha, or Doofus as they want to call you now," Ruka told me biting my leg. "As dogs, it's our job to keep our people safe, while making the world a better place."

"How are we going to do that?" I asked.

"You know, the name Doofus might actually fit you," she told me, rolling me over.

After several months of living at the warehouse, I was fitting into my new role well I felt. We woke up early and started playing around the RV after cacas. I had finally learned to poo in the rocky grass, but I would only do it on the edge where the concrete and grass met and I would do it in a long line, not a pile like Ruka. Why I would walk and poo confused Delux.

One hot afternoon while the Babes were painting more pictures instead of fixing the RV, Rob came to the warehouse to practice his drumming a bit. He asked the Babes if they wanted to test me for protection, seeing I was bigger and the cone was now off my neck, and the Babes said yes. I was confused. I didn't think I liked tests, and I already barked at the gate before Ruka noticed anything, so I felt I was making progress.

"This is more like a pop quiz, Doofus, not a test," Ruka told me.

"What should I do?"

"Do what comes naturally," Ruka said as she was called toward the RV.

Delux tied me up to a trailer that happened to be in the middle of the parking lot that day. "Make sure he's good and secure. I don't want him getting loose and attacking me," Rob said.

Attack Rob? Why would I do that? I like Rob. I think I like Rob. He'd always been a nice guy, and he too had a Rottweiler, so I wanted to show him respect, always, I didn't want to attack him.

Next thing I know, I was alone. Where did everyone go? While I was getting overwhelmed by the heat and thinking about Rob, I realized I was alone out there and tied up. I tried to walk toward the RV, but I couldn't reach because of the chain around my neck, so I went under the trailer in the shade and laid down.

"I really need to work on paying attention to the moment, in the moment," I thought out loud to an empty lot.

As I decided to take a doggie nap under the shade of the trailer, the door to the warehouse opened. I popped my head up instantly and looked. "Who did that?" A growl naturally came out of me. I didn't see anyone, but I heard the door open.
Now that the door was open, I could see it.

"Hey," I heard from the door in a dirty voice.

I crawled out from the trailer to see what was going on, and walked to the end of my chain in the hot sun until I could not walk anymore. I pulled, but the chain was tight. I was not scared like I usually was, and the sun was not a bother. This noise from the door was. I looked around and I saw nothing, and the door shut itself. I thought that was weird but there was nothing I could do so I went back under the trailer when the door opened again, and a man yelled. I instantly crawled back out to see what was going on. I ran to the end of my chain growling, then getting stopped by the length of the chain. It looked like it was Rob who ran back into the warehouse. What the heck was going on? What kind of test was this, to see if Rob is crazy? Because he sure was acting crazy if that was him.
It was hot out in the sun, so I went back under the trailer again wondering where the Babes went. My memory sucked. Mental note, pay attention to things. Maybe the Babes were right. They called me Doofus now because of the noise I made when I laid down. Maybe hitting my head was affecting the way I think?
I didn't know, but the door to the warehouse swung open again and some guy looking like Rob who had a big stick in his hand, was yelling and hitting the ground. I ran out from under the trailer all the way to the end of my chain barking and growling. I ran so fast, when I got to the end of the chain, the stop spun me around 180 degrees. I found my bearings and kept at him. The man kept hitting the ground

while I instinctively kept trying to attack him, barking and spitting. The man gave up and went inside.

"Ok, holy shit. That's good," Rob yelled and went back into the warehouse and shut the door.

The Babes came out of the RV with Ruka.

"Holy shit, kid, that was nuts. You got the job for sure," Ruka said to me in confidence, licking my face.

The Babes untied me from the trailer and told me "Great job" with their voices and their hands. Their attention felt nice, but again, something felt off. The energy I was feeling from them was different. I was not sure if it was because this was the first time I got aggressive toward something and was not punished for it, or what I was feeling.

"Wow, kid, that sounded as scary as scary gets. I'd say that you found your voice there, and if you build off of that, you're going to be something nobody wants to mess with," Ruka said.

I thought about her words. Was that why I was here? To be something not to mess with? I was free to roam around all I wanted, but I stayed close to the RV that was still parked outside, getting ready to be moved inside where they could seal the roof, and it would have a chance to dry without getting wet. The Babes were putting a lot of work into this thing.
They were trying to put work into me as well with "Doofus, come. Doofus, sit. Doofus, wait." All I heard was Doofus, so I would go and lay down. That was my Doof, remember?

"He will play with Ruka, but not us," Delux said disappointed.

"At least we now know, he'll protect the RV," Tess said supporting me.

The Babes would work all day and be wet with sweat while Ruka and I hid under the RV where it was always a bit cooler. Today, a video production crew showed up to film two couples have sex on motorcycles. The Babes were excited to watch their first porn shoot but then got mad because the actors used the Babes' towels to dye their hair blue.

The blue hair actor didn't bring the right shoes, so they had to rent the boots off one of the old guys who brought in one of the custom chopper motorcycles.

I walked into a scene they were shooting by accident looking for Ruka. The camera guy didn't mind, and they kept rolling and fucking as I passed by. I walked past the bootless old man, and he was chewing on a Backwood cigar and swallowing the juices. He smelled harmless, yet terrible at the same time. His socks had holes in them, and his toes were hanging out; he ended up renting his boots for $60 to the actor who dyed his hair blue. The sex actor took the boots and went barefoot into them. If there was a time for socks or a foot condom, this was it I thought, but the actor was a raw dog kinda guy from the looks of it.

After walking into the scene, Ruka and I watched all the sex go down from the comfort of our RV that was now parked inside the warehouse. Life as a dog is all about waiting. We waited for something to do, or we just did things without really thinking ahead too much.

A week later there was another video shoot with naked people walking around. Only this time they were shooting a condom commercial for some popular sex magazine. Funny how the week before they had sex without condoms and now, they're doing an ad for them. Trashy, to classy.

Again, Ruka and I were in the RV, only this time, the Babes joined us.

The Babes were excited to see if a ghost they once saw while playing pool, was going to appear during the commercial from the same fake wall that was now being used to make their fake room, where they were having fake sex.

The other night, The Babes were playing pool when all of a sudden, some man appeared from the top of the one of the fake walls.

"Doofus. You feel that?" Ruka asked me.

"Feel what? Holy shit, yes, I feel it and I can see him!"

Bark! I let out.

Tess screamed out while Delux was sitting on the couch looking up at a man in black coming out of the wall 12 feet up in the air.

The ghost man looked real to me. What was he doing up in a wall though? The ghost man was dressed in black and looked confused when he appeared, like he took a wrong turn or something as he looked right at us all. Delux was on the couch looking right into the man's eyes who was wearing a black hat like Zoro, and staring back at him.

"What the fuck! You see that?" Delux asked, as the man turned and disappeared back into the wall.

"What's going on, Doofus? Tell me what you see, because I felt something strong entered the room and it just left," Ruka said.
"Whatever or whoever it was, carried a lot of energy."

"Was that Zoro who just appeared at the top of that wall?" Delux asked Tess confused and laughing at the situation.

"I saw him too. He had on the Zoro hat and a cape," Tess said confused.

"Yeah, I saw the cape as he turned around and went back into the wall. He looked pissed off," Delux said.

"It looked like he saw us," Tess added still looking at the upper wall section.

"Yo, we really both just saw the same ghost? How was that even real?" Delux questioned.

"The dogs even barked before it showed up!" Tess added.

"What the fuck was that?" Delux asked getting up and looking behind the wall confused.

"Ruka, I saw what the Babes saw. There was a man dressed in black who just popped out of the divider wall."

"Well, if ya'll saw the same thing, and you and I felt something, it was something. What exactly, I don't know."

We were all in that moment together confused. After a thorough check of the wall, the Babes went back to their pool game talking about how Zoro showed up unannounced.

The condom commercial came to an end and no ghosts came out of the walls but the actor came when they needed him to. We all took a nap in the RV while the commercial was filming, and when we awoke, everyone was pretty much gone but a few workers the owner of the warehouse hired to clean up. The owner was a big guy named Judd, who rarely visited, but when he did, he got straight to the point.

"How much longer you kids gonna be here?" Judd asked the Babes.

"We would like to put the last bit of roof sealer on and let it dry inside the warehouse. Our plan was to be on the road before July," Tess told Judd.

It was the first week of June according to our calendar. This meant something I thought. It felt like a change was coming. Delux and Tess left us behind at the warehouse one day, and when they came back, they were excited. They wrote on their calendar that they got proper insurance and registration for the RV, making it 100% legal now. The Babes wrote everything they did on that calendar.

When they got me, when I got my shots, my belly surgery that also took my balls... a reminder that The Babes could not be trusted I thought, everything was on that calendar. Too bad I couldn't read, so I'd just have to remember not to trust the Babes after taking my balls off.

"Ruka, Doofus. RV," Delux shouted.

We had the "RV" command down. I'd kinda sit. I never stayed. And bring the ball back was still a hard no, but RV, that meant inside the box on wheels and not much else.

The RV looked nice inside now. It was very different now than when I first arrived here. No windows, the walls dangling down to the side, an absolute mess inside with a hole in the back floor and wall.

Two months later, we had a sealed art box that moved on wheels with a DJ booth. Under the countertop on one side of the RV hid all of Delux's DJ equipment. The U-shaped couch in the back stored all of his vinyl records. A separate compartment was built for all of their artwork and paint supplies.

The Babes each had their own small closets. There was a fully working bathroom and a kitchen with a cooler that acted like a fridge. We had running water, lights, and an exhaust fan in the roof that Tess made a cover for in case it rained.

"Doofus, get down," Delux said pointing to the back of the RV as I was sitting in my front seat.

"The driver's seat is my spot, but I can share," I said jumping out of the seat.

I felt like that seat was my spot after three months of sleeping in it, night after night. Delux sat in the driver seat and turned the key. The motor started up no problem and the Babes were extremely excited.

"They didn't seem so confident it would start, did they Ruka?"

"The RV sat here for over three months never being started. I'd say we're hearing a miracle right now, Doofus."

Delux drove the RV out of the warehouse, and then out of the lot onto the main road. Tess closed the gate and jumped inside the RV to the passenger seat.

"Doofus get down," Tess said, pushing me out of the passenger seat.

"I don't get any seats?" I jumped over Ruka and slid on the smooth laminated floor. I turned around and pushed my way up in the middle by Ruka between the two front seats. "Where're we going, Ruka?"

"Let's see how she handles," Delux said, pulling away and hitting the gas.

"A test drive, Doofus. A test drive," Ruka told me.

Delux hit the gas and sent us flying back a little, then he hit the brakes, and sent us forward. We got power and we can stop. He drove us around a few left and right turns, and over some railroad tracks twice that made the RV bounce around.

"Should be able to handle Costa Rica," Delux said jerking the wheel side to side.

We stopped at a store and got some food and snacks, and then drove back to the warehouse.

"That was weird driving her again," Delux said backing into their spot outside the warehouse.

"How do you feel she'll do?" Tess asked.

"There's only one true way to find out. Let's leave after the party," he replied.

"Party?" I asked Ruka.

"Yeah, Judd is holding the first annual, HoodStock Music festival here. Delux is going to DJ."

"What does that mean?" I wondered.

The Babes kept Ruka and I locked up all night in the RV while groups of people quickly started to fill up the inside warehouse and outside parking lot. Delux was on top of a big stage that was higher than the RV, making everyone who was outside, dance. Tess would come and check on us and every now and then, so would Delux. He would show me love when he saw me at the door, but I still wasn't sure about him, or Tess and their plans of going to Costa Rica, so I just jumped in the front seat and waited.

I'd still catch myself thinking about my first little friend back with my mom and how she was doing. "She's ok. Mom is keeping her safe," I thought while everybody outside was partying.

"Come inside and check out what we did to her," Tess told some older man who followed them in the RV.

"Well hello, doggies," he said to Ruka and me as we sniffed him out.

"Oh, watch out for our ganja tree there in the ground," Tess said, motioning the man away from it, but he stepped right on it.

"You call that a ganja tree? Ha, you should come to my house, and I will show you a ganja tree."

"Ahh, man, we spent months getting her all pretty."

"I do apologize," the old man said after stepping on the plant. "Wow, this is the same RV you bought from DL?"

"Yes for $800, and he left me with a note saying it's mine."

"Man, it was a piece of shit back then. Nice work," the old man said checking out the remodeling.

"What do you think about him, Ruka?"

"No, what do *you* think, Doofus"?

"He seems harmless. He has a good energy about him."

"I feel the same," Ruka told me. "Not to mention he smells like cats."

"What are cats?" I wondered.

CHAPTER 4

ON THE ROAD

After a very successful HoodStock, the Babes helped clean up what was left of the party the next day while Ruka and I sniffed out all the new weird smells that were left on the ground.

Ruka and I both got baths and we were dried off with a towel and left outside to dry in the sun, even though I would always find the shade.

"Ruka, Doofus, RV!" Delux called out, and in we went.

We were hitting the road. I was not sure what that meant, "Hit the road," but soon we were all in the RV and moving, and we didn't stop moving for a long time. Delux drove the entire time until we needed more gas. Ruka and I sat between the Babes on the floor, sharing her pillow. Ruka hated the moving RV.

"Why can't you relax while we're moving, Ruka?"

"I don't know. I just don't like the feeling of moving, or you pushing all around me because you yourself are having a hard time sitting still."

We stopped and filled up our gas tank that could hold a full tank of gas now. The tank had had a hole in it, but Delux was able to drop the tank down with Tess's help and fix it before we left. They were always taking care of each other or helping the other one with their ideas I noticed.

"Ruka, Doofus, outside," Tess said opening the side door after Delux parked the RV in a shady spot.

"Ruka, what is this place?" I asked as twenty new smells filled my nose all at once.

"I believe it's a rest stop... No, no, no, this is a gas station with grass. There will be many of these stops along our journey," Ruka said peeing in a random spot.

I don't know how she found her pee spot so fast. I had to search mine out. Preferably in the shade. Breakfast was shifting, and I could feel the urge to poo, so I handled my business while Delux waited to pick it up with a plastic bag.

"Good boy. Caca, Doofus," he repeated every time I poo'd.

What a weirdo I thought. "Why are you picking up my poo with your hands in a plastic bag and telling me 'caca' every time?"

"So you learn to go when he needs you to," Ruka said passing us.

"Ruka, Doofus, RV," Delux said after tossing our poo.

"I'll race you, Ruka," I said running off with an empty belly and a lot of speed. I was always the first one in the door of the RV if we raced. Delux loved it when I did so. Ruka hopped in next.

"What took you so long?"

"There was some chicken smell you passed by the trash can. I figured we're going to be in the RV for a while, so I took in a few extra sniffs and wiped my paw in it to dream about during my next nap."

"Oh, I can smell it on your face. Let me lick it."

"No get away from me."

Ruka never napped while the RV was moving. She sat between Delux and Tess, always making sure things were ok. This made me not want to sleep either, so I watched Ruka watch the Babes. If I walked up between them all, I would get some head scratches and pats, but then I would be told to back up.

"Doofus, back up, fool. You can't just push Ruka out of the way," Delux said.

"I don't mind, kid, just stop stepping on me like you love to do."

"I'll try not to."

"How much longer until the next stop?"

"A few hours most likely."

It was gas station after gas station, until the Babes pulled off at a rest stop where it seemed we were gonna stay for the night. We were let outside to do our business, and Delux tried to get me to bring him the ball back and play with him seeing as we'd been driving all day.

"Doofus. Fetch," he would say, then throw the ball as I stood there and watched the ball roll away.

"Doofus, you gonna get that?" Ruka asked me excitedly.

"No. I don't see the point."

"Yes," Ruka said tearing off in the direction the ball went.

Using her nose to sniff the grass to find the trail of the balls sent, Ruka would find the trail and then instantly find the ball. She would rush it back to Delux super proud.

"I got it, Papi," Ruka said in her Spanish accent, dropping the ball at his feet.

"Good girl, Ruka. You want to do it again?" Delux would ask.

Ruka jumped up on her back two legs, standing upright in the air. She loved this thing of bringing the ball back. When her front paws hit the ground, Delux threw the ball again so it would roll on the grass as she sniffed it out. She would bring it back, and get a bunch of hugs and scratches from Delux who was just as proud as she was.

I didn't get the concept as I thought back about attacking Rob. Delux and Tess touched and hugged on me all the time without me doing a trick. I didn't need to bring the ball back for pleasure. I was here to protect, not play, I reassured myself.

"How about you bring my balls back?" I asked to deaf ears, covered in Ruka's panting.

I realized, in that moment, I was hanging onto my past. My past was behind me, but I couldn't forgive the Babes for taking my balls.

"Ruka. Doofus. RV," Delux said.

Those words brought me present, and in I went, and Ruka soon followed. The babes fed us and gave us water. Fed themselves by heating up some noodles and getting some chips from a vending machine close by. Ruka and I laid on the floor, licking the new smells off of our paws, and falling asleep with the RV standing still once again in silence with the sound of the highway close by.

"Ruka!" I shouted.

"What, Doofus?" she asked, waking up from my shout.

"How did we get here?"

"What do you mean, how did we get here? For a dog, that's too deep of a question this early in the morning. The Babes ain't even up yet, go back to sleep," Ruka said letting out a deep breath.

"How did I get into the driver's seat?" I was puzzled. I actually didn't remember.

"You climbed over me last night, stepping on me several times trying to get your hind end up on the seat. You need to learn how to jump up. Now go back to sleep, we're gonna to be driving all day again today."

The Babes woke up before I could go back to sleep, and they let us out to pee and poo again.

"Sorry I woke you up early, Ruka."

"It's okay, Doofus."

The Babes gave us more food and water, and just like Ruka said, we were soon back on the road. The Babes pulled out their map book and found a location they were looking for. Tess gave Delux directions, and by midafternoon, we pulled off the highway and were driving into the woods on a dirt road. We found our way to a mysterious house, deep in the woods.
There was an old dog there to greet us.

"Ah, whooooooooooo the fuck are youuuuuuu?" the dog howled out as we narrowly drove the RV through some tight trees up the driveway.

Ruka got excited.

"That's another dog?"

"Chill, mamma. This is someone's house. We have to be respectful. No being a bitch here," Delux said bringing the RV to a stop.

"Wow, this place looks cool as fuck," Tess said taking in everything Ruka and I couldn't see.

The old man came outside his garage and greeted the Babes while we were told to stay in the RV.

"Who is this guy?" I asked Ruka.

"He's the stranger they met the night of their going away party."

"Ahh, that's why the scents here smell familiar."

"You can smell that?" Ruka asked me.

"I don't know, I think so. I smell something." There were a lot of smells coming into the open windows of the RV.

The Babes talked to the old man a bit, and he took them on a tour of his property while we stayed behind.

"Doofus. He has cats here," Ruka told me.

"What are cats, again?"

"You smell that sweet smell?"

"I think so. I actually smell a lot of new smells right now," I said sniffing the air around us.

"I smell cat shit. This guy has cats. We need to get outside," Ruka said with a sense of urgency. "Do your door trick and let us out."

"He has cats and a dog? I thought dogs and cats didn't get along."

"Just wait until you taste the delicious delights that come out of cats; now open the door."

I didn't understand why Ruka was getting excited about eating cat droppings. I still couldn't tell what smell was the actual cat smell, but I liked it out here in the woods. I moved towards the door.

"Delux told us not to open the door."

"You never listen to Delux."

She was right so I opened the door.

"Ah, Ruka, no!" Delux said catching us outside. "Ruka, no!" Delux said moving towards her like he knew what she was up to.

"Babe, what's she doing?" Tess asked as Ruka's nose was going psycho on the ground.

"She's focused on the cat shit. She loves it."

"Ruka, Doofus. RV. Lets go," he shouted, but it was too late.

"It's here, Doofus. It's everywhere!" Ruka said tripping out, finding pile after pile.

The Babes went and hung out with the old man and his family, while we stayed inside the RV.

"Ruka, your breath is stinking up the RV."

"Don't you love it?"

"No. Now what do we do?"

"We sleep Doofus, and if you hear something out of the ordinary, bark."

We were both woken up by the sound of the Babes returning for the night. They smelled like home cooked food and herbs. They were both super high, and full in their bellies. Tess more than Delux.

We got our food, and they giggled their way up into bed. After our last bite of food, Ruka and I did the same without all the giggles.

The next morning, we were let out to pee and poo again. Ruka went straight for the piles again. She went nuts. "Oh my gosh, it's everywhere," Ruka said finding a piece of dried-up cat poo, tossing it into the air and somehow catching it, then eating it.

"Ohh, a fresh pile!" Ruka said hitting the ground rolling it all over her neck.

"Now I smell like the wild, Doofus. Let's go hunt some small prey."

"Hunt some small prey? Ruka, what are you talking about? Are you okay?"

"Ruka!" Delux shouted and stopped her for only a second before she took one more body roll in the wet poo.

"Ah, Ruka, not again!" Delux said disappointed but knowing she would do it.

Delux walked over and grabbed Ruka by her collar that was jammed with poo on one side. He walked her over to the hose and gave her a bath.

"Ruka, why?" both Delux and I asked her.

"The smell, Doofus. The smell makes me do it."

"I found out she would do this when I first got her after I took her on walks around South Beach. She would eat and roll in any cat shit she could find, then come home breathing hard, stinking up the whole apartment," Delux told Tess, cleaning the poo off of Ruka.

"I hate the hose too, Doofus, but the poo's worth it," Ruka said getting hosed off.

"Ruka, your breath smells like shit. Lick your feet," I said walking away.

After the Babes filled up their water tank and digested the home cooked breakfast from the family, we were back on the road with promises to come back and visit them again after Costa Rica.

Back in the noisy RV that swayed in the wind at a steady 60 miles per hour, we continued north, to Minnesota. We had an event to get to that was going to help the Babes make money for this Costa Rica trip. If we were going to make it on time, they had to drive all day and night. The RV was slow and consumed a lot of gas, making us stop to fill up a lot. Delux would let us out to pee and poo if we had to, but then it was back into the RV, and back on the road. We drove all day, and late into the night. Delux did all the driving while Tess navigated.

"You wanna drive?" Delux asked Tess out of nowhere.

"What? Really?" Tess was surprised.

"I mean, we're on a road with nobody on it. It's two a.m., and you should drive your RV after we fixed her up. Get a feeling of her again. Appreciate her."

Tess had gotten her driver's license taken away because she was a bit of a crazy person behind the wheel, accumulating twelve negative points on her license in less than twelve months. She was a super model, but also super wanted in two states for not showing up in court, due to things she did while driving. It was mostly speeding tickets and drug charges.

This RV went slow, and the Babes had just smoked their last bit of drugs.

"Oh My God! I would love to drive," Tess said.

"Great! Ruka, Doofus, move," Delux said as he got up from the wheel of the moving RV and left the driver's seat open for Tess to sit in.

"Oh my god, what are you doing?" Tess shouted in excitement and confusion.

"Drive," Delux said, laughing holding Ruka and I back.

"You're nuts!" Tess said, quickly grabbing the wheel and jumping into the empty driver's seat taking over where Delux left off.

"Hi, guys! So this is what it feels like to be in the moving RV," he said rubbing our faces.

"If the police catch us, we'll do that move again. That worked great," Delux said.

"Oh my god, I cannot believe you. You're so crazy," Tess said in utter happiness that she was driving her RV again. "She drives so smooth now," she said.

Delux sat himself in her passenger seat and got comfortable.

"It's kind of nice on this side with the foot up and one hand on the dogs," Delux said to Tess.

Tess changed the music and lit a cigarette.

After driving all day, Delux started to fade away and fall asleep. Ruka was sitting up, leaning next to the passenger chair, while I leaned next to the driver's seat, watching Delux close his eyes and drift away, trying to hold his head up. Delux fell asleep with his hand on Ruka's head.

An hour into Tess's driving experience, something changed in her energy that grabbed my attention. Tess looked concerned as she looked into her mirrors to see a car quickly approaching us. Tess stayed on course and kept the RV from swaying, when the car got alongside of us and flashed a bright light into her side window. A siren chirped, then red and blue light flashed for a second, then went off as the car got behind us.

"Pull the vehicle over now," a man shouted over a loud speaker.

"Babe!" Tess shouted and hit Delux to wake up. "We're getting pulled over!"

Delux looked behind him and saw the police car as Tess pulled off to the side of the road.

"Quick, let's switch seats," he said groggy-like.

"They saw me driving already."

"Fuck... okay, ahh... I'll pretend I'm still asleep," Delux said leaning his head against the window.

"Ruka, what's happening?"

"We're about to find out, Doofus."

A cop opened Tess's driver's side door and told her to step out, and she did. Next, a second cop tapped on Delux's window for him to unlock and open the door.

I got excited and pushed my way onto Delux to get a better look at the cop and letting out a bark.

"Doofus, relax kid, you're stepping on me."

"Sorry, Ruka."

This scared the officer, and he told Delux to keep us back.

"Are you on drugs? Look at your eyes," the cop said to Delux as he stepped out of the RV, shutting the door behind him, leaving us inside.

We could hear one cop asking Tess questions, and the other cop asking Delux questions on the other side of the RV.

"Ruka, what do we do?"

"We wait, Doofus."

Delux opened the side door and grabbed our leashes from under the passenger seat and put them on us.

"Come on, guys, let's go outside."

"Go stand at the front of my cruiser," the cop ordered Delux. "And hold onto your dogs. I don't want to have to shoot them."

"Dude, what the fuck? Don't threaten me and my dogs like that. My dogs are chill. Look at them just standing here not giving a fuck about you. Why are your patrol lights off?"

The cop didn't answer.

Tess joined us as we stood there while the two cops talked to each other then went inside the RV.

"Fuck, we're going to jail babe," Delux said. "What about the dogs? Fuck, they're gonna take the dogs," he said sadly looking at us.

"What did you tell them?" Tess asked.

"The truth. We're from Florida and driving to Minnesota to help my parents out with the Taste of Minnesota."

"He asked me about drugs. They think we have a bunch of drugs inside," Tess said to Delux.

"You. Give your dogs to her and get in here," a cop said pointing to Delux and hanging out from the RV.

Delux went inside. I could hear him talking to the police as their big clunky shoes pounded on the floor of the RV as they walked around searching it.

"I love you guys," Tess said petting both Ruka and I, holding our faces like it was the last time we would see her.

Delux came out of the RV pissed.

"Hey, get back here," the cop said to him. "We don't want to talk to her, we're talking to you!" he continued.

"The cops said they found white powder in your bong, and they're being assholes saying we have a bunch of drugs hidden somewhere."

"What? White powder?" Tess asked, upset to the max.

Tess stormed into the RV shouting "White powder!" and then continued to shout some more that we could not understand. Soon, she was back with us.

"Fuck, these assholes are gonna take us to jail for nothing," Tess said.

"What were you doing?" Delux asked Tess. "Why did they pull us over?"

"I don't know. They just appeared, sped up behind me, shined a light on me, and shouted for me to pull over."

Delux looked inside the police car.

"Well, it looks like they're real cops, but they're not acting like it."

The cops finally emerged out of the RV and walked up to us.

"Go on, get the fuck outta here," one cop told them as they walked past us.

"What?" Delux asked.

"You heard me. Get the fuck outta here".

"I'll drive," Delux said to Tess handing her our leashes.

Tess put us back into the RV, and Delux got in the driver's side. We drove in silence for a few minutes as the Babes kept an eye out behind them.

"They turned around... What the fuck was that?" Tess asked with some relief.

"How did we get away from that?" Delux asked also checking his mirrors in disbelief.

"They didn't even ask me for my ID."

"Me neither, just, where are we from and where are we going, and where are the drugs?" Delux said laughing.

"Check the back of the RV. Did they take anything?"

Tess got up and examined the mess the police made a bit closer.

"They tore the poster board we decorated the walls with to see what was behind it. Assholes. My pantie drawer is dumped out... All the papers, my pipe, and my bong are all still here, but I wouldn't be surprised if a pair of panties is missing."

"And the plant in the bathroom?" Delux asked.

"Yeah, still there."

"What, really?"

"Those fucking pigs just stopped to search us illegally, hoping they would score."

"And they got nothing."

"I'm glad we smoked the last of our weed when we did."

"I wish we had a joint right now," Tess added.

That night, they made a plan where, because the RV was in Delux's name and he had the license that was valid, Tess decided she would take responsibility for anything found in the RV that might risk them losing the RV. As long as nothing happened to Delux, they should be okay, they thought.

After a full day of driving, we arrived at our destination before the sun began to set. It was the Taste of Minnesota.

CHAPTER 5

MINNESOTA

It was beautiful in Minnesota during July. Delux timed our arrival perfect and was able to pull right up to where the event was happening. Delux said hello to his family, and they got to meet Tess for the second time, I guessed, because they seemed to know her. It was their first time meeting me, so I gave them a good loud bark of a hello when they got close to the RV.

"Doofus, chill buddy. This is family," Ruka told me.

That bark was chill, I thought.

Ruka knew everyone, and they were all happy to see her. Delux's father walked right up to us and instantly asked him for a favor, and he said yes with no hesitation. He needed a fridge picked up from back home, so Delux put us into the back of his dad's new pick-up truck that we needed to take. Because I had only been in a pickup truck one time when the Babes picked me up, Delux tied Ruka close to one side and me on the other.

"Now what, Ruka?"

"We go for a ride, Doofus."

"The whole way up here was a ride, no?"

"Not like this. You're gonna love it."

Tess jumped into the passenger seat and off we went. This truck went way faster than the RV. We were actually keeping up with traffic now, versus getting passed by everyone.

The summer air in Minnesota smelled different. I liked it way more than the air in Miami even though it was almost as hot.

"What you think, Doofus?" Ruka asked me over the air moving around in the back of the truck.

"This is nice," I told her while adjusting my head to let my ears fly in the wind.

We made it to a restaurant that had two warehouses in the parking lot. Delux jumped into a forklift while Tess untied us and held us to the side. With ease, he lifted the fridge off the ground, and into the back of the truck. The fridge didn't move, so he backed the forklift away. Delux got out of the forklift to secure the fridge to the truck. As he was gathering the straps, the fridge moved, and fell out of the back, face down.

"Oh, fuck," Delux shouted out helplessly watching it all happen.

He ran over and lifted the huge fridge off of its double door face using his own strength. There was a small dent in an upper handle that protected the face of the fridge and that was it.

"I think we're good," he said.

He tried again, only this time, he told Tess to put blocks of wood under the wheels that were carved out to hold the fridge in place, and they strapped it down.

Delux ran into the restaurant that he grew up in for all of his childhood, to use the bathroom, then came back out.

"Holy shit, this place is disgusting now!"

"What do you mean?" Tess asked.

"It looks like they don't clean. The place has always had a smell to it, but now it smells like shit in there. Sad to see. My parents put so much love and hard work into here."

"I tied the dogs up in the truck," Tess said.

"Ok cool, let's go," Delux said not checking to see how we were tied up.

Both Ruka and I were in the very back of the truck. The fridge was tied up close to the cab. We were fine coming to get the fridge, because Ruka had her side, and I had mine. Going back, I had too much reach on my leash, and I don't know what happened to spook Ruka.

"Doofus, what are you doing? Stay on your side," Ruka told me.

"I don't like the wind on this side. It was nicer up by the window."

"Yeah I know, but the fridge is there now. So just relax and chill until we get there. I don't like you this close to me with all this noise going on around us."

I nervously sat down next to Ruka, pushing her a bit. She moved around and stood up.

"Doofus. I don't want to tell you again, move over to your side."

Her standing up, made me stand up, and I bumped into her again. I don't know what happened, but next thing I know, she was outside the tuck.

"Doofus!" Ruka shouted, falling over the side.

"Ruka! Shit!"

Delux must have seen what happened because he instantly pulled us over on the highway, crossing three lanes of traffic with Ruka dragging on the ground behind us.

"Oh my god, Ruka!" I yelled out as she was being dragged.

Tess jumped out of the truck's window and was climbing into the back of the truck's bed before the truck even came to a stop. She was like a crazy stunt woman crying instantly when she noticed her mistake of giving us too long of a rope.

"Ruka… Fuck, I'm so sorry!" I cried out, afraid to look over the edge.

Tess untied Ruka, and carried her into the front of the truck, and Delux took off for the next exit. We found a gas station and used the phone book to find an emergency vet. They found one close to where we needed to go, so we headed straight there. It all happened so fast.

The Babes took Ruka into the vet while I waited outside tied to the truck with the fridge. I felt terrible sitting there alone, looking at the rope Ruka used to be tied up with. I was trying to process how it happened.

The Babes came out of the building without Ruka. Tess had Ruka's blood all over her clothes and her collar in her hand. Delux came straight to me and tied my rope with less wiggle room.

"It's my fault," Tess said.

I could see she was sad. So was Delux.

"It's okay, it was an accident."

"Where's Ruka?" I whined out, but the Babes didn't answer.

The Babes dropped off the fridge to his dad explaining what had happened and why they were back so late.

Everyone was going to have a big day tomorrow starting this fair, and I just pushed Ruka, my only friend, to her death. I was living up to my name, I thought as I now sat in the RV alone and ashamed.

"Am I really a Doofus? I didn't mean to push Ruka out of the truck. It was an accident," I said to myself, looking at my reflection in the back window.

The Babes drove somewhere close by, and we parked for the evening. I was too ashamed to get up and look out to see where we were.

Tess reassured Delux that after we worked the two fairs, everything would be fine.

How was I going to be fine without Ruka to show me the way? Ha… show me the way. I was being led by a blind dog. My head filled with all the memories we created together as I let out a sigh on her pillow.

Tess left the RV and went to the vending machine or something. I was still too ashamed to move off the pillow to watch her like I usually did. Then Delux left right after, and I was alone again in the RV. They hated me for sure now. I just killed their Ruka, I thought, looking down the narrow walkway to the back of the RV.

Something made my neck tingle after some time of sulking. I sat up and jumped on the driver's seat and looked out the front window.

"Oh my gosh, Ruka!"

She was walking on her own with the Babes as proud as she could be. Was I seeing her as a ghost, or was she really there? The door to the RV opened.

"Ruka!" I let out, full of emotion.

"I'm fine, Doofus. Nothing but a flesh wound. I'm fine."

Delux lifted Ruka into the RV. She laid down and licked her feet that were all covered in bandages.

"I can't feel my paws. I mean, I feel something, but I don't if that makes sense."

"Leave it, Ruka," Delux said softly, petting her head while starting up the RV. "Okay, let's go," Delux said.

"Babe, can we set an appointment for me tomorrow?"

"Yeah sure, if that's what you want to do," Delux said with a feeling of loss I sensed.

Ruka said nothing to me the entire ride home. She just kept licking the bandages on her paws and Delux would then tell her to stop.

"For the next thirty days, we have to clean Ruka's paws twice a day," Tess said. "And I don't think I can handle it."

"I'll do it," Delux said.

The Babes had a lot to do then next day before the fair started. We crept into the driveway of Delux's parents' house sometime after midnight. After the long day we had, we all crashed for the night as soon as we parked and put the big plastic cone on Ruka's head.

We awoke early that morning to the sounds of Grandpa getting a head start. Delux carried Ruka out to pee and poo, and told me to do the same. We were in the suburbs somewhere. Delux's parents' house was a small split level square home with two separate windows over the garage.

"Ruka."

"I know. Delux's house looks like a cat."

"Looks like a cat? What?" I looked at the house and I could kinda see it. "You remember this place?" I asked.

"Just before I started to lose my sight, Delux used to bring me over here and Grandma would doggie-sit me."

"Grandma sits on you?"

"No, she would just watch me, while Delux would go somewhere for a few days or something."

"Look at all these flowers."

"Stay out of them," Ruka told me, catching her cone on the ground.

I peed on the flowers to try to remember that.

"Doofus, get outta there," both Ruka and Grandma shouted towards me as I was back in them again.

Oh yeah, stay out of the flowers, I haphazardly reminded myself.

The Babes left early that morning for Tess's appointment after cleaning and re-bandaging Ruka's paws. Delux came home in the evening to clean her paws a second time, and they both returned later that night with Grandma and Grandpa. Something was missing from Tess and Delux I felt.

The Babes were gone the rest of the weekend except for when Delux came back to change Ruka's bandages. I was able to see her paws and they were barely there. Her toenails and the pads of her feet were all gone.

"Ruka, I'm so sorry," I said sniffing her wounds.

"Doofus, leave it,," Delux said softly.

He'd have to do a good job of cleaning them if they're going to grow back normal again.

Everyday Delux was playing doctor. Removing the bandages, cleaning out the green and brown puss from between all of her toes and what was left of the pads, then bandaging all four paws again. Ruka would just lay there and let Delux do his thing.

"I'm so sorry, Ruka," I told her again, but she would just lay there.

Delux put the cone on Ruka and set her back on the floor.

"I'll be back later. I love you guys."

Delux left, and Ruka and I were alone in the basement of a strange house. We had a big sliding glass door we could look out of into the back yard, but all we could do was look out, until the Babes returned. The weekend went by fast. Ruka and I both slept all day long after that long drive up here, only waking up when Delux came home to play doctor, and when they returned at night to let us poo and pee.

The Taste of Minnesota ended, and the Babes had a small break where they could enjoy themselves. Delux's sister came by and brought her two kids. We all sat in the front yard in the sun and rolled around in the grass, taking turns petting Ruka with her plastic cone on her head. It was nice to see Ruka walking around like nothing had happened. The kids were fun to interact with out in the grass. One child has trouble walking, while the other was a wild boy who thought he could ride me like a horse. We let him try, but he kept falling off me. I looked at Tess and Delux with the kids, and felt something was off with the Babes.

The break was over quickly, and the Babes went back to work at another fair, only this one was within walking distance from the house. They didn't have to leave so early in the morning like the other fair, so they dedicated that time to Ruka and me. Ruka would walk around the yard, and Delux would keep trying to get me to fetch the ball. Fetch a stick. Pull on the rope, but I didn't want to. All I wanted to do was catch one of the squirrels that were in the backyard.

Delux still had to come home every afternoon and clean Ruka's feet, which were getting much better she said if she did say anything at all. I was having a tough time not being able to play with Ruka, and I didn't know what to do to ease my nerves, so I began to chew on a piece of wood I found attached to an old reclining chair.

"If you wanna calm your nerves, you should play fetch with Delux," Ruka told me from her cone, watching me chew on the arm of a chair. "It's for you to chase and bring back... It's a game," she tried to explain.

"Yeah, I just don't get it. I'd rather chase a squirrel. If he wants the ball that bad, why's he throwing it?"

I went back to the chair. At first, I just licked it a few times. I could taste the history of Delux's family in the arm of that chair. I thought for a second that this might be a bad idea, but I kept licking it. Licking soon turned into biting. Biting soon turned into a small mess of wood chips.

"Dollhouse!" flashed in my mind.

My little friend popped into my head with the wood pile, and then Big Man hitting me. I swallowed all the wood chips to hide what I'd done.

Delux returned and didn't notice what I had done to the chair, or it didn't matter because it was an old chair. Ruka stayed silent with me. I felt like she was still upset with me, or she was not happy with my puppy energy that was in a bigger body now.

I was bored out of my mind sitting in that house unable to play with Ruka. Whenever Delux came home, Ruka was excited to see him, but not me while I sat with her all day. Delux and she would go out and play even though her paws were still bandaged up while I just sniffed around and was reminded to stay out of Grandma's flower beds.

"Doofus, what the fuck is this?" Delux hollered out seeing the wood chips I didn't swallow on the floor next to his grandpa's old chair. "Doofus, you have a bone." Delux pointed at my bone that Ruka would always trade me for when I had the big hard rubber toy. "You have a big, hard rubber toy," he said pointing at the big toy in the corner by the pillow I never slept on. I didn't care; I just laid down.

The Babes were not fighting, but there was some tension in the air when they were together in the same room. Now Delux was mad at me for chewing on the wooden arm of the chair that used to be his grandpa's. How was I to know?

There was a pool in the back yard with flowers beds around the trees. I wasn't allowed in any of them, but I still found my way inside some. I was careless one afternoon and broke too many of Grandma's flowers where she noticed, and boy, was she upset. She spent all year preparing flowers during the cold winters, inside the basement we were now occupying.

Delux kept trying to throw the ball for me to fetch, and I kept going the other way, to lay down in the shade. He tried to get me to bite a rope he was hanging onto, but I didn't care. Ruka still wouldn't talk with me like she used to. She laid around with the lamp shade on her neck staring at the wall.

"How are you, Ruka?"

"I'm fine, Doofus."

"Are you ever gonna reply to me with more than those words? I don't feel things are fine."

"I was in what you could call a self-induced trance. Dogs feel pain differently they say, but there was a time I couldn't even feel my paws. I felt like I was walking on clouds. Then, it felt like I was walking on hot glass, and going into a meditation for a while was my only reward from my reality seeing the Babes are not smoking their herbs."

"They said you might not get the feelings back," I said, feeling sick to my stomach.

"Well, I'm definitely feeling something under these bandages."

"Really? This is great news!" I said, feeling my tail begin to wag itself.

"Help me get them off."

"Ahh wait, no. They're supposed to stay on Delux says."

"Delux also told you not to chew on the arm chair, and you did it again anyways."

I looked at the second wood pile I created.

"You wouldn't talk to me. You just sleep all day. I was going crazy inside."

"I was in a trance, Doofus. Now I'm healed. Help me get these off."

Delux came home and saw what we had done and figured now was the time. After cleaning Ruka's feet for 30 days, Delux took her to the vet where she got a clean bill of health that cost the Babes a lot of money. After helping Delux's parents with the two fairs, the Babes had some money.

"Doofus. I'm gonna try to convince Delux to take us for a walk."

"How you going to do that?"

"Watch and learn."

Ruka went over to Delux who was going through some of his records. He had a DJ gig somewhere that weekend he was getting ready to spin at. Ruka went over to Delux and sat down next to him, putting her paw on his arm.

"What's up, Ruka? What you want, baby girl? How's your paws?"

"I want to go for a walk in the park, D."

"You call him D?" I asked her.

"D is easier to feel. He can't understand me, he can just feel me. Once he feels, he will understand."

"Yeah but you call him D, not Delux."

"We all have our name for him—now watch."

Ruka went back to Delux and put her paw on him again and whipped out her puppy dog eyes.

"Ruka, you are so cute."

I walked over to Ruka and put my head close to Delux's hand.

"You want to learn how to swim, buddy?" Delux said rubbing my head and then standing up.

"Ruka, what does it mean to swim?"

"It means we are going to the park."

Delux put the leashes on us while Tess rolled them a joint. Ruka was walking fine now as we made our way down the street to the park entrance. I liked the park. There were a lot of trees and bushes with rabbits and squirrels everywhere. We made our way down a double row of perfectly planted pine trees, to a small dock that was on the river.

"Come on, Doofus. Let's see if you can swim," Delux said to me in a way I could tell he was still mad at me about the chair.

"You're gonna love this one, kid," Ruka said.

"Go on. Go swim," Delux said to me pointing to the river that was in front of a boat ramp.

Ruka found her way to the water and drank some, but she didn't go in it very deep.

"He wants me to go in the water?"

"Yep."

"I hate water."

"No, you hate baths."

"I don't know how to swim."

"All dogs can swim. It's a natural reaction once you're in the water."

"Come here, boy." Delux picked me up under my belly and walked me onto the dock. "In you go," he said tossing me over the railing.

I sank to the bottom like a rock. It was dark brown and colder than I imagined. I could see sunlight above me, but I didn't know how to get off the bottom. I kicked and I clawed at the water above me, but nothing. Then both legs touched the bottom at the same time, and I was able to kick myself towards the surface, which was just a few inches above my head.

"There he is. Good boy, Doofus, now swim," Delux told me from the dock.

"Babe, it looks like he's drowning," Tess said.

"It does, doesn't it," Delux said, laughing. "He'll figure it out."

I somehow got my rear end to stay afloat, then I was touching the shore with my front paws and able to climb out of the water. I gave myself a good shake, which led to it looking like I was wagging my tail, but I was just trying to get the water off.

"Oh, you liked it, did ya. Well, let's try it again," Delux said, grabbing me under my belly.

With one big toss, he threw me over the railing again into the water a bit further this time. He was enjoying this a little too much, I thought, as I sank to the bottom thinking about the chair, the flowers, the pillow, the shoe. I found my way back to the surface and got myself to float. I swam in a small circle and found my paws on the shoreline again. I gave myself a good shake crawling out, and another one just for good measure.

"Good job, Doofus. You wanna try it again? Let's go," he said, pointing at the seat he used to stand on to throw me over.

Before Delux could grab me, I did it myself. I ran up to the bench, jumped on it, then sent myself over the railing, falling into the water below.

"What tha… You see that?" Delux said to Tess.

This time, I stayed in the water and swam around.

"Ruka, this is great out here. You should try it!"

I realized in that moment, I loved water.

"I don't think this will change my mind about baths, but I love swimming!" I told Ruka as we walked home.

After I had a good swim, I was met with a garden hose and a bath. Yep. I still hated baths.

"Ruka. You notice something different with the Babes?"

"Like what?"

"Like something is missing from them."

"Tess was pregnant. She decided now wasn't the time for her to have a baby seeing she was living in a RV with a man and two dogs."

"You say it like it's a bad thing… What happened to the baby?"

"It's gone, Doofus. It's not here anymore."

"Ruka, are you okay? Your energy changed too just now."

"This happened to me as well, and I guess I'm still not over it."

"What do you mean this happened to you?"

"The guy who gave me to Delux, owned my boyfriend at the time."

"You had a boyfriend?"

"Well, he was just a friend," Ruka laughed. "He was ugly as fuck now that I remember."

"Do you remember his name?"

"Little Man Bronson. He had a big underbite."

"Was he a big dog with one of those silly names?"

"He was an ugly, skinny fucker. Smaller than me, and almost as tough. Now that I think about it, it was probably a blessing I lost all my pups. They would've been ugly as shit."

"What do you mean, you lost them?"

"I was pregnant with about eight puppies they thought. Delux kept me closed off in the kitchen so I could give birth on a clean floor, but I could no longer feel the pups alive inside of me as we waited for them to come out."

"What do you mean?"

"I don't know. One day I felt them all alive and well, and the next day, I didn't feel them move around anymore, but they were still inside of me."

"What did you do?"

"Delux took me to the vet, and they said that I would absorb them back into my body. They were gone just like that."

"How did this happen?"

"The doctor said it can happen sometimes. I might have been too stressed. I don't know. While I was pregnant, Delux moved us from Miami to Minnesota."

"Why'd you move?"

"He had no choice. His car was stolen and there was no way for him to go to work. He waited, hoping they would find his car, but they didn't until the last day the insurance ran out."

"What does that mean?"

"I don't know. I just know he was upset when he got his van back. It was destroyed, and the insurance only covered a carpet cleaning when the motor was now blowing smoke, the car was wet inside and full of mold with all of his stereo equipment missing."

"They stole his music gear?"

"No, his car stereo was missing, but it was a nice one."

"Oh."

"Crazy part is, Delux left his turntables and records in his van several days in a row because he was DJ'ing a lot in those days. The night his van was stolen, he went downstairs and brought up all of his gear right before we went to bed, and that night they stole it."

"Woah, he almost lost all of his music?"

"Music, turntables, mixer... all would have been very hard to replace."

"So what happened?"

"Thirty days after the theft, Delux's father drove from Minnesota to Miami, to help him move what was left of his life, back home to Minnesota here. I was pregnant during this time, so as I went from the warmth of Miami to the frozen tundra of Minnesota, I lost my puppies."

"It's not frozen here now."

"It's called seasons. We don't have them in Miami. It's always sunny. Or rainy. Here in Minnesota, it gets to be frozen like the ice cubes Delux puts in our water sometimes."

"No way, like ice cubes?"

"Yeah, ice cubes."

Ruka was a good distraction, and a great storyteller. She filled me in with all the details of Delux sneaking her into the hotel room, so she didn't have to sleep in the cold truck on the move back to Minnesota.

"I'm sorry you lost your puppies, Ruka."

"Thanks, but like I said, it was probably for the better."

"Do you think the Babes will ever get rid of us?"

"No way. They're stuck with us."

"Do you think the Babes will be ok?"

"Let's see, Doofus. Time is the only true teller of any story."

The Babes put us into the RV and drove us to a tattoo shop. Delux wanted a tattoo on his arm, and Tess decided to get one on her leg. Ruka and I waited in the RV while the Babes went inside. Soon a man and a woman came outside with the Babes from the building they went into. I didn't like the energy of this couple, and it made me want to bark, so I did, rocking the RV from side to side.

"Let me get the dogs so you can come inside and look," Delux explained.

"Are you sure the dogs will be cool?" the man asked.

"They'll be on leashes. Tess can handle them, don't worry."

Delux let us out on the leash and handed us off to Tess, who was waiting outside. This guy going into the RV reminded me of the police that pulled us over and went through everything.

"Bark! Bark!" I let out.

Turns out Delux was just showing him how he wanted his tattoo to look. It was something from his turntables that he had locked away under the countertop. They got out of the RV, and Ruka and I went back in. Tess let us off our leashes and closed the door behind her as we listened to their muffled voices slowly fade away and into the building.

"What's going on, Ruka?"

"The Babes are getting permanent reminders of temporary feelings."

After the tattoos, the Babes packed up the RV once again, and they decided to head to the east coast before Costa Rica. Tess had some things at her mom's house she wanted to pick up to take with us, so we headed that way.

The Babes said their goodbyes to Delux's family, and that morning after breakfast, we hit the road again with a stash full of mix tapes and an ounce of Minnesota's best blueberry herbs that when smoked, smelled nothing like blueberries and more like a fruity skunk.

CHAPTER 6

PENNSYLVANIA

We moved at a slow steady pace in the RV. Ruka always took the middle spot between the Babes, and I would sit on either side of her trying not to push her out of the way, which I seemed to do often while we drove. It was hard to sit still. To try and calm myself, I would lick and chew on Ruka's ears, but was often told to stop by one of the Babes. I had a lot of energy inside me, and sitting in the RV while we drove around all day was not fit for me. "Ruka. Doofus. Outside," Delux would say at every stop. Delux always had the stick that threw the ball in his hand for Ruka. He tried to throw the ball for me, and I just stood there wondering why he would throw it so far.

We drove into the night, stopping off at a rest stop with no trees. It was just a bunch of concrete. The sign said we were in Ohio. The Babes went to bed while Ruka and I laid on the floor licking the fresh smells and tastes off of our paws after eating dinner.

"I remember the first time we drove through here, we got stuck in Chicago."

"How'd you get stuck?"

"We broke down in the middle of the night on a back road through Indiana. No cars were out, and the one guy that finally came past us, owns a tow truck and a mechanic shop. The Babes thought he might have been a serial killer, but I felt he had good vibes, so I remained calm. He gave the Babes hot chocolate and let us all sit in the warm cab while he worked in the snow hooking up the RV. This was the night the babes fell in love with each other I think."

"Why do you say that?" I asked, half asleep from her long story.

"It was the first time they did it," Ruka said, snickering.

"Ahh, okay."

I had no clue what she was talking about, I just let Ruka keep talking.

"When we made it here, to Ohio."

"You stopped here before?" I asked, moving myself in a circle on the seat to find just the right spot for my hips.

"No, we were on another old country back road that resembled a winter wonderland."

"Winter wonderland?" I asked, confused.

"It had been snowing all day and night. There was about eight inches of fresh snow on the ground. Everything was white."

"Ah, okay." I said trying to imagine something I have never seen.
"That night we slept at a random trailer park where in the middle of the night, we heard gun shots."

"Gun shots? Like the ones in Miami that time at the warehouse when the gangsters let off two clips from an AK-47 around one p.m. *Bang bang bang*. And the police sirens after?"

"No. This was a shotgun. It blasted off twice, and they weren't followed by sirens, but the silence of the winter ground covered in snow."

"What does that sound like?"

"The key word in that sentence was silence, Doofus."

I was so tired. I just wanted to sleep but Ruka kept talking.

"What did you do after the gun shots?"

"There was nothing to do. The Babes looked around a bit from their window, but they decided to stay still, and they went to sleep. The next day we left."

"Why are you telling me this Ruka?"

"I don't know. I think we're are in the same spot, just on a busier road."

"And?"

"And that's it. You were supposed to fall asleep. Good night, Doofus."

Sometimes Ruka shared the oddest of things with me.
Before I could put any thought into what she just said to me, I faded away into a deep sleep, waking up to the heat of the next day.

"Damn, it's hot in here," Delux said.

"We need to find some shade for us and the Dogs, hot damn," Tess said jumping out of the bed.

"Maybe at the next truck stop on the other side of the border there might be more shade? We're close. We should try," Delux said, letting us out to pee.

"Okay, but let me roll us a blunt first."

"Sounds good."

Delux took us out for a pee in the hot sun, and I instantly made my way back to the RV once I finished peeing. Ruka did the same. It was extra hot that summer morning. Delux put us back in the RV and sat in the passenger seat looking at the map to verify the next stop and how far it was.

"You wanna drive? The next stop's not that far away," Delux asked Tess.

Tess jumped into the driver's seat in her short panties and small top that she never wore a bra under. She was excited. I could tell she missed driving her RV.

"Ok, if we get pulled over while smoking, which we will not, I'll stash the blunt here in the air vent, and later we can fish it out," Delux told her.

"Okay, good idea. We'll be fine, but good idea," said Tess. "And if anything does happen, I will take the fall because we cannot lose the RV."

"We'll be fine. We can do our Mississippi Switch if need be," Delux told her.

"That's right. That was so crazy when you did that."

We pulled out of the rest stop to look for shade before any of us even brushed our teeth or ate breakfast. It was a windy morning with beautiful blue skies. The sun was up, and the day was starting out hot as we pulled onto the highway with Tess behind the wheel, and Delux sitting in the passenger seat, falling more and more in love with her. I could see it in his eyes.

They passed the blunt back and forth as Tess turned up her punk music she sang to instead of Delux's hip hop. The back windows were open to help keep the RV fresh and aired out. Ruka sat on the floor with her nose in the air and tail wagging from the positive vibes going back and forth with the Babes. Ruka loved when the Babes smoked.

"It helps my eyes," Ruka said, sniffing the air between the Babes.

"Oh shit, there's a cop way up ahead with someone pulled over. You see him?" Delux pointed out.

"Yeah, I see him. I'll get in the other lane so we don't pass next to him," Tess said switching lanes using the blinker.

"Everything's cool," Delux said, putting the blunt out before we passed the cop.

I looked out the front window and saw the cop car with an overweight cop making someone sign a ticket. The cop stared at our RV the entire time as we passed him. He seemed to be paying more attention to us, than the person he already had pulled over. Delux looked back in the side mirror as Tess moved us back into the slow lane.

"Shit. He ran back to his car."

"Fuck, I see that. He's pulling out and chasing us with his lights on."

"Mother Fucker."

Delux never hid the blunt in the air vent, he panicked and tucked it under the carpet behind the passenger seat. The babes quickly rolled down the windows, and Tess sprayed some sort of air spray to make it smell nice, and then lit a cigarette.

"Fuck, he's pulling us over, Babe."

"Let's switch seats. You don't have a license," Delux said.

"He saw me already when we passed him. He looked right at me, then at the RV."

"Fuck. Okay, we didn't do anything wrong, so we'll be fine," Delux said sitting back in the RV petting my head.

"You put the bag of weed back in its hiding spot right?"

"Yeah, it's between the cups, in the cupboard."

"We got this."

The cop arrived at the window out of breath and with an attitude.

"License, insurance, and registration, ma'am."

The cop didn't even say please, hello, good morning, nothing.

"Ruka, what's happening?"

"The police is what's happening."

"I don't have my license on me right now, but here's my ID and our insurance and registration," Tess handed him.

"Ma'am, please step out of the vehicle. Sir, you sit right there and mind your dogs."

"Why did you pull us over?" Tess asked getting out.

"You were swerving as you passed me, and you are driving without a driver's license," the cop says putting handcuffs on Tess's wrists.

"Wait, what are you doing?" Delux shouted out.

"We weren't swerving. We changed lanes to give you space. It's the law," Tess said while being spun around.

"That's not how I saw it, and you're driving without a license. Stop resisting," the cop said putting cuffs on Tess. "You, wait here," the cop said to Delux. "You, come back to my car," the cop demanded, taking Tess away.

"What the fuck?" Delux sat there watching the cop take Tess.

"Can I put some clothes on?" Tess asked while being pushed away from the RV.

"No, get to the back of my car," the cop insisted.

"Ruka. What the fuck is going on. He's talking Tess?"

"Don't worry. Delux will get us out of this," Ruka said calmly.

"Sir. Open the side door here, and control your dogs, or I will shoot them," the officer demanded of Delux.

"What the fuck is this guy's problem, Ruka? Neither one of us has barked. Should I bite him?"

"This is just another asshole cop, Doofus. Relax, and don't do anything stupid. This cop's an overachiever it seems."

Delux put the leashes on Ruka and I and opened the side door to the cop and stepped out.

"Have you been doing any drugs or drinking alcohol?"

"No. We just woke up from the rest stop there, and we're just looking for more shade for the dogs. Why are you harassing us like this?"

"You passed me swerving. She does not have a license, and I think I smell marijuana."

The Babes did find some good weed while in Minnesota, but even I could hardly smell the weed after they sprayed that can. They had a small stash to get them to the Big Apple, that Delux confirmed was stashed away safe. All you could smell with this RV, was the motor and the oil that was in it. There was a slight vintage smell around the glove box, but not much.

"Go stand over there and hold your dogs. If they come close to attacking me, I will not hesitate to shoot them."

"Man… I am so tired of you fake cops telling me you're gonna shoot my dogs if I don't comply. My dogs are chill, you're being the asshole."

"I look fake to you? Go stand over there while I search your RV," the cop demanded.

"I think you need a search warrant or something. You have no probable cause to do a search. Where's your dog?" Delux yelled walking away.

"Your girlfriend was driving without a driver's license. I can do what I like."

"You discovered that after the fact. We were just driving for more shade, you dick."

Ruka and I were chilling while Delux did all the barking. From my guess, Ruka was still just as tired as I was after driving all day yesterday and waking up early with this heat. We were chill and not ready to cause any problems with this hyped-up officer out here in this morning sun.

"Fucking asshole," Delux said, crouching down to us.

Delux sat there with us while this fat police officer's backup arrived and stood alongside of us.

"This is bullshit. We weren't swerving. We moved over to give him room while he was giving someone else a ticket. He ripped my girlfriend out of the RV, instantly put cuffs on her, and didn't allow her to put on any extra clothes. We did nothing wrong for him to stop us and now search us like this. What is it with all you cops wanting to search this RV like we are shipping drugs around or something. We are just two artists, with dogs, trying to get to Costa Rica. What the fuck."

Delux was upset. You could hear it, you could feel it, and you could see it in his body language.

"I'm so sorry this is happening to you right now," the second officer said.

The second officer was an old man. The one tearing the RV apart was a fat, young man who if we were put to a foot race, he would lose even if we walked. I sat there looking at Ruka.

"What do we do?"

"There's nothing we can do, Doofus."

"I found a weapon!" the cop yelled out the door holding Delux's BB gun.

"It's a BB gun, you idiot. Those are not illegal. Use your common sense and you'll see. It's in your own fucking hands. Look!"

"Control your dogs. I don't want to have to shoot them," the cop replied again walking back to his squad car.

"Why did he just say that? Again! I'm so tired of cops telling me they're going to shoot my dogs. Look at them, they're chill even when I am yelling and pissed off."

"Again, I am so sorry this is happening to you guys," the old cop repeated.

"You. Hand your dogs to my officer and come in here," the fat cop told Delux after returning from talking with Tess locked in the back of the squad car.

"That's Doofus, and this one is Ruka," Delux said, walking away from us.

I saw Tess give Delux a head nod from the back of the car, then looking towards the cop as Delux walked to the RV. Delux went inside, and all I could hear was muffled noises. Moments later, Delux came back, and the fat cop exited the RV with their small bag of weed that was hidden.

"What just happened, Doofus?" Ruka asked.

"The cop couldn't find the weed, so Delux had to show him."

"You. Get in your RV and follow us to the police station if you want to see your girlfriend again," the cop demanded in a now dripping wet uniform.

The old-man cop handed our leashes to Delux as more officers arrived on the scene. Obviously, there was not much going on Canton, Ohio, for all these guys to show up.
Fat cop sped off with Tess, the other two squad cars then pulled out, and Delux followed. The cops drove fast, and it took everything our motor had, to keep up. The cops pulled off the highway and into a small city street. Our home didn't move like the cop cars, so it was a struggle. I was watching Delux's face from the passenger seat as he drove. He was worried. He was scared. Then I saw time slow down for him and his face shift. He turned his head right. Then left, then back right again as the police cars in front of him ran a yellow light forcing him to decide to stop and lose the police, or follow the car that stole Tess from us, and go through the red light.
He followed.

"What the fuuuu..." Delux couldn't even get the words out as time slowed down in that turn. "I've been here before," Delux said out loud looking at the familiar scene to his right.

"Ruka, have you been here before?" I asked.

"No, and neither has Delux. Well, not with me anyways."

We made a hard left, then an immediate right after running the red light, and time sped back up for us all. Up a hill a ways was the back of the police station. Tess was already inside, and Delux was ordered to go around front and talk to the front desk.
Delux came back to the RV after a long wait.

"Well guys. It looks like we are gonna be spending the night here."

Delux made himself lunch and took us out to play, although I still hadn't figured out what play meant, so we took a long walk and were put back in the RV parked alongside the courthouse. We sat there, not knowing what to do. Everything revolved around the Babes being together. So far, they had never been apart since I met them. 24 hours a day, 7 days a week, we were always all together.

"Except for the Taste and the Fair where we were left at home," Ruka said reading my mind.

"How do you do that?"

"Do what?"

"Read my mind. I know I was thinking that in my head."

"I'm not sure if being blind helped accelerate the ability, but I'm pretty sure all dogs can read minds. You can't?"

"No."

I looked at Delux again who was drawing some landscape from his mind in a book on the floor with us.

"What is he thinking?" I wondered.

He seemed worried about Tess.

Dinner time was about, and he made us all food. Delux walked us a few more times around the building Tess was being held in overnight.

"How're your paws, Ruka?"

"They're healing, Doofus. Thanks for asking."

Delux called us back into the RV where we called it a night. Delux crawled up into bed alone. He tossed and turned for a long time before he was able to fall asleep. Ruka and I both stayed awake until he fell asleep.

The next afternoon, Tess was finally released around 3pm after Delux paid a $420 bond to get her out of jail, promising that they'd go back and fix the situation.

"Oh my fucking god. Get me the fuck out of here," Tess said, getting into the RV.

"Where you wanna go?"

"Anywhere but here," Tess said.

"When I paid your bond, everyone in the office was talking shit about the cop who pulled us over. Apparently, he is known for writing the most tickets and carries a shitty reputation. They told me to take this all to court, after they thought my tattoo was a weed wacker."

"That fucking pig took me practically naked. He kept staring at my body, I didn't get a shower, and the place was freezing cold".

"I'm so sorry, babe."

"It's fine. It all worked out; we kept the RV and the dogs are safe."

"Is it true, you told him we had a bag of weed in here that he spent twenty minutes looking for and couldn't find?"

"Yes, I told him. He threatened me, telling me we would lose the dogs and the RV if I didn't tell the truth. I figured he was lying, but I was scared for you and the dogs, so I told him. That's why I looked at you from the car."

"That's what I thought. The fat fuck was dripping sweat all over the place when I came in here, and he threatened to shoot the dogs... twice".

"Fucking assholes," Tess said still frustrated.

"Babe, the old cop who stood next to me told me he was sorry this was happening to us."

"Ugh, such a prick!" Tess said, lighting up a cigarette.

"Hi, doggies! I missed you so much!" Tess said hugging our faces and squeezing us together. Ruka and I wagged our tails and tried to lick her face between head rubs.

"We'll go to the next rest stop, and I'll make you a hot shower and some food."

"I cannot wait. I'm so hungry."

"I have a surprise for you."

"What is it?"

"Reach your right arm back, and look under the carpet flaps there."

Tess reached under the two flaps that came together and there was the blunt she rolled that they barely smoked from yesterday morning.

"Oh my god, Babe. How?"

"The cop told me that you told him there was a small bag of weed in the RV, not a blunt as well. So, I just opened the cups and gave him the bag like he asked and he was happy with that."

"Oh my god, you're the best. Can we smoke it now?"

Delux looked behind him in the side mirrors.

"I don't see why not. The next rest stop is 40 miles."

"I love you, Babe," Tess said lighting the blunt with her foot on the dash in her new jailhouse plastic flip-flops. "I can't wait to take a shower!"

We found ourselves in the next state, but it wasn't New York. It was hilly, with lots of forest and mountains. The air was fresh out here. We pulled into a two-story apartment complex that was full of smells from all sorts of things. We were instructed to stay in the RV while the Babes checked things out.

"Where are we, Ruka?"

"You know, for a dog who can see, you sure ask me a lot of questions I shouldn't know."

"Sorry, Ruka. I just have a hard time figuring out what's going on."

"What's going on in your head?"

"What are we going to do next?"

"Live in the moment, Doofus. We're waiting for the Babes to come back from Tess's mom's house, or in this case, apartment."

I had more questions, but I didn't want to ask them. I just sat on the driver's seat and waited for the Babes to come back, while Ruka laid on her pillow.
"Ruka, I see something."

"What do you see?"

"I think it is one of those squirrels we saw back in Minnesota. Holy shit, I actually see three of them, no four."

"It's okay, Doofus. Our job is to protect the RV. Those squirrels are not a threat."

The Babes came back. The side door opened, and they came inside the RV.

"Do you think it'll work?" Delux asked looking at us.

"I think we try to leave the dogs in the RV first, and if it goes well, we leave them here, if not, we'll try them inside and they can stay in my room."

The Babes left us in the RV while they went inside to have a hot shower and eat some food.

"What do you think, Ruka. How long are we going to stay here?"

"We're dogs, Doofus. Anything over a week will feel like a month to us. Like I said, you need to learn to be in the moment."

In that moment, some person walked by on the other side of the street with a dog.

"Bark! Bark! Bark!" I let out without really thinking about it. "Ruka, there is a dog walking by us. Bark! Bark! Bark!"

"Doofus, it's okay. We only bark when they're really close or trying to open the doors."

I tried to control myself, but it was difficult. I liked it when I let out my barks, and I watched people jump. I laid down in the front seat with my head on the steering wheel. The person with the dog had come and gone, like the rest stops we stopped at along the way. I thought about them all while the Babes were inside the apartment building. I could hear Ruka twitching below me. She was finally falling asleep after a long drive. Ruka wanted me to be in the moment, but she couldn't chill. She sits the entire time, next to Delux, looking at him with eyes that don't see.

"Bark! Bark! Bark!"

"Doofus, what is it now?" Ruka asked jumping up and letting out a few barks herself.

"Someone parked their car over here."

"Bark! Bark!"

"Doofus, are they coming towards us?"

"No, but they're looking at me."

"How far away are they? I don't smell or hear anyone."

"They're on the other side of the parking lot."

"Bark! Bark! Bark! You better stay over there."

"Doofus, chill out. They're not trying to mess with us."

"They keep looking at the RV. Bark! Bark! Bark!"

"They're looking at us, because we're new here. We don't belong here. Doofus, we need to blend in and not draw attention."

"I got the attention of the Babes. Here they come."

Delux opened the door to the RV.

"Doofus, what are you barking about, buddy? Calm down."

"There's people!"

Delux put his hands nicely on me. I think he liked my barking.

"Come on, let's try them inside I guess. You can't be out here barking at everything," Delux said, looking down at me.

The Babes took us into the apartment building. There was a cat in the small living room that was attached to an even smaller kitchen. This place was small and tight like the RV. Around the corner, down the hallway, was the litter box. Ruka found that first and stuck her head in it pulling out a turd and eating it before Delux could say no. Down the hallway was two rooms, and a bathroom. The room at the end of the hall was Tess's mom's. The room across the bathroom was Tess's. It was still how she left it a few years ago.

Ruka and I were instructed to leave the litter box alone, but Ruka already had her head in there twice, so Delux turned the box around, so it would face the wall. The trouble was, the kitten that was in the house, was also blind.

"Ruka, she's blind like you."

"I know, Doofus."

"How can you tell?"

"She told me."

"How'd she do that? You understand cats? How do you understand cats?"

"Doofus, leave it," Delux interrupted as I was sniffing the corner of the litter box.

We were put into the bedroom, and that was gonna be our new home for a few nights. It was nice being so close to the Babes. We got plenty of cuddles in the mornings, good food in the evening, and the RV was sent off to a mechanic the first night. Apparently, something was wrong with it, and it needed attention.

I did escape the bedroom while the Babes went to pick up the RV. I could hear the neighbors talking outside the door, so I barked at them and pushed on the front door letting them know, I was in here. When they quieted down, I moved the litter box and tried one of these so-called cat poo's Ruka loves so much. They were actually pretty good minus a few litter chunks stuck to the edges. I jumped on the couch in the living room and had my way with two pillows spreading the insides out all over the floor.

When the Babes returned, they found paint, pillow stuffing, and wood chips on the floor from me clawing at the front door. Apparently, I was unable to control myself.

"Doofus, what the fuck did you do?" Tess asked me, looking at the back side of a torn up wooden door. Even though the door was still there, they didn't like that one.

A week later, we took Tess's mom's car to the state where Tess got arrested. It would be quicker and cheaper in gas using her mom's new, four-door sedan than the RV. The Babes put blankets in the back to protect the seats from our hair, gave Ruka and me a bone, and a big rubber toy to chew on. I didn't know how the Babes didn't see it, we didn't play or chew on things while we were moving. We just sat and watched them.

The car ride was smooth from the back seat compared to the RV. It was relaxing. Ruka finally laid down behind Tess after trying to get into the front seat a dozen times and blocked every time. I laid down behind Delux with my head on the armrest of the back door. It smelled good. It had that new car smell they said.

I took a nap and dreamt about eating a big giant cake made out of smooth liver with an eggshell topping. I bit and chewed on the meat cake as I slept. The meat was tough and didn't taste like meat at all. It was more polyester-like, with a hard foamy texture.

Hours later, the car stopped, and I awoke from my nap. Delux got out and opened the back door for us to get out to pee.

"Doofus! What in the actual fuck did you do?" Delux said questioning me.

"Oh my God... Doofus! How the fuck did we not hear or see him do this?" Tess asked.

"Oh, Doofus. You're in trouble this time," Ruka told me, getting out on Tess's side.

Delux bent down and picked up pieces of the car door that fell out after opening the door. I guess I was chewing on the door, and not a meat cake. The Babes were so upset with me.

"Doofus, they're probably gonna leave you here on the side of the road after this one," Ruka told me sniffing what had fallen out on the ground.

"Your new name is 'You Fucking Fuck.' What the fuck is wrong with you, dog? I gave you a cow's leg to chew on. A hard rubber toy. Ugh, you fucking idiot. We should just leave him here tied up somewhere with a sign that says FREE," Tess said in anger, looking at her mom's car.

"I told you, Doofus," Ruka told me, giving me the side eye with eyes that don't work but still had the same effect.

I felt terrible. Kinda. I didn't realize what I was doing.
Tess went into her court hearing with a lawyer and a judge, while Delux held us outside.

"Doofus. I cannot believe you. Ugh... You fucking... How did you chew up the entire door?" Delux asked, looking around for a place to tie me to. Tess came back out before he found a pole.

"So, we go back to Florida and fix it, or I become an outlaw in multiple states now," Tess told Delux.

"Tess is an outlaw?"

"She got investigated after she ran the RV into a pole when she first came to pick up Delux. She received three tickets and was supposed to show up to court, and she never did. Seeing she recently got arrested, trouble probably follows this woman," Ruka told me.

We spent another two long weeks at the apartment with Tess's mom, her blind cat and her mom's boyfriend who said he would replace the inside of the car door I destroyed. Delux left his computer with Tess's brother to try and fix something that recently happened to it. For some reason, the computer he recorded all of his music with, would no longer turn on. After the RV was fixed and ready to go, the computer was not. Delux decided waiting for the computer was not an option, so they left Pennsylvania for New York City.

"New York is huge!" I told Ruka who was wagging her tail.

There were so many huge buildings everywhere. Most were under construction it seemed, and a lot of them looked like they were from a different time period.

By now, Delux became a pro at driving the RV. He could parallel park the RV in two moves without hitting a car. The Babes left us in the RV behind a baby gate so we were not able to reach the front of the RV where we could see people and start causing chaos. With the shades drawn, we could not see the distractions that outside can bring.

The Babes returned from one of Tess's friends, and we were off to meet the weed man. Even though the Babes got busted once already, they thought they would never get caught again I guess, or they liked to live on the edge with their herbs.

As we drove through a long tunnel that went under water, Delux started to freak out like he did back at the warehouse when I was choking on a ball.

"Holy shit," Delux said in a weird shaking move, moving the RV side to side.

"What is it? You okay?" Tess asked.

"I just saw, something terrible here. People dying or something crazy like that. Buildings exploding and falling... Bombs going off and this tunnel filling up with smoke or water... I don't know, it feels so, real... What the fuck is happening right now?" Delux yelled out, focusing on the road.

Everything was normal for us. Traffic outside was moving steady. The music was relaxing. Tess had her foot up on the dash and a smile on her face, moving her hand up and down out the window while Delux was freaking out.

"I've never seen him do this besides when you choked. What the heck is going on with him?" Ruka asked.

There was no smoke or water in the tunnel, but as we exited out into a clear fall night, Delux was still in a panic.

"What the fuck am I feeling? I don't like it. Look at my arms. My hair is standing up. I have goose bumps all over!"

He was covered. His body was reacting to something. I let out a whine. Delux took in the world around him while taking a few deep breaths. He realized, in that moment, everything was normal and fine.

"What the fuck?" Delux let out a deep breath. "I see we are fine. I feel fine, but a second ago, what the fuck. It was like a panic attack. I was seeing a bunch of horrible shit in my mind."

We parked the RV in front of the two tallest buildings downtown where the Babes met a guy on a bicycle. Tess got out did all the talking. She exchanged a small book, for a large bag of film, and got back into the RV.

"Wow, you just did that on the street, in front of the World Trade Center, and got away with it?"

"It's just film, let's go," Tess said.

We left New York City and drove south on 95. It was a one-way to Miami from there. The Babes got high, turned up their music, and pushed us south. It was late, and a long day, so we pulled off at a rest stop, and called it a night. Delux was cooked. I could smell the weed they were smoking was a lot stronger, and it hit Delux and Ruka differently. For the first time, Ruka laid down while we were moving tonight. As long as I didn't bump into her, she would stay lying down and relaxed.

We were headed back to Miami for more opportunities to make some good money before their Costa Rica adventure.

"Ruka, what do you think we'll do in Miami?"

"Tess will model again, and Delux will DJ somewhere until they fix her license."

"What about us?"

"What about us, Doofus? Or, You Fucking Fuck, as they now call you."

"Don't call me that."

"You deserve it."

"Why?"

"You don't listen. You're pushy. You never live in the moment, or you never want to take part of any moments, but you love to have your own destructive moments, by yourself when everyone is trying to get your attention. You're a fucking fuck for real."

"I've always asked you to join me."

"No you haven't, and nor would I. You need to learn how to respect this place, the Babes, their things, and whatever else they tell you."

I thought I had been doing pretty good. Delux tried to get me to go fetch the ball, but Ruka and her level of excitement, were too much to compete against. I didn't have her enthusiasm. I sat and watched her run and sniff out the ball, then return it to Delux where he would roll it on the ground some other direction. They played well together, so I stayed out of the way.
The next morning, we were let out to do our business and we got back on the road again early that morning. Along the highway, Delux drove past an electronic sign that caught his attention.

"What?!? Building One of the World Trade Center collapses, is what I just read on that sign?"

"What?" Tess asked.

"That sign back there, it said the World Trade Center fell."

The Babes shut off their mixtape and put on the radio. Every station was talking about the collapse of one of the buildings because it was hit by a plane. The Babes were in disbelief. We were there yesterday.

Delux had a stone silence about him as he listened to the radio. He was right about whatever he saw or felt in the tunnel the day before. Tess just looked out her side window with her hand holding her chin. I could tell they were processing a lot, but I couldn't get inside their heads to see what it was. He just kept driving straight.

"Are we at war?" Tess asked.

"If not, it's gonna be. There's no way an airplane can bring down one of those buildings. No way, and two just fell!"

"What are we gonna do?"

"Let's call JC at the next stop. See if we can gather our thoughts with him for a bit before we head down to Miami. If the Country's going to go to war, JC's spot is the best to be at."

"Good idea. The modeling season, if it starts, starts back up in December, so we have some time," Tess said.

CHAPTER 7

TALLAHASSEE

The Babes got the go ahead, and drove straight to JC's house, deep in the woods. There, we watched all of the footage of the attacks, and the interviews of the people at Ground Zero that JC recorded form the news.

"That was not because of planes. You can see, it was planted explosives. Look at the windows blow out. That's the only way to bring three buildings down on their own footprint with two airplanes," they were saying slowing the video they recorded down.

I didn't know, but it felt right what Delux was saying. He had a way of looking at things and figuring them out in his own weird way.

"This is going to send us into a war," JC said.

Delux did the math sitting there on the couch smoking a joint with JC and Tess.

"If I had stayed in the military when I did, my contract would have ended this November, right after these attacks."

Delux was somber after watching all of the footage JC had recorded of the event in New York City.

"I would have been forced to re-enlist while on reserve." Delux leaned back in the couch silent, watching the TV screen.

Not knowing what to do, JC offered Delux a job, and the Babes decided to stay in the woods for a bit. With the new rise in terror level, the modeling industry was on hold, and who knew what would happen next.

"Babe, I'll work here. I can work with JC, or I'm sure he has some friends looking for someone to help them. There seem's to be a lot of private contractor work here."

"And what do I do?" Tess asked not wanting to stay there.

"Paint. Hang out with the dogs, help JC out around the property, I don't know. One of us needs to work, so I'll go until the modeling starts up again, or come hang siding with me, or chip paint off boats like JC wants, I don't know."

JC gave us a spot to park the RV on his huge property, down by a mud-capped sink hole. A burn pit was close by that the RV could fit inside of, it was so big. He drove his tractor around that dragged something behind it that made a lot of noise I didn't like. It cut all of the tall grass, weeds and baby trees down that were trying to overtake each other. Once JC finished cutting, we had a nice little yard to call our own. We were surrounded in nature out here. There were no traffic noises, no gun shots, no crack heads arguing about crack outside. No sirens, no horns. This was peaceful.

I found the mud-capped sink hole right away. It had a layer of water on it making it look like a pool, but as I laid in it, I could feel my body sink down into thick mud.

"Well, look who likes water now," Ruka told me, peeing before the hole to remind her it was there so she didn't fall in it. Ruka was not a fan of water, swimming or mud on her feet. She was pretty dense and sank like a rock she said.

"You know they're going to give you a bath after that mud, so enjoy it."

"Oh I'm enjoying it," I said, digging at it with curiosity.

I got up out of the mud and ran around the newly cut grass area we had. It all smelled amazing, so I rolled it all over my body then jumped up and ran around in circles some more, barking as much as I could. Delux shifted the RV around a bit to make the inside more level while I ran in circles around Ruka, trying to get her to chase me.

"Bark. Bark. Come on, Ruka, try to find me."

"Doofus, you're easy to find, you smell like muddy shit. You are right there." Ruka jumped out and bit my side.

"Ahh, I let you get me."

"No, you didn't. I got you fair and square."

With the RV settled in, Delux came out with shampoo and a towel.

"Ah shit," I said, running back into the mud.

The next few weeks, Delux would get up early in the morning, make himself some lunch to take on the road, and try to eat the breakfast Tess would make him before he had to leave for the day. He would leave when it was dark and return home when it was dark all week long, and sometimes on the weekends.

Ruka and I would play in the yard, sniff out cat poo, and play tag around the RV. Ruka loved laying in the sun when it was out, and I liked my shady spot under the RV. We were so opposite.

The ball Delux would throw for us was left out in the yard, and I learned to grab it with my mouth and throw it myself. Is this what Delux wanted? I'd rather learn to throw the ball like he does for Ruka, then run and go get it. I would paw at the ball as it lay on the ground, and I soon discovered, I could dig holes. I pawed and pawed at the ball until I had a nice hole the ball would roll back into. Now this, was fun.

If Ruka didn't want to play with me, I would just hit my ball in the hole.

Tess would leave the RV and hang out up at the house. She loved the kittens that were there and taught us to be kind and gentle to the small little creatures. Ruka was nice with the cats, because they provided her all of her treats when nobody was looking.

"Ahh Ruka, your breath smells like cat shit," Tess would say after Ruka and I got done with our adventures walking around the forest.

Delux was always too tired to play with us when he got home from his long days working construction. He was always dirty and smelly, and his first obligation was to shower the hard day off.

Tess or JC's wife would make food and have it ready for them when they returned. Tess would also have a joint rolled up, as well. After the joint, Delux would always come to the floor with Ruka and me, and lay on the floor with us.

"Did you guys find all the cat shit today while I was away?" Delux asked pulling us closer to him.

Ruka loved these moments with Delux on the floor. She would roll to her back with her paws in the air waiting for Delux to rub her belly, her tail banging on the floor.

I could tell something was different with the Babes still. Was it the abortion? Was it me and the way I struggled with not listening when they wanted me to learn?

Delux had a book that stated my breed can be difficult for the first year or so. I thought I was living up to the "or so" part. Delux would call me to come to him, but if something had my attention, it was hard not to be pulled away from it. My curiosity always got the best of me in most cases.

One weekend, when Delux had the day off and we were all hanging out around the house, I led Ruka right into a bucket of oil that was on the floor of JC's shop. We were not allowed in the shop, but some smell brought me in there. I didn't think Ruka would follow me. I forgot she could not see, and I walked her right into a bucket of used motor oil.

"What the fuck? Doofus, what is this? What am I standing in?"

"Ah shit, Doofus, out!" Delux pointed his finger out of the shop.

"Oh no, Ruka. How did you do this? We gotta get you cleaned up."

Several baths later, Ruka was finally somewhat oil free. We were not allowed in JC's workshop, because he had a working Tesla coil in there that generated energy out of thin air or something. JC turned it on one night and told Delux to hold a light bulb, and walk towards the machine. As he got closer, the lightbulb in his hand got brighter and brighter.

"Ruka, do you hear that? That's energy flying around Delux."
I barked.

"It's okay, Doofus," Tess told me as she watched the energy spark around the room.

"Wow, Ruka, I wish you could see this. It's like magic," I said, looking in from outside the shop.

Time ticked away, and I forgot we were supposed to be driving somewhere. Delux was working and saving money. Tess was chilling, trying not to pull her hair out with boredom.

"Babe," Tess said.

"Will you shave my head?"

"What? Really? What about modeling?"

"My hair feels completely dead from that last shoot in Miami. I should just cut it all off and start over. If not, I will have new hair, with dead or damaged hair at the end and it will all be shit. Just shave it."

The Babes set up the clippers by the house outside under the shade of the trees. Ruka and I laid down and watched them as the kittens played around us in the plants. Delux grabbed his clippers he used for his hair and cut Tess's hair for the second time. Only this time, all the way off. When they were done cutting each other's hair, the Babes looked the same with shaved heads.

One of the guys Delux worked for stopped by to pay Delux and saw them finishing up her hair cut.

"You know a woman is beautiful when she still looks good with a shaved head," he said to the Babes. "Look at my head. I have a blockhead."

"You also have a nice head of hair," Tess told the hardworking hillbilly.

"I do pride myself in my mullet I must say," the guy said.

He was right, Tess still looked amazing, even with no hair, and he did have a nice mullet. But would she ever model again? How long would it take to grow her hair back?

The Babes met JC's brother who lived down the street. He started inviting the Babes over for dinner and poker nights. When Delux got home, they would leave and go to the brother's house for dinner and play cards. Ruka and I hardly spent time with Delux anymore, he was working so much. After poker nights, the Babes would both come home smelling of cigarette and wine. They would give us love and pets, then we all went to bed, and this would repeat a few nights a week.

One afternoon, Tess got mad at me for not listening to anything she wanted. Ruka and I were playing all day, and Tess left the door open to the RV as she was up with the cats. I ran inside the RV covered in water and mud from the sinkhole while trying to hide from Ruka. I didn't know if I wanted to sit in the driver's seat, or in the back on the couch, but I left wet mud in both areas. I decided to grab one of Tess's "nice" pillows from the back, and I took it outside and tore it open in my hole that I had been digging with the tennis ball. Tess was very upset when she saw what I did. She was even more upset when she saw I didn't care. She grabbed her pillow and took it inside to discover the mess she had to clean up.

"Doofus, you fucking fuck. I just cleaned all morning. I wish you would learn to listen," she told me.

When Delux got home from work, I knew I was going to be in more trouble when he found out what I did. Tess got mad at Delux for how he hit me with the pillow I'd destroyed and the way he grabbed me and asserted his point. It was rough yes, but I could take it, and it was nowhere near what Big Man would do to me when I was a puppy.

Tess hit Delux after he hit me with the pillow and told me no. "How would you like it if I hit you, and shoved my hand in your face?" Tess yelled out to Delux inside the RV. She kept trying to hit him while he blocked her several times, then he grabbed her and held her as they both fell out of the RV to the ground.

"Yo, what the fuck? Chill out Tess."

"Fuck you. Aghhhh!" Tess said grabbing some things of hers and leaving the RV.

"Ruka?" I asked watching Tess walk away.

"See, Doofus. You need to stop disrespecting our things. All this happened because of you."

"Me? I think something else is bothering the Babes."

"Oh, for sure. Tess decided to abort their child because of their current situation and it's causing trouble for both of them. Then, she cut all of her hair off, which she has identified with her entire life. Delux is working two jobs all day long while Tess has to force herself to stay busy in the woods with a dog who doesn't listen."

"Ruka, are you mad at me, too?"

"No, Doofus. I just don't like seeing Delux like this. He used to take more control of things, yet Tess seems to be controlling it all."

"Come here, Doofus," Delux interrupted.

"Buddy, you gotta stop chewing on our stuff, man. This was her favorite pillow she traveled everywhere with, and now look what you did," he said holding the pillow in my face.

"Let it sink in, Doofus," Ruka said pushing her way into my attention from Delux.

"Hey Ruka, it's my time now."

"Hey, Doofus. Delux is mine, and I'm sharing him with you. Move out of the way."

"No. I want my ear scratches."

"Dammit, Doofus," Ruka said as I pushed her away.

Ruka started to bite my neck. I tried to bite her back, but she let go and went for my back leg. I was forced to sit down. Ruka laid on her back and now insisted I play with her. If not, she would not stop biting at my legs and neck. She was like a little alligator grabbing my legs and trying to spin around. Our play looked like we were fighting and the sounds we made, sounded like we were killing each other, but we'd both figured out each other's boundaries. We tried not to cross any lines with each other by being too rough.

"Now if you can just find the Babes' boundaries and stick by them. Agh, dammit, Doofus," Ruka said coughing.

"Not so tight on my neck," Ruka coughed up again standing upright.

"Let me show you what it's like," Ruka said, lunging at me with her mouth open.

I ducked, I dodged, and then I ran and jumped up into the front seat.

"Doofus, you're forever going to be a puppy," Delux said to me going to bed alone that night.

Tess came back to the RV the following day where she and Delux were able to talk things out and they seemed to be able to play again. I guess people are a lot like dogs, one of them just pushed the other out of the truck and with a little butt sniffing, everything gets cleared up.

That weekend, the Babes drove the RV to a college campus where they tried to sell some of their art.

They sold a few original pieces of art to some students, but what stood out, was an old man who walked up to Delux while he was painting. "You ever heard of quantum physics?" the old man asked looking at Delux paint.

"No. Never. What is it?" Delux asked.

"There's a book sale over there. Ask the woman in charge and she'll show you where to find some good books. Based on your art here, you may find it interesting."

I could tell you now, Delux was not a reader. He didn't even read the instructions of the electronic inverter. He just hooked it up and it worked. Well wait, they did have a big book that was the instruction manual for the RV and all of its parts, and he and Tess both looked at that thing all the time, and that was a mechanical book.

Delux set his painting aside to dry and took me for a walk.

"Imma go check out the books, Babe. I'll take Doofus with me."

"Ok. I love you."

"Love you, too."

We walked through the college kids going to school, and through the market to where the book sale was. Everyone was looking at me. More than half of the kids wanted to pet me and get all up in my face, but Delux politely told them no for me as we found the books. These quantum books were just as big as our RV book and seemed just as complicated.

Delux got our RV working again, so maybe he could get quantum physics to work too, I thought as I watched him flip through the pages.

He told me to stay by his side every time, as I tried to pull away. I had a hard time listening and staying focused with all these people around. Plus, he walked too slow for my pace, and he walked in the sun. I hated the sun. I would pull him in the shady directions, but he would stay firm with me and keep me by his side.

"Doofus, heel," he would say pulling the leash when I drifted.

I watched his every move, hoping one move was to let me go.

Delux put the science books down. "I'm smart, Doofus, but not this smart. Besides, these books are expensive, hot damn. We need to sell more art to buy one of these books. Let's go back to Tess," he said rubbing my face after he saw I was watching him.

I was kept by his side on the leash until we got to the RV, where Delux unclipped me.

"Doofus, RV." I ran inside.

"See, Ruka, I do listen."

"Listening only to what you want, is not listening, Doofus."

"What?"

"You only go into the RV so fast because it's always cool and shady in here."

"Whatever," I said, sitting on the front seat and lying down with my head on the steering wheel.

The Babes seemed happy driving us back to the woods. Tess wanted to feel like she was contributing after sitting around for weeks with us. She sold the most art while at the college event and was ready to do some more.

Later that night, the Babes came into the RV after a night up at the house with JC and his family dinner. Delux was frantic to find a pen and paper. "Holy shit, where is this all coming from." He let out and just started writing.

"Babe, tell me what's going on," Tess asked.

"My mouth is too slow for what is coming into my brain right now, I have to write it down. Try to write it all down. Fuck, my hand is even too slow."

Delux said he got some sort of download that night about something he was having a hard time explaining. Something about bugs and insects and the frogs that were outside making noises and making them all into a movie. He sat there for over an hour explaining things to Tess and writing them all down.

"Babe. This is a fucking movie!" Delux said closing his book.

Every time the news was turned on, it was still weapons of mass destruction and terror, terror, terror. Everyone around us thought it was bullshit, but we stayed hunkered down in the forest. There was a knock on the door that startled me as Delux and JC were playing a game of chess, passing a joint back and forth. JC told the knock at the door to come in. As the door opened, time slowed down again for me and I saw a car outside with the letters POLICE written on it. There was a man in a uniform standing at the door.
The cop tossed a bag of weed he pulled off some kids they both knew to JC and they laughed about it.

"Why don't you two come outside. I want to show you something," the cop said to us, turning around and walking out the door.

"Let's go. I was kicking his ass anyways," JC said.

We all went outside, and the cop popped his trunk. There, he pulled out a brand new M16 gas suppressed rifle.

"You boys feel like shooting?"

These boys were high and shouldn't have been shooting anything. And where were we? Was it safe to be shooting automatic machine guns out here?

"Why don't you go ahead and put this here dime in that there tree down there," the cop said to Delux in the most southern accent I had ever heard.

I followed him, sniffing the ground and watching our surroundings. This felt natural to me for some reason.

"Put it chest-high," the cop yelled out once we were by the tree.

Delux wedged the dime into the tree while I peed on the tree next to it. We walked back up to the cop when Tess joined us, with Ruka following.

"What's going on up here, boys?" Tess asked.

"This cop just walked in on us smoking a fatty and gave JC a bag of weed, and now he is letting us shoot his new rifle. What world are we living in? You wanna shoot it?" Delux asked Tess.

"Fuck yeah."

Delux put us in a pick-up truck where the neighbor's dog was chilling.

"What's up, hippies," Blanco asked as I jumped in and Delux set Ruka down.

"You know this cop?" I asked Blanco.

"He's a sheriff, and yes, I do. He runs these parts of the woods here."

"It hits high and to the left," Sheriff said after two shots missed the dime.

JC tried and missed twice as well.

"Wow, that son of a bitch has no kick at all."

"Ladies first," JC said, handing the gun to Tess.

"Then why'd you go first?" Tess asked sarcastically.

"Ohh, she's a sassy one," the cop said looking her body up and down as she crouched down to take her shot.

"Wow, that was not what I expected," she said with surprise as she missed as well. "This isn't for me," Tess said after one shot.

Delux took the gun and sat on the ground different than all of them. The cop walked up to the side of Delux's ear and whispered something drawn out. Delux turned around and looked at the cop.

"Yo, chill. I'm from Miami, but I'm not that guy you're whispering about in my ear, nor do I know him or run with his crew. Now back up because I don't take kindly to threats. You hear me? JC, come get your guy who thinks I'm associated with DL, while I show him how to shoot his own gun," Delux said turning back into his firing position.

I could always tell when Delux was being serious and when he was being playful… he was not playing.

"Leave him be. Let him shoot," JC said to the man.

Delux took a breath and, on the exhale, he took his first shot. He was a natural.

"You're right about one thing, Copper. It's high and to the left."

Delux took another breath and at the exhale, he not only knocked the dime out of the tree, he put a hole in the center of it.

"And that's how it's done, boys. JC, he thinks I am part of DL's crew and threatened to bury me out here in these woods if I did anything bad to you. Can you tell him to relax because, nobody talks to me like that," Delux said handing the gun back to the cop looking him straight in his eyes.

"Okay. Sorry, I just thought…"

"No you assumed, and look what happened," Delux said sternly.

"I don't know what happened just now but Delux was a badass to that cop."

"Delux is just being Delux. He's sees the world a certain way and has no problems expressing it."

"What's up, Blanco, you wanna play with us? They keep saying you're this bad ass pitbull, but you seem pretty chill to me."

"I am chill, but I'm down to wrestle."

The rest of the afternoon, Ruka and I took turns playing with a dog we could both bounce off of. Ruka would take his back legs, and I would go for the front.

The reality of going to Costa Rica was getting closer, so the Babes took the money Delux had saved up and decided to put a new motor in the RV. And as they say, the road to hell is paved with good intentions.

The motor was machined incorrectly or something and caused the Babes a bunch of headaches and breakdowns that never should have come with a new motor. The local hillbillies in the area helped them out and got the motor fixed and running like a race car. They even tore up an old car to use its steel to weld under the RV to make a better supporting frame in the back. They made a metal bumper that was never there, and they even put a metal rack on the back of the RV that would hold their generator in a locked compartment.

"With all this extra weight in the back, you should be able to do wheelies with that new motor," Hillbilly Davie said.

Delux tried it, and yep, the front wheels wanted to come off the ground as the RV went tearing forward.

"Oh, we're good now. Babe, this thing is Costa Rica ready!"

The Babes seemed happy and confident with their relationship, and the RV. It was our home on wheels, and it has to be good to keep us moving towards Costa Rica. With everything almost new and the terror level down a notch, it was time for a new adventure.

CHAPTER 8

MIAMI

On the road again. Windows down, breeze blowing, music flowing. Ahh, the good old smells of Miami. Depending where we were at, was dependent on the smells coming in the windows.

We pulled into South Beach and Tess let her modeling agency know she was back in town and ready to work with natural, short, thick blonde hair.

We then headed off to Key West because, why not, Tess suggested.

There was not much shade in Key West. If there was shade, there was usually a homeless person there already enjoying the 5-degree difference the shade provided.

Delux parked the RV in a temporary shady spot, where some homeless people told us we couldn't park there. Delux said it would only be for a short time and to leave us alone because it clearly was a parking space. We waited only five minutes when a different parking spot on the street opened up that was under a large tree providing shade.

Delux ran back into the RV and moved into the open spot for the steamy afternoon. We now had shade and a breeze coming in through the windows with the position of the RV. We were set.

Tess walked to the store, and Delux stayed back with us and the RV ready to pay the parking meter if the meter police walked by. There were a lot of people around walking on the streets. Laughing, drinking, eating. Delux took a nap with us on the back couch where the breeze was the strongest. When Tess returned, she put the food away she bought and joined us. After the nap, they took us for a walk around a park where a lot of people were gathered. There were artist selling art of all sorts. The Babes walked us around the event, where everyone thought Ruka and I were the most beautiful and well behaved dogs.

"Babe. We should sell our art tonight on the street where we're parked," Delux mentioned to Tess.

"You think so?"

"Your art is way cooler than what's here. We should give it a try."

"Okay, let's do it."

We walked back to the RV, which was already in the perfect parking spot to sell art. There were already a lot of people walking up and down the sidewalk looking at the RV, which was a piece of art in itself. All the Babes needed to do was stand outside and be themselves. They kept us inside locked up behind the baby gate. Even though Ruka and I could jump over it, we were instructed to stay on the other side. When the Babes were building the RV, they'd put up some hard metal mesh over the windows so Ruka and I couldn't break ourselves out. I liked to push on things when I got excited, including the window. All it took was one time of me pushing on the window barking at someone for Delux to see they were gonna have a problem if they didn't do something about it. So, they did.

He screwed the metal mesh on from the outside, keeping the inside of the RV looking clean with nothing to poke us.

While Tess made a sign advertising their art for sale, Delux made up a sign, "*Do Not Touch the Dogs*," and stuck it to the back of the RV window where people were walking by.

I was curious about everyone. I had never been around this many people before. So many of them had so many different types of energy. Most were good, which I paid no attention to, yet some... some were bad, and those I barked at. One bad guy, walked up right to the back window where Delux put his sign.

"Do Not Touch the Dogs. Ahh, but you guys are so cute," the guy in the leather vest said.

"Bark Bark Bark! Who are you calling cute," I asked him, charging at the window hitting the metal designed to keep me in. I knew the metal could hold me back and the window was open so I charged at it with some force.

"Holy crap," the people around him yelled out and screamed.

After I let out that bark, the leather vest guy still stood right next to Delux and stuck his finger inside the window. I didn't hesitate and bit his finger. I felt it in my mouth, but he pulled it away too fast for me to get a bite on it. Instead, the guy tore his finger open on the metal he squeezed his finger past, opening his finger up for some stitches.

"Man, you fucking idiot. You don't see the sign right here in your face," Delux pointed out to him.

"Your dogs look so sweet," he drunkenly said.

"Someone, please get your drunk friend before there's another accident," Tess told the group.

"I almost got him, Ruka. I could taste the chicken wing hot sauce on his finger."

"I love chicken wings," Ruka replied. "Let me lick your face."

The Babes met a lot of different people that night. One of them, invited them on a sailboat. The Babes were concerned about us dogs, but the guy said we could come too. He said they would stop at an island to let us run around and they would go fishing to feed themselves.

"It all sounds too good to be true, and what's this guy's name? Mountain?" Delux asked.

"They were nice. Think about it, it could be fun."

"They just want to stare at you in your sexy bikini all day."

"Im gonna wear the one I made just for you."

"Ahh shit. Sexy time," Delux said grabbing Tess in a playful manner.

The next morning after a night of selling only one piece of art, we parked the RV by the marina. We were forced to park at a parking meter and the Babes only had enough quarters for an hour's worth of time. It was 5am, the meters turned on at 7am, and boat leaves at 6am.

"This better be worth it, cuz we're gonna get a parking ticket."

Delux was not always a positive sounding guy. He was more of a realist in most cases, and in this case, he's probably right.
We saw the meter police all day yesterday walking past the RV and other cars looking for expired meters. While we were all going to be away, nobody would be here to feed the meter when the parking police walk by.

"Doofus, let's keep our toes crossed and hope the Babes don't get a ticket. They didn't sell much last night, and they can't afford any tickets."

"Ruka... you excited for this boat trip?"

"I don't know. I've never been on a boat before."

Moments later...

"Ah this shit sucks. Is the boat ever going to stop moving?" Ruka asked me, not sure what was going on as we rocked back and forth.

"This is not even the boat yet. We are taking a boat, to the boat."

"This was a bad idea," Ruka let out.

"Thanks for letting the dogs on. This should be a fun trip," Tess said.

"Fun my ass, this is already starting out bad," Ruka said not liking the constant movement of the boat.

Things went from good, to bad, to worse real quick. Ruka and I never got much food that morning. That was probably a good thing because we would have puked it up with all the rocking back and forth. We peed before we got on the boat, but we never poo'd, so both Ruka and I were pinching off our own turtleheads from the start. As the day progressed, we never went to any islands to, "let the dogs run around." Like Mountain said.

We went out to sea, and this Mountain guy parked the boat over a reef where the Babes got to go snorkeling. While they were in the water, Mountain kept looking at Tess's ass, and then at me like he wanted to fight me or something.

Delux was right, Mountain's a creep.

When Mountain wasn't staring at me, he was staring at Tess in her tiny self-made leather bikini.

I didn't like the vibe of this Mountain guy one bit.

I could tell the other guy, the one Tess met who invited us all on this trip, was the less powerful of the two men. One word though and he would fully throw us overboard if he was told to do so by Mountain.

The Babes finished their snorkeling, then Mountain decided to toss in a fishing line and proceeded to pull reef fish off of the bottom and use them for food.

I wasn't sure who he thought he was going to feed with these small, skinny fish that looked like they belonged in a fish tank, not on our plates. The Babes tried the fish and neither one of them liked the taste, and neither did we.

Mountain ate all the fish while Ruka and I kept pinching off our farts in fear of an accident. After dinner, Ruka and I still hadn't gone to the bathroom yet, or eaten all day. We both were afraid to go potty on the boat. We didn't want to make the babes look bad.

Tess noticed her bikini bottom was missing from the bag she stuck it in after snorkeling.

"I watched her put it in her bag," Ruka tells me.

"How Ruka?" I asked.

The Babes looked all around in the boat and couldn't find it. They went up above where we were and looked but Ruka and I never saw it on deck. The Babes went below and started to accuse one of two guys on board of stealing her suit. They both denied it, then Mountain locked himself in his room for a nap.

At this point, there was no communication between Mountain and the Babes. Tess pounded on his door demanding that he come out and take us back to shore.

"No. I need to take a nap," Mountain said through the door.

Tess pounded some more on the door and threatened his life a bit.

Delux was on deck with us smiling, looking at the other guy.

"Man, I highly suggest you find her bottoms, then turn this boat around and drive us back to shore," Delux said in a serious voice.

You couldn't even see the shore. The sun had set, and the sky was getting dark quickly as the stars began to pop out. Tess came up from below upset and started shouting at the other guy to figure out where her suit was. She knew she put it in her bag. It was obvious these two guys were perving out on Tess. I mean she was pretty, but she was also 6 feet tall and strong.

"I'll tell you what," Delux calmly said. "We'll wait here, and you go downstairs to Mountain. Talk to him and let him know, I will no longer play games after your conversation with him."

"We will lock you in your boat and burn it to the ocean floor," Tess added.

"Ruka, can they do that?"

"I saw Delux fight the winner of a tough man competition. I don't think these two guys will be an issue, but we may need to bite them and back up the Babes, so be ready," Ruka said just as calmly as Delux.

"Have you done this before, Ruka?"

"What, bite somebody? Yes."

"Have you done it while trying to pinch off a poo?"

"No, first time."

I could tell Ruka was lying to me about biting someone before. I think she just wanted me to feel like we could do this. We could help if need be, I thought.

Lucky for the two guys, they figured it out on their own. Mountain came out and tossed Tess's swimsuit back in her bag. Delux watched it happen from one of the boat's side windows he stalked the bedroom door from. Tess was pissed and went down to Mountain, but he locked himself back in his quarters again. So she grabbed her things and came up on deck.

"You turn this fucking boat around right now and bring us back."

"We don't have enough gas, we are going to have to spend the night here and wait for the wind."

"I don't trust this guy," I said to Ruka.

Delux stood up and walked right up to the other guy and grabbed him by his throat as he held a small knife along his side.

"Now that I have your attention and your life in my hand, you'll know how serious I am. Turn this boat around and drive us back, or I will do it myself, without you on this boat."

"Yeah, but we don't have enough gas," the guy repeated realizing Delux also had a knife in his hand.

"Ruka, where did the knife come from?"

"It's Delux, Doofus. Just watch."

"Then you take us as far as you can. Let's go," Delux said letting the guy go and turning the wheel of the boat.

Delux moved the guy behind the wheel.

"Start the motor and let's go."

"I just need to get something."

"No. You sit the fuck down and Tess will go get whatever you need."

I could see in that moment, Delux was holding in a monster that wanted to come out to play.

After three long hours, we made it back to the marina. Both Ruka and I were dying to get off the boat.

"Either we take the dingy, or you drive us back in the dingy. Fuck, you're running out of gas story, we're getting off this boat."

The guy anchored the boat while we all got into the dingy to motor back to shore. The guy went below and got a small tank of gas to fill up the motor on the dingy.

"I thought you didn't have gas?" Delux asked.

"Man, you're so lucky you made it this far with us. It took every ounce of me not to throw you off this fucking thing. I trusted you," Tess said looking right into his eyes.

"I didn't. That's why I brought my knife. You're lucky I don't stab your fucking dingy and sink you right here, you piece of shit," Delux said lifting us out onto the dock as we made it back to land.

Ruka and I got lifted off the dingy first and as soon as our paws touched the solid, non-moving dock, we both peed and poo'd and the same time.

"Doofus, I have never had to pee and poo at the same time before. I never knew it was even possible."

"Oh my god, it feels so good to let it all out."

"Jeezus, Doofus, that is the biggest pile of poo I've ever seen."

"Yesterday's dinner and leftovers... Oh and maybe a little bit of that one guys finger too."

"Doofus, I think I gotta shit again."

"I know I gotta shit again."

Ruka and I left four big piles of poo on the docks that early morning. We walked back to the RV and Delux was right. We had a $25 parking ticket waiting for us. The Babes were running out of money faster than they were making it. Between gas for the RV, and food for themselves and us, money was becoming tight. They only sold one painting while in Key West, so they decided to drive back up to the Miami area and try their luck there. It was nice in the Keys, but there's no shade for a dog.
Ruka was excited to be back in Miami. She knew a lot of people there and perked up as we got closer. I started to think about my first little friend. I wondered how she was doing, and if that asshole little boy was keeping his hands off of her.

"We're getting close, Doofus."

"Close to what?"

"Miami Beach. I can smell it."

I didn't know what Ruka was smelling. She spent way more time in Miami than I've been alive so I'll take her word for it. Ruka was a proud dog. She sat up from the floor leaning into the chair of Delux while I sat next to Tess and received pets on the head.

"This is the area we got you from, Doofus. Do you remember?"

"No, I didn't."

I tried to get a big whiff of the air outside to see if it reminded me of my mom, my dad, my little friend, but nothing. I could only smell the burning oil of our slow moving, gas guzzling RV, that was driving better, but still sucking up a lotta gas.

"I smell gas. Do you smell gas?" Tess asked.

"Yes I do. I'll look next time we stop to get gas."

We almost didn't make it to the gas station.

Delux pulled us off the highway when we needed to refill, and as we were pulling into the gas station, the RV shut off.

"Ah shit. I think we are out of gas," Delux said trying to start the RV with half of the RV sticking out into the street as it slowed down.

"You drive, I have to push her!"

Delux jumped out of the RV while it was still moving, and I jumped into the driver's seat.

"No! Doofus, get down," Tess said pushing me out.

"Yeah. Got it. It makes more sense if you drive," I said jumping down.

"I'll use the momentum to push us. Steer us to the right there," Delux yelled up to Tess.

"Does Delux ever think, or just react?"

"His reactions are correct most of the time, and if not, he fixes it."

Delux got behind the RV and pushed us into the gas station while Tess steered us into the back corner out of people's way. Delux took a look under the RV, and it turned out our fuel pump had stopped working. There was an auto parts store across the street, and thankfully they had the part we needed. There was a sign that said no mechanical work in the parking lot of the gas station, but Delux did it anyways. He dropped the gas tank, put in the new fuel pump, and then put the gas tank back where it needed to be, and we were back on the road in an hour.

Delux could fix most anything in a matter of moments. He loved driving the RV, and I think he loved fixing all of its problems even more. I could see a sense of satisfaction in him when he fixed something that he felt was actually fixed.

Tess got a message that she had a casting to go to, and that became the next thing on our to do list. After the RV was fixed, Delux drove us into Miami Beach.

"Wow, Ruka, this is where you're from?" I asked as we drove over the bridges into South Beach.

"Yep. Right over there to be exact."

"Do you miss it like I miss my mom?"

"No. Not anymore."

"Why not?"

"Delux is my family now, and Delux has you and Tess and, you guys are all I need," Ruka said.

"You make it sound so simple."

"It can be simple if you choose simple."

Delux drove us to Tess's modeling agency, and waited in the RV with us while she ran inside to check in.

Delux gave us all of his attention when Tess stepped out for any reason. I loved the times when Tess was away and Delux was all ours. I was starting to notice how much attention he does actually give us when he can give it.

When Tess came out, we were told she had a few castings she could go to tomorrow morning. The afternoon was running away from us, so we decided to look for a place to park the RV for the night. It was Miami Beach, so parking was by permit only, or parking meters. I could see that finding solid parking somewhere frustrated the Babes, but they soon figured it out, and found a system within the system.

We could park on the neighborhood streets during the day for free, and we would look for a loading zone spot for the nights to sleep. No permit was required in the neighborhoods until 6pm and the loading zones were not active from 6pm to 7am the next day, so we made any loading zone on the beach, our spot for the night.

Sleeping in Miami Beach was nice, but there were always cars and their stereos, or people and their conversations waking us up at night, keeping us all on our toes.

Our days were now spent, with Tess waking up to go get a coffee with her cigarette, and then Delux would drive her around to her castings. Tess got a few jobs here and there and while she was getting her picture taken, Delux hung out with Ruka and I by a park. We would sit in the coolness of the RV, parked in the shade somewhere while he wrote out his movie ideas.

Delux drove us to a different park by the ocean where he found parking meters that shut off at 7pm. There were many beach showers close by, and there was hardly any people around and the traffic... none because it was a side street.

"Babe. I think I found us the perfect spot to park," Delux told Tess once she finished work and got into the RV.

"Yeah? Where?"

Delux drove us back to the park he found, and parked the RV.

"What do you think?" he asked Tess

"This is way better than South Beach," she said.

This was, better than South Beach. We were on the beach, it just wasn't South Beach with all the traffic, people and their noises. Our RV faced the ocean when we were parked providing lots of wind flow. There was a small wall of stones in front of us the Babes could sit on, some grass that lead into sand mounds, and just over the mounds was the ocean. There were beach showers all around and it seemed like the perfect spot with trees to hang a hammock. Looking at the location, it didn't appear to be a camping spot, but after several nights there in a row, nobody said anything to us about being there all weekend. We came to visit this parking spot frequently over the next two months.

Some nights we would stay in south beach at the loading zone spots if Tess had an early start with a job. If she didn't have to work, we would spend most our time up here in this quiet little haven.

After any meal, the Babes would let us eat all the scraps, then bring their dishes outside and wash them at the beach shower, always saving the RV's water for emergencies. It was a daily routine for the Babes to wash the dishes and the cooler at the showers.

The Babes would even shower at the beach showers in front of strangers, using natural soap and brushing their teeth. It was normal for people to shower at the beach, but not using soap and shampoo. They even gave us a bath there from time to time with a special hose Delux made to attach to the shower to make it easier and more efficient to rinse us off.

We met a man who called himself Nature. He was homeless and he would trade the Babes weed for cooked food. Delux and Nature would sit on the sea wall playing chess, while Ruka and I would play with each other in the grass next to them, ripping apart fallen coconuts.

Ruka and I would play and she would stand in one spot as I would run around her and figure out a way to attack her but when I did, she attacked me back. I think the anticipation of always getting got by Ruka, became my thing. I loved knowing I can run around her and she can only get me if I get close. And I wanted to get close. I would let the anticipation build up inside of me and then out of nowhere, my head would explode with joy, and I would run around in a state of nonstop "zoomies" as the Babes called it.

"Man, what's up with your dog?" Nature asked as I darted in circles around Ruka.

"He's living his best life. This is how he has fun, and he does actually protect the RV so we accept him how he is, even though he destroys everything he shouldn't."

"Babe, I have a casting at Universal Casting tomorrow," Tess told Delux after returning from a call with her agency.

"You know one day they offered me a job to be one of their casting directors?"

"Really? Why didn't you take it?"

"They were just starting out and the job paid less than enough to survive here, and I was not in a position to gamble with my paychecks at the time."

"Well, it's an open casting tomorrow so you should come with me."

"For sure. They'll be surprised to see me here in town."

The next morning, we drove down to South Beach.
Delux found us some shade and left us in the RV with the windows open while they went up into a large building.

"Do you think they'll get the job?"

"I hope one of them does. They keep running out of money."

"Why do they keep running out of money?"

"Because they're spending their money on weed, then smoking it all away."

"Well, they did put a lot of money into the RV's motor, let's not forget," I reminded Ruka.

"Having a RV with a good motor, but no gas to have it take you anywhere, is not how you do it Doofus."

"How would you do it?" I asked.

"I'm a dog. All I know how to do is support the ones you love. You'll learn, Delux is going to do what he does, or what he wants to do, no matter what. He has lessons to learn, or lessons to teach. Some are easy, and some, some are hard. This might be a hard one for him because Tess is in control a lot when usually he is."

I sat there in silence in a RV that did not have much gas. The Babes wanted me to chew on the bone they left on the floor, but I loved chewing on the seat, or one of the pillows in the back, or the arm rest. All I wanted to do was see outside, so I took down the shades that covered our back windows and started barking at everyone I saw.

"Bark! Bark! Bark! You feel this guy, Ruka. He has some bad energy. Bark! Bark! Bark!"

"All I feel is you shaking the RV, calm down, Doofus. Let the bad energy come and go. It's like you're distracting yourself from what's going on inside of you."

The sunlight was coming in through the back windows now so I moved back up to the driver's seat.

"The Babes are gonna love this one," Ruka told me, letting out a deep breath laying on the fabric I tore down.

The door opened, and like every time the Babes returned, it was nothing but love for us.
Then they saw what I did in the back.

"Doofus, what the fuck, man?"

I hated when they used that tone.

Delux brought me to the back of the RV and scolded me for tearing up the curtains. Then they saw the driver's seat that I tore up a bit.

"Doofus. You fucking fuck. Stop chewing on the RV!" Tess yelled pointing at the seat.

We drove back to our parking spot up north and called it a day.

While sitting in our usual spot, the police came and parked right behind the RV. They were making this their habit it seemed because it was happening more often. The Babes would just sit tight and not move around while peeking through the curtains to check out what the police were doing. With the window tint and curtains drawn, there was no seeing inside our RV even if you tried to look.

The following week, we all watched a local guy break into the restaurant behind us across the street and stole all their liquor using three big garbage cans to carry it away. He then hid his stash on the roof of the lifeguard headquarters. The Babes couldn't believe what they were seeing and how well he hid all the bottles in the rain gutters.

Later that afternoon, the police paid us a real visit and started asking us questions.

"We don't believe it was you, we just need to look inside, that's all," the cop said casually and nice.

"You can go inside but stand right there so I can keep an eye on you. You can look, but you can't touch or open anything," Delux told him.

"I'm pretty sure you don't have what I'm looking for, and don't worry, I don't need to open anything, I'm pretty sure it wasn't you two. Did you happen to see anyone today do this?" the cop asked, looking around.

"We didn't see anyone. We were at the beach all morning." Tess said.

"I see this RV parked here a lot. Are you guys living here, or something?"

"We actually bought a warehouse in Miami, but it's not ready yet. It has asbestos and it needs to be removed fully before we can move in. Until then we are stuck out on the street in this thing," Delux casually told the cops pointing to the RV.

"Ruka, when did the Babes buy a warehouse?"

"Delux is just saying that as a good excuse to be out here living on the street for free. He's hoping to create some sympathy from the officer," Ruka told me.

"How much longer do you think until the warehouse is ready?" The cop asked.

"Maybe a month or so, that asbestos shit is everywhere," Tess added to the lie.

"Would you guys mind parking down there a bit, then?" The officer pointed to the far end of the parking lot.

"Yeah, sure we can do that," Delux told him, and the cops left us alone.

"What? Look at it down there." Delux said.

"It seems almost better down there, than here." Tess added.

"Yeah it does. Let's go."

We moved the RV to a new location 900 feet away. We now had our own two trees to hang a hammock, and a beach shower we never saw anyone use. We were set.
The Babes were notified that they got the job they casted for the other day when I chewed up the seat waiting form them.
Even Delux got hired and he's no longer a model.

"Ruka, why's Delux not a model anymore? He has a nice face, hands and armpits. His legs too, he's like the whole package."

"Except for the hairline if I remember," Ruka said.

"Yeah I see that, but it kinda fits him though."

"I do remember him handsome... Back in the day, Delux punched a famous photographer guy in the face for molesting him as he was trying to become a model."

"What?"

"I don't know, I wasn't there, it's just what I heard after it happened. Delux was even going to be the Marlboro Man at one point but after the punch, the industry didn't like him."

"What's the Marlboro Man?"

"It's the cowboy guy in the magazines always smoking a cigarette holding a horse."

"But Delux hates cigarettes."

"I know, and he's not a fan of horses either, but he doesn't hate money, and that job would have paid him a lot of it."

"He punched a guy in the face?"

"He shoved a guy in the face who forced himself onto him. When the guy touched Delux, Delux pushed him in the face making him drop his own camera, showing Delux he was taking photos with a camera that had no film in it."

"What?"

"Delux came home pissed that day. He took me for a walk and told some friends of his down the street. The next week, the job he had for cigarettes canceled on him."

"Dang."

"I don't think he would have done the job anyways. He said he would never promote cigarettes, and he really was having a hard time making a decision in the moment."

"Now, look at him... Delux and Tess are both gonna promote an alarm, or car or something."

Later that night we drove to a big house on South Beach.

"I know the guy who owns this house. I used to drop packages off for him when I used to work for Rob."

"Really?"

"Yeah. You've never shot here before?"

"No."

"You Don't know ****** *******?"

"Never heard of him."

"He has a cool wall library with a ladder and a loft inside this place. This guy trusted me to hang on to $10,000 cash that I was allowed to pick up from his bank."

"You held onto it?"

"I tossed the money in the air and rolled around on it in my bed acting like a fool. I even took pictures doing it. I was rolling up some bills up and stick'em in my ears. Then I had to stack all that crinkled money back up and hand it to the guy the next day like nothing happened."

Delux told the security outside that we were part of the set, and they let us park our RV right out front of the house with no questions asked.

"Ruka! We're at the set of a TV commercial!"

"Yeah, and?"

Ruka was not as excited as I was.

The Babes left the RV and ate a dinner that the set provided for them while we stayed in the RV.

"It smells good out there," I told Ruka.

"And you're all excited, but it's not for us. They never feed the extras this well."

"How you know that?"

"Delux was an extra in a Hollywood movie and TV commercial back in the day. He came home from both super hungry."

"I'm hungry."

"Doofus, you're always hungry."

When the Babes were done eating, they brought us some rib bones to chew on. The production crew put the Babes into clothes and sunglasses, then, told them to wait. The Babes were like us now, waiting in the RV for something to happen. We arrived on set at 5pm. They didn't use the Babes until 4am the next morning.

Between 5pm and 4am… the Babes had most of the crew of the commercial, in the RV.

Delux powered on the generator, opened up his turntables and started a party with everyone while they waited to be called on set. Ruka counted 30 people inside the RV, but it was more like 15 people once you divide all the legs by two. Delux had the music goin', while Tess had the weed and the beers flowin. 4am hit, and everyone was called to go to work. The Babes were called in soon after and it was just Ruka and I left at the after party.

"Doofus, people love us and the RV, don't they?"

"Yeah they do."

"Why do you only listen when there're people around?"

"What?"

"When people are around, you almost want to show off, but when it's just us, you never want to listen or do what Delux asks you to do?"

"Delux is always telling me what to do. He's not asking." I paused and thought about it.

"I don't know why, Ruka. I think I'm still trying to figure all this out."

"There's nothing to figure out Doofus. Wherever you go, there you are, some say."

The Babes returned as the sun was starting to come up.

"Holy shit! I thought we were in trouble when the director pulled us aside and told everyone else to go into the room," Delux let out.

"You were perfect for that role!"

"No, you were perfect for that role! How did that even just happen?" Delux questioned.

"They wanted people from a party, and you are the party," Tess told him.

"Babe, they put us directly on camera!" Delux said spinning around.

"Hi, Doggies! How are you? Everyone loved you guys. You were so, so good," Tess said.

"Babe, you know we're both now primaries because of that, right?"

"Yes! And, we got to say a little dialog," Tess said hugging and kissing Delux.

"This is just what we needed."

The Babes were running low on cash, and this commercial would help them out intensely.

"They won't be paid for like eight weeks though," Ruka told me.

Tess wasn't getting much work due to her hair being so short. This was stressing the Babes out a bit because her modeling was their plan. Tess could always pick up modeling work, but now, it was proving difficult with her hair.

The Babes had $25 to their names and another $25 parking ticket from our last trip to the beach with Ruka and I.

We drove into the neighborhood streets of South Beach, and parked under the shade of a tree, waiting for more calls for more castings. You could feel the energy in the RV shifting down with every day that passed where there was no art going out, and money coming in.

The Babes had not spent any money on weed in weeks. When they needed weed, they would buy themselves food, cook it and go find Nature and make a trade. Nature hadn't been around, so the Babes were outta luck, sitting there sober with us. I popped my head up because I could hear something.

"Ruka, you hear that?"

"Yeah. Someone's outside checking out the RV."

I let out a low growl, waiting to see what was going to happen next when we got a knock at our door. Tess got up to answer it before I let out a bark.

"Excuse me. Sorry to bother you, but it says you have art for sale on the back of your RV. Is it possible I can see some?" the man asked.

You could feel the Babes were shocked.

"We don't have much left, but I can show you what we do have," Tess said excited.

While Tess pulled out a few pieces, Ruka and I checked out the man.

He was older. He had a sweet energy about him that made Ruka want to show off how we play together and she started to bite at my neck.

"Doggies, not now," Delux stated, and Ruka stopped, while I kept going.

"Doofus," he added.

"Sweet dogs," the man said as Tess presented him some of their art.

"Oh, wow. These are really nice. Can I buy these three from you?"

Tess paused and looked at Delux.

"We usually sell them for $30 each, but if you want more than one, we can do $25 each," Tess said.

The guy opened his wallet.

"How about this. I'll take these three, and this one, and I'll give you $400 for the four?"

"Ahh sure. Okay. Oh my god, that's amazing."

"And my wife, she's the president of the condo association here that you're parked in front of, and she's looking for someone to paint her metal gate. Would you be interested in a job like that?"

"Yes we would," Tess quickly told him.

"Great. Use the money I just gave you to get whatever supplies you need and I'll pay you each $20 an hour to paint it and reimburse you for the supplies you buy. Can you start tomorrow?"

"Yes, we can," Tess said again without hesitation.

"Excellent. We will see you tomorrow then. She wants the gate white," the man said walking away with his new paintings.

"Ruka, what is the luck of that?" I told her as Delux jumped into the driver's seat.

"I think the Babes just got tricked into painting a fence, but it's good. This will be good for them."

"Babe, let's go pay this stupid ticket first. Pay our insurance, get food for the dogs and us, then we'll get the paint on the way back."

"Ruka, Doofus, let's go, in the back." Tess motioned to us.

It was that simple for the Babes. Every time they were running low, the universe would jump in and help them out without them even asking.

The fence got painted and the Babes made an additional $400, and a free bag of weed that the man's wife gave them as a tip. Weed would seem to just show up, and the Babes were no longer spending money like they used to on it. They took some extra cash and painted Delux Djing on one side of the RV, and a frog on the other. Tess even painted a white picket fence around the bottom to make it our home.

The RV now looked like it had a purpose and it didn't just have homeless kids with dogs living in it.

The Babes needed to check into Tess's agency, and they were lucky enough to get the loading zone parking spot right out front.

"You guys chill, we'll be right back," the Babes said, and they both went inside.

Ruka and I did the usual, sit and wait, only this time, I told myself to pay more attention to the world around me. People were always looking at the RV, so I had to learn to control myself a bit with my outburst of barking at everyone.

While parked and waiting for the Babes out front of the agency, I saw a group of people walking along the sidewalk coming from behind the RV. Their energy got me excited, they had no clue I was inside, and they were gonna walk right past me. After spotting them from the back window, I moved from the back of the RV to the front, and jumped onto the passenger seat to wait for them.

I used the side mirror and watched them get closer and closer.

My tail was wagging hard. If I don't stop wagging it, they'll probably know I'm here. It took all I had but I was able to hold still while taking in a big breath.

Just like Delux when he shot that gun, on my exhale, as the group walked past the passenger door, I stuck my nose out the cracked window and gave them the scare of their life.

"Woof. Woof. Woof. Woof!"

The group jumped back, and they all screamed and scattered. Some guys protected the women, while another man ran for his life. Like they say, you just gotta be faster than the slower one, or the one's who wants to be the hero.

"Doofus, who the fuck says that?"

"I don't know, I heard it somewhere. Sounds good doesn't it?"

The group was laughing to calm their nerves and moved along quickly as my tail showed my satisfaction going side to side. I couldn't control it as I stood there watching the group try to piece themselves back together looking at me, look at them, look at me.

The group hurried away from the RV and carried on.

Other people walked by that I didn't get as excited over.

I noticed how intensely I could feel a human's energy now and from so far away.

The Babes returned, opening the door and giving us a bunch of love as we greeted them.

"Doofus, you goof ball. I watched you scare the crap out of that group from the window up there," Delux said getting back into the RV.

"Come on, guys, let's go for a ride."

The Babes went to a record store far away, and Delux bought some records. Seeing it was so late, the Babes found a parking spot between some warehouses to call it a night instead of driving back to Miami. While there, a car rolled up to the RV and a bunch of guys got out and started to talk loud. Delux recognized a few of them and said hello.

"Dj Delux! What is this thing?" a guy asked.

"It's our home slash mobile DJ booth slash recording studio," Delux told them.

"And art studio," Tess added.

I wanted to get involved in the conversation, so I let out a whine to say hello because I was being ignored.

"Holy shit, you got a dog in there," one of the other guys said backing up.

"Doofus, chill man," Delux said to me.

"I have two in here, but they cool though. You're Cutty Ranks right?"

"Yes, Bredren."

"Man can we cut a dub plate real quick? I can record you in here, it will take me five minutes to set it up."

"You can record in here?"

"Yeah, I have a little set-up."

"Bredren, if you didn't have those killer dogs inside, yes I would. This thing is cool Bredren, but not with Cujo's in there," he said making the whole group laugh.

"We'll be in the studio. Come in the studio and leave your dogs outside," Cutty said.

By the time Delux got to the door of the studio after thinking if it would be worth it or not to spend the money, The door was locked, and nobody answered his knocks.

"Ahh, sorry babe. I know that was important to you."

"It's okay. It wasn't meant to be," Delux said, driving us to a different spot around the corner.

"Yeah, but what are the odds of a reggae star pulling right up alongside of us?"

"Right? But if I go into the studio, I'll have to pay the studio guy as well as the dub plate guy later on. I'd rather save the money.

I felt I messed that up for Delux. He was really bummed he was not able to record one of Jamaica's biggest Reggae artists. Ruka told me that guy was famous and to have a custom song from a famous person, is a big deal when you're a DJ.

"Thanks Ruka, now I feel worse."

Delux's parents reached out to them and offered the Babes an opportunity to make some money again up in Minnesota. His parents ended up getting their old restaurant back, and it needed some serious cleaning.

The Babes agreed it would be a good idea to go up to Minnesota to help get the restaurant back up and running with the modeling season coming to an end in Miami. They had money coming in from the commercial still, but they were also slowly running out of what they were trying to save for Costa Rica.

"We'll clean the restaurant then we'll train in the new employees as we get the place running. Babe. We're gonna be able to save so much money for Costa Rica doing this. If we spend three months there working and saving our tips, we can go to Costa with thousands of dollars saved up. We're gonna escape this concrete jungle were in. Imagine what we can do once we get there with a good chunk of change?"

Delux was convinced and Tess went along with his excitement like he was going along with her plan to drive to Costa Rica.

"Babe. We're on our way for real this time," Delux added.

Delux found a long piece of wood in the trash that was four feet long and a foot tall while Tess talked to the manager of the bar that was at the hotel her agency was in.

"I did it, I talked to the manager here and got you a DJ gig playing music for free but we can keep 100% of our art sales," Tess told him.

"What? This is epic! Look what I just found in a dumpster. It makes the perfect canvas, don't ya think?   I'm going to paint it black and paint four different pictures on it."

"That's a solid canvas," Tess said. "Hurry up, and we can sell it at our show this weekend."

"Not bad. Delux and Tess have an art show, and he gets to play some of his music," I said to Ruka.

"Did you see how happy Tess was to talk to the manager?"

"Ruka, how can you see that?" I asked.

"I feel it Doofus, you need to use your eyes to see it while learning how to feel it."

They came back from their art show with some weird energy. The Babes were both happy. Delux sold his dumpster dive painting for $1,000 and Tess sold several of her's, but something was up.

"I'd say, we made the gas money to get to Minnesota," Delux said counting the money they made.

The excitement was real, but something was off, Ruka and I could both feel something might have happened that night at the bar, but we were stuck out in the RV so we didn't know what it could be.

"I think it's more Tess then Delux," Ruka told me.

"No way. I bet it was Delux and his opinions and tellings and the way he speaks so direct, and..."

"Ok Doofus, I get it," Ruka stopped me. "Delux can be a bit much at times, but something happened tonight between the two of them."

"Yeah, something did. I do feel it."

CHAPTER 9

MINNESOTA

We made it back to Minnesota with no issues and the babes seemed in good spirits. No police, no breakdowns, nada. Everything was going great with the RV. The Babes were happy together and excited to go help out Delux's parents who were soon going to impact their future.

"Babe, I'm telling you, two months of cleaning, and getting the restaurant ready... then we work there for two, maybe three months... we're gonna make bank."

"And our commercial check is coming in soon too," Tess said excited.

"With that, and what my dad will pay us to clean, and then what we will make in tips once people meet us, we should have more than enough money to make it to Costa Rica, buy some land, and stay a while, who knows." Delux was excited.

"And maybe I'll get another modeling job before we leave for Costa. I'm grateful, Babe. We're doing it."

"Yes, we are," Delux said, pulling us into the driveway of his parents' house. "But what are we going to do in Costa Rica?" he asked after putting the RV in park.

"I don't know, but you could for sure DJ there on the Caribbean side, we can sell our art to tourists, and we both could learn how to surf. Let's just get away from society and all of it's bullshit, we'll figure the rest out when we get there. The RV has done well in two-and-a-half years. I know we'll be fine."

"Ruka, we're here," I told her.

"I know, Doofus. I know this smell like the back of your ass."

Delux opened the door to the RV, so Ruka and I ran out. We'd been driving for hours, and it always felt good to be on flat ground that was not moving and we could pee on it. Don't get me wrong. I loved the RV. But I also loved the stable ground.

I ran, I jumped over Ruka, all the memories of this place were coming back to me. I stopped and pee'd some more.

"Ruka! Watch out. I'm peeing here," I told her, but it was too late.

She walked right underneath me and got sprayed with my pee.

"Ahh shit, Doofus," Ruka let out.

"I was already here peeing, what you want me to do?"

"Make a noise or something."

"My pee was making the pee noise, and besides, I thought you knew my butthole. It was right there."

Grandma came outside and was super happy to see us.

Grandpa was too, but he showed his emotions in a very different way, like, not at all. Maybe just a little smile and the word "Ok" said slowly, or "I don't think so"... Oh I was happy to be back!

"Ruka. How good does this grass feel?" I said sliding myself down the small slope in the yard.

"Oh my god. Oh my god. Oh my god." Ruka didn't know what to do, rolling it all over her back. She sniffed her way to Grandma and laid down by her feet, wagging her tail hoping for a Grandma belly scratch.

"We made you guys a bed in the basement in case you didn't want to be in the RV."

"Mom, the RV has been our home for two-and-a-half years. It's where we live."

"Well, it's there if you like it," Grandma said.

"Thanks, Mom."

"What do you think? Do you want to move inside the house?" Delux asked Tess.

"It'll probably make things easier," she replied.

The Babes were put to work right away. They went and looked at the restaurant that night, and the next day they started cleaning it. Apparently, it was a mess inside. The place was practically ruined by the previous tenants who never cleaned it the two years they were in there. Between the tiles on the floor and walls, there was a thick layer of grease everywhere with the downstairs walls full of mold where they stored the food.

Ruka and I both stayed outside under the RV while the Babes worked inside. Ten hours a day for three weeks, the Babes worked hard. Ruka and I noticed the Babes were not as free flowing with each other like when we were in the RV traveling around. They spent 24 hours a day, seven days a week, in a box together with Ruka and I, and they were fine as long as they were moving or parked on the street. When they had more space, or stopped moving, something always seemed to happen to them.

"They're humans, Doofus. They have a lot of feelings and emotions," Ruka told me, trying to stay out of their way as they argued about something with Delux's father.

"Babe, he's been to war and he's practically deaf in one side of his head. He doesn't even say hi to me, and I am his son. You have to let it go. He is who he is. He means well and appreciates the shit outta us, he just does it in his own way. Can you please accept him for that?"

"I can't. It's disrespectful. I said hi to him and he just ignores me."

"Babe. My dad is always thinking. He's got a lot of things in his head, let it go."

She couldn't.

Tess kept arguing her point with Delux, and you could tell they were both getting frustrated with each other the first few weeks they were there.

Several weeks into the cleaning, The Department of Homeland Security came to the restaurant and surprised everyone. They were looking for the previous owner. Nobody knew where he was, and I heard he owed Delux's father a lot of money. Grandma was glad Ruka and I were around, because apparently the previous owner came to their house and threatened them in their driveway.

Delux kept threatening me that he was going to give me away if I didn't pull my head out of my rear end. I couldn't keep myself out of the flower beds, and I could not stop chewing on things that weren't mine like shoes, doors, pillows and whatever else attracted my nose.

Delux brought his music collection inside and set the crates of records on the floor. That entire day, they left Ruka and I home, instead of bringing us with them to the restaurant.

"I wouldn't do that if I were you," Ruka told me.

"What?"

"Doofus, I can hear you messing with Delux's records. Don't."

I swear Ruka could see. The way she caught me before I did anything, was like she could see. The way she ran and got the ball, was like she could see.

Tess and I were both frustrating Delux. She wanted to leave Minnesota when they'd just gotten here, and I still wouldn't bring the ball back, play with any of them, or keep my mouth off of what's not mine. I started to sit and stay, but I would not stay long, even if I was in the shade.

"Look at you. Are you that dumb? Go get the damn ball. What the fuck is the matter with you, dog?" Delux said to me frustrated while on his break from work and Tess.

"Doofus, make his life better and just do what I do, and get the ball and bring it back to him."

"Ruka, that's the dumbest thing ever. I don't know why you do it, besides I'm here to protect and keep an eye out for trouble remember."

"There is no trouble here, just play," she told me.

Frustrated, Delux put us back inside, and went back to work.

Ruka always took a nap after his visits, so I waited until she was asleep. I went over to Delux's records and slowly started to pull the records out of the crate. They all smelled like a smokey club and Delux. I pulled the vinyl out of the crate, then out of its protectant sleeve and licked the fingerprints of Delux clean off. It tasted and felt nice against my tongue. I couldn't resist. I was imagining how crunchy the record would feel breaking in my mouth like a potato chip, so I took a bite. I was right. It cracked, and pieces broke off into my mouth. I swallowed two of them and went for more records.

I woke up to the sound of the Babes coming home. They were now using Delux's father's car, because the RV used too much gas for local driving. I saw what I had done, and stuck my head under the bed hoping this is all a dream. This was a dream, right?

"Doofus! What the fuck?" Ruka asked me, waking up to my record mess first.

"I ahh…." I said, pausing as the door to downstairs opened and Delux walked in.

"Ohh, Doofus, you mother fucker," Delux instantly said, seeing what I had done.

I tried to stay hidden. This for sure would get me a hand on my backside.

"Oh you stupid fuck."

"What happened?" Tess asked coming into the room.

"He ate my records… the fucking old school classics," Delux said piecing the records back together.

"The ones hard to find, Doofus!" Delux said shaking a broken record at me.

"Look, some pieces are missing," Delux said turning to look at me. "You stupid fuck. You're gonna have to shit that out, man. I'm not taking you to the vet. You're now officially on your own. You're in god's hands dog."

Tess and Delux had a conversation about me while they were fighting themselves. Delux made flyers that night and printed them the next day. *"Free Dog"* they said with my picture and Delux's phone number.

"Doofus, we tried, but you're just not getting it," Tess said to me, touching my head.

"Getting what exactly?" I asked Ruka.

"If you sit, you don't stay. If you stay, you don't come. If you come, it's only because you want food," she told me.

"Yeah, and?"

"Did you forget you have a mission to do here?"

"My mission was back in Miami with that little girl when an ad in the paper took me away from her."

"That was a test mission you accomplished. Your real mission is here with the Babes and I."

"We're not doing anything but driving around. The Babes seem lost. Tess is acting different now, and Delux is blind to it all. No offense. And it doesn't seem like we're gonna leave for Costa Rica anytime soon."

"The Babes are making good money now with the help of Delux's father. Delux is your father figure now. You should show some appreciation, because those fliers they're printing are to get rid of you... For free!" Ruka said, just as upset as the Babes.

Delux kicked me outside and tied me to a post on the concrete deck where I couldn't ruin anything. That weekend, the Babes went out and put my fliers up in town. Delux came home and played with Ruka, and ignored me, leaving me tied up still. He fed me. I had water and a place to sleep outside, but both him and Tess stopped touching me that day.
Tess's frustration with me and Delux grew so much she wanted to leave for real now.

"Remember when we were at my mom's and you wanted to leave because you could not handle her, and we did... Now I want to leave. I don't like this here, and I want to go."

"Tess, please. We didn't have this opportunity at your mom's like we do here. Relax with my dad please, he's hardheaded, and likes things his way, but he's helping us. He knows what he's doing, and look, he's cut from a different cloth then most of us. His resting bitch face just looks scary, give him a break. He's trying to help us, don't you see that?"

"I want to leave."

"Babe, we can't just leave. We just got here. We have to stay here to help my family. They need us."

Tess thought about it for a day while she sat outside cursing me out and smoking her cigarettes. She was not happy, and I didn't understand why. I didn't chew on her stuff this time.

Delux's dad was old school. He was raised different, but through his thick skin, I felt his heart of gold. You could see his heart shine with the opportunity he gave them.

"I'm going to my mom's and try to get work in New York. You can pick me up there when you're finished here, but I don't want to be here anymore."

Delux was sad. Anything he said to keep her there was not working. They were making money and had more saved up now than they ever did, but Tess didn't budge.

There was a knock at the door downstairs.

"You guys okay down here?" Delux's mom asked, probably hearing the whole drama unfold from upstairs.

"Some mail came in for you today. It looks important," she said handing him three envelopes.

"Three?" Delux asked.

"Open them," Tess said in a different energy than she just had with Delux when they were alone.

Delux opened the first one. "$1236.45? That's way more than the $125 we were supposed to get."

"Check your bank, see if you got the same as me. We were both on camera," Delux told Tess.

"You were on camera more than me," Tess said.

"Yeah, but we were both called aside and the camera was put on both of us," he said opening up the other envelope.

"Holy shit, another $1236.45... This is so amazing. We for sure have our money now for our trip," Delux said in excitement while opening the other envelope.

"This one is $861.03. This is like three grand. All from us just being ourselves. Hahaha, we need more jobs like this!"

Delux was right. He and Tess looked great together. There was something about them that was so charismatic.

"Congratulations," Delux's mom said going back upstairs, leaving them alone.

"Nothing's in my bank account yet. The money has to go to the agency first and then they pay me after they take their cut."

Delux didn't have an agency, so he got 100% paid to him out directly. He took his new checks and paid off his old credit card debt that was always lurking over his head. He owed a kid from high school $100, but he didn't know how to get ahold of him or find him.

With some of the money he had left, he bought a new laptop to replace his computer Tess's brother never returned. Delux had lost everything he had recorded, and or created, and needed to start over.

Tess made her decision and was over it here. Delux chose to stay, so Tess found herself a plane ticket to her mom's, promising to be picked up by Delux in exactly two months.

"Let's get cell phones and keep in touch with each other," Tess mentioned.

"Ok. I promise I'll only stay two more months until everybody is trained in, and then on October 17th, I will come and pick you up wherever you are."

"Ok," Tess said. She hugged Ruka and I. "Good luck trying to figure it out in your new home, Doof," she said, tapping me on my head.

I could feel Tess had given up, but Delux still had hope for her, not me. I was left tied up outside as they left for the airport. Delux came home sad. I could feel it when he untied me from the post outside so I could go pee. He was still upset with me, but his sadness of Tess leaving, outweighed his anger with me destroying everything I shouldn't, and not listening to him when I should.

I was beginning to see that there was a fine line between everything. If you cross it, sometimes there was no coming back.

Nobody had called yet to take me off Delux's hands, and Tess didn't want to take me, so here I was waiting outside for what was next.

"Doofus, now would be the perfect time to bring the ball back," Ruka said to me looking out the downstairs window at the ball outside just out of reach.

"Forget that stupid ball game. Delux and Tess no longer want me here, why should I even try?"

"Because I need your help, Doofus."

"You need my help?" I asked shocked to hear that from her.

"Doofus. I might be tough and not take any shit from you, but to be honest, I need you. Delux has been great to me, and I never thought I needed to connect with another dog before, but I feel I'm connected with you. And if you get sent away, I don't think I'll like that and honestly, neither will Delux."

"Why didn't you tell me you felt connected before?"

"I didn't know before, but now I can see it, and more importantly, I can feel it. I'm gonna need you, and Delux is going to need the both of us these next two months without Tess."

Delux was quiet, sitting downstairs alone for the first time in two-and-a-half years.

"Delux wanted a family and that was taken away from him. We need to be his family now," Ruka told me.

Delux spent all of his time working. He would now take us to work every day with him in the RV because he would be gone so long. Ruka and I would sit outside in the RV while he trained the new cooks in the kitchen and the servers on the floor. Delux always came outside smelling like food, and we loved it. We would get a piece of meat or a french fry every now and then when he took his breaks. Seeing there was no Tess around, Delux gave Ruka and I most of his free attention.

Delux got a cell phone and updated Tess that nobody had called for me yet. They both expressed how much they missed each other, and Tess told him how much she missed me and Ruka and the RV. Delux reassured her that he was on time and they would see each other very soon. They talked every night after Delux played with Ruka outside in the back yard.

"Now's your chance, Doofus. Race me to the ball."

"What?"

Ruka ran for the ball, and I watched her go right to it, and bring it back to Delux who was waiting with joy.

"See fool, look how happy he is because of a stupid ball. And look at all the extra scratches he gives. You're missing out, Doofus. You really are a doof."

Ruka ran again for the ball, after Delux threw it again and again for her.

"You don't want none of this," Ruka shouted out towards me jumping into the air, waiting to be told to find the ball again.

"I'll race you, Doof." Ruka shouted out.

Delux threw the ball.

"What, race you? Oh, I'll beat you."

I ran towards the ball, and when I got to it, I saw Ruka hadn't even left Delux's side.

"Now pick it up, and bring it back here Doofus," Ruka told me.

I looked at the ball. I looked at Ruka. I think she tricked me.

"Get the ball, Doofus," Delux said to me in a way I could tell he had no hope for me.

I looked at the ball, then I looked at Ruka again.

"Doofus, now or never," Ruka's voice entered my mind.

"Fuck it." I grabbed the ball.

I squeezed the ball in my mouth, and it fought back. It was a tough ball. It had to be if it was in Ruka's mouth.

"Holy shit. Good boy, Doofus. Bring it here," Delux said in shock.

I ran straight back to Delux and dropped the ball at his feet, and looked at him in his eyes. I've never seen him happier.

"Good job, now do it again," Ruka said to me.

"Doofus. Fetch."

Delux threw the ball again, and I didn't even think twice about it. I ran towards the ball and jumped on it, squeezed it in my mouth, and ran it back to Delux and dropped it off at his feet, tail wagging.

"Holy shit, Ruka, this shit does feel good."

"Well, I be damned. I think you got it," Delux said surprisingly.

I looked at Delux. I could feel in my entire insides, the connection I normally felt early on in life, was happening now.

"Ruka. It's happening!" I barked out in excitement.

"What's happening?" she asked me.

"Wait," Delux said with his palm facing me.

"Ruka, find it," Delux said rolling the ball on the ground.

"This is great, Doofus. Wait here and feel it. Feel the connection!"

Ruka ran off after the ball, and I looked at Delux. I waited. I watched Ruka, and then looked up at Delux. He was so happy, I could feel it inside me, and see it all over his face.
This made me excited. I barked.

"Good boy, speak," Delux told me.

I barked again and again as Ruka brought the ball back and laid it down next to us.

"How's it feeling, Doofus?"

"Ruka. I feel it now. You guys really are, it," I said in disbelief.

Delux picked up the ball again. I watched his hand intensely, then his face. He was looking at me. I looked at him and no longer the hand. What was his face gonna do? I watched.

"Doofus fetch!" Delux said to me tossing the ball, and I ran.

"I'm gonna find it first," Ruka said to me, and came running after me.

I got to the ball first and picked it up. Ruka was right there to get me and fight me for it. I ducked. I dodged. I learned. I like this.

"I think we'll keep him now. I feel he finally connected to me, and it's so awesome, babe. I wish you were here to see it," Delux told Tess over the phone.

"Just gotta keep him from chewing on shit that's not his to chew on!" Delux said with happiness in his voice, rubbing my head.

The Babes called each other every day for the first month Tess was away. Delux would work all day and night and would call Tess late when he got home from work. They would laugh about old memories and talk into the night, falling asleep on the phone with each other.

Then one day, Tess never picked up Delux's call, and didn't call him back. I could feel Delux got a sinking feeling in his stomach.

"Ruka, you feel that?"

"Delux and his stomach? Yep."

All he could do was leave her a voice message telling her he missed her, he loved her, and he would see her soon. Tess finally returned his call, but something felt off about how Delux was responding to her. Normally he was happy to hear from her, but it seemed like he was trying to cheer her up or something. He then bought a plane ticket to prove to himself he was not crazy with his gut feelings and went to see Tess.

Ruka and I were left with Grandma and Grandpa. Grandma considered us like grandkids, so she treated us like grandchildren and spoiled us. She never let me run through her flower beds, but she would let us run around the entire house inside and give us treats. Even though this was a house and not an apartment like Tess's moms place, Ruka and I were too big for most spaces.

"Ruka. The Grands are watching TV. What should we do?"

"I'll tell you what we're gonna do," she said, grabbing my leg and pushing it backwards so I fell over after hitting the table with my bum.

"Ruka. What are you doing?"

"Let's wrestle."

"Here in the living room?"

The Grands loved watching Ruka and I play together on the floor. They laughed, watching us bite, pounce, and roll around on each other.

"These two are so cute, aren't they?"

"Yeah, I guess," Grandpa said, agreeing with Grandma.

I got the zoomies and ran all around the upstairs. In and out of the kitchen and around into the living room where I jumped over Ruka and ran the loop again.

"Doofus. Doofus. Calm down," Grandma said, worried I would run into something of hers and break it.

I didn't hit a thing, except a sweet spot in both their hearts.

I could feel it from them even though Grandpa had a hard time showing it. He had no idea, but his love poured out of him.

"Ruka," I said trying to catch my breath. "This feels like home."

Delux returned a few days later happy he got the chance to see Tess. We didn't know what happened while he was there, but he seemed happy, and he said one more month and then he was going to go pick Tess up in Miami and they were going to drive to Costa Rica.

A month flew by. Ruka and I did the same old thing and waited in the RV while Delux worked in the restaurant. Delux would pull us out and show us to people sometimes. I guess I would make a lot of ruckus barking at people, and those people became curious about me, so Delux introduced us. Ruka would sniff her way to the new person, giving them more love than they bargained for, and having zero accountability of personal space. Delux would throw out our street cone, and Ruka and I would put on a show, fighting over it. We were more bark than bite people would say, but then Delux would tell them the story of me biting the guy in Key West.

Ruka was fun and full of love, especially to every human, but she was a bit of a "fuck around and find out" kinda dog, if you were a dog who didn't submit. Ruka loved it when I submitted. I had to. If not, she would just keep humping me from behind with her pitbull death grip from her front legs around my waist until I did. If I tried anything, she was already ready to bite my neck. She couldn't see me or catch me, so I had to submit if I wanted her to play with me or give me attention. I was now too fast for her nose and ears, and her brain stopped letting her just run around because she was bumping into too many things, but me. I only played with her now in open spaces, unless we were in the RV, then it was fair game until the Babes said stop.

Delux let us do what we wanted, now that I started listening to him. He spent all of his free time with Ruka and me in that last month he was working in Minnesota. He was happy, he was in love, he was loved, he had money saved up for traveling, and he had Ruka and me. He was set.

On the weekend, Delux drove the RV out to the city to meet up with some DJ friends. We went past where Ruka and he used to live in a really tall building that faced a really old looking church made of large stones.

"Ruka, how was it in that tall building and the big city?"

"It was amazing. Delux went to see a psychiatrist to get permission for me to live with him in that building."

"You had to get permission to live?"

"Delux needed a piece of paper that says I'm his companion, and he cannot live without me."

"Sounds like a romance novel?"

"Yep. He even brought a picture of me and everything."

"And it worked?"

"Yep. After twenty days or so, the people who hired Delux to live and work onsite, appreciated his help so much, they not only let me live there with him, they let me move in early."

"Where were you while he was working?"

"Here, at Grandma's house, living the life like we are now, only without you taking all my attention."

"Whatever. You take all the attention when I'm getting it."

"Grandma was super afraid of me back in the day because my breed has a bad reputation, but after ten minutes with me, she melted. If I couldn't stay with Delux at his new job, Grandma said she would have kept me. I can't say she'd say the same for you."

"What do you mean? They all love me now."

"It took me ten minutes, not two-and-a-half years."

"You gotta point there."

"Ruka, Doofus. RV."

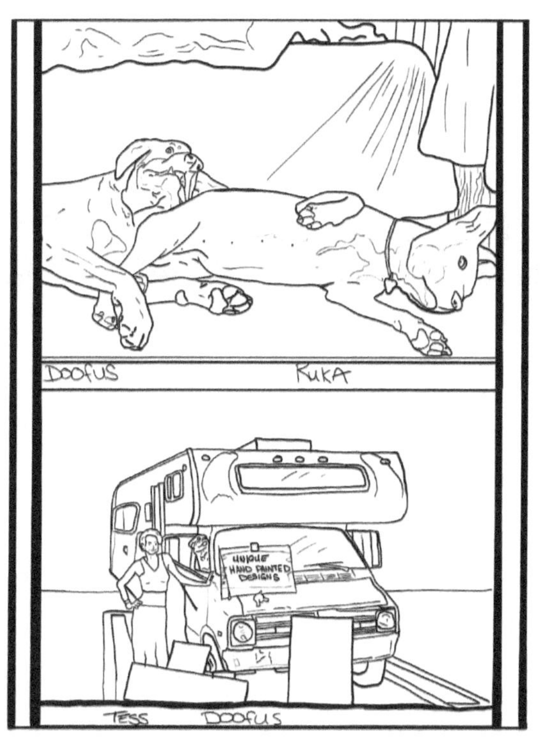
DOOFUS
RUKA
UNIQUE
HAND PAINTED
DESIGNS
TESS
DOOFUS

CHAPTER 10

TESS KNOWS BEST

We were back on the road, headed to Miami to pick up Tess. It was strange not having her in the RV with us for the long drive.

"Doofus. *Necesitarás aprender algo de español.*"

"What? Bless you Ruka."

"No, dummy. I said you will need to learn some Spanish."

"Learn Spanish? Really?"

"*Si mi amigo.* They speak Spanish in Costa Rica."

I was more concerned with the pit in Delux's stomach. I loved this newfound connection I was having with Delux, I thought as I looked up at him focusing on the road, yet still not knowing what was going on with him.

"What do you think it is, Ruka, love or fear?" I asked, sitting on the floor, letting her have the passenger seat.

"What?" she asked, clueless like she couldn't just read my thoughts like she always did.

"The pit in Delux's stomach. Is it love or fear?"

"It's the fear of love. I don't think he's sure what he's driving himself into, or why," she told me as the wind outside pushed on the RV.

For one month, he and Tess talked every day; the last month, they spoke maybe twice a week.

"Delux can be an overthinker, so he's probably overthinking everything, creating the pit in his stomach," Ruka added.

"Yeah, or he really feels something, because I feel something," I told her.

"It took you two-and-a-half years to 'feel something.' Are you sure of what you are feeling, or you just gotta poo, because we're stopping soon."

"Oh I gotta poo."

We were just dogs, so we sat back feeling the cool fall air turn warmer the farther south we drove, waiting for Delux to stop so we could go out and smell the world, and pee all over it.

Delux didn't play around and drove straight down to Miami. He only stopped once to sleep a few hours in a rest stop, but other than that, we just stopped for gas and food to go. He called Tess along the way, only to get her voicemail. The pit in his stomach grew bigger the closer we got.

When we finally arrived in South Florida, Tess called Delux back, and gave him her address, and told him to meet her in the alley on South Beach. Delux was happy on the outside, but I could still feel his pit getting bigger the closer we got to her destination. Once in the alleyway, we parked and Tess came outside with a cat and a cigarette in hand.

"She still smokes, and she just put a cat down," I updated Ruka.

"Oh maybe we're going to take a cat with us to Costa Rica?" Ruka said.

"The cat does seem to like her," I said as I watched the cat move around her feet.

Delux went to get out of the RV.

"No, stay inside. I'll just finish this cigarette, and we can drive somewhere. I know you don't like the smoke."

"You don't want to invite us inside?" Delux asked.

"No, my roommates are home. We have cats that are weird, and I'd rather go with you and the dogs in the RV somewhere."

"Ok," Delux said, sitting back down into the chair with the pit in his stomach.

Tess got into the RV without the cat. She was happy to see us and gave us a lot of pets, but it seemed like an act as she reeked of something other than cat, that I couldn't put a paw on. She told Delux to take us to the park, so he did. He was always happy to do whatever Tess wanted. From building the RV, to driving somewhere, to stopping for breaks, to having sex, Tess took control a lot.

With all their small talk aside as we drove, we made it to the park receiving the most amount of love Tess has ever given us.

"So what's up? You ready to come back to the RV and fulfill your dream of driving to Costa Rica?"

"No, I'm not?"

There was a short pause that felt forever.

"What's going on?"

"I started waitressing at the hotel where my agency is, and, I started dating my manager."

"I told you something was up, Ruka," I said turning my attention to Delux with my head cocked sideways.

"What? Dating your manager?" Delux asked as the pit in his stomach turned into stone, making him burst into tears confirming what he was feeling.

"I'm sorry. I wanted to tell you before you came down, but you were so excited. I didn't know what to do." Tess paused as Delux cried.

"I don't want to go to Costa Rica anymore. You can keep the RV and Doofus. I don't mind. I still can't drive the RV anyways; my license is so fucked up," she said petting my head with her soft touch, feeling little emotion for Delux's pain.

Delux couldn't stop crying. He was sobbing, siting there alone with her in the house they built together. He was confused, and angry.

"How long have you been together?" Delux asked.

"Maybe a month?"

"So you were with him, when I flew down here to visit you a few weeks ago, and you lied to me?"

"I'm sorry."

"You know... I knew it, too. The day you didn't return my call is the day this pit in my stomach arrived, and I somehow... Somehow, I knew it. How could I be so fucking dumb?" Delux said putting his head down.

"I'm sorry," Tess said sitting next to him.

"What the fuck am I gonna to do now? I gave up everything for you and this Costa Rica dream of yours," Delux said.

The Babes spent all night going back and forth with their love for each other on a rollercoaster of emotions. They'd spent two-and-a-half years together in this box I was calling my house. The Babes and Ruka felt like my roommates and Delux was my personal driver. Ruka is my friend, and now, now I have to move Tess into the same box as my mom and my first little friend.

Tess spent the night in the RV with Delux in the park holding him while he cried all night long. If he wasn't crying, he was boiling with anger, covered in a thick blanket of hopelessness.

The next morning, we drove up to a friend of Tess's. Tess wanted to finish the curtains inside the RV, before she left it, and us, with Delux.

Delux couldn't get his emotions in order. How could he? I could see he was driving us all around in a state of shock as he continuously tried to keep himself together. He waited as long as he could to bring Tess back to her home with cats and the other man she'd replaced us with. Delux begged her to reconsider and stay with us, but she was cold, and didn't seem to care.

Everything we knew about her had changed. Both Ruka and I saw it, we felt it. We knew it.

We pulled back into the alley and dropped Tess off at the back door where we found her. She said goodbye to us all, and got out. Delux sat there in tears, feeling the hole in his chest where his heart once was.

"Go," Tess said.

Delux pulled away with us and the RV, but his heart was left in that alley, cut into pieces.

"Ruka, this ain't good."

"She replaced us for cats. What a bitch. You know, I saw us in Costa Rica," Ruka says.

"Yeah, me too. Delux had a beard."

"A beard? No way, I didn't see him like that, he was clean-shaven and ripped like Tarzan."

Delux drove us to a loading zone that was closed for the night and we slept there until 7am. He didn't sleep. He cried.

He cried for days. He became lost in his own body. He didn't want to go back to Minnesota and work at the restaurant he just left. He was too heartbroken to be social or even play his music. He just sat in the RV all day from one parking spot to another, just looking out the windows while lying on the back couch. He stopped smoking weed. He stopped doing everything.

"Tess was his everything," Ruka said.

"How do we help him?" I asked.

He'd given up everything for her and her dream. Now he was lost, sitting there with us and a broken heart.

Delux drove us up north to a record store. Of course, we stayed in the RV, and an hour later, he came out with a huge stack of records in his arms.

"What not a better way to heal a heart break, than shopping and music?" Ruka said.

Delux parked us back behind some warehouses we went to back in the day. He turned on his studio and he got lost in the music until the early hours of the morning. He slept in late while the place we parked, turned into a busy loading zone area for businesses. With people all around, Delux let us out to pee and poo, but today, he didn't pick it up. You could say, he didn't give a shit. He packed up all his music and drove us south to the beach parking lot. The same place where the Babes spent a lot of their time when Tess was around.

Delux parked down the way a bit by a different shower and faced north so we could see the ocean from our side door. There was a lot less traffic going by us here making it easy for us to all relax.

Beach days became our everyday.

We would go to the beach early in the morning, and when the parking meters turned on, we would drive somewhere where there weren't any. I could feel Delux hated driving into South Beach. He figured he would run into Tess anywhere down there, but it was one of the best places to find free parking with shade until the evening.

Parking became a game. The meter police would drive by and put marks on our tire to see if we moved or not. Delux didn't want to pay any more tickets, so he was very attentive moving us around. With Tess not there to distract him anymore, he stayed on top of things.

He pretended to be happy sitting in the RV alone with us, paying close attention to the world around him. He wrote short stories about his movie idea he had and would draw out scenes when he was not playing music or playing with us. Getting lost in his bugs movie was all that kept him occupied besides us.

Our purpose as dogs became clear: Keep Delux happy.

It became easier to learn what Delux wanted without Tess around to change the energy he had at his core. I started to notice he would make hand gestures every time he told me something. Relax. Chill. Chill out. Wait. Heal. I had them all down. If he said *shake*, I would shake his hand. If he said *other one*, I would do it with the other paw. I felt he looked at me different now that I was looking back at him.

"It's because you're finally figuring it out Doofus. The eyes are the gateway to the soul. Use your eyes while you have them," Ruka added before rolling over and letting me chew on her ears.

Delux didn't want much, but he liked consistency and did everything he could to create it for us. We now spent so much time at the beach, I learned I love swimming, like I love it, love it. Even when the waves were bigger than me, I would jump over them and splash my belly on the other side having the time of my life. I wish I knew Ruka in my younger years so I could have played with her in the water.

"In my younger years, I for sure would have drowned you until you stopped breathing," Ruka added again getting into my head with her thoughts.

"Ruka," I growled at her rolling her in the sand.

"It's true you stinky mutt, get back here," Ruka said as I ran away.

There were so many laws about Ruka and me not being able to be at the beach. We were not allowed in a lot of areas, and where Delux was parking the RV, we weren't allowed on the beach there.

Delux didn't care and kept the leashes close and allowed us to be free to run and play. Ruka and I didn't bother anyone but each other and I might have been persuaded to chase after a squirrel. We stayed by Delux and were in our own little world. We wouldn't bark or yell at anyone or anything in public unless Delux told us to speak, or sing, which we had just learned to do.

"You just learned to do. I knew how to sing a long time ago."

"Okay Ruka."

I wouldn't run and chase anything anymore but Ruka. She never left Delux when we played in the big open areas, even when he would tell her it was okay to be free.

"Ruka. You can trust me, this area is totally open," I told her trying to get her to chase me and run a little bit.

"I know the beach, Doofus. I was running in this sand before you were a whiff in the air through your fathers nose and into his nutsack."

"What? Well chase me then," I begged, running in circles around her.

"Gotcha!" Ruka said, lunging at me when I got too close in the sinking sand that was grabbing at my paws, slowing me down.

You use up a lot of energy running in the sand and playing in the hot sun. I needed a break, so I jumped in the ocean. I was thirsty and drank up a bit of the sea water. It tastes terrible and goes down a bit weird I noticed after drinking some more of it, it doesn't really quench your thirst either.

"Come on guys, let's go," Delux said, calling us over to him.

I drank some more, and ran off. Ruka and I got baths at the beach shower with Delux's adapted hose, then we hung outside in the small plot of grass in the corner of the parking lot after getting brushed off. My stomach was feeling weird from the salt water, but I held myself together, keeping an eye out for the parking police. It was Christmas Eve, but the police were still checking and writing tickets.

Delux made himself a good dinner that night after calling his parents and wishing them well. He told them our day by the beach was amazing, and now he was going to play some music and go to bed. His mom was worried about him being alone on Christmas, but he reassured her, he was fine, he had the dogs.

Delux was not fine.

"The RV is clean for Christmas," Delux said petting our heads before going to bed.

We all fell asleep quickly that night, and I entered into the most wildest dream. I was swimming at the beach with dolphins. We were playing catch with each other. Every time I jumped for the ball, I would hear them squeak at me.

"Squeak, squeak," the dolphins said laughing and enjoying their time with me.

Every time I jumped, I felt like I was being pushed through the air by my bum, and then the dolphins would squeak when I landed. The ocean I was now feeling got warm all of a sudden by my tail, and this awoke me from my dream.

"Squeak," went my butthole and poo squirted out.

"Oh, shit!" I said, realizing it was me that was squeaking. I tried as hard as I could to keep what was inside of me, inside.

"Doofus, did you just..." Ruka started to say.

"Squeak," went my butthole, again with more poo shooting out as I stood up in the driver's seat, filling it with poo.

"Oh god, no," I whined out and jumped off the driver's seat, into the back of the RV splashing poo on Ruka.

Delux was sound asleep. I didn't know what to do so I ran to the back of the RV. I turned and looked at my butt. It was impossible to hold back my poo. More poo squeezed itself past my clenching hole and squirted all over the back couch.

Delux needed to wake up now, but if I barked, it would all come out. I couldn't bark, I had to hold it in. I couldn't even tell Ruka. I didn't know if she was awake or just traumatized and stuck there afraid to move, covered in shit.

"Oh Ruka I'm so sorry I shat on you."

"Squeak."

"Oh god," I said spinning in circles.

I went up by the side door that had the baby gate in front and looked up at Delux. "Please wake up," I thought out loud, looking at the ceiling above the bed.

"Squeak," my butt said as I was trying to send Delux my thoughts.

"Squeak," it went again, and again.

I ran to the back. I ran to the front.

"Squeak."

"Shit".

Delux finally looked down from the bed and saw me staring up at him.

"Doofus," he said, sleepy.

"Squeak," went my butt as I turned and looked at it.

"Oh shit. Doofus. Outside!" Delux said leaning down, pushing the gate aside and opening the door.

I ran out.

"Squeak."

Poo hit the stairs as I jumped out, and again it squirted out as I jumped over the sea wall. Once on the other side of the wall, I relaxed, and it all came out of me like you were emptying a bucket of water.
Pooing never felt so good.
How did swimming with dolphins turn into such a nightmare? Last time I saw dolphins, was when Mountain tried to kidnap us all. This must be a sign.

BAM!

"Ah shit," Delux said slipping and falling on my poo, hitting his back on the floor, getting covered in shit.

"Doofus. He told you to stop drinking the sea water and this is why," Ruka told me, trying to shake off my shit.

"I'm sorry, Ruka. I thought it was the dolphins," I told her.

We went to check up on Delux.

"Doofus, what the fuck? Are you okay?" he asked, super concerned and covered in poo.

I was feeling better, but my face said otherwise. I think I was just scared because Delux said the words, "what the fuck." That usually means trouble in my world.

"Thanks for the Christmas presents, buddy," he said rubbing my head and touching my empty belly.

He went back inside and assessed the mess.

"Doofus... Holy shit, you got shit everywhere, dude!"

Delux started to grab everything with poo on it and tossed it outside. After, he took a cold beach shower at 3:30 in the morning on Christmas. He washed himself then gave Ruka and I baths, and then washed himself again. He went inside the RV and grabbed his stash of herbs. I was proud of Delux. He'd spent the last week not smoking weed. He was trying to see how long he could go, and he didn't seem to be struggling with it.

"I was trying, Doofus, but I gotta get high for this shit," Delux said, sitting on the sea wall rolling his joint.

He rolled a fat one, then put his stash away inside the RV's wall, and came back outside with a lighter. He went back to the shower, rinsed his feet and came back to the RV and sat on the sea wall.

Ruka and I sat there watching Delux smoke, while cleaning our feet. After he got the joint going and took a few good hits off of it, we all turned and looked at some lights that were approaching from the next street down. "POLICE" it said written on the side of a car coming out of the next block with its blinker on letting us know they were coming our way.

"Fuck," Delux said, trying to tap the joint out and tossing it behind him on the sea wall seeing the police turn towards us.

"Ruka, what are the chances?" I asked.

"Just sit tight, Doofus. Everything will be okay. Just don't change that sad, pathetic looking face you have on right now."

"Sad face? Ruka how can you…?"

The cop car came right up to us and parked in the street, with its headlights looking us dead in the eyes. You could feel the tension in the air. Delux sat on the wall and didn't move as the cop stepped out of his vehicle, taking his flashlight in hand and walking towards Delux.

"If the cop arrests Delux for smoking weed, which he can, they will send us to the pound, and take the RV, that is full of shit right now."

"I'm sorry, Ruka. It was the dolphins I thought."

"What do you mean it was the dolphins?"

"Looks like you gotta shitty situation here," the cop said shining his flashlight into the RV lighting up where Delux slid and fell.

"It goes all the way to the back. The big one there," Delux said pointing at me.

"Well, it looks like you have it under control. Have a happy holiday," the cop said walking back to his squad car and leaving.

"Holy shit. That was a close one," Ruka said.

Delux reached for his joint.

"He's probably gonna radio his homies to leave me be so, Ruka, you wanna get high with me?" Delux asked Ruka, petting her head.

Delux spent all morning cleaning the RV. I felt terrible. We had to throw Ruka's favorite pillow away, a blanket, two pillows from the back, and both front seat covers.

Just after sunrise, the RV was spotless once again, only missing a few things.

"How you feeling, Doof?" Delux asked me, rubbing my head.

"I'm better now," I looked towards him ready to play.

After that shit, pun intended, I'm never drinking salt water again. For my belly, for Ruka—poor dog, I shat all over her—and Delux.

With the RV clean and airing out, we enjoyed Christmas Day, under the hammock with Delux outside. There were no busy crowds, no distractions. Just us and the coconut trees, with the breeze slightly making the hammock sway. Today was a good day.

It wasn't always palm trees and coconuts though. Delux was more lost than ever. He would spend all day parked somewhere doing nothing. He would walk us around, but Ruka and I looked so scary, not many people approached Delux for conversation to break him out of his head. He was never good with starting a conversation either.

"Ruka, was Delux always introverted like this?"

"Delux never lived in a RV alone with two dogs and a broken heart like this before so I don't think so."

He never had a problem hanging out with us all day doing nothing, but talking to strangers, that was not his thing.

"Ruka. We need to find Delux a friend."

"How do you plan on doing that?"

"I don't know. I'm just saying."

"Okay, let's find Delux a friend."

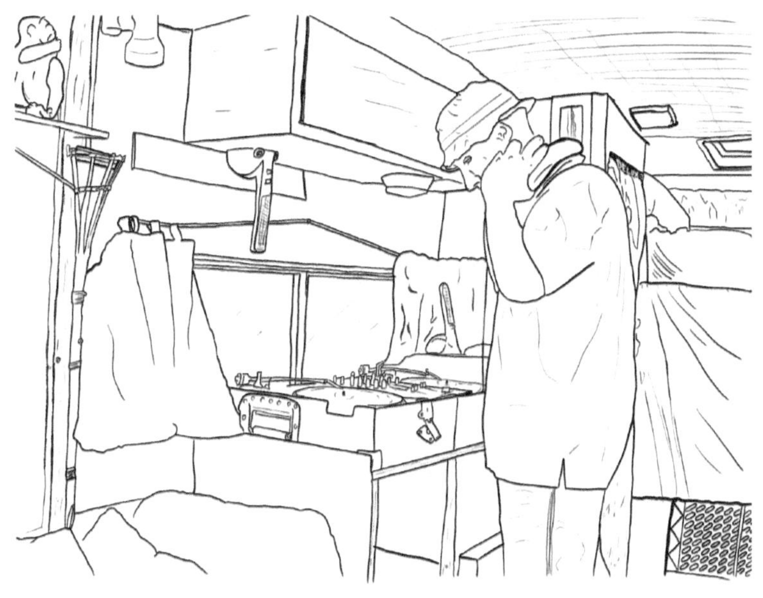

CHAPTER 11

GO DJ

We pulled into the record store Delux loved to visit up north.

"Ok guy's, I'll be back. You watch the place," Delux told us, rubbing our heads together then closing the door.

When he says to "watch it," I do. Anyone who pulled up next to us, anyone walking by too close, they'd know I'm here and to stay back.

Delux went into the store while Ruka and I sat in the RV watching him go inside. I took the driver's seat, and she was in the passenger seat.

"How much you think he'll spend in there?" I asked.

"It's been a while, so probably a few hundred dollars."

Ten minutes into Delux being gone, some big white Suburban pulled up and parked right next to us. You could hear the bass music coming from the dark tinted windows that were all the way up. I was ready. As soon as their door opened, I let out a bark, then I ran to the back of the RV and let out a few more barks and punched the metal grate on the back window as he walked behind the RV.

"Holy shit," the guy said, and he made a run for the door of the record store not realizing we were locked up. He opened the door to the record store and quickly turned and slammed it behind him, looking back at us.

"Haha. I sacred the shit outta that guy, Ruka."

"That's your favorite thing to do, isn't it, Doofus?"

"What makes you think that?"

"The way you bark just to bark, and the show you put on afterwards. It seems you like it."

"It's what I'm here for, right?"

I could see Delux in the record store listening to music. He walked over to the stranger and said something to him and handed him a record. Then they both listened to the records they picked, then they both bought some.

"Now they're walking out of the store together. Should I do it again?"

"Only if you truly feel the need, Doofus," Ruka told me, sniffing the air.

"Your dogs aren't gonna attack me, are they?"

"If I'm around, you're fine. The pitbull is sweet, the Rottweiler can be a bit much, but he's well trained, and also very sweet."

"Okay, if you say so. Follow me. Hi, doggies. Don't kill me," the new guy said, getting into his Suburban.

"Bark. Bark. Hi, guy," I said back.

"Oh shit, hot damn," he said, laughing before slamming his door.

"Doofus, relax, man. He's cool people," Delux told me, putting his records in the back.

He jumped into the driver's seat, and we started to follow the white Suburban.
We didn't have to drive far before we pulled into a driveway and parked.

"I'll be back, guys," he told us.

Delux got out of the RV and spoke with the new guy, as they went inside his house.

"What do you think, Ruka?"

"Well, if this guy is a DJ and Delux is a DJ, I think he might have found his new friend."

A while later Delux and the new guy came outside, and Delux opened the door to the RV to let us out.

"Outside," he said.

"That one is blind, and that one is…"

"Holy shit, that is a big ass dog man. Oh my god, Delux, please put them back. Please put them back," he said in fear, backing up and holding his arms close to his chest.

"They're good though, watch."

"Ruka. Come," Delux said clicking his mouth in the process.

"Yes, Daddy?"

"This is Ruka. She's super sweet. She looks crazy, but for real, my secret is, she'll never hurt anybody."

"Well, besides the little girl you bit," I said to Ruka under my breath.

"That was an accident Doofus, but this ain't," Ruka said lunging towards me.

"Ahh, dammit," I said trying to get away from her bite but unable to.

"Are they fighting?" the new guy asked.

"No, this is how they play and show off in front of people."

"Doofus. Heel."

I stopped playing with Ruka and went to Delux's side and looked up at him.

"Yes, Dad?"

Holy shit. I just called Delux dad. He wasn't my dad, but for some reason it felt like it in that moment. I looked into his eyes and waited.

"Doofus, go on," Delux called out, so I went in front of him a bit and turned around to look at him.

"Relax," Delux said making a fist, and I sat down.

"Stand," came next with a raised hand, and I stood up.

"Doofus, chill." I lay on my belly watching Delux flatten his hand.

"Good boy. Stand." Hand went up, and I stood up again.

"Yes. Now, back up," Delux said moving his fingers towards me, and I took a few steps backwards.

"Wow, you have total control of your dog like that? And you're using your hand," the new guy said.

"Doofus, back up. More. More. Back up." Delux kept motioning me into the street. I walked backwards looking Delux in the eye knowing something more was coming.

"Chill," Delux said, flattening his hand in a downward motion. I laid down on my belly on the warm street.

"Good boy. Chill out," Delux said rolling his hand over and tilting his head to the side. And just like that, I rolled to my side and put my head to the ground.

"Wait," Delux said as I let out my breath and waited.

"Holy shit. How did you do that?" the new guy asked.

"He grew up inside this RV with me, and we've spent twenty-four hours a day together, seven days a week, for three years. But honestly, he just figured all this shit out recently."

"You've lived in this thing for that long?" he asked, looking at the RV.

"Yeah. It was a girls idea, but she just left me with the RV and dogs. I came down here to pick her back up, but she was with another man already, so my plans have changed."

"Damn. Now what you gonna do now?" he asked.

"I have no idea. I can park anywhere. I just wanna DJ again so, where ever that is."

"Well, let me ask my homie. Maybe you can stay here, and you can join our DJ crew if he's okay with you parked out front."

"Man, I miss DJing a lot. That would be dope. Here, let me grab you those mixes I was talking about so you know I can back you up."

"Man, that record you passed me proved to me you know what's up. And look at this RV, man, it's like the real deal."

"You should see the inside."

"What about your dog?"

Delux turned and looked at me lying in the middle of the road as a car was slowly approaching.

"Watch. He won't move," Delux said as the car drove past me with the adults and kids looking outside the windows, checking to see if I was alive or there because I was hit by a car.

"Doofus. RV."

I sprang up, and ran into the RV, turned around and stood there on the top step proud as could be.

"Good boy," Delux said rubbing my face and jumping into the RV to find those mixes.

"Here you go. These are all recorded live with no edits. Let me know what you think."

"Maybe just park your RV over a bit in the grass there until I can confirm with my homie." He motioned with his hands.

"I think I found a new friend, guys. What ya think?"

"I think this is great, Ruka."

"Me, too," she said.

This sucks. Delux just keeps us in the RV all the time, while he hangs out inside with the boys. I wanted to hang out with the boys. Instead, I was stuck outside with Ruka and all she wanted to do was sleep, or clean her paws.

"I'm a lady, and I'm beautiful. I can't help it," Ruka said.

Delux quickly began DJing with his new friend, Lu. After making a new mix with the new records he just bought that afternoon in Lu's driveway, Delux was hired. Lu couldn't believe how fast Delux was able to record a mix, all while using a laptop and a generator.

"Told you, Doofus. Delux is a legend. You've never seen him really perform," Ruka said.

"I heard him at Hoodstock. At the warehouse, remember?"

"Yeah, he did great that night, but it wasn't a dancehall reggae crowd. That's what he likes."

It was all noise to me. Humans hear this music, and something happens to them.

Lu hung out with Delux as he mixed his new records, and from then on, Lu took Delux everywhere he went. If Lu was playing an event, Delux was at his side. If Lu was on the radio station, Delux was there with him. Before long, Delux and Lu started to get popular.

"Man, they hate us now," Lu told Delux rolling up a blunt in the back of the RV. "I can't believe I'm in here with your dogs. Please don't kill me," Lu said to me not making eye contact and laughing it off as I sniffed his leg.

Ruka and I liked Lu. He was real. He was authentic. And he was honest about his feelings of being scared to death of us.

I could sense a side of sweetness in him when he asked us not to kill him.

"He's harmless," Ruka told me biting at my paws.

"I trust him," I told her, putting her entire face in my mouth.

"Why do they hate us?" Delux asked.

"Because we are getting more calls than them on their own show."

"So now they're mad?"

"Yeah. People love us man. And they have no clue you're a white guy. This is great."

"Story of my life. Everybody judges me when they see me."

"It's because you look like a cop or something," Lu says laughing.

"You're like a hippy undercover cop," Lu adds.

"I went to school to be a cop, but I failed gym class."

"How do you fail gym class?"

"The teacher accused me of lying. I called him a bad name, and he failed me. Then, only one person passed the psychology class we had to take, and it wasn't me."

"So you became a DJ?"

"No. I discovered my girlfriend was cheating on me, so I decided to go into the Navy."

"Damn, how was the Navy?"

"Not sure how to answer that one. I hated my commanding officer while in training, but after I graduated, he was cool as shit, and funny as fuck. While I was in training, they wanted to send me to military jail twice."

"Why?"

"Umm I was arguing with a guy who lost a pin that holds his rifle together. Then in the end, before I got out. Let's just say, I left base one day and watched a DJ do their thing, and after that, it's all I wanted to do. I got lucky and the Navy breached my contract because of a medical thing, and then I got out."

"Damn."

"No the damn part is, I tried to go back into the Navy, but seriously, I got electrocuted by the door handle of the building you have to go into to be sworn in, and then I heard a man's voice in my head telling me not to go."

"What? That happened for real?"

"Yeah man, no lies. And thank god, I didn't go. If I had, I would have gotten out of the Navy the November after September 11th. Meaning I would have had to re-enlist."

"Damn, that's heavy. So that military training is what makes you look like a cop," Lu says laughing.

"I guess," Delux says getting high.

I never knew Delux's whole story. I still don't know. He was cheated on and went into the military, and now, Tess left him for another guy. I wondered what he was gonna do next. Go back into the military?

"No, Doofus. He will never go back into the military."

"How do you know?"

"Because he really believes god, or something spoke to him that day, and it made a lasting impact, and, he has us now. He won't do anything crazy without us involved."

Knowing Delux had us involved made it easier to sit around and wait for him to come back and open the door for us. He was never gone as much as he was when he was working with JC while parked in the woods. Besides DJing with Lu at a radio station getting hated on, or sitting inside the house getting high with the crew, Delux was always trying to include Ruka and me if he could. He would take us to the store with him on the skateboard. He would tie us up outside where most people who looked at us were intimidated, and nobody would ever walk by too close. Except one day.

Delux took us for a walk, then skateboarded to the store. While he was tying us up to the pole away from people so he could go into the store peacefully, a police car pulled up and parked right next to us before Delux was finished with his knots.

"Hi. Nice dogs you have there," the cop said, walking right up to Delux.

"It's cool, Doofus," Ruka and Delux both told me as I got very attentive with his quick approach.

"If you want, I can hold them for you while you run into the store," the cop said.

"Ruka. Did he just ask if he could 'hold' us while Delux goes into the store?"

"He means our leashes, so Delux doesn't have to tie us up."

"You're not going to take my dogs, are you?" Delux asked.

"What? No way. I love dogs. I have a few of my own I have to leave home when I'm out working. I see you around here with these two all the time lately. You're not from around here, are you?"

"I am, just not this area. It's a temporary thing, I think."

"You can trust me," the cop said.

"When people say you can trust them, you usually can't," Delux said, handing the leashes to the cop.

"That's Ruka. She's blind and sweet as can be. The big guy is Doofus. Don't let the name fool you," Delux said, laughing.

"Hi, guys. Got damn, you two are beautiful dogs. Do you know how to sit?" he asked me trying to pet my head, but I moved.

"Sit?" He said it like a question, not a command.

Ruka was already sitting down, not caring or paying attention to the cop.

"What are you talking about? I'm paying attention," Ruka said.

"Doofus, sit," the cop tried to command me.

"Ruka, you believe this guy? He wants me to sit down. Should I tell him the word?"

"Even if you did, he won't understand you."

Bark!

"The word is 'relax', you dummy," I said in my bark.

"It's okay, boy. Sit," the cop tried again with no luck.

I stood there looking around. I looked at the door Delux went into, but he was nowhere to be found. I looked out to the parking lot because people were watching us after my bark. I looked behind us. I knew we were safe with this stranger, but I still had to play my role.

"Way to stay solid, Doofus," Ruka told me.

"Really?"

"Yeah. Not too long ago, you were all over the place, and this is the first time I have seen you actually focused 100%?"

"Again, Ruka, I ask how, you can see me?"

"Your bum is in my face Doofus. It's pretty obvious what's going on."

"Doofus. Come on, boy. Sit," the cop tried again.

"Try with Ruka, she's already sitting," I said to the struggling cop as Delux came out of the door. Ruka stood up and joined me in the standing position.

"That wasn't necessary, but thank you," Delux said, holding his bag of goodies, reaching for our leashes.

"They're beautiful dogs. You're lucky to have them," the cop said, handing us over.

"Thanks, they really are the best, I must say. Have a good day officer," Delux said, skating us away through the parking lot, back home.

Delux would skate us around the neighborhood at night when it was cooler outside. The cop must have seen us on one of our midnight skates, I thought. We got home and Delux put us into the RV, and he went inside the house to cook breakfast for the crew.

Delux left for Tampa that weekend and left us tied up in the back yard, with the homie to give us food. He gave us food and water, but that was it. Ruka sat on her chain outside, I sat on mine. I didn't mind being chained up. All it meant was Delux would be back a little later than normal. But he always came back.

One night went by rather quickly alone with Ruka and the next evening, Delux returned like nothing had happened. Ruka and I realized we could handle Delux being gone, and I never caused any problems like I used to. But then again, what can I do on a chain outside, except find a place to dig a hole, which I didn't, I just slept. When Delux and the gang returned, they were super happy. Tampa must have been good to them.

Delux took us for the longest skate that night he got back. I loved pulling him on the skateboard. All he needed to do was watch Ruka while I pulled us at a steady speed where Delux could carve back and forth on the smooth streets, never putting his foot down. Both Ruka and I were on extendable leashes, so we were never too close to Delux. I was in the front, and Ruka was listening to my steps close behind. I was pulling Delux and guiding Ruka, I felt like I had a purpose. I was going to help Delux heal his heart and help guide Ruka through a life that is meant to be enjoyed. Life was feeling good with this new routine we developed.

"Hey, Lu. I just got word that MTV is looking for new TV show ideas, and they're holding an open video casting," Delux said.

"I heard that, too. What you thinking?"

"I'm thinking, we should submit the idea of you and I driving this RV from New York to LA, and we can only make money by DJing events we promote to get there."

"So I would have to live in this RV with Ruka and Doofus?" Lu questioned.

"I love the way Lu say our names… Doofus. Hahahaha," I said to Ruka as we laid on the floor listening to them figure it out.

"Yes. And the best part is, you have to shit in that tiny ass bathroom there," Delux said laughing.

Last time Lu was in the RV and they were talking, he admitted to Delux that he had to shower after every poo, and do them naked.

"What if you're at work?" Delux asked Lu in the moment.

"I don't go. I wait till I get home."

"Yeah, but what if you really gotta go? There's no holding it."

"Then I gotta take it all off."

"Shoes and socks, too?"

"All of it," he admitted.

"Ruka. If you and I both poo naked, and Lu poo's naked, then does that make Delux the weird one?"

"Yes. That's why they would both be good for any TV show," Ruka told me.

"You're black with dreadlocks and play hip-hop super dope," Delux said.

"And you're white and goofy looking, no offense, yet you play dancehall music like nobody else. I swear, you're like a black guy stuck in a white guy's body, and you got these dogs," Lu said laughing.

"Thanks, I think. My friends run the casting company they're doing this out of. I will get more info tomorrow when I drive down there."

"Cool."

We drove to Miami the next day. Delux drove around and looked for Tess, and we never found her, thank god. It probably would have set him back in his healing process. Just being in South Beach was hurting him I felt. We walked up and down the famous Euclid Ave, which was just a bunch of fancy food places with shops and a Starbucks on every block. Tess loved her coffee, but she was nowhere to be seen. Delux quickly got the info for the casting, and we headed back to Lu's.

"We could have done all that with a phone call, don't you think?" I asked Ruka.

"He misses her."

"She stabbed him in the back, then stabbed him in the heart!" I said, confused.

"She left us the RV, I have you, and we have him," Ruka reminded me. "Tess was a blessing."

Lu had a busy life. His roommates/crew, his day job, his night job, and trying to be a DJ in the clubs, and on the radio kept him on his toes. Lu was happy to have found Delux and tried to help him as much as he could, but Delux was running out of money, and they were both running out of options unless they started their own radio station which they talked about often. Our only transportation was the RV, and to move us all around at once for anything, was a lot.

If we did go somewhere, people never took Delux seriously when he looked for jobs. He had no local address to write down on applications. He was living in his car with two dogs, when most people weren't choosing to take on this lifestyle. For most, it was hard to accept a lifestyle that went against what society was embracing as normal.

Before we could make our video submission to MTV, Delux chose to leave Miami and go back to Minnesota where the family restaurant could provide him some opportunity. Lu was sad, but he understood and supported Delux and his decision to go.

"Go make some money, and come back. If we don't get picked for this MTV thing, we'll do something else."

"They're going to pick us. This is the best idea. It's never been done before in the history of reality TV."

Delux said his good-byes, and we were instantly back on the familiar road again, going north.

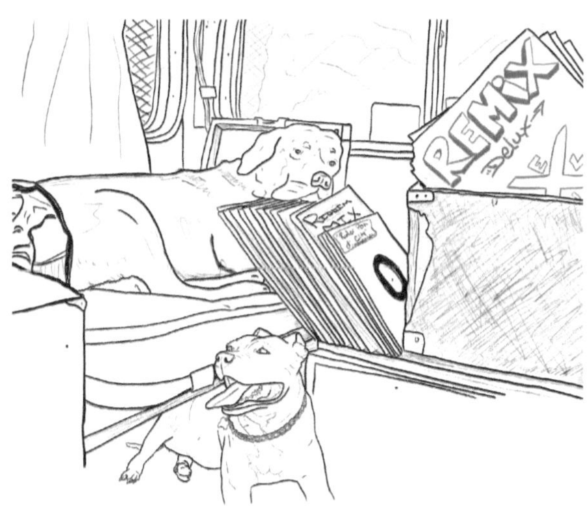

CHAPTER 12

MINNESOTA

"THE AUDITION"

Like always, as soon as we got to Minnesota, Delux immediately went back to work at the restaurant, leaving us in the basement. He was working both in the kitchen, serving on the floor, and even bartending because his father turned the once, small family restaurant, into a local bar. The two warehouses in the back, became the perfect backdrop for his MTV audition.

Even though Delux and Lu were far apart, they were still going to send in their audition tapes together. Delux positioned the RV so it was in front of the warehouses with the camera looking back at us. He had his vision and was setting it up. Ruka and I were instructed to stay in the RV with the side door open, so we could look out and watch him. The camera was on a tripod and Delux hit record and ran back into position with his back to us.

"Hello, MTV. I'm DJ Delux, and my friend Lu and I, have an idea for you," Delux said looking into the camera. He went on to explain how terrible it is for Lu to poo in our tiny bathroom, and he has to live with two dogs that he's authentically afraid of.

"That's our cue, Doofus, let's go," Ruka told me.

"No, I don't think it's time yet, Ruka," I said as she went out anyways.

"Ahh... Ok... Ladies and gentlemen, meet Ruka and Doofus," Delux said improvising.

"I go first," Ruka said, pushing me out of the way.

"You don't even know where the camera is to be in the scene. Follow me," I told her jumping out alongside her.

"I think we should go over here and..." Ruka said, walking away from me.

"Ruka. No. Over here," I told her with the street cone in my mouth, but I didn't think she heard me.

"And this, is Ruka. She's blind," Delux said watching Ruka walk right past him and into the camera's tripod, knocking the whole thing over.

"Ah shit, Ruka," Delux said, trying to catch it, but it was too late watching the camera hit the ground.

"Oops, I thought Grandpa was here. Smelled like Grandpa," Ruka said, coming over to me.

"We still rolling? That was not planned, she really just did that," Delux said speaking into the camera sideways as he picked it up then walked to the RV to show the inside. Fifteen seconds later, he was out of the RV and showing Ruka and I again on camera as we played tug of war with the street cone.

"Well thanks for watching, that's as original as it gets," Delux said, shutting off the camera.

"Ruka, you walking into the camera, made this audition the most real and authentic audition it could ever be," Delux said rubbing her face.

"What about me?" I looked at Delux with my head tilted.

"High five, Doofus. Well done."

"We got this," I told Delux, hitting his hand with my paw.

What MTV didn't know was, Delux was living in his parents' basement now, and no longer in the RV, which was kept out in the driveway. It wasn't what he wanted, but it was the best for all of us. That RV reminded him so much of Tess, it was still hurting him. Ruka and I would catch him just sitting inside, staring at the closet where Tess used to keep her things.

While we waited for MTV to call, Delux rebuilt the inside of the RV in his free time away from the restaurant to better suit him and Lu and maybe get rid of any memories of Tess. His time off wasn't much but he made the best use of it. He was working seven days a week for weeks straight at the restaurant. He went to work day and night, giving Ruka and me a lot of time together.

"And Grandpa."

Oh yeah. Grandpa would always be home with us most nights, but he would stay upstairs, while we were locked away behind two doors in the basement.

Grandpa came home from work one night with some BBQ rib tips just for me.

"No that's not true Doofus," Ruka said taking my bone from me when I turned to scratch an itch I had.

"Ok fine."

Grandma and Delux were at work, so it was just Ruka and me in the basement. Delux forgot to close one of the two doors to keep us downstairs. I managed to open the door a bit more and I had free range of the house. I was roaming around upstairs smelling everything I could get my nose on, when Grandpa came home from work. I knew it was Grandpa by the sound of his truck. I could hear him come up the stairs outside getting his keys out. I stayed silent behind the front door, like when I waited for that group to walk past the RV in South Beach. The keys in his big hands struggled to get the key in the door. As soon as the door opened, I barked and pushed the door shut.

"Dammit, Doofus. No," Grandpa said getting pushed back.

I lost my train of thought as to why I did that and he dropped his tray of ribs he brought home for himself, at the door. The smell of the ribs was enough to distract me from anything. I saw there was BBQ sauce everywhere as Grandpa pushed the door open.

"Well, you knocked them out of my hand, you might as well eat them now."

I could tell Delux came from this man. They were the exact same in energy when things didn't go the way they'd planned.

"Damn dog. I wanted those," Grandpa said shutting the door. "Go downstairs."

Yep. That's something Delux would tell me.

"Where'd you go? What you do? What'd you get, why do you smell like BBQ sauce?" Ruka asked, licking my face after I went back downstairs.

"I saved you a piece," I said to Ruka, dropping a bone in front of her with meat on it.

"I don't want it after it's been in your mouth."

"Yeah you do."

Ruka was happy with her bone. We both listened to Grandpa's TV downstairs, while he was falling asleep to it upstairs. We waited next to each other for Delux to get home from work.

"Doofus, you got something to do with BBQ sauce all over the front door?" Delux asked when he got home.

"How does he know it was me?"

"Everything is you Doofus," Ruka tells me with a strange look on her face.

I loved the RV, but backyard life at Grandma and Grandpa's, was amazing. There were the constant squirrels to chase, and Delux put the street cone in the back for Ruka and I to tear up into pieces. There were pieces of cone everywhere in the grass that Grandma said would be stuck in the grass for years to come. Delux would pick up the big ones and leave the small pieces for the lawnmower to suck up if it even did.

I got over being so nosy—wait, no I didn't—I mean, I learned to leave Grandma's flowers alone, and I began to poo in the same area, because here, here really did start to feel like home.

"Don't get used to it, kid. Delux is almost done remodeling the RV, and MTV is about to pick us thanks to my camera move," Ruka added.

"Ruka, your camera move was classic, but how do you know?"

"The added touches he made to the RV make it way more functional and flowing now. Plus, he added an air conditioner and a place for Lu to sleep," Ruka said from her front pillow.

Delux was done rebuilding the back, to be more comfortable and to hold his vinyl records better. Because his record collection was getting bigger, he needed to make some changes. We got a better fridge, and he made Tess's old closet into a permanent kitchen. Then… the RV was finished. The front seats and steering wheel were still the same, and that's all I really cared about.

"Hello?" Delux answered his phone and listened to the other guy.

"Mix Nizzle, what's good, homie?" he said, happy to hear from the guy. "I can't make you a copy, but I'll come down and play a set for you. Free of charge," he said laughing. He paused, kicking a broken tennis ball towards me. "Okay, cool. See you at nine." He hung up with a smile.

"I just got a DJ gig. High five," he said, and a high five he got.

Nothing changed for Ruka and me except now, Delux came home super late one night a week smelling like cigarettes. After his first guest appearance, the manager of the club wanted him to come do a guest spot every week, and he agreed. Two weeks later, the other DJ quit and gave Delux the night. Delux now worked full time at the restaurant and had a weekly DJ gig while he waited for MTV to contact him.

After his first night playing reggae and dancehall, he told his parents only 24 people showed up. The second week, eight people showed up. The third week, he said there were only four people in the club and three of them worked there.

"I got a plan," Delux said.

Delux drove the RV with us in it, to the Night Club manager's house to make a radio commercial. Delux went inside and got a tour of his house, while Ruka and I waited outside. The guy didn't like dogs, and honestly, Ruka and I didn't like him. When they came outside, Delux locked us up in the front of the RV with the baby gate.

"Are you sure your dogs will not attack me?" the Caribbean man asked.

"We're good, let's get to work. What do you think about this track, this track, and this track?"

"All that sounds good, but how do we make it into a commercial?"

"Easy. We record into this thing here and I can cut up the track and move things around to sound better."

"You can do that?"

"I think so. Let's try."

Delux recorded a few samples from his records he selected, and then a few instrumentals.

"Now let's do an intro and talk about the night. Use a nice clear voice, and sound hype," Delux said handing the guy the microphone.

"All right. People are you ready?" He said.

The guy sucked. He had no hype. No enthusiasm, nothing. He was as fun as driving through Iowa. Flat. They did several takes that were unsuccessful, so Delux did it once to give the guy an example. The manager still didn't get it.

"Man, I wish I had some of the commercials you could hear from Miami. It needs to be hype like them and like nothing like what's on the radio here."

"You did good. You try it," the guy told Delux.

"I hate the sound of my voice, I don't think so, and I don't have the accent we need."

I let out a bark. Ruka bit my leg. "Doofus, be quiet, they're recording," Ruka told me.

"But I agree, Delux sounds 100 times better than this manager guy."

Delux did a few takes, and before you knew it, they had a 30 second commercial done that sounded amazing. It was hype. It was clear. It sounded just like something we would hear on the radio in Miami, only we were in Minnesota and there was nothing on the radio like this.

Once people heard the commercial, they let Delux know by blowing up his phone. Most had no idea he was even in town again. He took Ruka and I with him the first night after the commercial ran. The club opened at 9pm and closed at 2:30. From what I saw sitting in my driver's seat perch, at 11pm, hundreds of people were left outside, not able to get in.

Delux sold out the place.

"Holy shit. That was fucking amazing!" Delux said getting into the RV with his records smelling of beer and cigarettes after his gig.

Delux never smoked cigarettes, but after a night of DJing, or bartending at the restaurant, he stank like them. They reminded me of Tess, and I didn't want to think about her.

Tonight, Delux was as happy and naturally as high as I've ever seen him. Delux drove home in silence with one hand on the wheel, and one hand on Ruka's head, every now and then rubbing mine with a huge smile on his face.

A few weeks later, MTV got back to Delux. They said they loved the idea, and they picked him and Lu for their show. He just had to sign some paperwork. MTV faxed it over, Delux signed it all, checked it twice, and sent it back.

"Now this is as happy as I have ever seen him. We are about to have our own TV show, Doofus," Ruka told me.

"What about the new club Delux just took over?"

"It's practice for what's to come. Shits like Destiny," Ruka said in excitement with a smile on her face.

I felt excited. What did this all mean?
After getting the news about MTV, Delux was feeling lucky, so he and a coworker drove to the casino one night after they closed the restaurant.

"Doofus. Look at her. She has the hots for Delux."

"How do you know?"

"Just look at how she looks at him."

I paused and looked at her listening to Delux talk about something.

"Ah yeah, I see it," I lied. "How did you see that, Ruka?"

"*Es una cosa de mujeres.* You been practicing your Spanish?"

"For what? We're not going to Costa Rica anymore."

"No, but we will be driving to Los Angeles, and that's the closest we'll be to Costa Rica so get ready. You never know with Delux."

I kept looking at this girl sitting in the passenger seat… All I saw was her looking at Delux. What's wrong with that? I didn't know what Ruka was seeing. To me, she was just some girl sitting where Tess used to sit. Tess flashed into my head again. I remembered the way she used to look at Delux when she was in love with him sitting in that seat. This new girl has the same smile on her face, huh… maybe I see it now, I thought as we pulled into the casino.

"Actually, let's park way over there where it's flat and no other cars are around for Doofus to create a scene," Delux said looking for a parking spot once they were at the casino. "I know my dogs. Doofus here will bark at anything too close to him."

"I don't mind walking," the girl said.

Delux and the girl got out, and told Ruka and I to be good, like he always did. He kissed us both on our heads and asked us to wish him good luck.

"What does that mean Ruka, 'good luck'?"

"It means he's gonna lose whatever money he brings in there with him."

"Well he didn't bring it all in there, I saw him leave some behind in his closet."

Delux and the girl walked through the parking lot and into the building. I took up my spot on the driver's seat and set my head on the steering wheel like I always do. Ruka took her usual spot on the floor between the seats and we chilled.

"Do you ever think of Tess?" I asked Ruka.

"At times something will remind me of her, but I try not to get hung up on the memories. You?"

"At times I think of her. I'm trying not to be upset about what she did."

"Like I said, we got Delux and the RV out of the deal. I think we're winning, Doofus."

"I hope Delux is winning inside."

"He's not. This place is rigged."

Before I could dose off like I usually did when I was on watch in the farthest, emptiest parking lot around, I spotted someone walking towards the RV with a flashlight. I growled as I sat up and then I barked. They shined the light on me. I barked again. They stopped, and moved the light around. I moved around, and next thing you know... the RV started moving.

"Doofus. Why does it feel like the RV's moving?"

"I think I bumped something."

"Well un-bump it!"

"I don't know how I did it."

Bark. Bark. Bark. I said to the flashlight man as the RV slowly moved on its own across the empty parking lot.

"We have a problem out here. I'm gonna need back up," the security guard said over his walkie talkie.

Bang! Crash!

I went flying into the dashboard.

"Oh shit, Doofus. What'd you do?"

"I didn't do anything. I'm just barking at flashlight guy here."

The flashlight guy I was barking at, never left us, so I kept barking.

He would get closer, and I would bark louder and more intense.

"It was his fault. He just had to leave us alone. I never would have touched anything if he would have just kept it moving, but he had to walk all the way over to us parked all the way over here," I barked at the guy.

"He's calling for backup on his radio again," Ruka overheard through my barks.

"Let him."

Back-up never arrived, but Delux and the girl from work did 20 minutes later. Delux ran up to the RV.

"Didn't you hear us paging you for an hour?" the security guard asked.

"Your page was asking for a Delux RV. This one's a Lazydaze model. See," Delux pointed out.

"It says Delux right there."

"No that says DJ Delux. This, is a Lazydazy," Delux pointed to the RV. "That one over there says Deluxe on it." Pointing across the parking lot.

"Do you know it's illegal to keep animals inside a vehicle because of the heat?"

"We're in Minnesota at one o'clock in the morning. It's rather cool out at the moment don't ya think? And if you actually investigated anything, you would see I have Florida plates, implying I and these dogs are from Florida, where it's a lot hotter than this at night."

"It's too hot inside the RV for animals," the guard shouted. "And they caused this accident."

"No, you caused this accident by getting close to my RV that was parked way over there and not leaving it alone when the dog started barking. He only acts crazy like this when people won't leave him alone. If we watch the tapes of the parking lot, what are we going to see, because like I said, I parked way over there to stay out of people's range."

"Well, your RV rolled all the way here and now caused an accident. I will need to report this to the police."

Delux got into the RV and backed it away from the car I ran into that ran into the car in front of it…

"Doofus 2 - Cars 0," Ruka added.

Delux looked at the other cars that were hit, and while doing so, the dent in the rear plastic bumper of one of the cars, popped out on its own.

"Well, look at that," Delux pointed out. "Looks like nothing happened here but a license plate fell off, officer."

Delux picked up the license plate of the other car and put it on the window with a note on both cars. "Hello. Sorry, my dog put my RV into neutral and caused a small accident. Here's my contact info if you would like to press any charges," the note said.

"What are you doing?" the security guard asked.

"I'm going to park the RV again. You're going to stay away from this area, and I am going back inside the casino. Now, if you'll excuse me," Delux said moving the RV.

"Ruka, you see he grabbed more money out of his closet?"

"I told you this place was rigged."

Delux and the girl came back an hour later. They lost all the tips they made that night, but they were still in a good mood laughing and joking.

"Nice driving, Doofus, but I got this," Delux said kicking me out of the driver's seat and driving us home.

Every Friday, Delux was filling his new night club gig to capacity before midnight. Delux was stoked things were going so well, then the phone rang and it was MTV again. They said Delux forgot to sign something. He knew he signed everything, and what they need is somewhere in their office with his packet of info. They insisted Delux forgot it and told him he needed to sign it again before end of day. He left work, got the fax from them, signed it, and faxed it right back without even reading it.

Some weeks passed and MTV never called again after that. Delux tried to reach them but was left on hold for hours. Before you know it, MTV aired the show idea of Delux and Lu, only it was not Delux and Lu. It was some C list celebrity host doing a terrible rendition of their idea, and all MTV did, was flash a photo of Ruka and I in front of the RV with Delux at the start of every episode. Delux was pissed. He felt like MTV played him. Lu saw what they aired and thought it was bullshit as well, but what were they going to do about it now they thought.

"I'll keep working up here, and once I have some money saved, I'll come back there with the RV and a car so I can go find a job easier," he told Lu.

"I talked to the homie, and you can park the RV in the back yard if you pay a little rent."

"Tell him thank you, that'll be amazing. Just give me some time. I'll save up, and we can start our own radio station this time. Fuck the haters."

Delux was missing Miami, I could tell. He was missing the RV life and most of all, he was still missing Tess even though he hid it well.

"You see the way that pretty girl from work was looking at him and he didn't even care?" I asked Ruka.

"I can't see, Doofus."

"Yes, you can, you pointed it out first."

"She is just his co-worker. Nothing more."

I was confused as to why after almost a year, Delux was still single.

"He hasn't found anyone to take Tess off of his mind."

"We take Tess off of his mind," Ruka added.

"No, I'm sure we… remind him of Tess."

"The only one Delux is looking for is himself, no other."

Ruka and I, the RV, everything reminded Delux of Tess, and I know he still wasn't over her yet. He started taking us to the restaurant all the time if he was working double shifts.

After the MTV disappointment, Delux and a few other employees including Grandma, all decided to go bowling. I had no idea what that involved, because again, Ruka and I stayed in the RV.

"Doofus. No driving this time, while you wait for us," Delux told me as they all left the RV sober.

"Ruka, you see that. The pretty girl from work is here again, and she keeps looking at Delux with those eyes of hers."

"I'm blind, Doofus, how am I supposed to see that? Besides, she's just a co-worker."

I could never tell with Ruka. One minute she saw everything and the next she seemed to choose to see what she sees. I didn't need Ruka, I could see this girl liked Delux.

"We've all been drinking except her. Maybe she should drive?" Grandma asked after they all finished their fun and returned to the RV.

"Nobody has ever driven the RV but me," Delux said.

"Think you can handle it?" Delux asked the pretty girl who didn't smell like alcohol.

"I can try," she said and got behind the wheel in my seat.

"I'll sit up in front with her and make sure she does a good job," Grandma said.

She smelled nice, so I didn't care that she was sitting in my spot. I understood, Delux was a bit too tipsy to drive so, this girl was my driver for tonight. The RV got on the road, Ruka stayed up front and I went to the back were Delux was with everyone else. He drunkenly pulled out some weed and rolled a joint in the back of the RV. Delux never got to ride in the RV, especially in the back. I enjoyed sitting with him after he rolled his joint which he lit, and then blew the smoke out of the back window, that did not go out the window. It went right up front where Grandma and Ruka were.

"What's going on back there?" she asked. "I'll be right back, honey. Don't worry, you are doing great," she told the girl driving before heading to the back with all of us.

Grandma joined the circle, and everyone lost their minds at how hilarious she was acting. To avoid the smoke, I ran up to the passenger's seat.

Tonight reminded me of the night the Babes did their TV commercial and invited everyone inside the RV to see their world.

Tonight, everyone who knew Delux, saw our world for the first time. I liked when people hung out inside our house on wheels. Delux seemed happy up here in Minnesota with all these people who knew and loved him. The smile that had been hiding his sadness, was starting to look more real. There were a lot of good people around him in Minnesota. His family. His coworkers, his friends.

"Ruka. Does Delux have any friends?"

"Of course he does."

"Where are they?"

"In their homes, doing their thing. Why?"

"We just never see Delux with people outside of work, or family."

"He has us, Doofus."

"And?"

"He has his friend Christopher."

"Who's Christopher?"

"The light skinned guy with glasses. I tore his shirt one day while he was wearing it. You weren't in the picture yet. Brother Jules. That's a homie of Delux. Lu."

"He just met Lu, and I've never met Brother Jules. Doesn't he have any childhood friends?"

Ruka thought about it. "No. He doesn't."

We pulled into the driveway after making it home safe. I was so caught up with Ruka and figuring out who Delux's friends are, that I didn't know we made it home.

"Come on guys were home. Let's go," Delux said opening the side door, stepping out of the RV.

Home is all I could think of. We were inside the RV all day and night with only two breaks to go outside while at the restaurant. That's more parking lot time, then grass, and Ruka and I had no time to enjoy any of it.

"So the RV's not your home anymore," Ruka asked me.

"No, no, no, it is. I just like it in here with Delux lower to the ground with us."

Delux showered and we got ready for bed. Ruka would sleep in the bed with Delux, and I would sleep next to them on the floor. I only liked sleeping in the bed when Delux wasn't around. For me, he was too hot to sleep next to, but Ruka, and her love affair with the sun, she liked the heat and snuggled the crap out of Delux now that there was a bed she could jump into.

Maybe Delux was too busy for friends I thought. Either way, all his work was paying off and so was DJing. Delux got a few DJ gigs outside of his regular Friday night, so he bought himself some CD players to DJ with.

"Ruka?"

"Yes Doofus?"

"Does this mean Delux is a button pusher, now that he has CD players?"

"Delux has been pushing people's buttons since he was a kid. And they say these CD players now a days, act like turntables so maybe it's a good thing."

"Delux says nothing can replace a turntable."

"Delux says a lot of things, Doofus."

I stopped chewing on his records after the first and only time, and found myself looking at a piece of dark chocolate sitting on Grandpa's desk that was wrapped in a shiny silver wrapper instead. I felt like I was being tricked as I couldn't resist its shiny reflections. I knew the candy wasn't for me, but I told myself it was left by the ledge of the desk for a reason, so I must try it. It was left by the edge for me like the BBQ rib tips.

"The rib tips were not for you," Ruka reminded me.

"You got some didn't you?"

I walked by the desk and threw my big head over the top and swooped the chocolate into my mouth.

Delux had left us home that night while he went to work at the restaurant. Within minutes of me eating that tiny piece of chocolate, I started to not feel well.

"Ruka."

"I know. I heard you take it off the desk dummy. Doofus... You're going to die if Delux doesn't find you in time."

"What? I'm gonna die?"

"You may be a strong, tough dog now, and you are a bit smarter, but…"

"Only a bit smarter?"

"Doofus. You just ate dark chocolate, so yeah, you're only a bit smarter than a dog biscuit."

"What do I do? It hurts."

"Can you vomit it out?"

I tried to push like I do when I eat some grass in the park.

"No. The pain. It's already starting deep in my belly."

"Hang on. We don't need another dolphin incident."

Just hearing the word dolphin made my butthole squeak.

"Oh no, Ruka."

"Doofus, go over there. Stay away from me."

There was nowhere to go. I didn't have to poo, but I had to do something. Liquid came out of me. Then loud farts followed by chocolate milk that was more chocolate than milk. It got on my own paws, because I was still in the habit of spinning in circles while I poo'd, and I walked right into the thickest pile. Now I had chocolate on my toes, which was not chocolate. Now you could see where I poo'd and where I stepped. Delux was gonna be mad.

"You'll probably die before he gets back. Don't worry about him being mad, he'll just be sad. But I'll be here for him, like always."

"Ruka, will you be serious. I feel like I'm dying here!"

"You are dying. Everyone knows, dogs can't eat chocolate. Maybe you'll finally learn your lesson to not to put things in your mouth that Delux doesn't give to you."

"Like you and cat shit?"

"Cat shit doesn't kill. We're not talking about me here."

"Ruka, are you gonna miss me when I'm gone?" I asked in pain as more poo was coming out.

"With my luck, you'll probably turn into a ghost and haunt me for the rest of my days, pissing and shitting all over everything."

I shit again and laid down in pain as things started to fade.
Delux came home from work early. I didn't realize today was Friday and he had to DJ tonight. I looked at his record cases, and there was a little shit on them.

"Doofus what the fuck, again?" Delux said after opening the downstairs door smelling and seeing my problem after picking the wrapper of the chocolate off the floor.

"Let's go, outside. Fuck! Why you gotta do this tonight?" Delux asked letting us out of the house. There was no more poo inside me.

Delux did his best to clean up the carpet downstairs. He was gonna need a carpet cleaner machine, but he didn't have time. He cleaned off his record cases, took a shower, then left me locked up in the bathroom downstairs where there were no rugs or carpet to soil if it happened some more.

"Doofus. You cannot eat candy off of Grandpa's desk, goofball. What were you thinking?"

I wasn't.

"I gotta go, buddy. If you're not better by tomorrow, we'll figure something out, but you're gonna stay in here."

He closed the door to the bathroom, and I was on my own. I felt like I was in solitary confinement. Ten minutes into my alone time, the pains came back again, unleashing even more liquid out of my system that I swear was empty. Where was it coming from? There was poo all over the wall and door. Poo was going out under the door into the hallway. I was left with only a place to sit by the toilet, or lay in the shower, but the shower door was shut, and I don't know how to open a sliding door, so I sat, and I shat myself some more.

This was the longest and worst night of my life. Everything started to get blurry. I wish Ruka was here, but she knows I would probably shit on her. As things blurred out, I passed out on the floor, dipping my toes into the chocolate poo mess one more time, fading into a dream of me and Delux in Costa Rica, running through the mud.

"Doofus, you are Chocolate Toes now," Delux laughed out falling into the mud with me, pulling the jungle around us in with him making me feel like we were falling and I woke up.

"Oh shit," Delux said hours later after he finished his DJ gig and saw what was coming out of the bathroom door as he returned home. Again at 3 a.m., Delux was responsible to clean up my diarrhea, and again, it was everywhere. He opened the shower door and put me in there, closing the door behind me. He then grabbed a dustpan and scooped up all my poo and flushed it down the toilet.

"Doofus, I am so sorry you feel this way, homie," Delux said to me kindly, wiping the floor.

It wasn't his fault, it was mine. When I let my curiosity get the best of me, it usually doesn't go well I'm discovering.

Delux opened the shower and started to wash me down with a bucket and his hands. I couldn't look him in the eye even though my vision had come back to me. He was concerned if I was okay. I felt by the way he was washing me down, Delux truly is my mission. He cares deeply for me.

"Please, don't ever eat chocolate again you dummy," Delux said, shutting off the water.

"How you feeling, Doofus?" Ruka asked me once I was out of solitary.

"Thanks for checking in on me while I was in there."

"Doofus, there was shit coming out from under the door. I love the way you smell my friend, but your shit stinks. I was not going down that hallway."

"Come on guys, outside," Delux told us, opening the door to the back yard.

Delux came with me. And waited to see if I would poo some more.

"You got caca's, buddy? Go caca if you have to." He watched as I sniffed my usual spots.

I tried. Just a drop of poo and a tiny fart came out. I was empty. I needed water.

"Let's go," Delux said going inside and getting us fresh water before bed like he could read my mind.

"I'm glad you survived," Ruka told me sarcastically.

"You would have missed me!" I tell her, biting her back leg, making her wrestle me.

"Did you see Delux bought a kayak?"

"No. What's a kayak?"

"Doofus. I'm the blind one, and I know he bought a boat. What're you looking at all day?"

"I'm looking at you. I look at you or Delux."

"Come on guys, let's go to bed," Delux said, closing the door after a long night.

The next morning, Delux hooked up his new kayak to a small trailer with wheels. He jumped on his mom's bike and grabbed the front handle of the boat and peddled away with it down the street.

"Ruka. What do we do, chase after him?"

"He'll be back."

"How do you know?"

"He told us to wait, and look."

I look down the street and Delux was turning around one way, then he turned around the other way.

"How'd you know that?"

"Because that boat's for us."

"How do you know that?"

"Ok guys. I think we got this". Delux said coming back into the driveway holding the boat in one hand.

He put the running harnesses on us and grabbed the leashes. Delux peddled us next to him on a bike, holding us, and the kayak on wheels in one hand. A few miles north on the back, neighborhood road, we went to an inlet where he could launch his kayak.

"Doofus free," Delux said taking the leash off me.

He took the front wheel off his bike and put the bike and the wheel in the front of the kayak.

"Ruka, let's go," Delux said, putting her in the middle of the kayak.

"Hell, no. I don't I like this!" Ruka said kicking and scratching.

"It's okay, Ruka, I got you. Stay."

"I hate boats, but ok. Here I am," Ruka said, trying to calm herself.

Ruka sounded like she wasn't happy.

"Ruka, where am I gonna sit?" I asked running around the boat.

"Doofus, back up."

Delux got into the kayak after pushing it into the water, sitting down with Ruka between his legs.

"Ok. I'm ok. I'm ok," Ruka said in a mantra.

"Doofus. Let's go buddy," Delux called out.

"What? Where do I sit?" I said with excitement, looking into the boat and barking out in confusion as Delux grabbed a paddle.

"No, you're gonna swim, buddy. Go on," Delux motioned with his hand as I tried to climb into the boat.

"I'm gonna swim where?" I ran into the water and made the biggest splash. I then paddled my way to the boat that was drifting away in the current.

"Good boy. Let's go for a swim," Delux said looking into my eyes.

I trusted him. I love swimming, and this was the river I learned in. I felt a true connection to this river. If I got tired, I could swim close to shore and my paws could touch. I could get out and rest, but I didn't need any rest. I swam in circles while Delux and Ruka slowly floated down the river with the occasional paddle to keep them straight. The sun was out on a beautiful summer day and I was loving it. The sun was warm, and the river was cool.

"How you doing, Ruka?" I asked swimming alongside them.

"I wish I had some dried liver with a duck fat latte with someone rubbing my knees."

"What?"

"I'm good, Doofus. How are you?"

"I wish I had a… had a…"

"Had a what?"

"I don't know. I don't need anything, I'm having the best time right now."

I didn't want the day to end.

We made it to the park Delux first threw me in at, and that's where we got out. Delux put the bicycle back together and strapped the kayak to the two-wheel trailer.

"Let's go, guys."

These are the best summer days, I thought to myself as we walked back through the park. I was gonna take a long nap when we got home, guaranteed.

As fall and winter set in, the days got shorter, and we were still in Minnesota. Delux had his plan to leave but was not sure when. While we waited for the right time to go back to Miami, Delux recorded a lot of his vinyl records to digital format so he didn't have to carry so many crates of music around when a lot of that music could fit onto a CD, or hard drive.

"I hate pushing buttons to DJ. I love the feel of vinyl," Delux mumbled into his phone talking to a friend, while recording his music late one night after work.

He loved his vinyl. When he played vinyl, he sounded well rounded and smooth with all his musical transitions. When he was pressing buttons using digital files… the music seemed to lose its soul.

Delux was still lost because of love. Tess really did a number to his soul.

"He was the best DJ back in the day, and the distraction of Tess guided him away from that, then, she didn't hold up her end of the dream she planted, and let him down," Ruka told me.

"Are you reading my mind again, Ruka?"

"I see you staring at him."

"No you don't. You're blind."

"I see you're wondering what he's going to do. What are we doing with him. And what is he going to do with us."

I had no idea how she knew all of that, but she was right. What are we doing but always waiting around?

"We're dogs, Doofus. Waiting around is what we do."

"Yeah but back in the day, we were always going somewhere."

I felt like I should be doing more. Every time Delux gave me a command, I did it. I would make sure I did it to the best of my ability. When he wasn't around, I started to run the commands through my head and saw myself doing them. As I did that, I realized, Delux says a lot more to me than just commands. I didn't understand everything, but I was starting to understand him and what Ruka was talking about. I just needed to let go and learn to trust Delux, I guess. I didn't need to be doing anything I thought. Just be in the present moment.

It was Friday night again, and Delux took us to his DJ night, only this time he stayed outside in the RV with us.

"Ruka, how come he's not going inside?"

"Last week he asked for more money seeing the club is doing so well because of him."

"Yeah, and…?"

"The manager he made the commercial with, fired him."

"What?"

We sat outside and Delux explained to the people going into the club that he was fired, and now leaving the State. If they wanted any of his mixes, he had a bunch for sale. Again, like after his first big night djing there, we drove home in silence, one hand on the wheel, and one hand on Ruka's head.

The next day, Delux took us to a store and rented a trailer to tow a car. We drove it home and he loaded his dad's car onto the trailer behind the RV.

"Ruka, what's this?"

"We're leaving today for Miami."

"What?"

"And we're talking Grandpa's car with us."

"Why are we taking a car with us?"

"Because Delux can't drive our home around everywhere he needs to go. It's not very efficient, easy, or appealing, so we're taking a car, that is not appealing."

I was excited. We now had a car, and a kayak, in addition to our skateboard.

"We're all set. I love you, guys," Delux said to his parents as Ruka and I got our hugs goodbye from them.

"We love you. Drive safe, and call us when you get there," Grandma said.

"I will," Delux promised.

And we were back on the road.

CHAPTER 13

PORK AND BEANS

Traveling the long distance to Miami was smooth and easy. Because we were towing a car, we took it extra slow. I never thought when we pulled out of the warehouse the first time in Miami, the RV would have morphed into what it was today and be able to tow a car.

We got back to Lu's house in Miami with no problems. The homie wanted us to park around the back of the house, so we did. The RV was safer and out of sight in the back yard. They gave us power and ran a direct internet line into the RV so Delux could promote his music.

Ruka and I just wanted to play, not watch him sit in front of a computer and edit music all day.

Because Delux had a car now, he quickly went out and found himself a job at a restaurant being a waiter. His first week was fine, but every day after, he came home talking shit about the place. It was nothing like the restaurant he grew up in he said. Employees were lazy, management was just there to flirt with young girls, and most of the customers were French, and French people don't tip. Delux was working for tips, and not making any.

He quickly started DJing again, only this time, for free or for money Lu was kind enough to split with him.

"Ruka, why'd we come to Florida again if it's always a struggle for Delux?"

"Winter Doofus. Winters. You have yet to experience a freezing cold winter."

"You keep saying that."

One of the guys who lived with Lu, had gotten a dog since the last time we were there. Her name was Queenie, and she hated life. She lived outside the RV on a raised slab of concrete that had a doghouse on it that she was chained to.

"Hi. I'm Doofus and that one over there is Ruka."

"Bark, Bark, Bark, I don't care," she shouted from the top of her doghouse.

"You don't gotta be such a bitch about it," I barked back at her.

"I'm sorry. My life here is shit with me tied up all day in the sun with only my doghouse for shade. It makes me wonder what I did in my past lifetime to deserve this," Queenie told us while going into her doghouse to lay down.

"I hate the sun too, so I get it."

"I rarely have fresh water. You two look like you live a good life in that RV. I'm sorry, I overreacted".

"Don't be sorry. It's okay. It takes a real dog to apologize, but no need. We're in your space. Your fight is not with us, but with your current owner."

"I know. Again, I am sorry."

Delux saw that she didn't have any water, so he grabbed her bowl, and gave her some.

"That's Delux. He's a good guy. I'm sure he'll help you if you need it."

"Thanks," she said drinking all the water.

I could tell she didn't want to talk, so we left her alone. We had our space, she had hers.

Delux started to leave us alone again as well. Now that he had a car and a job, he was working a lot to support us all. Ruka and I would be left in the backyard tied up under the RV or left inside if it was raining.

Delux installed an air conditioner in the back wall of the RV so during the real hot days, the AC would turn on and cool the RV instantly. It was nice, but I missed our beach parking lot, where the steady breeze always kept us cool and there was no job to go to.

"What? Always kept us cool? I remember plenty of hot days with no wind whatsoever and you complaining a lot in that beach parking lot. Oh it's hot. Ruka my mouth is sweating."

"What? Ruka, stay out of my head."

"I wasn't in your head, you were talking out loud."

"Was I?"

The only time Delux had to play with us, was at night. If he wasn't working, he and Lu were planning a party, or trying to set up their own radio station. Setting up their own radio station was illegal, but other people were doing it, so they started to look into it.

"Ruka, you miss Tess?"

"That's a strange question out of the blue. What makes you ask that question again?"

"Last time Delux left us alone this much, Tess was here to keep us company."

"What about when we were back in Minnesota in the basement on the days or nights Delux left us alone there?"

"It wasn't in the RV, so I didn't think of her that much."

"No, I don't miss Tess. I knew life with Delux before Tess."

"Tell me what life was like again before Tess?"

"Delux was rising to popularity as a DJ in Miami Beach before his car was stolen. Once back in Minnesota, Delux got back together with his ex-girlfriend."

"There was a girl before Tess?"

"Yeah, Aisha."

"What happened to Aisha?"

"It's what happened to Delux is the question. Late one night he went to a park and met Jesus and a bird. I don't know all the details, he'll need to tell the story again, but he asked Jesus something, saw a bird, then he broke up with Aisha the next morning after making pancakes."

"Delux met Jesus?"

"Jesus in the form of a bird."

"What?"

"Aisha told him to do it."

"Do what?"

"Ask for a sign."

"What do you think about while we wait here for Delux?"

"Our next skateboard trip."

Delux never missed out on a few circles around the block close by. The roads were smooth, free of rocks, and there were never any people around the warehouse that occupied those streets. We always had the road to ourselves. Delux would take me off the leash and let me be free while Ruka ran alongside of him still on the leash. He needed to protect her from running into the random light pole, or parked car. Almost every night, we took our trips around the block on the skateboard.

Delux must have had a rough night at work because he rolled himself a joint to take on our ride, which he never does. It was around 3 a.m. on a clear, cool night. Not a single person was outside. I ran and ran. Ruka chased me with Delux pushing the skateboard, rolling along the smooth surface. While he zig'd and zag'd back and forth with Ruka, her and him enjoyed the joint by themselves as the smoke floated away as they went down the street. I was ahead of them a bit and went running around the cornering the direction we always go with Ruka following close behind me pulling Delux who was finishing his joint.

I looked up, and in front of me down the street ahead, were a bunch of police cars in a circle with all of the policemen outside of their vehicles, in the street, in the dark.

"Doofus. Heel," Delux said getting a glimpse of the police lined up ahead of us.

"Doofus!" I heard my name shouted from the direction of the police.

"Who the heck knows me at this hour out here in these streets?" I questioned.

"Doofus. No. Heel," Delux said again quietly, but I pretended to not hear it and kept on running to the group of cops who'd caught my interest.

"Doofus, come back," Ruka said, but I ignored her too.

"Doofus! What's up, buddy? You guys, this is one of the coolest dog. He is so smart, watch," the cop said to the other officers, telling me to sit.

I could hear Delux clicking his mouth getting closer on the skateboard. That was his call for me to come to him, but I was too excited with all of this police energy. This whole time, I thought police were bad people, but these guys were cool.

Ruka and Delux caught up to me and the group of police.

"Doofus, you idiot. Delux smells like weed and is high as fuck right now, and you just ran us into a pile of police officers," Ruka told me.

"Oh yeah, this was dumb, huh?" I said looking around realizing what I had done. "I thought it was…" I started to say.

"You didn't think, Doofus. Delux smells like the fart of a ganja plant right now. He's probably going to get arrested."

Delux did look a bit nervous, but he was playing it cool and kept it moving past the officers who all looked at him but left him alone.

"That was the cop from the gas station. Remember?"

"Yeah, I remember, but you don't run away like that, Doofus."

"Ok. Sorry Ruka. What do you think that was all about?"

"Those cops are about to give someone a bad start to their day and lucky for you, they don't have time for us."

Living in the RV was a bit limiting for Delux with the small kitchen, so he ended up eating out a lot.

Delux came home early from work one day, covered in sweat and smelled like he was ill. Ruka and I stayed out of his way as he laid on the back couch. He had gotten food poisoning and right after he felt a little bit better, he came down with the flu. He was forced to stay home from work and everything for a few days. His work didn't like that he was missing his shifts, but Delux was actually sick.

"I've never seen him sick like this before. Ruka, what can we do?"

"He's gonna whine a lot and lay around but let him be and it will pass."

He would take us outside to do our business, but there were no skateboard trips while he was sick.

Delux sat in the RV all day and night while sick with his flu on social media. He spent a week connecting with thousands of people, posting his mixes to his website and promoting them to his new friends. He was doing the same thing other DJs were doing, when out of nowhere, social media shut him down. The social media site said he made too many friends too fast. Accused him of being a robot or something. I'd use the word militant, not robot for Delux.

When he was able to communicate with people again on social media, the social media site hit him with a copyright infringement and shut him down a second time. Delux was doing the same thing other DJs were doing, only they shut him down, not the other DJs. He was quickly over social media and how someone else had all the control. He was realizing, he lived in an RV in the back yard of someone's duplex. He hadn't really met any girls outside of work, since Tess broke his heart. He wanted to do something, but he didn't know what.

He lost hope in the movie he was writing, and even though he didn't need to practice DJing, he stopped making mixes to promote himself.

"Ruka, that food poisoning that turned into the flu, really turned him into a pile of lost hope," I told her as we both watched him just lay on the couch in the back of the RV smoking weed watching YouTube.

Grandma sent him a book to read about a dog named Marley. I'd never seen Delux read a book, and he read that book in a week or two. He laughed, he cried, he then took out his toilet and emptied it in the sewage pipe that was in the back yard and looked at me.

"Doofus, Marley was cool, but you got a way cooler story. I should write a book about you," he said passing by us outside playing with Queenie.

Queenie had nothing else going on for her, so she quickly learned to come and play with us when we were out and about. She was sweet. Her owner was not.

Delux lost his restaurant job because of the days he missed and a flu, that they said never happened. I could see he was tired of people not believing in him and by how his energy was sinking lower and lower. He was starting not to believe in himself.

His friend Arturo helped him out by giving him a job working as a pressure washer for some Peruvian guy who tried walking to America 17 times before finally sneaking in 15 years ago and turning himself into a millionaire.

Now, instead of Delux coming home late at night smelling like kitchen grease and other treats, he came home just after sunset, dirty and exhausted.

However he was, if he was not sick, he was good at giving us a lot of his free time, even if he was spending time with Lu after work. No more social media, no more promoting. It was just us, Lu, and an exhausted Delux.

Delux liked to take me with him places now that we had a car. I would sit in the back seat with his gear for pressure cleaning and his speakers for music with my head out of the tinted windows while Ruka sat up front. We'd go get ice cream. I'd bark. I'd sing. Ruka would sing. Delux would laugh. We made a good team. We made a lot of people smile when they saw us together.

He would take us to South Beach to walk around even though it was far, but there were more chances of meeting someone there he thought.

One day while we were walking down South Beach, we ran into Tess. She was pushing a stroller with a baby in it.

Delux died inside in that moment he saw Tess with a 1-year-old baby.

"Which means... She got pregnant not too long after her and Delux split up."

"Good math, Doofus."

I watched him talk to her and he did seem interested in what she was saying, but whatever was put back together of his heart, fell back into pieces seeing her with a child. When we got into the car, and we were alone, he began to cry, and he couldn't stop.

"And they call me a bitch," Ruka signed.

Ruka was too much to handle when both of us were together in new places. She wanted to go here, she wanted to go there, and because she couldn't see shit, she would bump into everything. Today, I was glad she was here with us. I don't think we could have seen Tess again without her.

One morning, Delux left Ruka behind and took me super early to go pick up a friend who needed a ride to the airport. Delux's friend called him a dozen times an hour before he was supposed to actually leave the house to go pick him up.

"I'm just making sure you're up. Come on man, I can't be late," the guy on the phone said.

"You have so much time, chill out," Delux said frustrated, getting in the car.

I looked for a place to "chill out" in the back of the car, but there was a set of rubber boots and a shovel in the way from his work.

"No, no, sorry buddy. Not you, dickhead on the phone here," Delux said putting the phone in his lap on speaker phone and rubbing my face with both his hands.

Delux pulled out onto the main road rather quickly and went from zero to 30mph a bit too fast for the police officer who was hiding that early morning to tolerate. Delux did look suspicious. Black car, tinted windows, and it was 3:33 in the morning. The cop put on his lights and pulled us over.

"Doofus, be cool buddy," Delux said, putting down the back window a bit to let the officer see inside while grabbing his phone.

"Great, now I'm getting pulled over because you're telling me to hurry when you have plenty of time," Delux shouted into his phone.

"You took off a little fast back there. License and registration, please," the officer asked, walking up to the window.

"Hold on, asshole," Delux said into the phone and dropping it on his lap.

"Not you, officer my friend here. Yes sir, here you go. I know I went fast, but I wasn't speeding or doing anything crazy, it's my asshole friend on the other line telling me I'm late when I'm clearly super early," Delux said towards the phone while handing the cop his information.

For just waking up, Delux was a morning person I must say. Every time I watched him wake up early, he was ready to take over the world.

"Your dog good?" the cop asked.

"Yeah, he's good."

"You mind putting the back window down a bit more?" the officer asked, and Delux obliged.

"You got any guns, knives, bombs, hand grenades, or dead bodies in the car?" The cop asked in confidence that Delux had one of something off of his list.

"I left the gun and knife at home. I don't have enough ingredients to make a bomb, grenades are impossible to find this time of year, and the dead body..." Delux turned around and looks into the back of the car.

"Good boy, Doofus," Delux said getting a nose bop in the face from me when he turned around.

"Looking at my boots and the shovel I have back there, I'd say ya just missed him," Delux casually said, turning back around looking at the officer.

"I'll be right back. You hang tight," the cop said, walking away.

"What you think, buddy, am I gonna get a ticket?"

I wish Delux could understand me.

I couldn't believe Delux actually had a pair of boots and a shovel in the car. I assumed it was from his pressure washing job but now I'm questioning him as the cop returned.

"You know, in all my years of law enforcement and asking that question to people, nobody has ever answered it like that. And the fact that you actually have a shovel in the car." The officer paused and laughed.

"You have a good morning. Slow down and tell your asshole friend there, you're on your way," the cop said, turning around and going back to his car.

"Good boy, Doofus," Delux said to me, rubbing my head. "That was a close one. Look I have a roach in the car. Stinky one, too!"

"I'm on my way fuck face," Delux said into his phone, hanging it up.

As a human, they say turning 30 is a big deal. For a dog, turning 30 happens rather quickly due to how we age. Today Delux turned 30, and Queenie tried to kill herself.

Queenie had had enough.

Even though she warmed up to us and we would play together at times, she was over it. She tightened her leash around a post that stuck out the top of her doghouse, and then she jumped. Her back legs barely touched the ground, so she was slowly choking herself out.

"Ruka!"

"What Doofus, what's up?"

"Queenie... and a kid?!"

"I know."

"Yeah, but I just saw a world in a dream or something where you and I were in a big metal box in the jungle. Police were there, and some boy was hanging just like Queenie is now."

"Stay present, Doofus."

I took a deep breath and exhaled, watching Queenie struggle.

Delux saw the whole thing go down and ran over to rescue her. She'd never received any real love from her owner, no free time off of her chain, nothing. Delux let her off her chain, and she ran over and played with us.

She lived in her own poo because the length of her chain was short. We all felt bad for her, but the owner listened to nobody, until Delux turned 30.

"So you don't respect me?" the owner shouted out to Delux who was standing in the doorway of the house with his hands in his pockets.

"No, I don't. It's hard to respect a guy who cannot take care of a dog, and when we go out in public, you act like a dog every time with the ladies. It's fucking embarrassing."

"So, you don't respect me?" he asked again, getting closer.

"No. I don't."

Delux saw it coming. I bet Ruka saw that shit coming. Delux moved at the last second, taking most of the punch to the neck, and not the side of his face. The blow was hard, but it did nothing to faze him. The guy then tackled Delux while Delux still had his hands in his pockets. I barked and wanted to get him, but I was locked on a chain to the RV, only able to watch.

"That was a cheap shot if I ever heard one," Ruka said from under the RV, not seeing a thing.

Delux stood up from the tackle, and the guy had him in a headlock from above. Dude was attacking Delux. Delux said something I couldn't understand, and the guy let go. Delux stood up and was laughing with a big smile on his face. The other guy was still mad and ready to fight. Delux had blood on his back from landing on a rock from the tackle.

"Man, you're gonna learn the hard way. I enjoy getting my ass kicked, but I will be the last one standing after those two cheap shots. You really wanna do this?"

Lu got into the middle and broke them up before any real damage could occur, but the damage was already done.

"You don't attack someone on their 30th birthday, just because they called you out for something you actually do," Lu said to him.

"You a piece of shit. With the girls. With your dog, and now with this bullshit," Delux said walking away looking at him.

Delux respected people, but if he saw you fucking up, he'd judge you, and let you know. Not to be a dick, but to make you better. When the truth had a chance to show itself, it did, and Delux got punched in the face for it. I'm sure he'd do it all again.

Lu was gonna be a dad soon, and his focus was turned to family. Delux was trying to keep a roof over our heads working two jobs because we were his family. He found another restaurant gig, but after two months of trying to juggle both the pressure washing job and the restaurant gig, he went back to waiting tables.

Delux finally started to go out at night after running us on the skateboard, to try to meet new people. He would go out alone and come home alone. Most likely, when the new potential women saw the key to his house was a small key to a padlock, they were no longer interested in someone who lived in a RV.

"That or his Dad's PT Cruiser."

"What's wrong with the PT Cruiser?"

"Doofus, I'm blind, and I can tell you everything wrong with the PT Cruiser."

"You are a bitch, Ruka. I like the car."

One afternoon, Delux finally brought a woman back to the RV.

"Ruka. Delux just came home and, listen, he has someone with him."

"Sounds and smells like a girl."

"She's a girl. She looks very business like in a skirt and heels. She looks like a lawyer or something fancy like that" I said looking out the front window as the side door opened.

"This is Doofus, and that's Ruka. She will come up and lick your face off so be ready to hold her back."

"I'll say hi later, I gotta pee. Where you been all day, Delux?" I asked, going over to the corner letting out what I'd been holding in all day.

"Doofus, he was gone two hours. Shake it off and come say hi. She smells like she has cats," Ruka told me excited, licking the lady's face.

If there were cats, Ruka was in, but something about this lady didn't feel right to me. Tess had a fucking cat the last time I remembered seeing her.

"Something don't feel right. Ruka, you don't feel that?"

"I feel she has cats," she said making love to this stranger paying me no attention.

Delux started to spend a lot of time with this new lady over at her house.
She never wanted to sleep in the RV with us and Delux. She had a nice condo with a hot shower and a toilet that flushed your shit away for good, so why would she?
She would come over some afternoons, and Delux would kick us out of the RV so they would have the entire inside to themselves. Then she would leave, leaving the place smelling different, and Delux all

tired and shit. Both Ruka and I knew what went down inside the RV.
We could hear it, we could smell it. I get it, Delux was lonely, but who
is this lady?

This was his first relationship since Tess left us over two-and-a-
half years ago.

Even though Ruka and I kept him busy and occupied when he
was around us, he needed the presence of another woman, or more
friends. Ever since Delux's birthday punch in the face, the energy had
been weird around the duplex.

Since Delux had been seeing this woman longer than we
thought, she had grown rather fond of him and us, and asked us to
move into her place.

"What about the dogs? And your cats?"

"The dogs can stay on the patio to start as long as they don't
bark, and we'll see how they do."

"Don't bark, who's she kidding," I told Ruka, holding back my
laughter.

We packed up the RV and moved out of the backyard of the
Duplex and into the parking lot of a condo association where shit was
fancy.

"Don't bark. Don't stand out," I told myself.

CHAPTER 14

CONDO LIFE

"No barking allowed," we were told as we were shuffled over fake wood floors and out into the screened-in patio area.

"Show her how good you two can be, and she'll let you inside. But for now, you're out here," Delux said rubbing my face.

"What the heck is this?" I asked Ruka, disappointed.

"Have you ever had a lake view before Doofus?" Ruka asked me lying down and looking out the window.

"This lake is fake. Dug as a drainage pond then made to look like all these condos have a view."

"Humans will be people, Doofus."

"Whatever happened to living with nature and all the trees? The world needs more shade."

"This world can be a shady place, believe it or not. It's up to you to bring the light," Ruka told me, lying down and giving into patio life instantly.

"Ruka, When Queenie tried to hang herself, that dream, or flash I had of you and I in a metal box in the jungle seemed so real. It had so much detail in it. It felt different."

"Do you still remember any details?"

"All of them. The place had two metal gates you could see through as a front. It was a metal sided garage for a truck and us. We were in the jungle and a dirt road was in front of us a bit down a sloped driveway. There was a young boy, a dad, a mom and the police took them away, and the boy was in a bodybag. They took you and I and put us into boxes inside a truck."

"And?"

"And that's all I can remember. I think someone died."

"Did you see Delux."

"No. You were the only familiar thing."

The cats got free range of the house. Yeah, cats as in two of them. A furry one and a not so furry one. They were on the kitchen table where people would eat. They were on the counters where they would prepare the food. The cats even got to sit all over the furniture all while we watched from the patio with a plant that subbed as an ashtray.

"Who the heck is this woman that Delux would move out of the RV, and into this cookie cutter lifestyle? Look at her furniture It's bright red. This is not Delux," I said to Ruka who ignored me and pretended to be sleeping.

Within the first three days of living at the condo with the RV parked out front, Delux got a warning that the RV could not be parked there, due to "rules and regulations."

"I'm going to have to put it into storage somewhere."

"Why don't you sell it?"

"Sell it? No way. That thing is one of a kind. It has a new motor, a generator, an A/C, and I custom build it, several times," Delux said, defending the last five years of our life in that thing.

"Bark. Bark. No way. That's my home," I said from the patio.

"Our home, Doofus."

"Bark. Bark. Our home," I shouted through the sliding glass door.

"Doofus, easy buddy. No speak," Delux came out and said taking a seat with us.

"I love you, Daddy. I support anything you want to do," Ruka said, wagging her tail pushing me out of the way.

"Ruka! Help me out here, that RV is all I know. I spent five years in that thing."

"I know, Doofus, but change is inevitable as your life has presented to you time and time again with us moving around."

"True."

"It's how you adapt to that change that separates you from everything else."

Ruka was right, but I felt a special connection to the RV. I didn't want to be on the patio.

Delux came home from a double shift at a restaurant he always had to wear a clean, pressed, long sleeve white dress shirt at. Today, his shirt was full of coffee stains.

"How was your day? Oh my, what happened to your shirt?"

"Someone spilled coffee on me during my first shift, and I didn't have another shirt to put on so here I am."

"Did you make it to the job fair for the interview?"

"Yeah."

"And?"

"They said they would call me tomorrow. Let's hope because I fucking hate this restaurant. The gay dudes be rubbing up against my dick for no reason as they pass by me behind the counter. I reported a guy and the manager defended him telling me it's fine. Then that asshole is the one who spilled coffee on me."

"The new job will love you and your resume was great."

"Yeah my fake resume."

Delux would walk us in the mornings and nights, around the group of condos alone. He would ask the lady if she wanted to join, but she rarely did. She was busy during the day, and just liked her wine, couch and cats at night.

"Ruka, this is not the woman for Delux," I said, peeing on a tree.

"A reason, a season, or a lifetime, Doofus."

"What?"

"That's the only three options when people meet people. Dogs too, now that I think about it," Ruka said, thinking about it deeper.

"What do you think this is with Delux and this woman?"

"There's no reasoning behind this, except for the fact that Delux is blinder than me, and dumber than you at the moment."

"But he just got a new sales job, and is no longer working in restaurants."

"Give it time, Doofus. The woman, the job, the RV... We don't always see the reason right away, but over time, you eventually do."

Ruka's mind would get in her philosophical roll, and she would roll with it whenever she could. I wish she would just be direct and simple with me.

"I'm bored out here on the patio."

"Let go, Doofus," Ruka exhaled. "We don't always need a thing to do, and nothing lasts forever."

This is where Ruka and I were different. All I wanted to do was something.

"Being here when Delux gets home with a wagging tail and a cold nose to bump him with, is absolutely enough, Doofus. Don't underestimate yourself."

"Delux is distracted with this woman and her cats. He doesn't make time for us like he used to."

"How much of his time would you like?" Ruka asked me.

I didn't have an answer. With Delux's new sales job that he lied to get, it came with three days of training in a city a few hours away. The company that hired him put him up in a hotel and paid for his gas so he could learn the tricks of the trade.

He asked the Lady in the condo to take care of us, and she did, but when Delux left, she was more concerned about a friend of hers than us. This one guy would come over a lot to be with the condo lady. He was a friend of condo lady and soon Delux was chill with him as groups of friends of hers would visit.

"We're like watching a sitcom through these glass doors huh?" I asked Ruka, watching everyone in the room including the cats.

"You're watching a sitcom, Doofus. I can't see. Remember?"

This Fred guy would try to pet me, but I wasn't having it. When he tried to pet Ruka, she wasn't having it either and would instantly start to play with me and ignore him.

"If we keep busy, he won't touch us," Ruka said biting my neck as he came out and smoked a cigarette on the patio.

"Who is he?"

"I don't know. Some long-time friend of the condo lady. He must be the one who's been using this plant as an astray. I don't trust him."

"Me, either," I said, biting her back.

While Delux was away for training, this Fred guy came over to the house. He and Condo Lady went upstairs, and they came down an hour later.

"Ruka?"

"Don't ask, don't tell, Doofus."

"But we gotta tell Delux."

"How? He can't understand us."

I had to come up with a plan. I thought I could think of something, but I was just a dog. All I could think about was the next walk or fetch time I got with Delux when he returned from his work weekend.

He wasn't supposed to return until Sunday.

Friday night, the Fred guy came over again and spent the night upstairs with the lady. Ruka and I needed to go outside but she forgot about us or didn't care to let us go relieve ourselves.

"The boat trip in the Keys prepared us for this moment, Doofus."

"I don't care, I'm taking a shit in here in the next five minutes if she doesn't come down and let us out."

The next morning, the lady let us outside, but it was too late. I had dropped a pile by the sliding glass door for her to pick up.

The guy came downstairs naked holding his clothes in his hands.

"Why's he naked?" I asked Ruka.

"Because she's more of a bitch than me, Doofus."

"Oh shit, he left me a message saying he is coming home early," the lady said reading her phone.

"Well, I better go. Until next time, cutie." The Fred guy kissed her and walked out of the house.

"Ruka?"

"I know, Doofus. This is terrible, and we don't have a way of telling him."

When Delux came home, he came right outside to see us. He was so happy to hug and squeeze us, I couldn't believe it.

"It sucked being away from you two for three days," he said blocking our bombardment of kisses and hugs. He came home from his work trip excited.

"This work thing is gonna be easy. I'm so happy I got this job," Delux said to the lady.

"How was your time with the dogs?" he asked her.

"Oh, they were great. I walked them and did as you said."

"What a lying bitch," I said looking right at her, but she ignored my stare.

"Good boy. Good girl," Delux said to us.

He was excited with his new job. He was feeling responsible and like a real adult with a new corporate job with corporate hours verses staying as a waiter in the world of the unknown.
He went upstairs to shower and change.

"Ruka, this is shit now with this lying bitch. What do we do?"

"We wait."

Delux got a weekly gig DJing on Sunday night at a famous local spot on South Beach. He would arrive home Monday morning at 5:30 a.m. after a night of partying for the people who provided the party. It was some kind of locals night for the people who worked in the night scene all week. It made his Mondays at his day job a bit rough, but he was a veteran.

Delux and Condo Lady were soon always arguing about their sales jobs. Condo Lady liked to drink alcohol. Every weekend, and twice during the week, she would be smashed most the time.

Delux tried connecting with us by sitting outside and painting the drunk lady a picture with us, but Ruka and I were tired of the patio life and just laid there.

The lady would know if Delux let us in the house while she was out. He did this often while she was away to keep us close to him, but our hair would be all over her fake wood floors mixed in with her own hair and that of the cats. I didn't see the big deal if we were inside, but the lady wanted nothing to do with it once we moved in.

"I do remember she talked a big game when we were back in the RV. Oh yeah, the dogs are welcomed too," Ruka said mocking her voice.

I wondered how the RV was?

Delux got a notice that the storage place where the RV was parked at, was getting shut down by the city, and everyone was being forced to vacate. Delux had to come up with a plan, and he needed to come up with one fast. He searched around for other storage places, but they were all out of his price range.

He was now splitting the rent with the lady at the condo. Paying rent was an issue he never had to face while living in the RV with us. At Lu's place, we only paid $50 a month to live in the back yard. The lady was charging Delux $600.

"Ruka, you notice Delux is still sad all the time?"

"It's probably because we're all living here and he hates it," Ruka said to me, licking her paws.

Delux came out onto the patio with us. I could feel he was sad. Ruka and I never knew what was going on anymore because we were shut out on the patio with a piece of glass between us, muting out all of Delux's essence. He was in his own world inside that condo, and we were in ours out here. Separated like two spectators watching each other in an experiment.

"Sorry, doggies, but I sold the RV today,"Delux said, sitting on the floor crying.

Both Ruka and I were speechless, cocking our heads to either side in confusion as we comprehended what Delux had just said.

"Ruka, my home?" I said as a tear came to my eye.

"I'm sorry, Doofus," she said to me. "I know you loved it."

Flashes of the RV came through my mind of all the times I spent in there.

"I'm so sorry, guys, but I had to do it. I can't afford to store it, and I can't park it here in this stupid fucking condo, and where are we gonna go?"

Delux was sad and confused. Tess had given him that RV, but it seemed like he was heartbroken again selling it. Turns out some old lady bought the RV for the price of the generator that came with it. Was the sale of the RV what was making Delux sad? He had lost money on the sale of his RV. Our memories in there were priceless, but he practically gave it away.

I wondered how long he had this weighing on his mind? It was hard for me to figure him out with this piece of glass between us. I felt so separated from him.

"Ruka. I hate this patio. I want to be able to hear and understand Delux. I feel so disconnected from him out here."

"A reason, a season, or a lifetime," she reminded me.

"This is feeling like a long season."

"We're dogs. Everything feels like a season. Sometimes it's up to us to find the reason," Ruka said.

Routinely we were taken outside, and I was run through my list of commands while he made Ruka sniff out the ball he would throw somewhere in the grass. After a few tricks of sitting, standing, walking backwards, and laying down on my side, Delux would throw the ball really far for me to go and get. I loved these times with Delux when we got them, but we could see he was still struggling with something.

Condo Lady would come home late from a night of "networking," and start arguing with Delux, yet she wanted to play with us. She only wanted to play with us when she was drunk. Delux would feed us and have dinner ready for her, but she would complain about how terrible the food was and go into drunken rants while drinking more.

A few nights Delux came downstairs to sleep on her fancy red couch that looked super uncomfortable. Ruka and I would watch him toss and turn all night from our patio. All I wanted was to lay next to him.

"Me, too," Ruka said, reading my mind and touching me with her paws as she rolled on her side.

Delux left for some more work training for a few days.

Although he was giving us all he could, Ruka and I were starting to lose interest in doing anything, and we were both getting fat with his new sales job taking up our walk times. I was concerned for Delux but at the same time, I was starting to get destructive with the lack of a good routine again, and I made a mess of the back screen door.

Condo Lady was inviting the same 'Friend' into the house as before when Delux would be sent away for work. The Lady got down on her knees and sucked on the man right in front of us.

"Ruka, be thankful you're blind," I said turning away from them in disgust.

"Not going to lie, it feels weird doing this in front of his dogs," the guy said unbuttoning his shirt.

"Let's go upstairs then," she insisted.

When I came into Delux's life, he was full of excitement and love. The chemistry and power he and Tess held and created was amazing every day, even when they disagreed with something like me, and my shitty behavior. My behavior was not the problem this time, and from what I knew of Delux, he was not the problem either.

Delux came home to an empty house after his work trip and ran out onto the patio to greet us first thing. He was sore and in some sort of physical pain in his shoulder, but he loved us hard like he always did and held us how he could .

Delux made his way upstairs ignoring the cat's meows for attention and he took a shower. He came downstairs pale, holding a pair of men's dress socks and laid them on the table.

"Ahh, shit," I said.

"Reason, season, or a lifetime, Doofus," Ruka reminded me.

When the Lady came home, she saw the socks and ignored them.

"Ruka, she's pretending that she don't see the socks."

"Let's see how that goes," Ruka said.

"Ahh… I may have a sales job now, but, these are not my dress socks. I don't have fancy socks like this. Who left their socks under the bed like a dog, pissing on its territory or some shit?" Delux said while she kept mumbling over him, not looking at him in his eyes, clearly giving all the signs of lying.

Delux didn't waste any time. That was it. Condo life came to an end just like that. With the money made from selling the RV, and not paying Condo Lady the last month's rent, Delux was able to afford the first, last, and security deposit on a new place of our own.

"Which means we're gonna be broke again, only this time with no RV," Ruka said.

"What? NO." I was nervous.

"Ruka. Doofus. Outside." Delux said letting us outside to pee as he was packing his things.

Driving to new places in the RV was fine, because I always had Ruka, Delux, and most of all, the RV. The RV was mine I felt. From eight weeks old past 5 years old, that RV was my entire existence. I guess I was happy I didn't have to see the RV leaving Delux's hands. After almost a whole year here in this patio, I almost forgot about the RV.
Looking back, I had nothing but wonderful memories, no matter if the RV was here or not. I realized, all that really mattered was Delux and Ruka. Delux played with me then, and he plays with me now. Ruka would walk under me while I pee then, and she still does it now.

"Ruka! Watch out." Delux said but it was too late.

"Ruka, just don't come near me when we go out to pee, and it will happen less."

"You pee on me so much I surprised you didn't bring it up sooner Doofus."

"No Ruka. You're blind, and you cannot resist going where I go. Use those floppy ears of yours and listen for my pee."

"It's hard to hear anything when I my inner voice is always reminding me you're just a Doofus, and I live with a forever three year old."

Ruka and I were the first to go to the new house and we could not wait to get out of this patio life. Delux put us in his car and drove us over to a tiny house under a giant mango tree, in a neighborhood of small houses. "Welcome to our first home, guys!" Delux said with excitement, opening the front door for us and his two bags of clothes, turntables, and his music collection.
What the fuck? Ok. Looking at this house, I miss the RV.

CHAPTER 15

TINY HOUSE, BIG HOOD

We had it all here. Single level home. One bedroom, one bathroom, a big kitchen, giant cockroaches painted over in the cabinets, and the living room was big enough for Ruka and I to play in. The best part was, we had our own fenced-in back yard! It was tiny, but it was there. There was no more glass partition between us and Delux anymore. We were now able to bump our noses into him and get his attention any time we wanted.

His sales job allowed him to work from home, so he did. Working from home meant 20 minutes on a computer, 20 minutes playing with us. 10 minutes on a computer, 20 minutes playing with us.

When Delux had to go to the office, Ruka and I had the entire house to ourselves. We were locked up inside the house and not able to see outside, but because we had more space, we felt free in there. There were no restrictions of not being allowed on the bed or the couch, because they were the same thing, a futon in the living room. Delux turned the only bedroom into his music studio and stored all of his equipment in there.

The Condo Lady came over after we were all settled in. Ruka could see Delux was no longer interested in her. Condo Lady would still deny that she'd done anything wrong, and she was calling Delux crazy for thinking she cheated. Delux didn't see her suck her friend off in front of us, but he found the socks under the bed and that was

288

enough for him to walk away. Condo Lady was the one making him angry and sad. She didn't realize Delux didn't have to see what she did to know she did it. He just knew, and so did we.

Ruka and I ignored the Lady when she came over. She tried to get Delux to be romantic with her, but he ignored her as I ran in circles around Ruka playing with her on the floor.

We were alone with Delux once again and had him all to ourselves and this made us happy. We had a small backyard where Ruka laid in the sun, and I had enough room to play catch with Delux and it supplied us with plenty of mangos.

Delux had to go to the office more and more these days because if he stayed home, he noticed he wasn't getting any work done and not meeting his monthly quota. Instead of filling his sales funnel, he was either playing with us, or playing video games, completely unfocused on his job. His new sales job should have fired him for barely making his quota, but after a few things got shaken up in the office, the higher ups made Delux the new operations manager instead.

Delux wasn't cut out for sales. He was too honest and nice even though his directness made him seem like an asshole at times. When he and Tess sold their art, Tess did most of the talking while he painted the smallest details that nobody would notice when they did buy one of his paintings.

Once Delux was promoted at work, Ruka and I would not see him for 12 to 14 hours a day. He was used to hard work like this, and he liked it because it was guaranteed money if he just showed up and did the work they needed because we were still living "check to check," he said.

All the new work hours helped him keep his mind off of things, but it also made him miss us. When he came home, he was all about the dogs. Taking us for walks after worked helped Delux focus on what he was going to do next in his life.

"So what do you think, guys? You like this new neighborhood?" he asked us as we walked down a sidewalk full of cracks because the old tree roots underneath were growing through.

This neighborhood was full of life and people and some of these people had dogs. Most of these people with dogs never picked up their dog's poo, making it smell like dog poo everywhere on our walks. Now

I could see, or rather smell, why Delux would always pick up our piles. Shit stinks.

On our walk, I noticed a woman with long dreadlocks walking on the other side of the street. That instant, time slowed down for me the moment I saw her. Have I been here before? I thought as I looked around us.

"Why do I feel like I know this woman that's across the street from us?" I asked Ruka.

"Is that who I'm feeling, Doofus?"

"I don't know, but there's some woman across the street with dreadlocks. She smiled and waved at us."

"Huh?" Ruka said puzzled. "I'd say she's just being nice, but..."

"There's something strange about her energy," I told Ruka as I watched the woman walk on her way.

"Life's weird like this, huh?" Ruka said casually.

"Weird like what?"

"Did you see something when time slowed down for you just now?" Ruka asked me.

"How did you know that time slowed down for me?"

"Doofus! Before you forget, if time slowed down for you too, tell me, focus and tell me, what did you see?" Ruka insisted.

I took a breath and tried to clear my mind to see what I was feeling.

"I see that woman, she's drowning in the ocean, just off of a beach with rocks. I see Delux in the water with her struggling. Holy shit, Delux is there, too. Ruka, did this happen already? What's going on?"

"No. This is a time shift we just felt, it usually means what we see is going to happen. This is a sign trying to communicate with us. Like a deja-vu, only it's a future 'I've been here before' moment."

"A sign? Do we have the same ability as Delux like when he saw the ball in my throat, or the buildings getting blown up? How do you know this is a sign Ruka?" I asked wondering if this is her having a senior moment in her old age or another lesson she thought I still needed to learn.

"Because I felt it, and saw the same thing too, Doofus."

"Yeah, but how do you know it's going to happen?"

"The same way Delux knew without knowing. The same way you just took a breath to clear your mind to remember what you saw. I know, when these things are inside me a certain way, it's a time to see and listen."

I paused for a second and took a breath. In my mind, I saw the woman across the street, fighting for her breath. "She's drowning in the ocean," I said.

"Turn around, what do you see?"

"I see a thick forest or a jungle or something."

"What else?" Ruka stopped to pee so I could focus.

"I see Delux running on the sand running to go help her. What does this all mean? Why is this scene playing in my head like a movie?" I asked, shaking my entire body a bit.

"It means we're on track to keeping things right, Doofus."

"How'd you get so good at this, Ruka?"

"My first memory as a pup is always that I was once the assistant to a king back when a great unknown empire was at their peak. It was then I learned to calm my soul's mind, to see what 'Source' is, or what

God wants or intends for us. Life is bigger then us all sometimes, but never bigger then you, for you are It Doofus."

I turned and looked at Ruka. She was getting old and grey. She was starting to lose her mind, I swear. "Assistant to a king? An unknown empire? What god wants? Save that story for another day, Ruka, unless it can help Delux here find some routine in his life."

"I have a tomb build for me in what is now called Egypt. My name is carved into the stone even," she said, walking blindly. She knew I doubted her as a smell of another dogs pee distracted me from the dreadlock lady day dream.

"Doofus. Time slowed down for me, too. I saw you in a ghostly form pulling at Delux's leg on a beach next to a thick jungle forest. You are the one who alerted him to a woman who was drowning. That woman across the street, is that woman you saw in the dream, is she not?"

"If you saw that too, why didn't we do something when we saw her?"

"Do what exactly? She was just walking down the street, and we're dogs. You bark at her, she's just gonna think you're mean and crazy."

"Thick jungle forest? I had a ghostly figure? Does this mean we're going to Costa Rica with Delux?"

"You have the gift of real sight, Doofus. Use it to remember the people who cross Delux's path. Feel what they are about, and the messages will begin to be clearer when you focus. Costa Rica was Tess's dream, not Delux's if that helps you at all."

"Focus on what?"

"Focus on nothing. Then everything will come. Find what fits and put it together."

Sometimes I just let what Ruka told me go in one ear, and out the other.

Delux let us into the house after our mysterious walk and told us how amazing we were. He loves us. If Ruka and I had egos, there would be no room in the house for either of us it was so small.

Delux tried to make our little house a home, but there were too many insects, and they couldn't be stopped. Even the ones that came with the house that were painted over, had brothers, sisters and cousins that would come and visit.

When Delux said the word ROACH, Ruka and I knew to check the floor. If we found it, we ate it. The neighborhood was infested with multiple species of ants, flees, mosquitos, and roaches. This was a nice house, but it lacked proper screen doors, so the inside of the house was hot, and if you opened the door, well, all the bugs came inside.

Ruka loved eating the roaches when she was younger and could see them but with her lack of sight, it was all on me to point them out. Delux wished she could see them now. The lizards too. I thought lizards ate ants but not the ones in our house. The bugs would crawl all over the place biting Delux while he slept, and causing havoc on any food containers they could get into.

Lucky for Delux, the lease on this little house of ours was only for six months and time flies.

We barely had a chance to enjoy the tiny back yard with all the fire ants ready to attack, or the feeling of wet mango squishing between our paws in the muddy grass.

As soon as we unpacked into one house, we were packing back up again for another, making sure Condo Lady did not know the address to bother us anymore with her lies and annoying drunk behavior.

We did one last walk around the neighborhood where nothing strange happened this time with any people. We even walked the same route when it happened last time. I didn't pee on Ruka, and Delux did what the other dog owners did, and left our poo on the ground with all the other piles from the other dogs that we hardly ever saw. So maybe that was strange?

"Doofus, you're strange".

"You raised me Ruka".

"I didn't say it was a bad thing".

"Are we any closer to Costa Rica?"

"We're closer to Trinidad."

"Trinidad? What are you talking about?"

CHAPTER 16

THE MOLDY APARTMENT

Delux moved us within skateboarding distance to his job. Work was now right over a fence that went around a bunch of large apartment buildings. If you walked down by a little creek to get around the fence, you were in a big empty parking lot, which Ruka and I were free to run around in. I could already tell this home was going to be fun with all this room to play fetch and skateboard in.

There was a weird smell to our new apartment on the first floor, but it had no bugs and seemed super clean. There was carpet. Delux was not a fan of carpet, but options for living are tough when you have dogs. After having me for six years now, he learned I can stink up a rug real fast. Carpet and dogs don't mix well, but we had no choice. I'll call this apartment a definite upgrade from the last little house, the patio at the condo, and even the RV, this place is nice.

We had no clue how Delux was able to afford a place like this, and the fact that they allowed dogs like us, was amazing. There was a community pool, but we were not allowed in it. Delux mumbled that he would not be swimming in that pool, once he took us for our first walk around the place to check things out. Trees in little plots of grass were spread out all around the parking lot for us to do our business in. This place had it all. The roads were smooth and the wheels of the skateboard glided us home with no issues on our walks.

The main room as we entered was the kitchen and the living room that had a sliding door to the outside parking lot. Through a door on the right, was a large bedroom with the bathroom tucked away in the corner. Carpet was everywhere except, the kitchen and bathroom.

"Ruka, we're gonna have to stay clean in this new spot."

"Doofus. *You* are gonna have to stay clean in this new spot."

"I don't know, Ruka, you got a smell about you."

"I'm getting old dummy. It's what happens. You smell too punk."

Our routine at the new apartment was great. Delux would leave us five minutes before he started work. He would play with us in the parking lot every day. Delux would throw the ball for me, and the stick for Ruka. We enjoyed our time with him as much as he did with us.

A few hours after he left for work, he would return home for his lunch break and hang out with us watching videos online while eating his sandwich and chips and kicking my ball for me. Ruka and I would get a few play moments in with him, and then he went back to work for a few more hours. Before we knew it, he was back home again just before dark, taking us on our skateboard adventure around the empty parking lots that surrounded his job.

We would pull him past some of his work employees who seemed shocked to see Delux had dogs like us and was riding a skateboard.

Everyone stayed back.

"Are we still that intimidating in our old age, Ruka?"

"Who you calling old, Doofus?" Ruka snapped back.

Ruka was aging rather quickly now. Her eyes sinking deeper and deeper into her head. Her ears no longer perked up like they used to from all my chewing on them.

A guy in the building next to us got a puppy, and they were outside playing when we returned from our run. He was the cutest little thing. I just wanted to play with the ball, and this little guy was determined to take me for a walk when we just got back from one by grabbing my leash and pulling it. There was a lot of life and adventure here. The people in the buildings were nice, unlike the ones that occupied Condo Lady's place.

Speaking of Condo Lady... Delux was spending time with us outside after work. He changed out of his suit and tie and put on his play clothes for us. Condo Lady showed up to the new apartment a bit drunk. Delux was surprised she found out where he lived.

She drove over to our new apartment drunk, still talking about how she didn't cheat on him and that they should get back together. I was getting annoyed with this woman. Delux was too, but he let her talk while throwing the ball for me. It was easy to run away from her drama and fetch the ball.

"Who wants to live with a liar, a cheater, and someone so obsessed with her car and her cats?" I asked Ruka running back with the ball in my mouth as she found the stick.

"Please, don't show up here anymore," Delux told her. "I just want peace. Ruka. Doofus. Lets go," Delux said to us moving towards the apartment.

Condo Lady left, showing off her car's power and speed in the parking lot as she pulled away.

"What a crazy lady," I said to Ruka.

"She's Latina like me. We a little crazy like that. You been practicing your Spanish?"

"Ruka, we're not going to Costa Rica anymore," I said walking into the house, convinced her mind was going.

I was happy to see Delux stand up for himself with Condo Lady. I could feel he felt good about what he'd just done, when he'd been lacking self-confidence lately.

"Ruka. What is it with girls and cheating?" I asked her walking into the apartment and drinking some water.

"Boys cheat too, Doofus."

"Delux doesn't cheat."

"Delux's a special kinda man, not a boy."

Delux came home from work one day telling his neighbor and his puppy outside about how his job had another shake down. Delux ended up getting another new position inside his same office. The new position required him to be there less, yet he got paid the same amount. Whatever was going on there, he was happy about how it turned out for him.

An old friend of Delux's from Minnesota had moved to South Beach to work in hotels or something, and he passed by to say hello.

"Hey, I remember this guy," Ruka said to me sniffing him up and down, then jumping up on him.

"I met him when Delux lived in the fancy high-rise in Minnesota. Remember, we drove past it that one day. The place by the church?" Ruka said receiving tons of attention from him.

"I remember Delux got this fool a job where he worked, and he fell asleep in the middle of his shift, in the middle of the floor."

"What happened?"

"When I saw him again, I jumped up and tore his shirt letting him know not to make Delux look bad."

"Did he?"

"I have no idea, he and Delux have been on similar, yet different paths, and they don't see each other much. I'm surprised to see him here, but he cool people," Ruka said biting me, showing off in front of him.

I let this Chris guy scratch my butt, but that was about it. Delux needed a good male friend in his life, and he didn't have one. Lu is busy with his new family and work life, and this Chris dude lived in South Beach with the South Beach lifestyle.

Another day, another nap. Ruka would go from her pillow, to the blanket, to my pillow, to Delux's shoes in the closet, or his pile of dirty clothes on the floor.

"Come on guys, let's go," Delux motioned to me after his lunch break that he'd spent at home was over.

"What's happening, Doofus? Where are we going? He has to go back to work, no?" Ruka asked me.

"You don't know?"

Ruka always knew what was going on. I sat there looking at her clueless.

"Delux grabbed our leashes when he should be going back to work," I told her knowing she heard him grab them.

"It's 'bring your kid to work day', so you two are coming back with me," he said, surprising us. "Be good, okay. Don't be super crazy, Doofus. Ruka there's a lot you can bump into inside here, so you can just sit with me," Delux said to us.

We were almost a hit. Everyone in the office was afraid of how I came into their personal space and introduced myself, but as they got to know me, almost everyone fell in love. Two of the office staff were impossible to convince that Ruka and I were harmless. They would walk all stiff and give us the side eye the entire time they walked around.

We're dogs. Who cares, I thought, but this one girl, she could not accept us. Darcy... she didn't like us at all. When she realized we meant no harm, she pretended to be fine with us, but Ruka and I could feel she was up to something with some bad energy.

"Do you think she's trying to take his job or something?" I asked.

"No. She doesn't like her life, and she's for sure a back stabber, so just stay clear from her."

"What does that mean… backstabber?" I asked Ruka.

"It means she's already called HR at corporate, and filed a report, the moment we walked in the door."

"Is this the same girl who called out of work because Jesus spoke to her and told her not to go to work that day?"

"Yes, this is her."

"She and Delux should be cool if they can both talk to Jesus."

"Maybe, but, she's up to no good. I can feel it."

"Didn't Jesus really speak to Delux? Isn't there a story there?" I asked Ruka.

"No, a bird spoke to Delux."

I liked everyone's smell in the office but Darcy's to be honest. It was easy to avoid her and her attitude. Just her alone, I could see why Delux hated going to work.

Then there was this tall Jamaican woman who was afraid of us for a second. Then she saw us for how sweet we were trying to be, and she loved us as much as she did Delux, I could sense it. She listened to his advice on how to be with us, and she was quickly able to get close and feel all of Ruka's love. I could tell from how she spoke with him, they had a good relationship, and it only took a few minutes for her to warm up to Ruka bumping into everything in her workspace to fall even more in love.

"I like this lady's energy," Ruka told me.

"She's like ten times your size."

"I know I felt it when I bumped into her feet under her desk and when her hands touched me."

Then there was Kathy. She was a spicy one like Ruka back in the day. She was a hard worker in her own eyes I could sense. It took some time for her to warm up to us, but she didn't have dog energy, so she was also easy to ignore.

Ruka said Kathy also could not be trusted.

"She's Latina like me, Doofus. I know these things," Ruka told me.

Delux called out my regular bag of tricks to convince everyone I would behave and listen to him and not be a problem. Ruka, she was the one who misbehaved the most. She would never sit still. She wanted to say hi to everyone and bumped into everything, and everyone, on her way to do it.

"I'm gonna go say hi to Darcy and Kathy. You wanna come with?" Ruka asked me.

"No, Delux told me to stay. He told you to stay, too."

"Stay, schmay, I'm gonna show Kathy what a real Latina is, then say hi to Darcy just because she already called HR. What more can she do?"

Ruka was getting old and turning into a stubborn bitch. She would have this mask on that everything was okay, but when I looked at her, I could see she was aging fast. I was getting old too, but I wasn't showing it like she was.

"How you doing, Ruka?" I asked her under Delux's desk.

"I'd rather be at home. There's too much negative energy in this office. I see why Delux is stressed out all the time and comes home drained. It's draining me."

"Me, too," I said.

I looked at Delux and did a quick head gesture towards the apartment, and he actually picked up on it as we made eye contact.

"Come on, guys, I'll take you home," Delux said after sending an email.

"You guys, alright?" Delux asked us outside, walking through the parking lot.

"I think I understood him, Ruka."

"What did he say?"

"He asked us if we want some of his dinner when we get home."

"I don't think that's what he said, Doofus."

"Wag your tail and just go along with it," I told her.

I tried to be funny, but Ruka seemed like she was in another world these days. She was hiding something from me I felt. I could see it in her when she was in front of other people at the office. She was trying to experience everything even if she just experienced it. It was like she was now double and triple checking everything to make sure it was there. I could see Delux was concerned as he paid strict attention to her as we walked.

"Bark! I'm worried about, Ruka," I said, looking at Delux.

"I'm worried too, Doofus," Delux said to me.

"You guys, I'm fine," Ruka insisted.

"Delux understood me, Ruka!"

It was a lucky guess," Ruka said, lying down in the kitchen.
I felt him. I could see how he looked at Ruka. He knew Ruka was getting old and dying and there was nothing he could do, so all he did was try to spend as much time with us as possible. He would sit on the kitchen floor with us and make us sing with him. He would howl and that would make both Ruka and I howl. We loved it.

I could tell Delux loved his new life here with us, but he missed the RV. He'd kept the countertop of the RV as a piece of art, hanging it up in the apartment. It was full of pictures of Delux's DJ career. Besides a little hand drum and a Bob Marley curtain that covered his closet, the counter top was the only thing Delux kept.

"He kept the hear no, see no, speak no monkeys," Ruka added from the floor.

"Ahh, yes he did. I forgot."

I was seeing over and over again that life is all about change. Change is inevitable. It's going to happen whether we want it to or not. It's how we adapt to that change, that separates, or joins us, with everyone else Ruka always reminded me.

"Ruka, you need anything?" I asked once we got home.

"Part of that dinner you were talking about," she said looking around the kitchen.

Ruka's energy would come and go. She liked to sleep all day and just be active after Delux got home. Ruka was having issues holding in her pee, and she started to pee in the apartment on the carpet. Delux had no choice but to tie her up in the kitchen when he left, so if she peed, it was on the plastic floor, and not everywhere else.

"Don't judge me, Doofus. I can't help it," Ruka would say to me as she peed in the kitchen right before Delux came home on break.

"I'm not, Ruka," I said, smelling her pee checking to see how she was doing. She didn't have much time left. It was hard watching Ruka grow old.

Delux was distracting himself with work, and women, instead of writing his book or his movie ideas out, and that was hard to watch, too. What was he doing with his time I wondered? Why was he accepting this corporate way of life when his best days were in that RV? Now that he had a place to live without a padlock on a flimsy door attached to four wheels, more women were attracted to him, so the distractions came from every angle now.

Delux never let any women get too close though. He would hang out with them out in public, but rarely bring any of them home. Ruka and I could just smell the women on him when he got home. Some smells we liked, some we didn't. Either way, we never met any of them here. Delux wanted real love but was more afraid of it now than ever, and I bet he had no clue what real love even looks like.

Most girls just wanted to play around with him, or create an idea of him in their heads that didn't exist. The smells he would come home with reminded me of horny cats, but it was just horny women. You could tell by the smells on Delux what these women intentions were, and they weren't good.

Until one day Delux came home with a new smell. "Ruka. You smell that?" I asked her as her and I did our routinely timed attack on Delux, sniffing every part of him when he got home from his shift.

"Yes, I do."

"What is it?" I said, having flashbacks of Tess in my mind.

"That my friend… is something special."

Delux came home from work that day smelling like he ran into a beehive full of pheromones and tomato sauce. Three days later, he came home, again, smelling like that same beehive.

"What's he doing at work that has him coming home smelling like Italian food and sex?" I asked Ruka.

"I bet he met a waitress. This is too many times he has come home smelling like work, pizza, and sex."

"How are they having sex while he's at work?"

"Their souls are. Whoever this woman is, she's a reason, for sure."

That seemed like a spoiler alert, but Ruka was never wrong. That also seemed like a spoiler alert.

"How do you know she's not more than a reason?"

"We don't. Only time will tell us how far it will go. For now, she's for sure a reason."

Her name is Maria. She came over alone. I say alone because when she did come over, both Ruka and I could smell three other smells on her, and they weren't animals.

"Or are they?" Ruka added.

"What are they, Ruka?" I asked as I sniffed her butt and Ruka licked her face.

"This is definitely the woman who Delux's been seeing two lunch breaks a week with."

"What are these extra smells?" I asked as Ruka tried to lick her face some more.

"Kids... they're kinda like animals. Only worse."

My mind stopped. "She has kids?"

"Yep. Three of them from what I can gather."

"Ruka, can you stop licking and help me think for a minute."

"There is nothing to think about, Doofus. Just be. Time is short. Delux is happy. Be happy. Kids ain't that bad, especially when you can give them back to the owners."

"Delux wanted kids."

"Yes, he did." But maybe not anymore.

Maria did seem to make his life happier than how it was the last few years. She would stop by with her littlest one who just wanted to throw my ball, and I loved it just as much as she did. She was so adorable. She would pick up my ball and throw it regardless of how much slime I left on the ball.

"I'm gonna go get it," Ruka said.

"Doofus, wait," Delux told me, even though I was going to wait anyways.

I watched Ruka sniff out the ball, and she then sniffed out the little girl who was so happy that Ruka came back to her.
Maria was a natural with us and fit into our energy perfectly. Delux grabbed the hands of Ana, the little girl, and put her on his skateboard. Delux held her hands in the air while she stood on the front of the board as they did circles in the parking lot. She loved it as she laughed and screamed as I ran next to them. I barked running around them. She laughed even more. Everyone was having so much fun together. This was so unexpected I felt.

"Ruka, you see this one coming?"

"What, this woman and Delux?"

"Yeah."

"No, I didn't, but I think it'll be good."

Maria and Delux were falling in love. They started to spend a lot of time together when they could. Sometimes alone, and sometimes with one or all the kids.
Things were going so well between the two of them, one weekend, they took Ruka and I up north for a vacation to see Maria's mom. Maria brought her three kids, and Delux brought Ruka and I. It was the best car ride and reminded me of the RV days, only better.
Once we got there, Ruka was left with the kids while I was taken with Maria and Delux to a boat.

"Ah, I don't like boats," I said as I whined a bit, hesitant to get on.

"Come on, Doofus," Delux encouraged, pulling my leash to get me on the boat, but I didn't move. I didn't want to get on a boat again.

It was Maria's stepfather at the wheel, and I was sure he would do us no harm, but something inside me said don't get on that boat, it's gonna be a bad trip.

Delux got out of the boat and picked me up in his arms on the dock. There was no escaping this. Maria took our photo and then Delux carried me onto the boat.

"He is so cute," Maria said rubbing my head.

"We're actually going to an island this time, buddy," Delux reassured me looking into my eyes.

An hour later, we were at an island with no other people around. Stepdad pulled us up to the shoreline and I jumped out. I tried to hold my excitement back, but I couldn't and I did the zoomies around the open area. I was on an actual island!

"I think Doofus likes it," Delux said to Maria.

"Delux, Maria, and Doofus! We should write that in the sand and put our paw prints! I mean handprints, sorry," I barked out in excitement as I ran around.

We dropped our stuff behind some bushes and explored the island for a campsite. There was only one campsite we could find that looked flat enough to lay on, so we set it up there. Delux quickly set up the tent and gathered whatever dry wood he could find to start a fire later. After everything was all set up, we went exploring some more. The little island we were on was covered in trees. Some were blown over and the entire root structure was peeled off the ground and now sticking up. It was amazing being there running around like a lone wolf. The smells, the taste of the ground and the grasses that grew here. It was our own private paradise, and I was the only dog.

Maria and Delux swam naked in the cool, clear blue water that surrounded us. They made some food before it got dark and told each other more stories about themselves in front of the campfire.

Delux was fighting with a huge headache from being in the sun too much that day, or dehydration maybe, but he was pushing through it. He made sure I always had enough fresh water, but he didn't drink enough himself I don't think. Maria was concerned for him and tried to soothe his pain by rubbing his head, but there was nothing she could do. His hair, his eyes, it all was hurting him.

They tried to make love under the stars, but couldn't. Delux's head was pounding so bad, all he could do was hold it in his hands, and the stars were not out for some reason.

Something caught my attention, and I started to sniff the air.

"I can smell rain," I whined out.

And not just any rain either. A full-blown thunderstorm opened up right on top of our island. Our fire was instantly out, and the rain cover that was supposed to push the rain aside and keep us dry, did the opposite. The rain was coming down so hard, it was crushing down the tent. I got scared and didn't know what to do. I jumped over Delux and Maria, causing even more water to come into the tent.

Delux was lying on his back with his legs in the air trying to hold up the falling tent while still holding his head up. Everything inside was getting wet. The lightening was coming down all around us, lighting up our failed attempt at setting up camp. The thunder shook the water soaked ground we were all lying on. Reminder to self: Getting on a boat, always leads to something bad.

The next morning, Delux's headache was gone, but he was exhausted from not sleeping through the storm. I was exhausted from not sleeping either, but now that Delux was awake, I could sleep, so I found myself a somewhat sunny spot to dry up a bit, and I took a nap. When it gets too warm, I will get up I thought as I drifted away thinking of last night's rain and thunder.

I started to dream about more and more thunder, when I was awakened by the sound of a giant sea plane circling next to the island.

"What the fuck is this?" I asked Delux after jumping up to see.

"Energy drink. Really? This early in the morning?" Maria asked, watching the plane circle around us at dawn.

"Are they shooting a commercial right now?" Delux asked, looking at a small boat with a big camera on it that was following the plane.

The plane swooped around and did a few passes through two smaller islands, next to the one we were camped on.

"It's too early for this shit," Delux let out.

"How's your head?" Maria asked.

"Not as good as yours," Delux said, embracing her. "It's better, but the sound of this plane and these guys on their loud walkie talkies in the boat is bringing it back."

"In that case, I can help you again," Maria said to Delux, hugging him.

The loud plane was too much that early after no sleep, but there was nothing anyone could do. I let Delux and Maria do their thing, and I went back to my nap that didn't last long. The boat with stepdad showed up and it was time for us to leave our little island with its own commercial. Delux picked me up again, and we all got on the boat.

"How was your trip, Doofus?" Ruka asked me when we got back.

I told her all about the smells, the bugs, the birds, the boats, the plane, and the rain. I tried to describe it all to her the best I could so she could understand it and see it within her own mind. I would have liked to know what she would draw if she could, based off what I told her about the world around us.

"How was your time here? In this stranger's house?" I asked, jumping in excitement to see her again.

"My time here was well spent waiting for you to return. I chewed on the bone a lot and laid in the sun out front next to their sign."

"Yeah, you did. The bone looks a bit smaller, and your tan line on your belly is nice," I said, checking her out.

We went home after our weekend sleepover that I think was more for Maria's kids than Ruka and I. Delux dropped Maria and her kids off at her house, and the three of us went back to our moldy apartment. The smell in the apartment was strong now after a weekend of fresh air in our faces.

"Ahh fuck, it stinks in here," Delux said opening the house once we got back.

The work week returned for Delux and one afternoon while he was home on lunch break, a police officer delivered papers to him at his house.

"Here you go, you have been served," the cop said.

"Served? This ain't even my name on the envelope. What is this?" Delux asked.

"Look, I'm not here to give you any advice, but these are eviction papers. The guy you are paying rent to, is not paying the bank, so the bank is taking back the property. I would call your landlord if I was you and maybe stop paying rent. Good luck," the cop said walking away.

"What the fuck is this shit?" Delux said, looking at the envelope.

"What does this mean?" I asked Ruka after Delux went back to work.

"It means, we are going to have to find a new place to live."

"Ruka you smell that smell?"

"Yes."

"What is it?"

"Mold. If you listen carefully, there's a leak in the wall from one of the upstairs apartments. Give it time, and the mold will show itself through the walls."

I was upset. I liked our ground-level apartment with not a lot of tenants. I wondered if everyone was paying rent to someone who was not paying the bank. That meant that someone was making a lot of money off of all of us, and now we had to get out.

Delux tried calling his landlord, and the call didn't go well. "No, no, no. You have the lawyer whose name is on this piece of paper call me. Not your lawyer, the lawyer on the paper saying I have to move out," Delux said, pausing.

"The rent? No. I'm not paying the rent until you straighten this out," he said, hanging up the phone.

When Delux stopped paying the rent, water, and electric bills, he instantly started to save money. First it was one month, then it was two months, then it was six months he stayed living there, rent free with only one other phone call from his landlord asking for money.

"I got a second notice for you to be evicted. I'm not paying you shit," Delux said, hanging up the phone on the guy who was clearly scamming us in this shitty place.

With all the new money Delux was saving, he got rid of his father's car and got himself a slightly used Jeep. Not too long ago, Delux was hit by a drunk driver coming back from the beach. Delux was fine, but the accident messed up the front end of the car. His insurance company said he was 10% responsible for the damages just for being on the road.

The car was fixed but ever since the accident, the car wasn't the same. So, he got rid of it. The Jeep he got was not much better. The day he drove it home, it had issues with the oil sensor going up and down rapidly, so he brought it back. They said they would fix it, and they did.

Delux had a plan to pay off the Jeep quickly with the money he was saving not paying rent. Within a year, he'd have it paid off he thought.

He kept working, and Maria kept coming over with her kids on his free time, and we would all hang out and play in the parking lot together. All the kids were old enough to entertain themselves, even though they all wanted their mom's attention or to throw my ball. I remember being like that when I was a pup. All the pups wanted Mom all the time. Even me, but I didn't want to deal with the crowd, so I always hung back and just observed.

You observe everything from the back of a jeep. Especially when the top is down, and the doors are off. We went for rides in the jeep to get ice cream when it was just Maria and Delux and no kids. When the kids were around, we would all skateboard somewhere close by. Delux would hold the youngest's hands and help her balance on the front of his board while I pulled them down the sidewalk.

"Excuse me. You know that's very dangerous, right?"

"What?" Delux said, stopping us to talk to a stranger in her car.

"It's very dangerous with that poor little girl on there like that with these big dogs around."

"Ma'am, this is what we do. The dogs, and the kids, love this. Everything's fine."

"It's dangerous. What if she falls, or the dog gets in the way..." she continued.

"Lady, you are the only car who got in the opposite lane to get close to us just to talk some shit. You are on the wrong side of the road telling me something you know nothing about. Please, carry on and have a good day before I say something else," Delux said to her.

"Doofus, let's go," Delux called out to me.

I went. I pulled them. The little girl loved it and laughed with joy.

"I'm calling the police," the angry lady said.

"What is it with people?" Maria asked in her happy self.

"What is it with this lump in Doofus's throat that bounces around?" Delux asked. "You see this thing?" he said taking a closer look at a ball sticking out of my neck.

Something was wrong. He took me to the vet. I was never a fan of the vet. They want to stick a thing in my butt to see how hot I am, cut my nails, look at my eyes, gums, and finger up my ears.
Fingers in the ears though… I kinda liked it to be honest.

"Everyone likes a finger in the ear," Ruka says.

"Not if it's wet," I reminded her.

Turns out I didn't have cancer. It was just a swollen gland, that should go away they say. It did, but then it would come back again, sometimes bigger than the last. I got used to this ball in my throat when it was there. It was like a small ball was attached to my throat and would bounce around whenever I ran or walked quickly. Delux would tell me it looked like I'd swallowed a tennis ball.
I could tell he was concerned about it. He was filled with concern for me, and for Ruka who seemed like she was entering her last days. I still felt like a puppy while I was watching Ruka age pretty quickly. Dogs are these forgiving and full of love creatures, but it's all so temporary.

"We just do our short time here and leave," Ruka would remind me.

In that moment, I felt like maybe we didn't leave. I kept coming back here to this world to help humans. I could feel it was my job or something. But I also thought how much I loved to run, bite, and chase. That was my job.

"Who am I?" I started to wonder.

"Why are you Doofus?" Ruka asked me, interrupting my thought while she was tied up in the kitchen.

"Why am I what?"

"No. Why are you Doofus?" she tried to clarify.

"Because I would make a noise when I laid down. Why are you asking?"

"Doofus, you are Doofus, because you chose to be Doofus."

Oh boy... Here she goes again with her philosophical jargon and deep processing of my thoughts again.

"Ruka, Your body changed so quickly," I told her.

"I'm almost five years ahead of you, kid, that's almost half a lifetime for dogs."

"How old are you, Ruka?"

"I think I'm around twelve in human years."

I didn't know what that meant, but I wondered what I was for a second, then it didn't matter. Seeing how Ruka was I decided in that moment, I was just going to live the best life I could for Ruka, Delux, and whoever else came into our life.

"Sorry you're tied up here, Ruka."

"It's for the better, Doofus."

Water bubbles started to appear behind the paint the size of large balloons, and the white walls started to show signs of darkness in the bathroom. Then, Delux came home to a home full of water from a leak upstairs. After two weeks, the place was still not dry, and no real maintenance was around to fix anything. Just some drug dealer kid posing as a handy man only to come back and steal your TV later on.
Delux drove his Jeep to work. He never did that. When he returned home, he had good news.

"We're moving, boys and girls. High five, Doofus!"

A high five he got.

I got excited and spun in a circle, and Ruka stood up and barked, then howled while doing a downward dog stretch.

"I found us a nice little house, a fenced in yard ten times the size of the last one, in a quiet neighborhood with smooth roads. Are you two ready?"

Delux was happy, so we were happy.

Within days, we moved out of the mold, and into the new. With his malfunctioning Jeep that still had the same issue from when he bought it, Delux moved everything over to the new place one load at a time. Once we were all moved into the new spot, we got to meet the new landlord.

CHAPTER 17

NOTHING LASTS FOREVER

"So these are your two dogs? They're rather big, no?" she asked.

"They're average, like I said," Delux explained to a disappointed old lady.

"Not for around here. Everyone has small dogs around here," she said as a big guy with a big golden retriever walked by us.

"That's a big dog," Delux pointed out.

"If I would have known you'd have two big, dangerous dogs, I would have said no to you renting here."

"Like I said, they're the nicest, sweetest dogs you'll ever meet. Besides this one is really old and doesn't have much time left. Please, can you have a heart?"

"What? Ruka! You really don't have much time left?" I asked, looking at her tired body.

"Look at me, Doofus. I'm old. I smell. I don't have the energy for much anymore. When I sniff the ground too much now, I run out of breath. It's hard to get up. I can't control my valves anymore. My eyes can no longer take care of themselves and are starting to deteriorate even faster."

"Ruka?" I questioned feeling an overwhelming sense of sadness in my heart.

"Trust me. I'm not going anywhere, kid," Ruka told me.

"You told me to never trust anyone who tells you trust me."

"No... I didn't say that," she tried to tell me.

"Sounds like this lady doesn't like us," I told her.

"Story of our life, no?"

"Until they meet us."

The new house was great, despite the landlord. Two bedrooms and one bathroom. The kitchen had a counter that separated the kitchen from the living room. The yard was big, and the grass was soft. The grass was the best part of the house.

Delux turned one bedroom into his music studio. Setting up his turntables and organizing all of his vinyl records. I noticed he never touched his records like he used to.

"That's because all the music's on CD now, or a flash drive. Who wants to carry heavy records around anymore?" Ruka asked me.

I watched Delux set up the studio.

Our house was instantly a home. The furniture from the other apartment filled in the new home nicely.

Maria came to visit and added her touch telling Delux he was crazy for putting the bed where he did, so he changed it with her.

There was something different about them. They seemed like they were not a "couple" anymore, but still together a lot.

Delux got a promotion at work, but it still included working with three pregnant women and two not pregnant women. He would come home stressed after long days of fixing other people's problems. There were secrets at his job he was keeping, or destroying, that were starting to eat away at him. Maybe they were just records and not secrets; I didn't fully understand his work, but that office was weighing on him.

I would nap and dream of the RV while I waited for Delux to get home. Ruka and I still greeted him at the door when he arrived. Our happiness to see him, was 50% happy, and 50% we need to go outside and pee.

Our new house was all tile, so Ruka could have her accidents as she pleased, and she was no longer tied up. Delux celebrated my nine years around the sun, and I was now understanding what Ruka was talking about when it comes to age, your bladder, and holding it in.

The landlord met Maria and one of her children as we all played in the front yard.

The landlord showed in her body language that she was upset about Maria being at the house with her little one. The landlord let Delux know she rented to him with his dogs only, not also with a girl and her kids.

Turns out the landlord was spying on Delux and saw that Maria was coming to visit, and at times she would have her kids with her. She never stayed the night at our new home or stayed a long time for that matter. She was a single mom with three kids, she had a lot going on already.

"Can you see that Delux and Maria are no longer a couple, but just friends?" Ruka asked me.

"I thought I was feeling something. I don't see them hugging on each other anymore. Not even in the house."

Maria felt like she was holding Delux back from something great. He spoke about writing a movie, and how people were telling him to write stories.

He was managing two dogs, a full-time job, and a DJ career that he was giving up on. His story was still going for him. It didn't make sense to stop to write about it.

Delux and Maria had an honest connection, so they remained friends and supported each other in ways most would consider crazy. Maria was not like Tess, or the Condo Lady. Maria loved Delux and wanted nothing but him, but she knew that she and her three kids were a bit much for him to handle at the moment, and she wanted the best for him.

"Well, since you brought it up, you might as well talk about, Jobe."

"Brought what up?"

"She's what this chapter's about, isn't it?"

"Ruka, wait, I was going somewhere with that," I told her, trying to get back to what I was thinking.

"Just get to it, Doofus. I don't have much time."

Jobe was this tall, beautiful dark-skinned woman who, once she met us all, she fell in love with Delux.

"Once she met me, she was in love," Ruka added in.

"She liked you a lot. That's true."

"Did? Don't give away the story. She likes me."

"Oh shit. Right."

Jobe was just like Delux, they were on a similar path. How their paths crossed was strange in its own.

"What are you doing home?" I asked Delux who was home from work before his lunch break.

"Why be at work when I can be home getting high with you two?" Delux said putting his keys on the table and starting to cry.

"Ruka, what's wrong with him?"

"He's sad, Doofus. He wants to find someone to love like Tess loved him when she did."

"But she cheated on him and broke his heart for years."

"True. But the love was an experience of love like no other."

"I'm having a hard time understanding this human love thing?"

"You saw what just happened with Maria. You can find the most amazing, awesome person, but if they're not the one for you, they're not the one. But it can still be love. Some people are great, but want different things, or they're at different stages in life. Also, Delux just ain't ready yet. Hence the reason I'm trying to teach you about a reason, a season, or a lifetime, Doofus."

Delux smoked a bit of weed while sitting on the floor, petting our faces. "Why am I crying?" he asked out loud, petting us. "Why am I getting high at home, when I could be getting high at the beach?"

"Doofus, you wanna go to the beach?"

"I always wanna go to the beach."

"Ruka. I love you girl. I wish I could take you."

"It's okay, daddy. Go with Doofus, I'll be waiting here for you."

Delux and I jumped into the Jeep with the hammock, a book, a notepad, his weed and some water. Since it was 11:30 a.m. on a Wednesday, the beach was empty when we got there. Finding two palm trees to hang the hammock was easy, and there was parking right next to them. Delux set everything up, then took me for a quick illegal swim in the ocean.

Dogs weren't allowed at this beach, but today, Delux didn't care. We both swam around each other a bit, playing with the tennis ball, then returned to the hammock that had a little shade from the palms covering us. The breeze was perfect, and the ocean was smooth like glass. I dug away the hot sand, then laid down in the cooler sand I found below.

The beach was empty. Not a single person was besides us so it was easy to fall asleep under Delux in the hammock.

I awoke to a girl setting down a blanket not too far from us. Delux didn't see her at first, but after about 30 minutes, he poked his head over the lip of the hammock and checked in on me.

"How you doing, Doofy?"

When he called me Doofy, I knew he was in a playful mood. I could tell he was trying not to be sad. He was trying to distract himself from what was going on with him and Maria, or work, or Ruka, or who knows what.

Delux then saw the random beach goddess as well. She was beautiful, sitting there on her blanket writing something in a book. Delux tried to ignore her and went back to his own writing and hiding himself inside the cocoon of his hammock.

I kept an eye on her. She sat on her blanket, reading a book with a large drum that was next to her in the sand. I'm sure Delux saw the drum. He loves to drum. He had been traveling with a small drum since we had the RV. He could talk to her about drumming, I thought to myself pretending to be him walking up to her. He likes to drum not start conversations. They both had drums. They were both here alone. I was getting overwhelmed with my thoughts, so I took a deep breath and continued to watch her while I turned my thoughts to just being present like Ruka would want me to.

"What do you think, Doofus? Should I go talk to her?" Delux asked, leaning over the hammock.

She's been sitting there for an hour I thought. She could have sat anywhere at the beach, yet she chose to sit not too far from where we were. How do I tell Delux yes?

"What do I say to her?" He paused.

"Fuck buddy, she's beautiful isn't she?" Delux said rubbing my face and sitting up in the hammock. He drank some water. "Doofus, wait," he told me.

I stayed while he walked back to the Jeep and grabbed something from inside.

"Is he doing what I think he's doing?" I wondered out loud.

Delux came back to the hammock zone. "Good boy, Doofus. Nice wait," he said proudly holding a seashell he found on a beach 150 miles from here. Where was I gonna go? I have shade under this hammock I thought. The rest of the world around us is on fire with this 1pm sun, yet I'm chilling at the beach, in the shade with a breeze, on a workday, I'm good, Daddy.

"Okay, here I go. Wait here just in case she's afraid of dogs," he told me, walking over to the girl.

Ah to be a human, I thought, horrified. I didn't think I wanted anything to do with being a human. I loved the fact that all I gotta do is sniff a dog's butt, and let them sniff mine, for us to figure out if we'll get along or not. Butt sniffing does get a little more complicated with any dog that's a bit timid, but what is a good life without a little complication to figure out, right?
Delux had his solutions, but he loved to complicate things, so I kept an eye on him. He walked right up to her and asked her something and then pointed to her drum. He then proceeded to talk, and she smiled and laughed. He never took the shell out of his pocket. Instead, he pointed at me.

"Oh, he's so cute. Yeah, call him over, I would love to meet him," I heard her say.

"Click, click," went Delux's cheek muscles, signaling me to go to him, so I did.

"Good boy," Delux said to me holding my face as I tried to smell her energy.

"This is Doofus. He's really smart. Don't let the name fool you," he told her.

"Hahaha, Doofus? Can I pet him?"

"Sure. He's a bit sandy and stinky though. Sorry."

"It's okay, I love dogs."

Her touch was nice. There was something about her though. I had smelled her before. I knew I'd never met her, but I had smelled something on her that I remembered. Shit, Ruka always told me to try to remember people... Who had this smell before?

Jobe and Delux talked about how her ex-girlfriend took her dog when they broke up. Delux didn't say anything about what he'd just heard and stayed listening and kept the conversation going. When she said girlfriend, the dreadlock woman I saw on our walk from our first tiny house flashed into my mind.

That's it! I got up and sniffed her some more while they were talking.

"Doofus. What are you up to, buddy?" Delux asked me.

"Hi there, sweetie. Oh my god, he's so soft," Jobe said touching me and the strange ball in my neck but didn't mention it.

It was not her, but it was kinda her. The lady from the walk a year ago. I could smell her on this Jobe woman. That's why she smelled familiar, or something about her is familiar I thought.

My head flashed to the dreadlock woman drowning. She wasn't panicking as she struggled in the ocean water, but she was going down. We were at the ocean now, but there was no jungle behind us like in my dream. Just the concrete jungle of the city.

When I came back to the present moment, I looked around towards the sea. Again, glassy water, and nobody was swimming or even walking on the beach.

I turned towards Delux and I could see he was in love already.

"Shit," I whined out loud.

He admitted to her that he was going to lie to her and say he found the shell he pulled out of his pocket, and was going to use that as a way to start the conversation.

"Well, a hello did just fine for you, didn't it?" Jobe told him smiling, sending him mixed signals after her girlfriend taking her dog, comment.

They did hit it off nicely I thought. And very organic. They talked for two hours or so when they suddenly saw the parking meter police and they both got up and ran to their cars because they both had expired meters. Turned out they parked right next to each other. She got into her SUV, and pulled away, waving goodbye.

"Sure, Doofus. The only girl I finally get the balls to talk to, turns out to be a lesbian."

I'm a dog. I didn't know what to say to that.

We packed up our things off the beach and made our way home to see Ruka. We got caught up by the drawbridge that the boats would pass under.

While the bridge was up, Delux would pull out his skateboard that he always left in the Jeep, and go down the hill on the empty, opposite lane of traffic. At this bridge, there was a hairpin exit to the right that shot you back towards the bridge at the bottom of the hill. Then, all you had to do was run up the side of the bridge to get back to the top and do it again.

"Doofus. Wait here," Delux told me excitedly, as he ran to the other side to ride down.

I waited. This wasn't his first time doing this with me. I loved watching him go down the hill and pop back up again. He always came back so I had nothing to worry about, so I barked and howled, to cheer him on when I saw him. He kicked a few times and got some speed. Then he zig zagged a few times before going wide into the hairpin turn with a lotta speed and control. He would go out of sight for a few seconds that felt like minutes, then pop back up at the top and do it again.

"Good boy, Doofus! Good wait!" he yelled out as I watched him take his second run with plenty of time to go as there were two large boats waiting to pass under the raised bridge.

As Delux started to go down the hill, Jobe jumped out of the waiting traffic, waving her arms in the air. "Oh my god, you skateboard, too?" she yelled out, holding her hands on her head in disbelief.

"Woot, woot!" Delux yelled out going past her, and into the turn.

When he popped back up at the top, he went and met Jobe in the middle of the road. She was happy. Delux was happy. This was fun to watch I felt.

"Bark. Bark, Bark." I was happy to see him authentically happy.

"Good boy, Doofus. Oh my god, she's a goddess! She skateboards, too. What the fuck?" Delux said getting back into the Jeep with me, rubbing my head.

Delux had met his match. She drummed, she painted, she skateboarded and she said she started paddle boarding recently. Then she pulled up alongside us in traffic at a stop light blasting some reggae music.

"And you listen to reggae music? Who are you, and who is that you're listening to? I've never heard him before," Delux said across the Jeep into her car.

"It's some new guy. I just went to his show and got his CD. It's so good."

"Let me borrow it," Delux told her.

"What? No way. What if you lose it, or scratch it? What if I never see you again?" she yelled out laughing, wanting to say yes.

"You live in the same neighborhood as me, and here, you can have my phone number and email. Besides, you said you know where I live when I told you, so, let me borrow it, and come get it tomorrow. I promise it will be in good hands."

"Oh my gosh. No way."

"Here, take my CD, it has all my info, I will give it to you for that CD. Come get it tomorrow, and keep my CD for free," Delux said handing his mix out the doorless Jeep.

"I cannot believe I am doing this," she said handing him her CD.

It worked. Delux got the CD from her. It's funny how the world works out. Too bad she's into girls and not guys. I couldn't wait to tell Ruka when we got home. Delux was shining so much, I probably didn't even have to.

"How was the beach?" Ruka asked, running past us to go outside to pee. "Ugh, I was struggling to hold that one in. Doofus... Why do you smell like a girl?"

"I should smell like two girls."

"No, you smell like one girl. Who is she?"

"It was someone Delux talked to at the beach, and guess what."

"I don't guess, just tell me."

"She smelled like that dreadlock lady from the other house. The one that gave us a flash or something in our minds of her drowning."

"I don't smell two girls, I just smell one, and she was all up in your neck, on your chest... What happened to you out there?" Ruka asked happily.

"Delux met a woman."

CHAPTER 18

THE CLIFF HANGER

Jobe came to the house to retrieve her CD that Delux had already made a copy of. She saw his artwork and fell in love with it instantly.

"We have to paint together," Jobe said flipping through Delux's pieces.

Once Ruka sniffed out Jobe, Jobe fell in love with her right away.

"And I wanted to fall in love with her... She smelled and tasted so good when I licked her," Ruka said.

"You do that to everyone."

"Until I find out they have on too much make-up. Yuck. They need to make makeup taste better. Could you imagine being someone kissing another person full of makeup. Gross," Ruka said laying back down on the ground.

"This is why I don't lick strangers. I don't trust them," I told Ruka

"And I don't trust her," Ruka said looking right at Jobe.

Jobe didn't wear makeup. She was a natural, free flowing kind of woman, with an energy about her that would make everyone in the room stop what they are doing when she walked in. She was strong. She was independent. I felt she was lovely. She was in our living room, getting to know Delux.

When she left, it didn't take long for her to return some other day or evening to hang out with him some more. Delux and Jobe started painting together when they hung out. They liked the same music. They played their drums together and they started cooking together.

Delux would go out with her at night sometimes, and then one night, she stayed the night and snuggled Delux in bed all night, into the following morning. I loved these kind of days.

The work week ended, and Delux had two days off to just be home with us. Even though Jobe was in the picture now, Delux always made time for Ruka and I first thing every day. He then made a big breakfast for Jobe and he shared some with us. He always shared his last pieces with us.

Ruka and I liked it when there were people in his life. After Tess, Delux was alone with just his thoughts and us. This new energy was exciting. Delux's energy was different, in a good way. After a few weeks of Delux and Jobe hanging out together, things between them got even more serious.

For the first time after being molested as a young girl by her father, Jobe decided to trust and be with the first man she ever chose to be with. Delux.

"Look, if you like girls the way I like girls, I know you can't just shut that off. If you want to be with a woman, that's fine, just keep me informed. Don't be afraid to talk to me about your feelings, your needs, your wants, and desires. I don't need to watch or to take part in anything, I just want clear communication, trust, and for you to be happy," Delux told her.

"Wow, he just said that to her?" I asked Ruka in shock.

That was all Jobe needed to hear, and she was in love. Or at least willing to try out what love was like with Delux.

Delux and Jobe became one of those powerful couples. Jobe became friends with Maria the first time they met, and Delux easily became friends with Jobe's friends and family that had a music gathering one evening they went to.

Life was simple until Delux started to follow her to a Mystery School she was going to. There they started learning about secret traditions of an ancient world before all of us existed or something like that.

"So they think," Ruka interjected.

"What do you mean, so they think? I thought you were once part of an 'unknown empire,' or something like that, your royal highness?" I asked Ruka.

"The mysteries of this world are not meant for the average mortal person to know. All people are doing at these schools is listening to someone else's opinion of the world based off of older opinions written in a few books. What they need to do is just go out there in the world and truly experience it. Experience the mysteries yourself for what they are—live life."

"Do you think we are "livng life," as you say?"

"We're all dying in life, until we acknowledge the sacred mysteries of it." Ruka said from her pillow.

"But I will say, this has been the best life."

Jobe and Delux would come home talking about strange things after school like giant buildings, old rocks, frequencies, and flowers of life. They would come home, put on music, and paint together, talking about the teachings that night.

Jobe was actually a beautiful painter. All of her art was a picture of something with purpose. Delux painted abstract and confusing chaos, while she painted figures and beauty.

It was nice, watching them get close to each other. Delux seemed happy again in his life. I didn't even notice the switch from him being sad to this new current state. When you're in the moment and you have your purpose set forth, life was just moving along.

In the days of the RV, Ruka and I and Tess became his purpose as he navigated life and its many options. He was happy and full of adventure ten years ago, letting Tess steer him towards Costa Rica. Now he was slowing down and looking for that family or tribe that humans are supposed to find or create.

Delux trading his time for money at corporate America was starting to pay off with him making extra payments towards his Jeep to pay it off sooner than later. We always had food at the house, and life was more stable now than it had ever been for us. Ruka and I could both settle into this energy and know we were safe and not going to have to go anywhere.

And then it happened.

"Ahh, fuck!" I yelled out in a bark, feeling something inside me send my back legs to the ground as I ran through the grass on the home stretch to our house during a run.

"Doofus!" Delux shouted out, running over to me with concern. "What happened—you okay, buddy?" he asked me.

"What happened, Doofus, you okay?" Ruka asked me, sniffing my legs.

"I don't know, Ruka. Something hurts inside my waist. I don't know what happened, but it felt like I got hit by something in my insides," I told her, looking at my belly.

"Where?"

"My belly, I think, or my waist. I don't know, it happened so quick."

"Does it hurt now?"

"Right now, staying still, no, but if I get up, I don't know."

"Well, try to get up."

"Doofus. Easy buddy. Just wait," Delux said, putting his hands on my body touching me all over while I sat there in the grass.

"I'm fine, Dad. I'll be okay," I told him with my eyes and smiled as I stood up.

"Ok, you can stand up. Can you walk home, or should I carry you?" Delux asked me.

I seemed to be okay, but something was seriously off a minute ago.

"I should carry him home," Delux said looking at Jobe.

I knew he wanted me to go back to the gate of the house, so instead of running there like I was about to before, I walked home like nothing happened.

"What the heck? Now he's walking fine."

"Do you think it has something to do with the cyst in his neck?"

"I don't know, it's still there in his neck like normal. I saw his back legs go down. It was like his hips gave out, but he's walking home fine, look at him."

"Doofus, don't try to be a tough guy and hide anything. Are you okay?" Ruka asked me.

"I'm okay."

We got home, and Delux and Jobe talked more about their new relationship and what their expectations were while looking over my body. Jobe wanted to go to Columbia and live in the jungle. Delux wanted out of his corporate job and was up for anything at this point. Their plan was, Jobe was going to keep selling weed to her friends, and Delux was going to work any overtime available at work to save up some money to go to Columbia.

"How you feeling, Ruka?" I asked her.

"About Delux and his new lesbian girlfriend that he's moving too fast with?"

"No, you. Wow, you can't be happy that Delux is finally happy? How you doing, Ruka?"

"I'm tired, Doofus. It feels like I could be reset at any moment."

"Reset? What do you mean?"

"It really is a dog's name, that makes the dog," Ruka said to me.

"Ruka, what are you talking about?"

"Doofus, you really are a doofus… Reset. This body will go away, but my soul will go into the start of a new body somewhere, to be with new people, with a new purpose when the time is right."

"Ruka, I hate thinking about you not being here."

"You better practice your Spanish, kid. You may not be going to Costa Rica, but it sounds like you might be going to Columbia."

"What are the chances you come back into our life here if we go out and buy a new puppy afterwards?"

"I would love that, Doofus, but that's probably not possible. Delux seems to be following another woman and her dreams, instead of finding his own."

"Look at your face, Ruka, you are so gray now all over. And your ears don't stick up like they used to."

"You spent a lifetime chewing on my ears, licking them, pulling on them. What did you expect?"

"I just want you in my life forever, Ruka."

"I know, Doofus. You always say that. I'll miss you and Delux very much, but this is how life is, and honestly, I don't know the odds of coming back into your life again."

"I feel like we finally have a home here. I loved the RV and all the moving around, but I have fallen in love with our routine here with Jobe around."

"She can't be trusted, and the landlord hates all of us so much, I doubt she will give Delux another year, even if I am no longer around as a 'vicious dog,' like she says I am."

"Your love's the only thing that's vicious about you Ruka."

"Thanks, Doofus."

"You need anything?"

"I got everything I need. How you feeling? How's your belly or hips or whatever's going with you?"

"I feel fine."

"You guys wanna go outside?" Delux came in and said.

That word. Outside. It was a trigger that always took us out of our realities inside the house and put us "outside." Both Ruka and I jumped up and went to the door that Delux was already opening. It took Ruka a bit to get up and out, but she made it. She walked out to the sunny spot, and I went to the shade next to her chewing on the deflated football I popped some time ago.

The landlord was upset she saw a new person with Delux that was not Maria. To make the landlord even more upset, Jobe and Maria were instantly friends when they met, and we all started to hang out together skateboarding down the street with all the kids and us.

"Ruka, are you tired yet? You doing okay?" I asked pulling Jobe next to Ruka who was in the care of Delux.

"I'm great, Doofus! These moments are more important than how my body feels."

"Ok," I said, pulling Jobe faster while Delux guided Ruka.

We stopped to get ice cream. Maria and Jobe talked like little birds while Delux managed us and entertained Ana, Maria's youngest. Jobe loved talking with Maria, you could see it, and Delux was happy there was no tension between his past lover, and his new one. They were all something special. Seeing love without judgement, or jealousy from them was something to remember I thought watching them all communicate in harmony. Life moved fast yet slowed down to these moments we all shared together.

Ruka and I were watching him be vulnerable again, as he was starting to open up. Jobe was opening up to him as well. You could feel they were bonding and getting closer and more comfortable with each other even though it was rather fast.

Ruka started getting sicker with her old age seeping in. At any moment she could pass and that would be it, she kept reminding me. It was hard to watch her face turn more and more gray and sunken in. Her eyes seemed to be melting away in her head from the inside out.

Ruka hid her pain well, but there was no hiding what she was feeling. She was ashamed she would poop and pee on herself in the house still. She tried to hide her feelings by being tough, but I could see now, it bothered her. I would try to talk to her about her accidents, but she would always put on a tough girl mask and say she was fine and it was all part of life. She was worried about something though I knew it.

"Ruka, tell me a story."

"A story. What kind of story?"

"Tell me something you remember about yourself."

"My life flashed before me once. All of it I thought. Even this future we live together now, I saw it before when I was younger."

"You saw us together, before we were together?"

"Well, I didn't know if it was you, but yeah. In one moment, I saw some kind of story with Delux and you, and it turns out yes, here you are. It all came true. I can't believe it."

"How did it happen... the flash?"

"I was hit by a car and flung into the air. It spun me around so fast my collar came off, and shit came out my butt. I was hit so hard, I didn't know up from down when I landed."

"Holy shit, Ruka."

"I ran around the block dragging my butt, watching my future unfold. I stopped at Delux's friend's house because it was the first familiar thing I smelled. In my head, I was in the future with you here somewhere, but as soon as I smelled something I remembered while I was running, I woke up and ran to it, slowly forgetting what I was seeing in my head. Delux finally caught up and found me there as I was processing if I was dead or alive, and what I had just seen."

"You could see back then?"

"Yeah, I could see everything."

"Everything but that car coming," I told her, laughing.

"Haha. I turned my back to traffic, and as I looked up to Delux, I had backed up a bit and a car just got me."

"Were you okay? Did you get hurt?"

"I had a tiny scratch on my leg and I was a bit sore all over for a few days, but I was okay. I had a daydream of my future life with a Rottweiler that made no sense, because I hated Rottweilers."

"Was the dream correct?"

"Here you are, Doofus."

"I mean with everything else in the dream?"

"Now Delux is going to help me go to sleep to take away my pain."

"Ahh, you're going to snuggle in bed with him."

"Something like that, yeah."

"Ah, I'm so jealous," I said, rubbing my head into her.

A few days went by with some strange feelings in the air. Ruka had her mask on saying she was fine, and Delux was sad. Ruka couldn't move from where she was laying down. Her body was giving out on her.

"You guys wanna go outside?"

"Yes!" Ruka and I both said.

Delux helped Ruka get up.

"Once I'm up, I got this," Ruka said, walking herself outside the house, peeing in a shady spot, and then laying down in the sunny one.

"You wanna chew on my football?" I asked her, laying the football down next to her, and laying down with her in the sun.

"Thanks, Doofus. I just wanna feel the warmth of the sun right now."

"I have to admit, it does feel kinda good."

"Wow, I never thought I would hear you say that the sun feels good."

"There's a lot about me, you don't know, Ruka."

"Doofus. I know everything about you. I've known you all but eight very short weeks of this dirty, wet, stinky, muddy, ass exploding life of yours."

"That's all you think of me, Ruka. My ass explodes?"

"Your name was Buddha, and you hit your head making a 'doof' noise so many times, they called you Doofus... Yet you actually turned out to be the smartest, kindest, most loving, loyal dog, a friend could ever ask for."

"Ahh thanks Ruka, stop it," I said blushing, because I could feel she meant it.

"You're here to be Delux's best friend, not mine," she told me.

"I can be both."

"You know... You actually turned out to be pretty smart for a Doofus."

"Tell me what Ruka means again."

"It's short for Ruquita, which is slang for a 'fine bitch'. Imma fine bitch."

"Yes you are," I tell her, looking at Delux.

"You been practicing your Spanish?" she asked me.

'Click.'

Delux took our photo lying next to each other in the grass with the sunlight.

"Fuck, I love you guys," Delux said, rubbing our heads together then wiping a tear from his face.

"Are you ready?" Jobe asked.

"No," Delux said sadly.

"Doofus. In the house, let's go," Delux called out, so I ran inside.

I turned around to look outside, and the door was already shutting. I could hear him call out to Ruka, and pick her up, placing her into the Jeep, and they drove away.

I sat there looking at the back of the closed kitchen door. I pushed on it with my nose to see if it was open, but no. The house was quiet as the Jeep pulled away. The neighborhood was quiet.

I walked around the house and sniffed Ruka's pillow with only the sound of the ceiling fan present. Even though I lay on her pillow sometimes, all I can smell on it is her. I wonder if they were taking her for ice cream? Or maybe to the beach, or both.

They take me alone sometimes, so maybe they were taking Ruka because it was easier with just one of us. I didn't mind sitting home alone so Ruka could be out in the world experiencing it like I did with Delux.

She was here first, I lay and pondered. I tried to lie there, but I couldn't sit still. I chewed on my bone a bit, but I just ended up putting my head on Ruka's pillow again, waiting for them to come home. I wondered if getting hit by that car when she was younger, made her go blind? I had to remember to ask her what she thought when she got back.

I dosed off and had a quick dream of my childhood. Meeting Ruka for the first time when she walked right up to me with her nose down, and said I wasn't the one, then walked away mumbling that I'd do. She was always telling me to relax when I had to poo. She showed me how to bark at the gate at people we didn't know, or trust. She was the blind one teaching me to jump into the RV as soon as the word was said. She encouraged me at the river's edge. She kept telling me not to chew on things, to divert my energy into different things, like the bone I was meant to chew on or playing with Delux.

I awoke to a sound from outside. I was feeling like Ruka taught me acceptance. I pictured her at the beach with Jobe and Delux. I wished I was there with them. I drifted back to sleep thinking of all the times Ruka helped me. Nagged on me about everything I was doing. She was right about everything, I thought, smiling and laughing to myself.

"I'm gonna tell her," I said to myself, appreciating my memories and falling back asleep into another dream on her pillow.

"What was that?" I felt something waking up. The house was quiet. Just the sound of a small hum from the refrigerator and the ceiling fan. The street outside was even quiet.

I stood up. It hurt my belly. My heart hurt for some reason, too. I was feeling sad, I think. I walked around the house and checked every room. All seemed normal. The bedroom was clean and organized. The music studio, nice and tidy for all the records Delux had. The bathroom was good. Delux liked a clean bathroom and so did we. We didn't like to follow him into a dirty stinky bathroom I thought, turning around back into the hallway.

"Said the guy who lays in the mud," Ruka's voice said.

"Ruka?" I turned my head around and looked.

Nothing. I ran to the kitchen, nothing. I sniffed the door and still didn't smell the Jeep was back yet with them.

"I know I heard her. Where the heck is she?"

I let out a bark. I turned and looked at the living room. I sniffed around the skateboards, the surfboards, the paintings, the plants, the couch.

"Ruka," I called out again, but never heard an answer.

I laid back down on her pillow, while trying to keep my eyes and ears open towards the front door. I tried to stay awake.

Tess was in the way. All I wanted to do was look out of the window, but Tess kept telling me to get down.

"Doofus. Stop stepping on me," Ruka said to me.

"You smell that? Where are we?" I asked.

"I don't know, but stepping on me is not going to help you any faster. Just be patient."

"Sorry, Ruka, I just get excited. Hey, for real, you smell that?"

"Yes, Doofus, I do," Ruka said after sniffing the air.

The Babes got out of their seats, and I jumped over Ruka into the driver's seat. Delux had rolled up the window, so this meant only one thing. "We're going outside!" I yelled, jumping out of the front seat, running down the middle of the RV, and spinning in a circle in the back of the RV, pushing Tess out of the way.

"Doofus. What the fuck man, easy!" Delux said to me.

I tried to contain myself but outside smelled like the great outdoors, and I love the great outdoors. The door opened.

"Outside, but wait, come here," Delux said.

Ruka waited, but I didn't. I started to sniff everything I could. There were millions of smells. So many I had never smelled before.

"Oh my gosh, Ruka, where are we?"

I peed on a sign that Delux was reading.

"Danger—Cliffs."

"Ahh, Ruka! Come here!" Delux said, trying to call Ruka over to him.

"Wow, Doofus, you're right, there're so many smells here," Ruka said, sniffing the ground at high speed.

"Watch out. Ruka, don't go that way!" I shouted out, but it was too late, she was going over the edge of the cliff.

"Ruka! No!" Delux shouted as Ruka realized she had no ground under her front paws.

"Holy shit!" Ruka let out, going over the edge.

"Ruka!" I ran over to her as Delux followed.

"Doofus, did I almost walk off of the cliff?" Ruka asked me.

"Yeah, Ruka, you did walk off the cliff. I thought you were a goner."

"Ruka. Oh my god, come here, girl. Holy shit. You almost walked off the fucking cliff, man," Delux said to her holding her tight with just inches to spare.

Delux quickly put the leash on her to keep her close to him.

"What about Doofus?" Tess asked.

"He can see where to go. He'll figure it out, or fall. I'm sure he'll figure it out. He was staying away while Ruka didn't see it. Oh my god, we almost lost Ruka."

"Oh my gosh, we almost lost Ruka," Tess repeated realizing what almost happened.

"That would've been terrible," Delux said, walking us away from the edge.

We all walked down a steep path to the bottom of a huge gorge that split the ground in half. You could fit a small city down here I thought, but it was just full of trees, tall bushes, and grass. I ran ahead making sure we were alone, and we were. I ran back behind us to check, and we were good, so I ran back to Ruka, and bit her in the back leg lifting her off the ground.

"How you doing, Ruka?"

"Ah, hey fucker. Don't do that while I am on a leash."

"I'm just letting you know I'm here."

"I can hear your doofy body running. I know you're hear. Just bump your nose into me or something, you don't need to bite my back leg and lift me up every time, Doofus."

"We're safe to run around and play down here, maybe Delux will take you off the leash now."

"Ah shit," Delux said.

"What?" Tess stopped in her tracks.

"Look, there's a tick crawling on my pants. We should get outta here with the dogs."

"No time for play, Doofus. Ticks suck. Literally," Ruka told me.

We made our way back up to the top of the gorge. Going up was harder than coming down that's for sure, but we all made it to the top. The Babes did a quick tick check on Ruka and I, and we came up tick free.

"All right, well, that was cool to see," Delux said laughing at the ten minutes they'd spent there.

"Let's go guys. RV," Tess said opening the side door.

We got back on the road and kept on driving.

"We should do that again," Tess told Delux.

"Do what, take Ruka to a cliff so she can blindly almost walk off of it?"

"No, but yes," Tess said laughing. "We should make more random stops like that to see cool stuff. I like it," she said holding his hand.

"Me, too. We will. Are there any more listed in the map on the route we're taking?"

"I'll check."

The Babes were so in love you could feel it ooze out of them. Maybe Ruka and I felt it more because we were always sitting between the two of them up front. The Babes were a force to be reckoned with. Everyone looked at us, wherever we went or showed up to. If the RV didn't turn your head, the Babes would, and if the Babes didn't, when they took us out of the RV, that would. I didn't know what it was, but there was something special about the Babes, I thought sitting there with Ruka while we got back on the road.

"Ah. Babe, can you look at my back. I feel something crawling on me," Delux said, leaning forward while he drove.

Tess lifted up his shirt. "Oh babe, you have a tick on you, and there is one on your shirt, here let me get it, oh wait. There's a few actually. We should take your shirt off."

Delux took his shirt off while still driving.

"Ah, shit babe, your shirt is full of ticks. You must have walked into their nest or something."

Delux pulled over to the side of the road and jumped out of the RV.

"Babe, check my body."

"Okay, there's some by your waistline. Maybe take off your pants, too."

Delux took off his pants and found many on the inside. He stripped down naked right then and there on the side of the highway. They put his clothes into a bag and tied it shut. Tess then frisked Delux's naked body for any ticks on the side of the highway while cars wizzed by. She didn't find any more ticks, but she found something else she liked. After a bit of time on the side of the road with the Babes in the back of the RV, we continued our adventure.

"You feel any ticks on you, Doofus?"

"No, you feel any ticks on you?"

"I don't think so, but feel free to check my ears."

Ruka laid down and I began to lick her ears and bite on them a little for her. The sound of the RV rumbled underneath us, as the wind blew past from the open windows out the back.

"My heart sank when I watched you get close to that edge."

"My heart sank when I no longer felt the ground under my paws, then found myself at that weird angle."

"Lucky you got a big, Latina ass to hold you up on that cliff's edge."

"My ass is not big. It was my quick response time."

"Either way, I'm glad you're here. I don't think I could do this random adventure without you."

"You wanna practice your Spanish?"

"Si por favor."

Bang.

I heard a door shut outside and it awoke me from my dream of Ruka and the cliff she almost fell off of back in the day with Tess.

"They're back," I said, jumping up.

"Ruka."

I had to tell her about my dream and remind her we almost lost her one day. I could hear them outside coming towards the door. I stood by the door to greet them.

"Hey, Doofus," Jobe said to me, hugging my face.

"Hey, Buddy," Delux said to me.

I looked behind Delux and there was no Ruka.
I can usually smell her, but her smell was only on Delux.
I looked at Delux.

"She's gone, buddy," he said to me with eyes full of tears.

CHAPTER 19

DOOFUS THE DOG

Ruka was gone, but Jobe was there to fill the feminine hole of loneliness I had without her.

Delux would leave to go to his 8-5 like normal, and Jobe would sit in the living room with me, listening to music, smoke like Tess used to do, and paint her soul onto blank canvases. With Jobe, it was almost like Tess all over again, only the RV was a house with more room in it, and our wheels were the Jeep, that was always in the shop.

Jobe decided to go somewhere for the day, and I was home alone for the first time since Ruka. I tried to sleep the day away, but I couldn't. All I thought about was Ruka not coming home when I thought she would. I never got to say goodbye to her. I was filled with sadness.

I laid on her stinky pillow trying to fall asleep so I didn't have to think about her while I was awake, but all I could do was smell her.

"What are you doing on my pillow? You miss me too?"

"Ruka?!?" I yelled out.

"Woof, you know how hard it is to find a place you've never seen and have no idea where it's at?"

"Ruka?" I said surprised looking through her body without seeing her insides.

"Wow, Doofus, you're better looking than I thought. Look at you, all tall dark and handsome and shit. You're a little thick in all the right places," Ruka said to me, walking around me smiling.

"Ruka. Is this really you? Am I dreaming? Why do you look, see through?"

"Yes, no, and because I'm a ghost Doofus. Wow, this place is kinda how I saw it when I was alive, but not really," Ruka said looking around the house as I saw the furniture through her ghost like body.

"Ruka. What's going on? How can you see? Where did you go? Why are you see-through? Delux said you were gone but now you're here...?" I was confused.

"Doofus, you wouldn't know a ghost if it walked through the wall."

"Walked through a wall?"

"Yeah. Like that Zoro looking fella back at the warehouse when you were a kid. Do you remember?"

"Ruka?" I said in disbelief.

Ruka walked through the living room wall into the bedroom and then back.

"You're a ghost?"

"I can see the actual world now for what it really is. This is amazing! I can't stay long. I have some work to do, but I will leave you with this. Enjoy your time with Delux, because there's not much time left. Change is coming."

"What do you mean?"

"You're sick and dying like I was. And if we don't act quick, Delux's going to die in a tree house, and we can't let that happen."

"Die in a tree house?" I questioned.

"Doofus, I gotta go, but I'll be back soon, I promise."

"Where're you going?"

"I gotta go find a restaurant guy. I think he can save Delux, if I find him."

And just like that, Ruka walked out of the house through the wall and was gone.

I stayed lying on the pillow. I must have been dreaming.

Jobe came home and let me outside to pee and play in the yard a bit. I looked out in the yard for Ruka, but I couldn't find her or smell her. Just a small whiff of her old poo piles that were picked up and thrown away, remained. I peed and went back inside because I was too sad to play by myself with nobody watching.

"I must have been dreaming. What a weird dream, it felt like she was here," I said walking back into the house looking at the wall she went through and every other room.

"Doofus. It's beautiful outside. You don't want to be outside?"

I looked at Jobe. She was exactly the hippy type that would live in a tree house I thought. I remember Ruka said she didn't trust her. Today, she smelled different, and I didn't know why. Ruka telling me about Delux dying in a tree house sat in the front of my mind. I laid on Ruka's pillow watching Jobe move around the house doing her thing.

Delux would come home and she would have dinner and a blunt ready for Delux. They would smoke, they would eat, and then take me for a walk around the neighborhood. Damn, I missed Ruka a lot. The walks weren't the same without her zigging and zagging around me. Bumping into me as I stopped to pee.

Delux did what he could to help me keep my mind off of her. He started to take me everywhere with him. He had a rental car because the Jeep was being fixed, again. He would lay down blankets inside the car and take me along for all the rides.

I actually got to go to the Mystery School where dogs weren't allowed and find out what all the mystery was about. Nothing much really, just a few humans trying to figure out who they were, and what was going on. The school's teachers would then play musical instruments while people did rhythmic breathing.

Dogs don't think this deep, nor do we play instruments, but we do breathe a lot. Dogs just need food, a little attention, the word outside, followed by some head scratches and more attention.

The who, what, and why of the world… not our business until it has to be.

Life is short for us Ruka taught me, so we don't have time for too much information, unless it affects us in the moment.

"Life is short for all when you look at the big picture."

"Ruka! You're back."

"Doofus. How you feeling?"

"I'm fine Ruka. What're you doing here? I know I'm not asleep."

"You're awake. I'm just checking in to see how you're doing."

"I feel fin… " I felt some pain in my belly and could not finish my word.

"Your time is getting closer, Doofus, but hang on as long as possible," Ruka said licking my head, then disappearing.

My stomach. It hurt more now than ever. Delux saw my pain. The next day he came home to let me outside, and I couldn't get up off of Ruka's pillow. I had pain written all over my face when he walked in the house. I whined when I finally stood up.

"Fuck, this hurts. What's happening to me?"

I hobbled outside, and peed and pood in the same spot… Something I'd never done before.

"Holy shit, Doofus. What's wrong with your poo?" Delux asked, looking at a sack of something that just came out of me. "I've never seen poo like that. I gotta take you in to the vet. This isn't normal."

Delux made some time and took me to the vet. Turns out my pancreas was giving out, and it was going rather quickly. I had no idea what a pancreas even was. There were surgery options, but Delux didn't have the money, and they said there was no guarantee it would work. He took me home, and I could feel his concern the entire ride.

The next day, I felt almost 100% better. I could stand up, I could play, I could pull Delux on the skateboard, all was good. It was just another day in paradise it seemed.

Delux went to work that morning concerned about me, but Jobe was there, so I was in good hands. Days would go by, and I would be fine, but then the feeling would come back hard, and I wasn't able to stand up without a lot of pain. I was getting all cramped up in my belly and unable to move without feeling like I would tear apart my own insides. I was pooping out these disgusting sacks of mucus that were freaking out Delux when he tried picking them up.

"Doofus, you're too young to be getting old like this. What's happening inside of you, buddy?"

Delux was concerned, but he was trying to stay playful. I could feel everything inside of him for me was true love. Some days I could hide the pain I was feeling, but most times I couldn't when it was bad, and I would lay in the same spot for two or three days. It was debilitating when it happened, but when the pains went away, I felt ok again. I was okay I would keep telling myself, but deep inside I knew I wasn't.

A few days later, the pains struck again while Jobe and Delux were out one night. I ended up pooping in the house like Ruka used to. I don't know why it happened, and I could now feel the shame she would always try to hide. I never poop in the house, I said looking at it. I got scared.

"It's your insides, Doofus. They're dying faster than your outsides. And you pooped inside the RV once and Grandmas house too remember?"

"You say outsides like I have more then one outside."

"If you only could remember, you'd know," Ruka said vaguely.

"Remember what?" I asked in pain, and full of shame looking at the poo on the floor.

"You'll see soon enough if we don't run out of time."

"Run out of time for what? My insides are dying. What can I do?"

"You already did it, Doofus. We did it together. We stood by Delux's side as long as we could while he discovered loss, himself, and love yet again."

"So then what are we running out of time about?"

"We have to keep Delux out of that tree house."

Delux kept making appointments for me to see someone every time I got ill, but I would feel better and be playful again, so he would cancel them.
I was trying to read the room when Jobe was there, but I didn't notice anything out of the ordinary with her. All I saw was love, and they both missed Ruka as much as I did.

"Ruka, do you visit Delux, or only me?"

"For now, only you, Doofus. I'll see Delux at a later time. Now, you need to get to that appointment he keeps setting for you. Trust me. It's better than feeling sick."

"They can cure me?" I asked.

"Yeah, something like that."

Delux got a phone call saying he was not allowed to miss the next appointment because he has missed three times already. He hung up the phone and said this weekend, we were taking a trip. Usually Delux was happy for trips, but I could feel he was not excited for this one, even though I was feeling better this whole week.

It was a beautiful sunny day out. Delux had his Jeep back from the mechanic and the top was down and the doors were off.

"What do you think, buddy, can you jump inside without hurting yourself?"

"I got this," I said to him.

I jumped inside and felt a slight pull in my tummy. Delux saw it happen, but he told me good job anyways and patted me on the head. Jobe and Delux got into the Jeep and off we went. We drove down the street, got onto the highway, and the wind started to blow my ears into the air. They both were touching me as I stood between the two of them rising my head out of the Jeep feeling the wind under my ears. I loved Jobe's touches. I felt I could trust her. I didn't see why Ruka couldn't.

"It is so crazy that he seems fine now, when it seemed like he was dying and in so much pain just the other day," Jobe said, holding my face.

"He's fine, he's sick, he's fine, he's sick... the cancer is killing him. It's painful to watch."

Was this cancer thing what was inside my pancreas? I thought I didn't have cancer? I wondered as we drove with the wind.

As we got off the highway exit, a fire truck was coming down the street with its sirens on. I began to howl into the air like I always did when I heard one. Ruka would do it too, and then add in a few barks to spice it up.

"Good boy, Doofus. Sing!" Delux said happily with a tear in his eye.

"Fuck, man," Delux said wiping his face.

I was so confused. Why was everyone so sad? We pulled into a building's parking lot, and Delux found some shade.

"Do you mind if I wait here?" Jobe asked, crying.

"Yeah, no problem."

"Doofus. You ready, buddy?"

I was always ready.

"What's up, Dad?" I barked.

"Oh my god, this is so fucking hard," Delux said to Jobe putting the leash on me.

We went inside the building, and they were expecting us. I waited a minute so Delux could fill out some paperwork to fight my cancer. A young girl approached and said they had a room ready for us. This place looked professional, and my cancer wouldn't stand a chance here I thought. I was able to walk myself down the hallway with pride into the room they had prepared for me. The room looked strange to me. It was a medical room that had candles burning and blankets on the floor.

"If you two want to just sit down there on the blankets," the young nurse said to us.

I was down to sit, I loved sitting next to Delux. Ever since I could remember, even if he was mad at me for something I did, if I sat next to him, he would forgive me and touch me with love.
I was feeling a slight pinch in my stomach as I sat next to him, but I'd had worse days. Delux sat next to me on his butt with his legs crossed. I sat next to his shoulder feeling his arm hug around my body. I bumped him in the face with my nose and gave him a few quick licks.

"I love you, Dad. I don't know what's happening, but I love you, Delux," I said looking into his eyes.

The nurse said something to him I didn't catch, and then she put a small needle into my arm. It was a small prick but nothing I couldn't handle.

Then it hit me.

I felt a separation, or something. At first, I felt my heavy dog body slump into Delux. He held all of me, and instantly started to cry harder than I have ever seen him cry before. The nurse even started to cry, and she had to leave the room as Delux held my increasingly heavy body in his arms.

I got heavier and heavier.

I leaned against Delux and realized my body was now below me, and I was sitting above it, watching Delux hold me tight, crying profusely with my head in his lap and his body over mine. Then right in front of my eyes, Ruka manifested herself in front of me.

"Welcome to the other side, Doofus," Ruka said in a dark scary voice, looking at me in an ominous way.

"What?" I said, looking up at her confused.

"Ha, ha, just kidding. This is more like an in-between than the actual, 'other side',"

"In-between what?" I asked.

"That life sitting in Delux's lap, and the one were getting prepared for."

"What's the next one?"

"I'm not sure, but we're still stuck with each other from what I gathered."

"Gathered from where?"

"A girl does not give up her sources, Doofus. Find your own source."

I was confused watching Delux hold my body, crying, yet here I was unable to get him to respond to me.

"Now. We don't have time to waste. We have some serious work to do, Doofus. Me dying, now you dying, sends Delux into a shit storm he was not prepared for, and if we don't act fast, it's not gonna be good."

"Act fast? What do we do?"

"First... We don't leave his side."

Delux held my lifeless body for some time in that room. He was so sad. He just stared at the body that was me, petting my lifeless head, sobbing.
In that moment, I had a realization... if that was me, then who am I?

"That's an age old question, Doofus, and we will answer it later. Now unless you want to get left behind here like I did and forced to find a home we don't know how to get back to, let's get to the Jeep."

I walked away from Delux still holding my body on the floor.

"That's the saddest thing I've ever seen," the young nurse said as Ruka and I walked out the room.

"How do you feel?" Ruka asked me.

"Strange."

"It's not gonna be easy at first, but you can touch things, and go through things. I'm gonna need you to figure out the difference between the two right now."

"How do I do that?"

"Focus on touching the door, and try to move the door."

I tried and ended up walking right through it.

"Ruka. Am I a ghost?"

"Yes, now try again. Move the door."

I focused. I looked at the door and saw the direction I wanted it to go in my mind, or not my mind.

"I don't have a mind anymore, how do I think?"

"I was asking that when we were both alive and you did just fine, now focus."

"Ruka, this is so weird."

"Doofus, you have to get this before Delux gets up and leaves."

I walked towards the door, and hit it with my shoulder, and the door moved a bit. Delux turned his head towards the door, then looked back down at my body, still in tears.

"That's it, Doofus. You did it! Let's go outside to the Jeep."

We went down the hallway and around a corner where there was a door. I watched Ruka run right through it. I saw myself running right through it, but instead, I bounced off of it, stuck on the inside of the building like I was still a dog.

"You're still in the past, thinking about the door. Move on in your mind, Dooufs, and come through the door," Ruka said from the other side.

I tried again and bounced off of it. I saw Delux coming form down the hallway, wiping his face.

"Doofus, Try again! Hurry!" Ruka said half in and half out of the building.

I made it!

"There you go, now just one more door, and then the Jeep."

"What's with the Jeep?"

"You have to focus the entire time you're in the Jeep, or you'll fall through the floor onto the ground, and the Jeep will keep going while you are trying to figure out touch and how to catch up. The more you try to chase what you want here, the slower you go. Like in a dream. So stay present and things will work out."

"You told me one time you saw the future."

"I did. Up to this point. From here forward, anything is possible."

"What about the tree house thing you were telling me about?"

"Like I said, we need to follow Delux everywhere. Now, try to get into the Jeep."

Ruka wouldn't elaborate on the treehouse, we didn't have time. I looked at Jobe sitting in the Jeep waiting for Delux to come out. You could see she had been crying hard, too. I focused on the feeling of jumping over the side like I used to when we went to the beach. I leaped.

"Yes. You did it," Ruka said, jumping into the Jeep, too.

"Wow, Ruka, you can jump, too?"

"I can do everything and more now that I can see again."

Delux came out of the vet's office wiping tears away from his face.

"Oh my god, that was the hardest thing I've ever had to do… His body…" Delux cried a bit more in Jobe's arms.

"He didn't cry like this for you, Ruka."

"What?"

"I'm just kidding. He was a mess. Fuck, he still is a mess. Now he's going to be a super mess!"

"This is why we need to act fast," Ruka emphasized.

"What needs to happen?"

"We need to keep Delux working at his job a little while longer. We need to get his landlord to like him and give him a second chance now that it's just him and no dogs."

"What about Jobe?"

"Yeah, Jobe…"

We got home to an empty house. Even though Ruka and I were there in spirit, the house felt empty. There were no happy dogs at the door jumping up and down to say hello. No dogs that needed to go outside and pee. No sick dog to take care of. It was just Delux and Jobe now.

"You want me to roll us a blunt?"

"Yeah, sure," Delux said going into the bedroom to lie down.

"Ruka?" I said, feeling his loss.

"Just let it play out. He needs to mourn us. Keep him going to work. Stay here and watch them, I'll be right back."

"Where are you going?"

"I'm still trying to find someone who will help. I want to make sure everything works out for him like it should."

"What do I do?"

"Explore what it's like being a ghost dog. Go snuggle Delux on the bed and try to make him feel you."

Ruka left through the wall. I sat and wondered how she knew what to do all the time. Had she really worked for an ancient empire's king? I wondered for some odd reason.

I looked at Jobe who was just doing her thing like she always did. Same energy, nothing different was coming from her. She was happy Ruka and I were gone I sensed.

I went into the bedroom to see Delux. I jumped onto the bed and lay next to him while he lay there, holding a pillow over his face. As I put my head on him, to let him know I was there, he lowered his hand down to me, and I watched his hand and arm go right through me.

"How does one get used to being a ghost?" I thought, looking at him.

I laid next to him and thought of all the times I felt the hands of him. He was firm. He didn't play around when it came to paying attention. At times, he needed to give me a few hard corrections for thinking I knew what he wanted when I didn't. He always made sure I was successful at what he was teaching me, and praised me for it with gentle, yet excited hands once I learned. I thought of all the times he told me no and pointed his finger at me. He would always see the look of shame in my face under his fingertip and end up giving me lots of love instead of discipline. He looked for ways to train me that fit my situation, and it always involved these hands of his.

I felt him twitch. I could feel him, his warm body under mine, going softer with every breath he let out. His hand, getting more and more relaxed when Jobe entered the room.

"The blunt's rolled, babe," she said seeing no response from him. "Babe," she faintly tried and quickly gave up, closing the door behind her.

He slept all day, only to awake to Jobe making dinner. I bet it smells good, whatever she's cooking, I thought.

"I saved some of the blunt for you over there. Sorry, but you were out," she told the groggy Delux.

"Yeah, no worries. It smells good in here, what are you making?"

"Chicken for you, and potatoes, with a salad for me. How are you?"

Delux looked around the house.

"I can't believe they're both gone. I never imagined it like this. The house feels so empty now. I can't stop thinking about how Doofus's body fell into mine as he fell asleep… It was so fast… His last breath."

Delux started crying. Jobe held him, as he grieved us both now. It was hard to watch.

Corporate America never took a break, and Delux had to go back to work after one day of mourning me.

"Keep him going to work," Ruka told me before she left.

Monday came, and Delux was back at it, in the office early to get a jump on payroll. He was the only one trusted to do the company's payroll and bonuses. It was one of the things that frustrated him with his job I found out while tagging along with him everywhere he went now. Now that I was a ghost, nobody could call management and get him in trouble for me being there.

While in the office, I found out Delux was paying people bonuses on things, when the customer never paid the actual contract. Which meant the company was paying salary and bonuses to people who were selling a product to people, who never intended to pay for what they agreed to. I could see why Delux hated his job now. He didn't make a bonus, because his accounts receivable was out of hand. His receivables were only out of hand because of these fake contracts the sales reps were pushing through. And now his was paying them bonuses for it all.

The ladies working in the office, would only do the bare minimum and be in no rush whatsoever. Three girls were still pregnant while the other two, still had strong opinions. I could see the smile on Delux's face was fake while in the office.

The Jamaican lady was the only one who would tease him and bring out his real smile. She was the latest temp that Delux wanted to hire as a full-time employee, but she didn't want the full-time job. It was with her help that Delux was able to discover the accounting debacle the bonuses were causing with the overtime he was putting in.

Ruka thought Delux was planning to quit his job, we just didn't know when.

"How's work?" Ruka asked me, sneaking up behind me under Delux's desk.

"Ruka! You scared the shit outta me. There's something I wanted to ask you."

"What is it?"

"I don't remember right now, hold on."

"I don't have time. I was just passing by. Keep Delux working, and somehow, get him to go to the beach this Saturday."

"How do I do that?"

"You'll figure it out. Don't forget, like your question," she said fading away through Darcy's desk wall.

"Question? Oh yeah. Ruka?"

She was gone.

I was able to see and communicate with Ruka still, while Delux was feeling the most alone he had ever felt. I was feeling the "alone" now, too. I already processed losing Ruka once, and now I was losing her on a daily basis.

"Doofus. I'm here if you need me. Just call out to me, I will show up," Ruka said, coming back through Darcy's desk.

"How do you know what to do all the time? Who are you?" I asked.

"Doofus. I promise I will tell you. Better yet, hopefully you will watch Delux have one of the strangest days of his life and you can judge from there."

"What?"

"Actually, you're going to see a lot of things, but trust me, I'll explain more later. We'll be together again, I promise."

"How do I know that?" I asked Ruka.

"I'm here now, aren't I?"

She was right. Like always.

"I'll get him to the beach next weekend."

"Good. Hopefully I will see you before that."

"What are you doing?" I asked.

"Finding Delux his next friend."

"Is the new friend going to replace Jobe?"

"Nothing can replace Jobe," Ruka said, walking away.

It seemed like it took forever, but the weekend was here before you knew it, and getting Delux to the beach was effortless.

Jobe was doing what she could to distract Delux, and keep his mind off of Ruka and I. Clair, a friend of Jobe's, would come over and they would all play music together. This weekend, they were all going to the beach.

"Ruka?" I thought out loud, trying to call her.

"How's it going, Doofus?" she asked, coming in through the wall.

"Where do you come from when you just appear like that?"

"It's hard to explain. Let's just say, I come from nothing that is everything at the same time. That's why I can hear you and find you."

"Can I do that?"

"When the time is right, I'll teach you. But right now… get to the beach and you'll see," Ruka said.

Now, I've gone to the beach a bunch of times with Delux. We have gone paddle boarding with friends, done drum circles, swimming in the sea and some relaxing on the sand… During all those beach days, not once did a random stranger come up to Delux and say, "Hey, you guys look really cool and look like the kind of people I want to attract into my life. My name is Devin, nice to meet you."

Devin handed Delux a business card with his photo on it, and it said he was in real estate. Delux was in no shape to buy a house, but he could always use a friend.

"I have a business card too. Let me grab it for you," Delux told him, jumping off the sea wall and going into his Jeep.

"Man I love your Jeep, your paddle boards, your drum. Man, you guys seem like a super cool vibe. What do you guys do if you don't mind me asking?"

"If I tell ya, I'd have to kill ya… I create stuff," Delux said, handing him his business card, laughing.

"DJ. Artist. Producer. This is a cool business card," Devin said.

"Thanks, I designed it myself. Those are my paintings there and my music is at the website listed if you like dancehall and hip hop."

"Man, I'm so glad I came up to talk to you guys," Devin said, walking off.

"And the job is done," Ruka said, coming out through the rocky sea wall.

"Who is this guy?" I asked.

"Not sure. He's some sort of people person."

“What's he got to do with Delux?”

“Not sure. It all depends on if they call each other or not.”

“Is that my next task?”

“No, you still need to make sure, no matter what, Delux keeps his job in corporate America.”

“Ruka, you've been to his office. He hates it there. He thought people were stealing from the company, and he's now finding out, it's true. He's not going to last long there.”

“Well, if we don't keep him working there, he's not going to last long, period.”

“What does that mean?” I said a bit fearful.

“He needs this job, more than he thinks. Oh, and Doofus… Remember to keep an eye on Jobe, she's up to something.”

CHAPTER 20

HOLE IN THE SKY

Feeling accomplished that Delux had made it to the beach to meet this random Devin guy, I sat home with Delux and Jobe watching Jobe paint, and Delux go through his records.

"Ok, I'll keep these records. This one is my mom's, these two are my sister's, and I will keep these because Buju Banton signed them, and these are my dub plates. I will always keep these."

"And the rest?"

"This is like a $15,000 vinyl collection or more. There're thousands of records here. Yeah some are trash, but a lot will be classics, and it's a complete collection from the best era of music. Someone will buy it. I'll sell the turntables too."

I was shocked. I never thought I would hear Delux say these things.

His vinyl collection was his everything. He was buying Dancehall and Reggae music that was pressed in the UK and shipped to Minnesota back in the day. Ruka said Delux was the director of a record pool with Prince's DJ, Brother Jules, who supplied him with half of his rare collection. After years of recording all of his vinyl records, song by song, instrumental by instrumental, a cappella by a cappella, he finally had it all backed up on a hard drive. But I still didn't understand. He always stated he loved the feel of vinyl. Why was he selling it all?

"The landlord said I can't renew the lease, so we need to find somewhere to live in a month," Delux told Jobe.

"I know of a place at a community farm that has a tree house we can stay in for only $200 a month."

Tree house?!? Ruka said something about a tree house... What was it?

"Fuck, I don't wanna sell all my music and turntables, but what am I going to do with all of this stuff if we go to Columbia?" Delux was trying to figure out.

"You can put them in storage. With the money we'll save splitting $200, verses $1200. You can afford a small storage place."

"But when we leave, then what? Keep paying for the storage unit while we're out of the country?"

Leave? I questioned. Where are they going? Where is Columbia? I was confused like Delux was when he found out Costa Rica was in Central America, and not off the east coast of Africa.

"Oh, that's how we can drive to Costa Rica?" Delux had said to Tess looking at the map flashed back into my head.

Was I not paying enough attention, and here I was, having a flashback to Tess. All the things Ruka had said to me started to go through my head. You been practicing your Spanish? Keep him working, no tree house, keep an eye on Jobe.

What did I miss? I felt I was missing something. Did Delux need to learn Spanish?

Over a year had gone by with the Jeep malfunctioning, and it was back in the shop again, for the same issue it had since he bought it. The dealership gave Delux a nice rental SUV with unlimited miles free of charge while his Jeep was in the shop.

"We should drive somewhere with this fancy thing," Delux said talking about the rental car.

"Ok, but this weekend, we have the event I'm modeling at."

"After the event, I'll take time off of work and let's go surprise our families."

"Oh, that's a great idea," Jobe said in excitement.

The weekend came and I jumped into the rental car with them to see what this event was all about. Jobe was going to be a person lying on a table receiving a massage by a woman showing people how to massage with proper technique. There was a lot going on at this event with yoga and massage demonstrations, exhibits of natural medicines, with books, and other things I couldn't make sense of. There was a raffle at the event, and Delux bought two tickets from a small man with a big smile who was eager to sell. Everything seemed bright and glowing in that place.

"It's you! You ghostly hunk of see through burning plasma," Ruka said, startling me.

"Ruka, what the…?"

"Now I see why I spent all those years humping you. Do you remember?"

"Of course, I remember. Every time I started to win a wrestling match with you, you had to hump me."

"And every other time as well. Doofus, you are hot in that ghostly body of yours."

"Ruka, I think we're in a church right now."

"I don't think they give massage demo's at a church, Doofus."

"Well, they are at this one."

The event carried on, and when the raffle started, Delux won a prize.

"Are you ready for this, Doofus?" Ruka asked me.

"Ready for what?" I followed him to the prize table where the same little man who sold him the ticket, was there with the same big smile.

"Ah, you won."

"Yes."

"Pick anything that interests you on the table here. May I suggest this book."

"Mmm. Thanks, but I think I will take the massage here. Thank you." And Delux walked away.

"I think he should have taken that book. Delux should pick the book," I said.

"Keep watching, Doofus," Ruka tells me.

Jobe was still doing her part of the demo when after several other people had won the same raffle, Delux's other ticket was called, so walked up to the table.

"You again," the little man said excitedly. "May I suggest this book?"

"Mmmmm... No thank you. I have a girlfriend, so I'll take the other massage, and give it to her."

"Excuse me, sir," the little man said.

"Do you happen to have any more tickets?"

"No, that was my last one."

"God is talking to me right now and he is telling me that this book is meant for you. Are you sure about your choice?"

"Well, I want the massage for my girlfriend and you probably just want $10 more dollars out of me for another ticket because I won twice… so…"

"God is telling me this book is for you," the little man repeated.

I had never seen a man so convinced of something. I watched Delux's bullshit meter go through the roof with this guy. The guy was nice and had a nice smile, but what was he talking about, "God was speaking to him?" I thought I was God, having a dog experience because things are backwards?

"Wait, what did I just say?" Where's Ruka?

Delux handed the little guy at the raffle table ten dollars more for a ticket, and I watched the little man put the ticket into the bowl. I watched someone else mix the bowl up. Then someone else picked the tickets. That bowl was full. There's no way Delux would win again I thought.

"Hey, Ruka," I thought out loud to find her.

"Boo! My boo," Ruka said biting my back leg but just going through me.

"Look at this little man here. He says God is talking to him, telling him that Delux needs a book. Can that be true?" I asked her.

"That Delux needs this book, or that God is talking to that little guy over there?"

"Both."

"Well, let's see if he wins."

"What are the odds? There's a whole bowl full of tickets still needing to be drawn," I said.

"When it's meant to be, the odds, don't matter. Doofus, you got Delux to the beach, and I got Devin to meet Delux at the same time. The odds of that are what need to be questioned. Besides who cares if he wins or not, the money donated should be going to a good cause."

"And the winner is..." the announcer shouted out...

Not Delux.
They announced some more winners... none of them were Delux, and his odds of that book still being on the table were slim with the three new winners. A number was drawn and they were not in the room. They called the number several times but the winner was nowhere to be found. So, the girl stuck her hand into the bowl to pick out another number, she handed it to the announcer, who called out Delux's newly bought ticket.

"See, I told you this book was for you," the title guy said with a smile as Delux walked up to the table of prizes.

"Ok. I'll take the book," Delux said, walking away with his new book and two massages.

I always watched Delux. I learned how to read the room and situations because of him. Watching him pay attention to detail was incredible. It was hard to catch him do it, but once you saw what he was doing when he does it, you will see, he was doing the room scanning thing all the time.
He looked around the building for Jobe seeing the demo was now over. He was excited to tell her about the things they'd won.

"What's the book about?"

"I don't know. It's called the *72 Names of God,* and it came with this deck of cards. Plus, look, two massages we can use once we get back from our trip."

"Nice. This is going to be fun."

I couldn't find anything wrong or different about Jobe. It seemed like she loved Delux and maybe Ruka was wrong about her? Ruka is never wrong I thought and kept on watching but she cared for Delux deeply it seemed and he was on his own free will.

Right before we left for the road trip, someone finally called Delux and offered to buy his record collection. They offered only $400 for it, and Delux took it not knowing what life was going to bring him next. He'd lost his dogs, and he could not renew his lease on a house that suited him. His car was in the shop again, his girlfriend wanted to move to the jungles of Columbia, live in a treehouse and become a shaman, and he just sold his lifelong record collection for peanuts. Things were getting heavy for Delux to process. He was losing all that he knew. He wanted a normal life, but what did normal even look like for him and what was it gonna cost him?

Delux went to his 8 to 5. He was far from a shaman, and he had no clue what he would do in Colombia once he was there. His records and one turntable were now gone, and it seemed like part of his soul was missing when he walked into his studio and saw how empty it was.

Then, someone else lined up to buy the other turntable the following week. Delux was letting go of everything that made him, Delux. I was disappointed he was making these decisions. I tried to understand but I couldn't get my head around why he was getting rid of what he loved the most.

"It's because he lost us, Doofus. He truly loved us the most, and now he's lost without us."

"Ruka. Damn you always scare the crap outta me when you just pop in like that."

"Hahaha, it's called karma for all the times you jumped on me while I was blind in the RV."

"You always talked about how you could see without your eyes."

"I still can see without my eyes. Are you ready for this road trip?"

"How did you know about the trip?"

"Because I told you, I can still see without my eyes."

We left the next morning early. Ruka joined us and we all rode up to Jobe's family first. Delux met her brother, her mom who she didn't get along with so well, and her uncles. Everyone welcomed Delux into the family. Delux and Jobe went for a skateboard ride, while her family made fun of them for using such long skateboards. They swam in the pool and enjoyed barbecue that I wish I could have tried.

"Ruka, I miss BBQ."

"Yeah me, too."

Jobe's uncle had a small heart attack while they were there and needed to be rushed to the hospital. We were able to check in on him the next day, and he had a lot to say.

"Go live your life, follow your dreams, and do what's on that bucket list of yours because you never know," Uncle said, and the room agreed. "You never know when it is your time, so go do all the things you want to. Find a way," he said, looking right at Delux.

I could tell the way Jobe looked at Delux, she was thinking about Colombia.

"Delux is not going to Colombia. We have to get him to Costa Rica," Ruka said.

"What? Costa Rica? Again? Not Colombia? Ruka, you gotta tell me what's going on."

"Doofus, can it wait until the ride home?"

"What are you hiding, Ruka?"

"You know how I can see without my eyes."

"No, but tell me more."

"I saw Delux in a treehouse, and he dies there," Ruka told me.

"I'm sure he'll build a treehouse with his own hands once he's in Columbia. He will get old, and die there. That is a great way to go, don't you think?"

"He's not old when it happens."

"How does it happen, Ruka?"

"It's not clear. I have to see something first."

"See what?"

"I'm not sure, Doofus," Ruka said, concerned.

We got to Minnesota, and it was more pools, more BBQ's, and more kids running around yelling and screaming. Delux's sister had more kids now and the family was getting bigger. It was keeping Delux beautifully distracted from recently losing all that he loved.

"What are you gonna do?" his mom asked after hearing he wanted to quit his 8-5 job.

"I don't know, I'll figure something out. I always do."

"That you do. I'm just worried about you," she told him.

"I'll be fine, Mom," Delux said, convincing himself he was going to Colombia with Jobe.

Later that night, Jobe and Delux went out front, into the rental car to smoke one of their pre-rolled blunts Jobe rolled up before they left.

"Babe, I was reading that book we won at that thing you did, and it's crazy," Delux mentioned.

"How so?"

"So, a long time ago, when I lived in my RV, I got super sick and just floated around the internet all day for a week until I felt better. One day I came across a video of a guy in Las Vegas who could call UFO's."

"What? Was it real?"

"I thought so. It was like some 'Strange news of the week' special the local news station was doing, and they found a guy who could talk to aliens."

"Did it work?"

"Yeah, it worked. Or they faked it really well some said. I looked for other videos debunking what he did, and some said he sent up a balloon, but it had to be a big balloon, and it went side to side, in and out of a cloud, so I don't know."

"Wow, crazy."

"The news people were shocked, I was shocked and guess what..."

"What?"

"The guy on YouTube called himself the same name as this book says, is the name of god."

"What's the name of god?"

"This book said the letters YHWH, and that was the name the guy on YouTube used."

"That's crazy."

"Yeah. How come I remember watching that video years ago, and now I got this book that some little man said, God said I needed to have it?"

"It does seem like a lot of strange coincidences. What's the book about again?"

"Something about meditating on some symbols that they put together to manifest things into your life."

"Huh… And the guy at the center said you needed to have it?"

"He said god said I should have it. The first part of the book, tells a story of a wizard man who steals a kid's soul from god using 10 of the towns biggest thieves and crooks to break the kid's soul out of heaven. They used the name, YHWH. We should try," Delux mentioned.

"Try what? What do we do?"

"I don't know. Let's close our eyes, meditate, and ask the universe for a sign it exists, by sending us a light orb from space. That's what the YouTube guy did."

"Okay, let's close our eyes and try."

"Ruka, what are these two doing? What do they expect to see?"

"Not sure, but this is what I came here to see."

"What do you mean? You knew this was going to happen?"

"Not exactly," she told me.

Jobe and Delux both closed their eyes for a few minutes then opened them and looked out of the sunroof of the rental car, into the heavens that were filled with millions of stars on a dark night.

"If something happens in the next minute from them doing this, we need to step up our timeline," Ruka said seriously, looking up at the stars.

"Do you see anything?" Delux asked Jobe.

"Nothing but stars. You can see so many here."

"What's going to happen, Ruka? I don't think people can call UFO's," I said, looking out the sunroof at the nighttime sky with them.

"It's not a UFO that's gonna answer," Ruka calmly said.

A "holy shit" and a scream came next, followed by heavy breathing from Jobe.

Delux remained calm but was utterly surprised.

"Ruka! Did you see that?" I asked just as shocked as Jobe.

"Shit," Ruka replied, disappointed.

"I saw something! Holy shit, I saw something! Ruka what the heck was that?" I asked looking at Delux.

"What did you see?" Delux asked with eyes full of wonder towards Jobe.

"A hole just opened up like an eye right above your parents' house, the size of the house. It had every color going every which way inside of the hole that was lined with a thin black line, and a silver lining. What the fuck was that?!?" Jobe asked crying and trying to hold herself together.

"I saw the same thing. The colors, they were everywhere. The thin black and silver lining on the outside. It just opened and shut. What the fuck was that?" Delux questioned.

I saw the same thing as them. I felt like it was something, and it looked right at us all.

"What was that?" I asked Ruka.

"That, was the sign I was shown before Delux passed away. Time is running out, Doofus. Your death came too soon, and it changed the timetables."

"Who told you about the sign?"

"You did."

"No I didn't."

"The real version of you did."

"Real version? Ruka what are you talking about?"

"You, choose not to remember Dog, and because you're 'dead' now, I can remind you without any repercussions, I think."

"Repercussions?"

"I'm what you call, a helper. I help souls, your soul, here, to move through this realm and some of its experiences."

"What? I don't get it."

"You know you can stop being Doofus anytime."

"Ruka. What are you talking about? You sound so... weird."

"It's because you still don't remember Dog. You chose to come here to help Delux move his soul through this experience, Why, I don't know. That's on you. I am the safety switch for when things go wrong, because they always do, like your cancer."

"Safety switch? If you were sent here to help me, why do you hate Rottweilers so much?"

"Doofus, that's your next question?" Ruka said laughing at me. "Like I said. I would know it's you if I didn't want to kill you the first time I smelled you. It's part of the safety switch."

"I remember that first day outside Big Man's house. Him yelling at my little friend to go back inside. Setting me on the ground in front of you all."

"You peeing on yourself," Ruka reminded me.

"Yeah, I did pee on myself a lot, didn't I?"

"You were broken, and scared. Dog, you send me here every time, for you to succeed in your mission. Things have gotten out of whack because of your quick onset of cancer, so things are trying to change."

"What things? What does it mean?"

"It means the devil is real, but so are we. Since you still can't remember what I'm talking about, keep Delux working that 8 to 5, and I will take care of the devil. There's a way I think, but it involves another person, and honestly, I don't like how it looked in the dream."

"Wait, all this that we are doing is based off a dream?"

"Life is but a dream, Doofus. It's all you give me to work with, Dog. I'll be back," Ruka said fading away out of the vehicle.

"Life is but a dream," I said to myself, debating if I could chew on the back door of the car we were in.

Where is my mind? I asked myself. I was there, listening to Delux and Jobe try to figure out what they saw that night because it was not what Delux saw on Youtube.

That weekend, Delux left his parents wondering if their son was okay after he told them he and Jobe opened up a hole in the sky above the house.

The entire drive back to Miami was them debating their reality. We were all convinced that we saw the same thing. Jobe talked about their experience to the Mystery School teacher, and he advised them to never try that again, and gave Delux a different book to read.

"What is it with people giving me books, and telling me they're for me?" Delux asked.

"Read it," the teacher said.

"What do you think?" Delux asked Jobe in the car leaving the mystery school.

"I don't know what to think. What did we do that night?"

"I don't know. Maybe we can ask this Crystal Skull fella next week that everyone is so excited about," Delux said sarcastically.

"The skulls not a joke, babe," Jobe told him, defending the crystal that was not even here yet.

I ♥
N Y.

CHAPTER 21

A SPIRIT NAMED PANCHO

Delux always had a skeptic side of him that liked to ask a lot of questions.

"Where's this skull from?"

"Mexico."

"And some guy is just driving around with it?"

"Yes."

"How big is it?"

"It's like a skull size, maybe bigger."

While Jobe was away one afternoon, Delux looked up on the internet anything he could about crystal skulls. Some people say they're real, others say they're not. Then he found out the people that said the skulls were real, later apologized and said they were not as old as they thought they were, but still amazing.

"And why is this skull coming here to our school?"

"I don't know, but the guy is telling his story about it. It should be interesting, keep an open mind," Jobe said.

Following Delux to work was boring. His days there were busy, and the same over and over again. The only thing that changed was what he was having for lunch, but he always snacked on the same chips, soda, and chocolate bar late in the afternoon for that last minute burst of energy.

The Jeep was back in our life, so my seat next to Delux was more exciting on the way there at least. I was sitting on the seat again, and not floating in-between it, or on the ground like a lost ghost. I couldn't believe I was a ghost, and we were going to see a crystal skull from Mexico. If I'm confused about all this in this afterlife, I can't even imagine how Delux is feeling. You could see on Delux's face, he wasn't interested in this skull thing.

The room was full of hippie ladies in white, holding crystals in their hands, with a few guys who only ate blueberries for breakfast and legumes for lunch. Delux wasn't going to be fooled. While everyone else was clamoring over this skull, Delux stood back and just looked at it and observed everyone in the room.

The story went, some grandma apparently had this rose quartz, hollowed out, two inch thick, rustic looking crystal skull, tucked away in her closet. When she died, she put in her will, that her grandson Darlo was to get it. Darlo, not knowing what to do with the skull, decided to take it to the safety of a local safety deposit box in his area. It was a big skull, so he needed a big box he thought.

As Darlo drove with the skull in the back seat of his car, the skull began to talk to him. The skull told Darlo that Darlo needed to show the skull to the world. As the skull was talking to Darlo, the skull said his name. Darlo called him Pancho for short because he thought nobody could easily say the name the skull called itself.

When the skull was with us in the room that night, it wasn't talking. It was just sitting on the floor where grown women were bowing to it, crying, and pushing their own crystals, closer to him.

"Please don't touch him," Darlo said to everyone.

That's how the skull ended up in South Florida that week. Darlo was on a skull showing tour with rooms full of 6 to12 people who like rocks. I was trying to figure it all out. Why were these people so excited for this thing? Delux was even hired to DJ a birthday party with Pancho on his DJ table next to his mixer. The party was soon over, we drove back home, and Jobe couldn't hold in her excitement.

"There's going to be a big event held in Miami for Pancho."

"An event, cool," Delux said, driving us home.

I could tell a lot was on Delux's mind, but I couldn't get inside it no matter how hard I tried. He was a robot now. Go to work. Go home and do what Jobe was doing or had planned for them. Repeat. Weekend is here, go to the beach, go to some event praising the four directions. Repeat, then go back to work...
Delux was now going to some strange events with Jobe.
Some were filled with women where Delux and two other guys sat in a hole dug in the sand meditating, others where everyone sat around a fire and people were eating weird plants. Delux was always opening one eye, looking around at what the heck he was taking part in while saying no to any of the plants that went around.
When the skull event rolled around, Delux was giving a drum lesson with another guy to a group of people in a big circle. I loved when Delux played the drum. Even as a ghost I could feel the vibrations of his drum in my spirit, or soul, or whatever I am at the moment.
I looked at my paws. "What am I? Who am I? Why is Ruka calling me Dog at times and not Doofus?"

"You rang," Ruka popped in.

"No," I told her.

"Ahh, what's going on here?" she asked, looking around at the large crowd of people.

"Delux. Darlo wants to talk to you," the mystery school teacher abruptly interrupted the drum circle walking through my invisible self, interrupting my paw gazing.

"Tell him I'm busy teaching a lesson."

"He wants you to carry Pancho out through the closing ceremony."

"I thought you were gonna to do it?"

"Pancho spoke to him and wants you," he said.

Delux knew that was hard for him to say.

The teacher knew Delux could care less about that skull, and here Darlo was asking for Delux, and not him. The teacher was the one responsible for all of us experiencing this skull in the first place.

"Doofus. This next part was going to happen whether Delux wanted it to happen or not."

"Ruka, you stink. Where were you before you just came here?"

"I was watching a guy drink away his miseries after his girlfriend just cheated on him, and his job is screwing him over on a contract they signed. I'm trying to get him to help us with Delux."

"What?"

"Ghost stuff, Doofus. How's our boy doing?"

"He's about to carry this crystal skull thing that talks to people, through a crowd of people."

"Oh this is going to be good. Let's get closer," Ruka told me.

We followed Delux to the table that the skull was resting on. It was sitting on a light, to show the hollowness of it, facing outward towards the crowd. Delux looked at Darlo who was across the room talking to someone. When Darlo and Delux made eye contact, Darlo nodded his head and pointed down like it was okay for Delux to pick up the skull. Delux went to grab it and realized it was heavier than it looked. He adjusted his footing and tried again, picking up the skull, then carefully turning the skull in his arms to face outward towards the crowd.

"Anyone can touch it?" this young girl asked Delux as he turned around with the skull.

"No, he wants me to carry it through the closing ceremony that's happening now I guess."

"Can I touch it?" she asked, looking up at Delux, holding the skull.

Delux looked towards Darlo who was still distracted with someone.

"I've seen him let people touch it, so sure, you can touch it while I hold it," Delux said to her.

"In three, two, one," Ruka counted down.

"What?" I said, looking at Ruka.

"Look at Delux," she told me.

"What's the matter with him?" Seeing he was clearly in a different state of mind at the moment than when he grabbed the skull.

"He's in a trance triggered by that girl with her earrings, and the spirit inside that skull."

"Earrings? Spirit inside the skull? Do I need to bite someone?"

"Doofus, this is the last attempt, Spirit is using to get Delux to 'see'. If we don't get him to 'wake up', he may be gone to the 8 to 5 forever."

"I thought you wanted me to keep him at the 8 to 5?"

"Pay attention to Delux." Ruka motioned.

"He looks asleep," I said, watching him hold the skull with the girl holding her hands up to the skull.

"Ruka, look at that, she has the same symbol on her earrings as the tattoo on Delux's neck."

"Now you're paying attention, Doofus," Ruka told me.

"I think so," I replied as time began to slow down.

Delux was standing right there in front of me, but I could see he was somewhere else in his mind. The young girl stepped aside, and Delux began to walk slowly with the skull in his two hands, holding it against his belly. His eyes were shut, but he was walking the path just fine.

"Ruka, he's barefoot walking on rocks. How is he able to do that with his sensitive feet?"

"He's no longer here with us, Doofus. He doesn't even feel the rocks under his feet right now."

"Will he be back?" I asked looking right at Delux.

"Let's see," Ruka told me, following him.

I was confused. Delux made his way through the crowd, and out of the property to the parking lot where he seemed to wake up, confused like me.

"Oh my god. What the fuck?" Delux said looking down at his surroundings seemingly coming back to himself.

"What's the matter?" Jobe asked him surrounded by Darlo, the teacher and his wife.

"How did I get out here?"

"You walked. Just now. What are you talking about?" Jobe asked looking at him puzzled.

"Holy shit, some old man was talking to me just now," Delux said, wiping a tear that had ran down his cheek.

"Here," he said handing Darlo the skull. "What the fuck was that? Did someone drug me? Am I on drugs?" Delux asked, looking at his hands.

Darlo put the skull in a towel and then into a cooler in the back seat of his car haphazardly.

"That's how you keep it?" Delux asked, seeming more than concerned.

"Yeah, why? It's okay," Darlo said.

"No. Something bad is going to happen to the skull. We have to protect it. You, have to protect it."

Now that sounded like crazy talk coming from Delux. One minute he doesn't give a shit about that skull and now he's freaking out, that it needs to be protected and not just tossed around in a cooler with a towel.

"It's fine. This is how I've been traveling with him. I keep him safe," Darlo reassured.

Delux didn't sit well with this moment he was having.

"Him, or whatever that is inside that skull, just spoke to me and I saw it damaged, lost, and then destroyed. It said it needs proper protection. What the fuck? I was just talking to some old guy I swear, we were floating through time which looked like everything running together... How did I get out here? Holy shit," Delux said, looking around confused and distraught.

"He's fine how he is, trust me. Come on. Let's enjoy the party," Darlo said, turning Delux around and walking the group back into the event.

"Ruka, you think that skull really talked to Delux?"

"I know it did. The question is, did it work?"

"Did what work?"

"The awakening."

"How will we know?"

"Only time will tell us, and we don't have much. Keep Delux working and keep an eye on Jobe. I gotta go check in on the drunk guy in LA."

"Who's the drunk guy in LA?"

"A fallen angel who met the devil, and her crew of assholes. He used to work for Delux's father a long time ago, and there's some type of message or something, I can't quite put a paw on it, so I'm going back to figure it out."

Ruka was gone and I was alone out by car and the skull that said nothing to me.

"Doofus, one last thing. Try to get back home before Delux drives there. Use your mind to think you're there, before you're there, if you know what I mean."

Before I could ask her how to do that, she was gone. Who's this guy in LA, I wondered. Life was easier when I was alive and just a dog. I just had to look at Delux, and I could tell what was going to happen. I wag my tail... He pets me. He's going to the bathroom, follow him. He's putting on a shirt, that means we're going somewhere. He opens his wallet, that too means we are going somewhere. Now, I had no idea what was going on.

When we left, I tried to put myself back into the house like Ruka asked me to. I thought about it, nothing. I pictured the inside how I last saw it with the surfboards, the records, the tubes of paint on the floor and paintings leaning against the wall, Ruka's old pillow sitting next to the side door in the kitchen, and nothing, I was still standing in the parking lot.

"Shoot, the pillow's no longer there, neither are the records," I thought.

I pictured Ruka still lying there waiting to go outside to play. I took a deep breath and pictured everything inside the house again as I closed my eyes. As I exhaled, I tried to let go of everything in my mind. Where I was, and what was happening around me. I took another breath and on the second exhale, I started to feel something pull away inside me in the slightest way. I found myself in the house, next to Ruka's pillow that slowly faded away as I got there.

"I did it!" I said excited.

I was back at the house. Thirty minutes later Delux and Jobe show up after their event.

Weekend fun time was over, and it was time to go back to work tomorrow. I don't even work, but tagging along with Delux felt like work when we get to his office. Delux wore a shirt and tie at work. He sat up front and he was the face of the company when people came in the front door, but they rarely did.

It was not his job to go to the back of the building and help people who needed help, but he would randomly do it anyways because he hated sitting at his desk all day.

Today, a stranger out back needed help. Delux was reluctant to help him, but decided to anyways even though it was outside of his, "authorized work".

"Man, where did you come from?"

"Right over there through that door. You need some help?"

"Yes, please."

"No worries, this gets me away from my desk. Cool surf stickers on your truck there, you surf?" Delux asked looking at his truck.

"When I can. Last week I was surfing the best waves of my life in Costa Rica. Some of the set waves were almost double over head and trying to kill me."

"That sounds crazy. I've never surfed waves higher than my knees," Delux said to him laughing. "I'm going to need you to sign this piece of paper for me, saying what just happened back here," Delux instructed him.

"Yeah, no problem."

"Cool, thanks. It's protocol."

"I get it," the man said.

Delux looked down at the piece of paper as the man started to walk away.

"Wait, your name is Trinidad?"

"Yeah."

"For real?"

"Yeah."

"And you just told me about Costa Rica?" Delux said confused.

"Yeah, why?"

"Man, you got time for a story"?

"You just saved me time, I got time. Tell me," he said enthusiastically.

"Long story short, I was on my way to Trinidad, the country, to DJ a party, when I got stuck in Miami. There, I met a South African super model who punched me in the face for something I did a while back to her ferrets, it's a long story, but then two months later that same model surprised me on New Year's Day in Minnesota, in an old RV she bought from a gangster who was slanging glass pipes and drugs out of it in Miami. She met me for one week, and decided to drive across the country to help me move. My point is, her plan was to drive that RV to Costa Rica. I only met her because I was going to Trinidad. Your name is Trinidad, and you just told me about Costa Rica, so.... In my reality, I think that's weird, no?"

"You lived in an RV with a super model?"

"Yeah. Like the size of that van over there. I lived with her and two big dogs, one of them was blind."

"Sounds fun."

"The fun part is, you're another 'Trinidad', and you just told me about Costa Rica. That's a fucking sign," Delux said hating his job.

"I'm telling you man, this beach in Costa Rica is called Playa ********. It's magical, man. You should go visit. I can hook you up with a local guy I met there for a nice place to stay. He even has my surfboard. I'll tell him to let you use it," Trinidad said.

What is it with Trinidad and Costa Rica that Delux felt was speaking to him? He gets this way when something from his past comes back around and shows itself again.
Delux noticed 'Trinidad', happen twice and both times it involved Costa Rica.

"I can't go to Costa Rica, I'm going to Colombia," Delux said to himself walking back into where his desk was located.

I could see the wheels in his head spinning as he watched the clock, waiting for 5 o'clock to roll around. He was lost. From losing us and selling everything in a matter of weeks. His entire life was changing in every moment that ticked by.

"What am I gonna to do in Colombia?" he said out loud, sitting at his desk zoning out into his computer.

Delux sat at his desk pretending like he cared about his job, while he was working on a strategy to get out of it, and still have enough money until something else comes along. It was risky, but Delux took risks. His dogs were gone, even though I was sitting right in front of him. He didn't have to take care of anything anymore to distract himself, from himself. I didn't know him before the RV, but maybe he lost himself when he changed his life with Tess. Her Costa Rica plan was not his plan.

Now it's happening again, only this time, Delux was getting rid of everything that makes Delux who he is, and going to a place he didn't want to go with Jobe.

I remembered when he first brought me to work, he was full of love and life. I could see he was a bit emptier now. Looking back, he always seemed happier the further back you looked. Jobe was there for him, but maybe not enough for what he needed. He had the time now with Ruka and I gone to see who he really is, he was just distracted from seeing that with all of Jobe's plans. Maybe Ruka and I held him back a bit because he always needed to be there to feed us and take us outside. Maybe he did need to let everything go again and start over… Ruka would tell me that all the time, "just start over." Delux was good at starting over

"What would I tell you?" Ruka said, bursting into the office.

"Dang, Doofus, I wish this Darcy lady could see you sitting right next to her."

"Ruka. She's back. Yea," I said without excitement or getting up.

"Doofus, are you peeing in here?" Ruka asked, sniffing the chair Darcy was sitting in.

"I pee on Darcy every day. Look at her. She's always on her cellphone, and never wants to answer the office phone."

"Doofus, you've been in this office too much. Go out. Explore a little bit," Ruka said, peeing on Darcy's chair as well.

"Delux is lost, Ruka. He's become a robot at work. I don't know what to do. We're just here, working his life away in an office he hates while he waits for Jobe to decide what they're gonna do."

"I told you to keep him working, and keep an eye in Jobe. She's up to something no good."

"She smelled different the other day," I recalled.

"Ahh good, you are starting to smell things again."

"I also was able to leave the car, and get home before them like you asked."

"My gosh, Dog, any more good news?"

"Delux is starting to be a people pleaser in his office."

"That means he has something up his sleeve he is about to pull."

"He truly hates it here. What the employees are doing to this company is sad, to be honest."

"Try to get in his head. He needs to go home early tonight."

"Why?"

"Just get him home early, you'll see."

"Ruka, you got something against telling me all the details? I feel there's something you're not telling me."

"You're right, Doofus. There is something I'm not telling you. I'm not telling you because I think we can stop it. I think we can fix it."

"Fix what?" I asked confused but ready.

"Remember when Delux got that book *72 Names of God*?"

"Yes. The book he won, then him and Jobe opened a hole in the sky with it."

"He didn't open anything. The universe revealed itself to Delux, because Delux is that universe, just like you and I. We all are. We all hold some type of key that can open doors to witness it, it seems like he's got a real key that can."

"Like when he saw the future of me choking before I was choking?" I asked.

"Yes. And there are types of powers, or people, that want to keep these kinds of key-holding, door-opening people, shut. So keep Delux working here."

"This makes no sense. He hates working here."

"Here is not really here. Here is only temporary."

"Here is not really here? Ruka, what the hell does that mean?"

Ruka was gone. I was just as lost as Delux was.

Four-thirty came around and Delux was determined to get to the bottom of something in a file cabinet. He was in and out of one secure office, to another, locking the doors behind him every time. I didn't know what he was looking for, but he was looking for something.

"Dad. Go home. Do this tomorrow," I said facing him, looking over his desk as he organized a stack of files into two piles.

He ignored me with his intent focus, to getting the job done. He always looked up at the clock this time of day, but his gaze was at the task at hand. The phone rang. Darcy was in the bathroom, never failed this time of day. Delux answered it, got distracted helping someone on the other line, and then went right back to what he'd been doing.

5:00.

All the ladies left for the day. They said goodbye and walked right through me as I sat there looking at Delux, trying to get his attention.

"Yo, Delux! We gotta go! Ruka said so. She wouldn't tell me why. But she said we gotta go. Lets go!" I barked out and spun in a circle in front of his desk.

"Ruka!" I called out.

Where was she now when things didn't go how she needed them to? I tried to send myself home to check on Jobe. All I needed to do was use my mind. "I got this," I said, struggling to teleport myself.

When I opened my eyes, I was now in the living room of the house. The house was empty. Jobe wasn't here. She was always here. I decided to wait here instead of going back to Delux and his files.

"Ruka?" I called out.

Still nothing.

I didn't need her anyways. I was just bored sitting in the empty house. Maybe I should go explore but I'd already seen everything around here.

"But you haven't seen inside people houses. Dude, some people live like animals," Ruka said walking into the house.

"We are animals... or we were," I said lying on the floor where the pillow used to be.

"No, I mean people live like pigs. A lot of people are disgusting."

"Yeah... I don't want to see that."

"You don't know what you're missing. You know how many people have sex the same way we do. We should start a question: What came first, doggie style with dogs, or with humans?" Ruka asked.

"Wouldn't it be called human style if it was humans first?" I asked.

"How you doing, Doofus? You seem down?"

"You got me worried about Delux."

"Look, don't worry. All we can do in this life is try. You got me, and I have some answers."

"Answers that you can't share with me."

"The teacher doesn't tell the student the answers, while the student is still learning."

"What?"

"I gotta go. Jobe is coming home. Use that big nose of yours and find out what she's been up to," Ruka said fading away.

Ruka was gone out the wall, and the sound of Jobe's car door shutting happened at the same time.

"I swear I feel like I am dreaming."

Jobe walked in the house with a pizza and beers in her hand. For a lesbian, she sure knew how to make a straight male happy. Out of habit, I greeted her like I always do, but I fell right through her after jumping up. I don't think I actually cared enough to let her feel me. She seemed weird today, but I didn't know if it was because Ruka was trying to make me see her in a bad way or what. She started to roll a blunt when Delux finally came home.

"Hey babe, how was your day?" she asked, handing him a blunt.

"Ahh, thanks," Delux said leaning in to give Jobe a kiss.

"Why does your face smell like pussy?"

"What? No, it doesn't," she said cupping her face and sniffing in.

Delux leaned in to kiss her again and smell her face. "I know pussy, and your face smells like pussy."

"No way. That's impossible."

"Anything you want to tell me? Remember, I told you you can be honest with me. I'd rather you be honest than lie."

"I'm not lying. I don't know what you're talking about."

Delux leaned in again and took a smell.

"Yeah, that's pussy, but ok."

"Ohh my god, stop," Jobe said laughing the situation off.

I could tell Delux didn't want to argue. I knew when he knew he was right, and after I leaned in and got a whiff myself, he was right. Her face smelled like another woman, and she lied right to Delux's face about it.
Wait, how did I just smell Jobe?

"It's not pussy. Stop acting crazy. Look I got us a pizza and some beers. I figured we'd chill inside tonight maybe paint a little. What do you think?"

Again… Another woman who was lying to Delux. Why did this keep happening once he was so invested in the relationship?

"Because he hasn't yet taken time for himself to see who he really is," Ruka popped back in to tell me.

"Darlo invited us to New York. He wants you to present the crystal skull to the Mayan elders," Jobe said, changing the conversation.

"Doofus, you'll wanna go on that trip. It involves a plane so master your ghost skills," Ruka advised me then left again.

"What? Why me? That means I have to take time off of work," Delux asked, unhappy.

"Well, it's over the weekend, so maybe just take Friday off. Darlo really wants you to be there?"

Delux was annoyed. He was trying to get to a root of a problem at work and taking a day off to spend the weekend in New York with a crystal rock was not part of his plan.

"Look for tickets, and I'll request time off tomorrow," Delux added.

Jobe believed he was excited, but I could read right through it. He wasn't. He knew she just lied to him, and he chose to let it go.

New York was some special event with the calendar reading a bunch of 10's or something like that. I mastered my ghost skills and was able to fly on the plane just fine without falling through and losing Delux. I had to sit in the aisle, or sit on someone... I chose the aisle and just let everyone walk through me. When we got to the event center, Delux saw the skull again for the first time since he held it.

"Darlo. What happened to the skull?" Delux asked in shock.

"Oh, I dropped it while handing it across the table to someone."

"You never let people touch it I thought?"

"She was cute and I was a little drunk," Darlo said.

"Darlo, I told you this thing told me it would break, be lost or destroyed or something like that, and now here it is with the jaw broken?"

"It was an accident," Darlo stated and walked away.

Delux was disappointed and confused with his reality. Did that skull really talk to him like he says it did? Most of the people here had some type of skull they said was old and ancient. All the skulls looked homemade or like they would be used in a voodoo ritual except for Pancho. Pancho was the real deal I felt after seeing Delux's reaction to holding it, his story, and what I can see now with the broken jaw. Is this why Ruka wanted me to go? To see the future unfold? I didn't get it. If she knew something, why wasn't she telling me?

"Watch out, don't look at it. It can fly across the room and break your jaw or something terrible," some Indiana Jones looking man said. He was holding his hand over a pouch attached to his side, that was holding a baseball sized object in the pouch.

"I just wanna see it. Can I see it?" a woman begged.

"It's dangerous. I have seen it fly around the room and blind people. If you look at it, it can be triggered and go out of control," the man who owned it said mysteriously.

I could see Delux read the room, and he concluded this is where all the crazy people were gathered listening to this guy.

"Don't look at it," Jones said again, holding a crystal sphere to a lady's forehead.

She began to shake. Then cry. Then shake and cry.
The man rubbed the crystal ball that could kill people, all over her back, and she lost it. It looked like she was having an orgasm or something the way she was screaming and crying. Delux walked out of the room in fear of being hypnotized. I could tell he couldn't wait for it all to be over.
Delux presented the crystal skull to a short guy the people in the room were calling a Mayan elder. I was in a room full of people, some who claimed to see spirits, yet none of them saw me. I peed on the center podium just to make sure, and yeah, nobody here saw me here.
People talked, some shared stories, and then it was over. Just like that, a total waste of time. I saw a woman pull Delux aside, and tell him something, but by the time I got there, she'd disappeared into the crowd.

"Except now we know what the skull said to Delux was true," Ruka said while popping in and walking next to me. "It's about to get real, Doofus."

"Whatever you say, Ruka," I said in frustration not knowing what Ruka knew, or what this lady had just said to Delux.

Delux flew home Sunday night dealing with the thought that he really was shown the future when he held the skull and it came true. Jobe stayed a few extra days in New York with the Mystery School teacher and his wife who were presenting the skull at some more places around New York City with Darlo.
Wednesday when Jobe returned, she had horrible news. "Darlo lost the Crystal Skull."

"What? No way!?! It was true then, what I was told by it," Delux said in utter disbelief.

"Yeah. Darlo left the skull in the back of a taxi cab, thinking he was going to a party full of women. The taxi left with the skull still in the back seat. When Darlo realized he left the cooler with skull in it, it was too late. They tried to call the cab company, but they could not figure out who was his driver. The skull was gone. "

"So Delux was right. The skull was broken, and now lost," I said to Ruka who was sitting where her pillow used to be.

"Yep."

"What does it all mean?" I asked

"Hopefully Delux wakes up and can see that there's more to life than an 8 to 5 job, a home with a fence, and a cheating woman behind it."

"How does all this relate to that?"

"Hopefully he now sees there's more to this world than he can ever begin to understand or imagine."

"So if there's more to life than an 8 to 5, why do you want me to make sure Delux keeps on working his 8 to 5?"

"A lot of people need help in this life, and sometimes we knowingly help people, and sometimes, just the accidental eye contact and a smile is all the help someone needs to see the world a bit differently that day."

"He does look into your soul when he looks at you," I said.

"Yeah and because he pays too much attention to the world, he judges a lot of things in it."

"That he does."

"Looking into Delux's eyes was the biggest thing I missed as I was losing my sight. I felt like I was looking at myself looking into his eyes," Ruka said looking up at Delux from the floor.

"Now what?" I asked.

"Now we wait."

"Wait for what?"

"The Trinidad guy to appear."

"Shoot I forgot to tell you. He showed up here the other day."

"Ok, good."

"What does it mean?"

"Now, the restaurant guy in LA needs to call."

"The drunk guy?"

"He's not a drunk. Drinking was just his resolution to heartbreak and getting screwed over by the company he helped start."

"What's he got to do with Delux?"

"I don't know. They went to high school together and both of them worked for Delux's father at the restaurant when they were in high school from what I can gather."

"From what you gathered?"

"Yeah. From what I gathered, Doofus. I don't know everything."

"Ruka!"

"What, Doofus?"

"What's the point of all of this?"

She thought about it.

"The point, is to laugh, and fight for your right to party."

"I feel like I haven't laughed in a while," I said looking at Delux and Jobe talk about their future in Columbia together.

"Doofus… I know things I can't share with you, but that doesn't mean you're not part of it. You will know everything when the time is right, because you are Dog. You're the point of all of this. I just don't know how to put it into words for you to understand. You just have to trust me. People need Delux, and Delux needs people. You and I are gone now, and Delux has nobody. We're here, until he finds his, somebody. That's the point of all this. So laugh."

"Shouldn't he be finding himself?" I asked.

"Exactly. Now you're getting it," Ruka told me.

Time was up, and Delux had to move out of the house. The landlord kept his deposit because she said he left too many holes in the walls.

"They're small holes from hanging art on the wall. They can all be fixed for $10 and you should always do a fresh coat of paint before anyone moves in anyways."

"The holes are beyond excessive."

"Lady, I managed a luxury apartment complex with a high turnover rate. There's absolutely zero excessive damage in this house, and I'm actually going to go inside and take photos in case you want to go to court, like you said," Delux said upset.

Delux didn't get angry like this often. This lady was nuts and pushing all of his buttons. There was no damage besides small nail holes in the wall and a few scuff marks from the skateboards being put in the same spot. Nothing worth keeping Delux's entire $1200 deposit over.

"Ah fuck! You fucking bitch, I needed that money!" Delux said, hitting his steering wheel as he drove his Jeep back to the dealership with the same issue its always had.

"Look, Carmax. You sold me a lemon, admit that. Your fancy 'CARFAX' report is lying, or you missed something. Take your Jeep, and give me all my money back right now, or you'll face legal charges, because I'm gonna be that guy standing outside your building with a big fucking sign saying you guys are bullshit."

"Sir. Please calm down."

"This is calm. Go find your fucking manager," Delux stated, laughing.

"There is no need for that kind of language."

"This is how I talk, go get the manager please."

Carmax wrote Delux a check for the exact price he took on a loan to buy his Jeep.

The loan had a huge interest rate due to Delux's bad credit, so paying it off in full would help him out a lot. Out of the blue, some old hippy lady that was friends with Jobe, gave Delux her car.

"Here, you can have her," she said handing Delux the keys.

"You're just going to give me your car?" Delux asked her.

"I'm moving to LA. I haven't made a car payment on this thing in a few months, so the bank is looking for it. They could take it at any time if they find it, but I put crystals in every corner for protection to keep you safe."

"Wow. I don't know what to say. Thanks," Delux said to her looking at his free four-door sedan. And just like that, Delux still had transportation to and from his 8 to 5 I was so invested on him keeping. A week into having the car, someone broke into it and stole Delux's wallet he'd left in the glove box.

"Well the crystals didn't protect me that much," Delux said looking through the car to see what else they may have stolen.

Jobe talked about them moving into a tree house again. Ruka said something about a treehouse, but Ruka was nowhere to be found.

"Ruka!" I yelled out in my head.

Nothing. I sat in the empty house until Delux came back to put the last load into his car and move out completely. I jumped in the car, and we drove to Miami.

'Earth in us Farms', is what the sign outside said.

CHAPTER 22

THE TREE HOUSE

This farm place was cool. There were chickens, goats, trees with fruit on them, trees that looked like they were from an imaginary dream world, and tiny houses all around the edge. The entire city block was a fenced in community.

I didn't see any cult signs out front, just one that read 'Earth in us Farms'.

"What do you think?" Jobe asked Delux.

"So, people all share this space together?"

"Yes. This is our bathroom that we share with the two people who live in these rooms here..." Jobe pointed out in the main house.

"Share? I'm not used to sharing a bathroom," Delux said disliking the situation.

"It'll be fine. Come this way, just wait till you see the tree house."

What was Delux doing? He's allowing someone else to decide what his life was going to be like without thinking if he really wanted this life for himself. He just wanted the girl and the love that came with it, but she was a liar, too. And he called *me* Doofus, I thought as we turned the corner and bumped into Ruka.

"Ruka. What brings you back here. Did the restaurant guy sober up yet?" I asked.

"He's good. He's making better decisions but these two guys, both he and Delux, have been letting these women decide what is best for them, when these women don't have their best interest as their best intention," Ruka said looking around the farm.

"Humans."

"Exactly, but dogs aren't perfect either. How's, the job going?"

"It's going. Delux has discovered a huge mess in the financials and is debating on quitting or letting corporate know. He also keeps looking at waves in Columbia, and surfing photos all day, so I don't know what's going through his mind."

"Doofus, keep trying to connect with him. Whatever he does, he cannot lose this job. He cannot quit, and for god's sake, he cannot get fired because of this discovery, or Darcy, or anything."

"Well, you know Delux, he's pretty unpredictable."

"That's why you gotta keep trying to get into his head and help him make the right decision to keep at it. Help him find the solution since he already found the problem."

"Yeah, I get it... Keep working," I said just as depressed as Delux from the energy in the office.

"He's lost almost everything in the last 30 days, you have to get him to hold onto something that's not related to Jobe. Like music, or surfing, something that was his, before her."

"He's talking about selling his surfboards to a guy at work."

"His drum then. Don't let him sell the drum."

I remember when Delux bought the drum. It was a djembe sitting alone. He asked if it was for sale and the women went to the back to check the price. It turned out to be cheaper than Delux thought, which was perfect because he had been saving all his money and not treating himself to anything special.

The drum sounded amazing. It had a deep bass sound when hit in the middle, and a nice sharp high pitch slap on the edges. I had no clue Delux could even play the drum at the time. He never practiced or mentioned he wanted one. He just saw it, tried it, and bought it. Once the drum was home, he barely played unless someone else wanted to play too. When Delux played the drum, he played with seamless rhythm. A sense of tribalness flowed through his hands and fingers that all seemed to move separate from each other forming a perfect beat that morphed and changed. Delux loved playing that drum.

"I'll just get a new one in Colombia. I have too much stuff to fit into this tiny tree house. Look at all my surf boards just sitting at the bottom here leaning up against the tree, looking like trash. I just need my CD players, and music, that's it. I can always play music somewhere with those, and make more money than with a drum," Delux said to Jobe trying to consolidate their things for their trip.

"You love that drum," she told him, banging on it.

"I can get a new one," Delux insisted.

And just like that, Delux sold the drum to someone at the farm. Delux was so focused on making and saving money, to support both him and Jobe, he was losing everything that was him. Jobe wasn't working, just hustling a little weed here and there, so saving money for everything was Delux's burden.

"Great. There goes the drum," I said upset, watching him walk back empty-handed from one of the tiny houses.

"Delux is learning to let go," Ruka told me looking around.

"But you told me he needed to keep the drum... Now what?" I asked Ruka.

"So this is the treehouse?" Ruka said, looking up at the thing not answering my question. "It's just as I saw it, which means we don't have much time," Ruka said seriously.

"Keep him working. I gotta get to restaurant guy now," she said fading away.

"I'll do what I can," I said watching Delux climb up the stairs to get into the treehouse.

What can I do? I kept asking myself. I wished Ruka would tell me more details of what she knew. Then, in that moment of reflection, it came to me. If Delux kept working for two more months, between what he has saved up already, they could probably make it to Colombia and live like kings and queens due to the exchange rate. This is good I thought. I would share it with Ruka once she returned from LA.

"I wonder what this restaurant guy needs to talk to Delux about," I said exploring the farm some more on my own. Delux knows about restaurants. Maybe they can work together or something. Oh, Ruka is smart, I have to hand it to her I thought. She knows Delux so well.

There were cats here. They ran from me like they could see me. I tried to play with them, but they would run every time. After some time, I got them to see that I wasn't a threat and they began to play with me, and began chasing me back, or hitting me on the bum when I wasn't looking, then ducking into the bushes.
I could hear Ruka in my head… "Doofus, you should be focusing on Delux, and not playing around."
These cats were so adorable and so playful, I knew she would do the same. Ruka was the one who told me to go explore, so that's what I was doing.
The treehouse was in the center of the farm. I had no idea what kind of tree it was, but it was huge. There was a small wooden house on the bottom of the tree that someone was staying in, but they were not home. There was a steep set of stairs outside that zig-zagged its way up to a door, outside a large, section of the treehouse. I couldn't

believe this is where Delux and Jobe would be living until they left for Colombia.

The farm was full of tiny houses spread out along the edges with one big main house as the entrance for the public. Yeah, even the public could come and visit this place during the day. The farm was a cool concept. There seemed to be a few people living around here, but who was actually working here?

Delux did all of his work somewhere else. He just needed a place to sleep, shit, shower, and shave before work. He was a real trooper for moving here I must say.

Inside the tree house, the wind blew right through the open sides that only had a thin sheet to keep out the wind or rain. One side had a window with a big, wooden peace sign in it that Delux hung his bob Marley flag over. The other side was wide open, looking out over the trees of the lower neighborhood and open sky. I will admit, it was kinda nice and unique. There was enough room inside to set up his traveling DJ equipment, and the treehouse even came with a squirrel inside. If I was myself again, that squirrel would have been dead.

"Dead? Shit!" I forgot Ruka told me Delux dies in a treehouse, and she said earlier, this place was just how she saw it. I gotta find Delux!

He was working. He was always working. I walked into his office where he was busy sending off a report about how short the accounts receivables was. I looked at him sitting at his desk and I felt my mind melt into his, and I was able to get into his head for some reason.

Delux had worked in that office for five years. He learned every aspect of the job in the shortest amount of time. He started in Sales, was moved into Operations, then he became the Office Manager because they didn't want to lose him by burning him out in Operations. After a year in his "office manager" role, Delux was pulled aside by his bosses, boss, Chris for a one on one, private conversation.

"So, I hate to say it, but we did a random background check and found out that your college degree here is bullshit. I don't know how you managed to get this job, and make it this far, so can you please tell me how you did it?" Chris asked directly.

"As you know, I started here when Russ was in charge. After my interview, he asked me if there was anything else I wanted to say. I looked him dead in his eyes and told him, 'That degree on my resume that you're holding is a B.S. in bull shit.'"

"Ok." Chris waited for more.

"Then I told him to think of me like Playdough."

"The philosopher?" Chris asked.

"He asked the same question. No, the kids toy. You can take me out of the box and mold me into whatever you want. Then leave me there and tomorrow, that's what you got. And the fact that you left me outside the box, that's exactly where my mind is at, outside the box. This is why you should hire me and overlook that lie in my resume."

It was clear to me now why Delux came to work every day. He was at a job that required something he didn't have. Delux was well appreciated from upper management, but not the ones in his office. Everyone there just wanted to get what they could at the cost of the business. Make a fake quota to get that bonus, but at what cost?
Delux had enough. When I got to the office that day, it was too late. Delux was on the phone calling Chris.

"Chris. How you doing? Thanks for taking my call this late on a Friday."

Delux had never called Chris. Chris was one of those regional managers that just shows up unannounced, or calls you. In Delux's role, he was required to tell his boss first, not Chris.

"What's going on, Curb Head?" I overheard Chris ask Delux who looked upset.

Curb Head was the nickname Chris gave Delux because he caught Delux skateboarding to work one day.

"I fucking quit, man. Take this as my two-month notice. I love this place, so I'll give you two months to find another person I can train and test in to be like me, but I fucking quit. I can't do this anymore," Delux said into the phone painfully.

"Ah what's the matter, there's not enough waves for you down there in South Florida. Why you wanna quit?" Chris replied sarcastically.

"What? Waves? No." Delux laughed, a bit caught off guard.

"I'm sorry to sound so harsh, but if you, being the boss of my boss, can't see what's going on around here, I don't wanna work here anymore. This office, and how people do shit around here, I can't be part of it, man. I don't want to be part of it. I also don't want to just leave you high and dry because you gave me a chance, and I've spent five years here. I find that I do actually care so… consider this my two-month notice," Delux said in disbelief that he actually finally said it.

"You wanna go work in Hawaii?" Chris replied without hesitation.

"What?" Delux asked completely caught off guard.

"I know you like to surf, and we need a guy like you to run the branch in Hawaii, not just manage the office. There's surf in Hawaii right? You could surf there right?" Chris asked.

"Did you just offer me a job in Hawaii?"

"Yeah. What do you think? It's a small office with 80% Military contracts, and 20% civilian, you'll love it."

"I don't know. I wasn't expecting that as your comeback to me wanting to quit."

"I wasn't expecting you to be in the office after 5 o'clock on a Friday. What's up? You just worked all week and waited all day to call and tell me that you wanna quit?"

"No. I've been trying to fix our accounts payables that ya'll keep pressuring me about."

"I hear you've been trying. Keep it between me and you but seriously, think about the offer a few days because I know I can make it happen for you. It's late, go home and enjoy the weekend, call me on Monday," Chris said.

I can't wait to tell Ruka I can get into Delux's head now!

Delux drove to his treehouse in the gypsy girl's, crystal laced car, now seriously thinking about his job offer in Hawaii.

When he got home to Jobe, he never mentioned anything to her about the Hawaii offer, just that he put in his two-month notice at work. Jobe seemed happy to hear the news, but there was something different about her energy after he told her.

That weekend, they took the surfboards and paddle boards to the beach with some friends. As a ghost dog, I could fully stand in the sun and enjoy the entire day with them in and out of the water. I could feel Delux was thinking of me. He was looking right at me and didn't even know it. I would have given anything to feel him see me again.

"Be careful what you say there, Doofus, it might just happen," Ruka popped in.

"Ruka!"

I jumped on top of her, showing her how good my ghost skills have gotten by shoving her to the ground.

"Doofus. What are you doing?" Ruka said shaking off the attack.

"What do ya think? I'm getting good, huh?"

"Doofus. You were supposed to make Delux keep his job. What have you been doing, playing with the cats?"

"How did you know?" I asked.

"Doofus, Delux cannot quit this job, remember!"

"He got offered a job in Hawaii, that's not quitting."

"Doofus, he can't go to Hawaii," Ruka said upset and left.

"Ruka! What did I do? Wait, I got into his head!" I yelled out, but she was gone.

New Year's Eve came, when Jobe and Delux went on a sailboat with a large group of friends. Delux had to work all day and was tired through the night's parties. Jobe got him stoned with a blunt, and Delux was ready to pass out at 9pm.

"Jobe, I'm going below deck and rest a bit. Come get me at 11:30 so we can celebrate the New Year together."

"I will baby. I love you," Jobe told him.

I stayed on the lower deck with Delux. I could hear people celebrating upstairs, and nobody came down to get him. Jobe never came down. The party above us was winding down and still, nobody came downstairs to get Delux. Jobe left Delux alone.

At 5:30 a.m. Delux woke up and realized he was in the same spot as his nap down below. He woke up with me at his side, but without his lover. He went to the bathroom and then went up on deck to find everyone up there lying all around the top deck. Delux walked around all the people looking for Jobe. He finally found her at the front of the boat, snuggled up with the girl from New York who was at the Crystal Skull thing.

"Jobe?" Delux whispered. "Happy New Year."

"You left us all," Jobe said pretending to go back to sleep and snuggle the girl right in front of Delux.

He stepped back, and I watched his heart break in that moment. He worked so hard and dedicated so much to the relationship, and he felt so pushed out in that moment as she rolled her back towards him.

Delux went back downstairs and sat in meditation alone until more people awoke. Other people began to get up and they could feel the awkwardness on the boat, because Jobe was not hanging out with Delux like she always did. She was always hanging with him, always hanging on him, and showing him love, but this moment, she was all about this girl from New York and had no shame in front of the group. Delux's pain was seen and felt by everyone on the boat. I could even feel it. Jobe apologized to Delux haphazardly. What was done was done. Delux was hurt by how she did it, and I could see he felt confused in his head.

"Let her go!" I barked into Delux's face.

He touched the side of his face I was closest to as he played the drum with some other people who were sitting in the back with him. Did he feel that? Did he hear me? I needed Ruka, but when I thought of her, she wasn't showing up. That restaurant guy must be keeping her busy.

The fun and deception on the boat was over, and Delux had to go back to work. He was making work more his life, than life, his life. And at the moment, he was hating both. Now with Jobe acting a fool with another girl and lying about her to Delux and everyone else, I could feel something was bound to happen.

"Babe. I saw you two on the boat together. I know what I walked up on. Just tell me the truth."

"She's nothing to me, I swear. I just met her, and we had a great conversation all night because you were sleeping," Jobe said barely looking him in his eyes.

I felt I was receiving punishment for something I did in a previous lifetime to have to witness this kind of betrayal happen to a person over and over again. Everyone knew it was more than just great conversation. I remembered when Delux met Jobe, he told her to just be honest with him, and all she'd been doing was lying. She was up to something, I could see it now.

She was using Delux's savings to buy weed from her friend, and re-sell it to other friends, making Delux's money back and a little extra for herself, but she always owed Delux money. He was helping her with everything, and all she was doing in return was pretending. Was she pretending this whole time? I wondered.

I followed them to a gathering where Delux was introduced to Dre, an ex-girlfriend of Jobe. Dre looked down at me, I thought. I wondered if she saw me. It was quick, her glance towards me. In the small window of eye contact, and the way I watched her long dreadlocks move with her body gestures, I suddenly remembered that she was the same dreadlocked woman walking down the street back at our first house.

"Delux this is Dre," Jobe said.

"Hello."

"I finally get to meet the man who stole my woman away from me?" Dre said.

"What?" Delux said, startled by her energy.

"Ha, ha, ha, I'm just messing with you," Dre said, laughing and touching his arm.

"You were crazy, I was already on my way out," Jobe said jokingly to Dre.

"Whatever, you were crazy, bitch," Dre added.

"It's so funny. You two should have met each other. You both have so much in common," Jobe said about Dre and Delux.

"I don't do dick, darling," Dre said in a firm manner still laughing. "And why are you trying to pawn off your man?" Dre asks.

"Be careful with her. I hear a lot of nice things about you, Delux. Nice to finally meet you, and I don't have to stay hidden anymore," Dre said, looking at Jobe.

There was a bit of tension between Dre and Jobe, but also some resolution between the two of them. I felt I had just witnessed two human souls healing. Too bad one of them wasn't Delux's. I gotta tell Ruka I met the Dreadlock Lady from our first little house.

Shoot, there was something else I was supposed to tell her, I thought as another morning rolled around.

Waking up in the tree house was magical. The birds that chirp and sing early in the morning were enchanting. Delux got up super early for a Monday and jumped his naked body into his wetsuit. There were waves, so he wanted to get some before going to work and having to deal with payroll, the reporting of last week's numbers which were usually false, and the staff that loved doing the bare minimum.

He grabbed his work clothes and shoes and put them in Jobe's truck. He strapped the surfboard to the roof and put a gallon of water in the back to rinse himself off later. Going surfing is a mission, I thought. And for what, ankle high waves?

When Delux got to the beach, the waves were exactly that, ankle high. Maybe a knee-high wave would come every ten minutes or so, but it was flat. Delux had to work though, so he had no time to waste. I sat in the sand and watched him try to surf the waves that weren't there. I was wondering what enjoyment he was getting out of this. He had a nice warm bed, with a warm woman who was lying to him. Ahh ok, that's why he was here.

I would still snuggle up next to his legs every night, but he didn't realize it. I bet if he knew I was there, we would still be in bed and not here chasing waves that are more ghostly and invisible than me.

"He loves surfing, even if there're no waves," Ruka said, fading in and watching the sun begin to show its first light.

"Ruka!"

"You should see the waves in California. They're huge compared to these!"

With his job offer in Hawaii, the waves are the biggest."

"Did he take the job?"

"I haven't heard him talk about it to anyone. He's looked up the cost of living there, and places to live, but he sees it's expensive even with the pay increase they will give him," I said, watching him stand up on a tiny wave.

"Delux has a drifter's soul. The change will be good, but Hawaii is not for him," Ruka insisted.

"Can we manifest ourselves back into his life?" I asked.

"I'm not sure if that's possible," Ruka said looking around.

"I've seen it in the movies," I tell her.

"This is not the movies, Doofus," she said, looking right at me.

"No, it's not," I said, watching Delux try to stand up on another wave and falling.

"Looks like he's still finding time for himself doing what he loves," Ruka said.

"He loves falling. He's been coming here early in the mornings even if there's no waves. Turns out, he has better days when he starts it at the beach first."

"That gives me an idea, I'll be back," Ruka said.

"What you gonna to do?"

"I'm going to get the restaurant guy into surfing. He needs to find happiness, and the waves there are way bigger than these tiny things here."

"Yew!" Delux yelled out as he kicked out of a knee high wave all the way to the shoreline.

Delux showered a bit at the beach, but still had his wetsuit on his hips and legs for the drive to work. I stared at Delux in the truck going to the office in his wetsuit. He stopped at the drive-thru for a breakfast sandwich. I was trying to get into his head, but I couldn't. He drove and ate his breakfast sandwich as he skipped the song on the radio and put on one I liked. I wished he knew I was there. I reached out and touched his leg with my paw. He picked up his sandwich and took another bite. I missed him so much, and he was right here in front of me all day long. This sucked.

We pulled into work and like always, Delux left a bit of sandwich that he would usually give to me. He paused and looked at it.

"I love you, Doofus," he said and put it into his mouth.

"Delux!" I woofed out going unheard.

He looked around like he heard something. The parking lot was always empty this early in the morning and nothing was there. Delux was there an hour before start time. In this extra hour, he would get a lot done at the office, having no distractions from phones or people and their weekend stories in the office.

He stood outside and put a towel around himself and took off his wetsuit. It was a bit of a struggle to get the wetsuit off his legs and ankles, but he did it without flashing any animals that may be watching from the nearby wooded section. He grabbed his gallon of water and splashed his face, armpits, back, chest, and then a good rinse on the crotch area while he held the towel open. Delux was a master at the gallon jug rinse off from the RV days. If there was ever a competition in extending the life of a gallon of water, my money was on Delux.

He proceeded to put on his underwear, pants, socks, then shoes. Now with his lower parts covered, he stood there with no shirt on. He then hung up his wetsuit on the back of the truck to dry, and the towel over the door. He put on his undershirt, then his nice shirt, and then the tie. He put one foot at a time on the front seat and tied his shoes. He had no hair to comb, so off to work he went.

Delux had the master keys and unlocked the front door, where normally he had to deactivate the alarm, but it was already deactivated.

When you walked into Delux's office building, to the right was Delux's desk that faces the parking lot with floor to ceiling windows that let you see out with ease, but not into the office. To the left after you entered was the conference room.

That morning at 7 a.m., his boss, Chris, the regional manager, and a few VIP's from another country, two of them being older women, were in the conference room that faced the parking lot where Delux had parked.

"You're here early," Delux's boss said.

"So are you," Delux replied, shocked to see them there unannounced.

Boss didn't like that comment I could tell, as I peed on Darcy's chair and watched Delux get settled in.

"Good morning, Curb Head, you catch some waves this morning?" Chris said from the conference room.

All these people were there, but no cars were out front. This here looked like an audit or something was going down. I smelled everyone in the room. Only the Boss was sweating at 7:00 a.m. in an air-conditioned room. This for sure was an unannounced visit of some sort. Did they come because of Delux wanting to quit?

"Dang. You guys scared the crap outta me. Yeah, I got a wave or two."

"Do you always get ready in the parking lot like that before work?"

"If I go surf first, yes. If I had known you were in here watching me, I would have parked down a bit, sorry."

"What are you doing here so early on a Monday if there're waves?"

"It's payroll, and the Send Report day."

Everyone knew what that meant.
Payroll was difficult with a branch that had 48 employees, and the Send Report was always difficult to match at the end of the week, and still be in the green.

"You trying to get here before me to shine in front of management?" Delux's Boss said jokingly.

"It's payroll. I'm always early on payroll days."

"We'll keep it down so you can get some work done," Chris said, and Delux got to work.

I looked outside from the conference room and there was a clear shot of Jobe's truck with the towel and wet suit hanging from it. All the senior VP's watched Delux change in the parking lot. I smiled.

Boss man was upset about Delux's comment of always being early and let him know when they were alone. "Hey, don't make me look bad in front of management. It looks bad for you when you do that, or make comments like that," he said, grabbing his pants and pulling up his waistline.

"I said the truth. When are you ever here this early unless it's that once every three month operations meeting?" Delux said straight to his face.

"Well, you better hope you got your department in order because it looks like they are doing an audit on you and your account receivables."

"I'm good. My department will pass," Delux said, walking out of his office.

Delux did things his own way. He discovered certain documents in a person's file were private information and required a separate storage location outside of their personal file. This was already a practice put in place, but there was a hole people didn't see. There were rules to follow, and Delux followed them, yet when the VP's found the info they were looking for was not where it was supposed to be, they looked to Delux for an explanation.

"So because of this hole, I added a new filing system with the basic information here, that is secured with payroll. All other hardcopy information on employees is separated into these three folders depending on the type of request you need," Delux explained.

"How did you learn of this?" one VP asked.

"Some government security agency with no warrant came to our office to get some info on an employee. It was that day I discovered there was personal information not relevant to a search in his file. When I searched other employee files, I noticed they were all like this, so I took it upon myself, and separated the info. Basic info is here locked up, personal information is there, also locked up, as required."

They were impressed. I had no idea what Delux was talking about, but after they reviewed all of his payroll for the last three years, his methods for keeping track of people's vacation, sick and personal days was beyond perfect and easily understandable and comparable to their audit.

He also presented the spreadsheets his office staff had put together of their top 50 customers that were past due on their payments. Plus all the bonus payouts that were applied even though the customer was not paying.

Delux was keeping his job for sure I thought. A few days after the audit, Chris called Delux and asked him if he still wanted the Hawaii job.

"Who's up for the position, just me, or anyone else?" Delux asked.

"There's a local guy, and you, and you are the most qualified, and you surf. It's a perfect fit for you," Chris said trying to convince Delux.

"I'm gonna have to say no."

"No?"

"Yeah. And I still want to quit in two months."

"Can I ask why?" Chris asked.

"Hawaii is expensive, and they don't need another blonde haired, blue eyed gringo like me telling'em what to do. From what I hear, the locals are not of fan of us mainlanders."

"80% of your customers are Military, and their accounts receivables is all in the green."

"Yeah but I bet 100% of the workers are native Hawaiians, and I still say no. I don't know why, or what I'm gonna do, but I can't do this anymore. Sorry. I quit."

"Ok. Hang tight, kid. Don't quit yet," Chris said.

"You have two months. I can't do this anymore," Delux repeated as I could see him thinking deep about his current situation.

"What if I get rid of your boss?"

"It's not just him. It's the sales force selling bullshit contracts that don't pay, yet they get bonuses for them. The account manager is doing the same thing. I'm tired of the op's guys doing shit their own way and not getting the job done how we tell them. I'm burnt out."

"Don't quit. You're gonna get a phone call this afternoon between 4 and 5 your time. Be there to answer it," Chris said.

"You got two months," Delux said to Chris, laughing.

I could see Delux had a different energy about him after turning down the job offer of a lifetime. It's not everyday someone will pay you to move to an island paradise to surf. Delux barely knew how to surf anyways.

"So it's official, Delux put in his notice?" Ruka jumped in from Darcy's desk.

"And here she is again, the disappearing, reappearing Ruka. You know, what's so important that you can't hang out here with me and Delux?"

"Pretty soon there will be no you, me, and Delux?"

"What do you mean?" I asked, concerned.

"I mean, there will be you and me maybe, but Delux? Delux is going away, kid."

"Ruka, stop speaking in code. Tell me what you're doing. What's going on, and where's Delux gonna go?"

"Delux might look like he's enjoying this win at his job, that's making him feel important, but he's still making plans with a woman who…"

Ruka got interrupted by something that was not there.

"Sorry, Doofus. I gotta go. Delux can't quit. He has to keep this job."

"If you were here watching him, you would know, he hates this job," I yelled towards Ruka, but she was already gone.

It was 4:30 p.m., and a call came into the office.
Darcy took the call and forwarded the call to Delux who was at his desk, finishing a report.
He hated this job, but it was a job. It was an easy job for Delux. He learned everything and could do everything, yet was not at the top. Was he a fool for turning down the job in Hawaii where he would have been placed at the top?
Who was calling him, I wondered?

"This is Delux, how can I help you?" he said into his desk phone.

"Ahh… sure… If you can make that happen, I can do that," Delux said listening for what came next.

"Ok, I will. Thank you."

I tried to listen in, but I couldn't hear what the guy was saying on the other end.
Normally I can.
Did this guy know about me?
Did Darcy snitch on me again, and the guy made it so he couldn't be heard?

I was confused as I tried to get into Delux's head. Delux still had this weird energy about him that I could no longer put a paw on.

Back at the treehouse, Delux was excited to tell Jobe the news.

"Work offered me a new job that may require a bit of traveling. They're gonna fly me to Canada this Monday, just to interview me."

"Why didn't they just do it over the phone?"

"He kinda did. He asked if I would like to take a traveling position helping the company restructure their way of doing business. He said it would pay very well, and they would take care of all my travel and hotel expenses if I take the job."

"What are you thinking?"

"Well, I'll go to Canada and find out exactly what it is I'll be doing. They're gonna pay for it all, so why not. If I take the job, I'll be able to save a lot more money with the pay raise and all expenses paid. I think doing this temporary is better than staying in the office for two months like I planned," Delux said, still processing it all.

"Whatever you think is best, babe, I support you," Jobe said.

No, she didn't. She didn't support Delux at all. Jobe was always hanging around this girl from New York who just happened to be in town.

Delux went to Canada for the interview. I went with him, but I was denied access at the building he went into. It was so secure even a ghost couldn't enter. I tried to wait for the double doors to open, but there was always a failure once I got to the second door, and nothing I could do would get me past it. I had to wait outside.

"This is snow, Doofus," Ruka said appearing out of nowhere, rolling around in it.

"That's what all this white stuff is?"

"Lucky for you, you don't have to feel how cold it is on your paws."

"I'd be lucky to feel anything right now."

"Don't wait for Delux, he'll be fine. Feel your way back home. Find Jobe as soon as you can. Something ain't right if you can't get into this building."

I closed my eyes and sent myself back to the warm treehouse that was actually feeling cooler in the onset of winter in Miami.

"How'd the interview go?" Jobe asked Delux when he returned.

"I can't talk about it," Delux told her laughing.

"What?"

"They made me sign a non-disclosure. Twice."

"Why twice?"

"The first one was to make sure if I said no to the job, I wouldn't say anything about the changes that are coming to any staff within my office."

"And the second one?" she asked.

"The second one is the actual job itself. I can't talk about it. And when I quit, I can't go work for the competition, or share information. I'll get in trouble or something."

"When do you start?"

"I did already. They will begin to fly me up there Monday, and I'll be back on Friday."

"Wow, that's fast!"

"Right? Shits crazy. What are the chances I try to quit, and instantly I get my salary doubled?" Delux said in excitement.

"Speaking of crazy, the bank found your car."

"They took it?" Delux asked semi-shocked.

"Yeah."

"Fuck. I liked that car."

"We can use mine."

"You wanna go to the beach this weekend with the surfboards?" Delux asked.

"Are there waves?"

"Who cares, let's just go," he said.

Jobe's a bitch. All Delux needed to hear her say is, "Babe, I met a girl, she's super cool, and we have something between us that I can't explain."

The entire time Delux was away in Canada, she was with this New York girl in her hotel room. I wanted to bite the both of them, but I couldn't alert my presence to these two bitches. This girl Jobe was messing with, had met Delux and she knew he was in love with her.

I remembered a mysterious woman at the event in New York City who pulled Delux aside. I had gotten into his head to hear what she said to him. "Your girlfriend is not who she pretends to be. She's an energy sucking vampire and she's lying to you. I hate to see this happening, and I can't be quiet about it."

So others felt that Jobe was bad as well. Why was it when Delux goes away, these women like to play?

I watched her lie to Delux's face about how she just, "hung around the farm and helped out while he was away. All lies. She didn't do shit around here but drop two shits in the bathroom they had to share. The rest of the time she was with this New York girl at her hotel. Jobe was pretending to love Delux, and he believed her. She was so good at manipulation.

The third week Delux returned from Canada, Jobe picked him up from the airport, and brought him back to the treehouse. He showered and changed into something comfortable getting ready to go out with Jobe and a friend of theirs for dinner. Delux locked up the treehouse and got into Jobe's truck.

"All right. I'm ready. Fuck it feels good to be back here. I can shut my brain and body off. Where do you wanna go eat, the Thai spot?" Delux asked watching Betty, the mutual friend of theirs, came around the corner and began walking towards the truck.

"There's Betty. Maybe let's ask her," Delux said.

"Babe, I want to break up," Jobe dropped on Delux.

"What?" Delux said turning towards her, unprepared for this.

"Look, this isn't working out right now, and I just think it's better for both of us."

"Right now? You think it's better?" Delux paused.

"You choose to tell me this now? Betty is about to get into the truck, and you choose now to break up with me? What the fuck's the matter with you?" Delux asked as the statement sunk in.

"Hi guys, how you doing"? Betty said opening the back door and sitting alongside of me.

"Hey, girl," Jobe said like nothing had just happened.

"S'up, Delux? With the new secret job. How are you, secret agent man?" Betty asked rubbing the top of his head.

"Ask Jobe."

"Ahh, what?" she said surprised.

"Yeah," Jobe said casually like it had zero effect on her.

"I changed my entire life up for you. And this is how you do it? You tell me just before Betty gets in the truck? I'm just gonna get out. You two go on," Delux said getting out of the truck.

I jumped out, too.
Jobe drove away, leaving Delux standing there alone on the side of the road in front of the farm he now lived at on the weekends. His heart was never fixed from Tess. Then the condo cat lady had men's dress socks under her bed, and now Jobe. The only thing Delux loved and that loved him back were his surf boards. At least he has those. He could stay living in the treehouse, or maybe rent a spot he would only be at one day a week to do laundry.
Nothing made sense at the moment.
Delux walked back up into the treehouse. He looked at his surfboards and then grabbed his phone.

"Gary. If you still want all my boards, I'll sell them to you right now. What you got?"

I couldn't believe it. Delux was selling the last of what he identified with.
He still has his DJ console and music to mix with, but in this moment, I just realized, if Delux sold his surfboards, he would have lost everything in 30 days, including me and Ruka.

"Did someone say Ruka?"

"There you are. I was wondering when you'd show up."

"I wish I could smell the cat shit in this place."

"No, you don't. I got some bad news."

"I know. Jobe broke Delux's heart."

"How do you know? It just happened."

"Sorry, Doofus, but I knew it was going to happen a long time ago. I just couldn't tell you directly."

"Ruka, stop hiding things from me. Maybe I can help."

"You can't help yourself with what you don't remember yet, Doofus, only I can do that," Ruka said.

"What I don't remember? Ruka, I can help."

"So how you gonna help?" Ruka asked.

"I don't know. Delux is about to sell his surfboards. Maybe I can stop him. He needs to hold onto something, right?"

"He needs to hold onto his soul."

"His soul?"

"Yes, the soul. Sorry I didn't fill you in on the deceptive ways of Jobe. Maybe I should have, but I was told not to."

"By who?"

"You."

"What? When did I say that?" I was confused.

"When you were Dog, or god or someone... Remember now?"

"No," I said after thinking about it.

"Keep Delux working and everything will be explained," Ruka said and faded away into her classic exit.

Keep him working? It's the only thing he's got, I thought.
The following week Delux came back from Canada and sold his surfboards to the guy who cleaned the vehicles of his company.

"Yeah sure man, a short board, a fun board, a beautiful custom longboard, and a professional stand up paddle board with paddle... all for $700. That's a fucking steal," Delux said transferring the boards into the guy's truck.

"For real man, thank you! These will be in good hands and used proudly." the new owner said.

To Delux, selling the boards cheap was a future investment to a possible friend who surfed. I couldn't believe he sold all his boards for only $700. He was losing money left and right on everything he was selling. Only his Jeep had paid him back exactly what he put into it.

When everything was said and done though, Delux had a small savings account with four grand in it. The most he'd ever had at once in his life. Delux sat there in Jobe's truck wondering what to do next with himself since he had permission to use her truck while he was in town for the weekend. She lied and broke his heart, but she wasn't a total bitch.

While in the parking lot, watching his boards drive away, his cellphone rang.

"Hello."

"Yes. This is he."

Devin was calling Delux for the first time. It couldn't have come at a more perfect time.

"Devin… Yeah…. The guy from the beach who sells houses. I'm shitty, how are you?" Delux flat out said, watching his boards leave.

"Man I just sold all my surfboards for $700. I'm watching them drive away as I speak to you."

"I would've sold them to you, but your call's five minutes too late," Delux told him.

"Better late than never," Ruka chimed in from the back seat.

"Ruka. He sold all of his boards… he has nothing left. I failed."

"You didn't fail. He hasn't sold his soul, and Devin finally showed up. Devin is the 'someone' Delux needed to meet. Everything should be good now."

"You think so."

"I know so. Soon you and I should be fading away into the next life you signed up for."

"So this really is all about me?"

"Yep."

"You just don't remember. It's how you want it, you tell me. It's always you and I, kid."

The next weekend, Delux came back to the treehouse after a long week in Canada. I was still around with him, and I hadn't shown any signs of fading away. He was deeply depressed when he arrived home alone in the tree all by himself. He hid his depression from everyone. As much as he wore his heart on his sleeve, he was good at hiding the fact that he was empty inside.

It was hard to feel, but it was cold and miserable in Miami that weekend. Rain. Humidity, and 40-degree weather don't mix well in a treehouse open to the elements.

Delux borrowed a space heater from a friend to help keep him warm, but it wasn't working. Jobe wasn't staying at the farm on the weekends, to give Delux the treehouse to stay in. He hated it there, and the weather wasn't making it any better.

He opened his safe and counted the money he had saved up. Half of it was missing. Jobe.

Delux left for Canada, and the following weekend he returned to the treehouse where the weather was still cold and shitty. Delux checked the safe again. The money was there, but there was still $900 missing. He was sad. He was lonely. He was depressed. He didn't want to be a burden to anyone. He needed help with his mental state but he didn't know how to ask .

Devin came into his life, but Delux wouldn't call him…

"Ruka! Help me!"

"What's up, Doofus?"

"Look at Delux. He's super sad. What can we do?"

"It's not up to us anymore, Doofus."

"What do you mean?" I asked, watching as my see-through green color was fading away a bit. I could see more of the treehouse through both my paws and Ruka's entire body.

"Ruka. What's happening?"

Delux grabbed his gun out of the safe. You could tell he was cold and miserable sitting in the treehouse alone. The rain was blowing in on him keeping him cold and wet. He sat in front of the heater checking out his gun. He slid out the clip. He removed the round that was already in the chamber and stuck it on the floor in front of him. He looked at it. He began to cry, but he pulled himself together. He took out all of the rounds from the clip and stood them up in front of him.

"It just takes one," Delux said, putting them all back in.

He chambered a round and stuck the gun to his head with his finger on the trigger. I barked as loud as I could in his face. I tried to bite his arm and pull the gun away.

"Ruka! What the fuck, do something!"

"There's nothing we can do, Doofus. What's done is done."

"Ruka!" I yelled out, jumping through Delux still trying to get his arm.

"Why can't I stop this?" I said fighting to pull the gun away.

"We gotta stop this!" I yelled out.

Delux put the gun down and locked it back up in the safe. I was relieved. My biting and barking worked.

He was crying. He was sobbing like the rain outside was falling. He looked around the treehouse and found a rope he used to tie the surf boards down with. "I'm in a tree house. There's a limb. This is much better than a bunch of blood everywhere," Delux mumbled out loud as he tied the rope.

"Ruka, what the fuck is happening right now?" I said, watching Delux throw the rope over the limb.

"Destiny, Doofus," Ruka told me.

"No, this is bullshit. We went through all we did with him, only for it to end this way?"

"You told me not to tell you our future, Dog. No matter what happens. Everything comes to an end, Doofus. Even us, look at you," Ruka said too casually.

I was fading away more and more not understanding.

"If you knew all the answers, Dog, you never would've learned what you have, or enjoyed the life you got to share with him. It's why it took you two and a half years to accept him. You didn't really know, you had to see him first. See it to feel it."

"Ruka, this is so painful to watch," I said as I thought back to the day I brought Delux the ball back for the first time.

"This is Delux seeing," Ruka told me.

"Seeing what? Something has to happen. He can't go out like this!"

"Something is happening, Doofus. Look at you. Besides, it's his choice to make, not ours."

"I'm going more and more transparent. Just like you."

"That means our job here is done."

"It can't be," I said feeling helpless unable to stop him.

Delux held the rope and made sure it would hold his weight.

"I should write people a note or something," Delux said looking around. "At least to my dad," he said.

"It's sad, but this is what destiny actually looks like, Doofus."

"No, not like this," I begged.

"Just like this," Ruka stated.

He stood on the stool and put the rope around his neck without writing anyone a goodbye letter.

"He's so fucking broken, Ruka. Why can't we stop this?" I cried as Ruka and I started to fade away even more.

"Our job here is complete, Doofus," she kept repeating.

Delux's work phone made a strange noise and got his attention as he put the rope around his neck.

"Ruka, I can hardly see you now."

"We did it, Doofus."

CHAPTER 23

PURA PURGATORY

"We didn't do shit..."

"Trust me, Doofus, yes we did."

"Anytime someone says trust me, you shouldn't, you always told me."

"Doofus. You can trust me, I promise you."

"Then why are we locked up behind these bars for this lifetime of ours?"

"Because, that's how they do it here."

"Here. What is here? Where are we?"

I was tired of this life in this man-made cell we were in. Locked away in a metal and concrete box with a gate on one side like we did something wrong in our past life.

"What is it, day 1,809 today we've been locked up in here?"

"As in dog days, or people days?" Ruka said sarcastically.

"They're the same thing."

"Doofus, can you please look at the bright side and accept at least we made it back here together with all our memories, and I can see again."

"What good are memories doing us, Ruka? How do you know Delux is still alive, because that's all I can think about."

"Dead or alive, you taught him what you needed to teach him, Doofus. You helped heal his soul."

"Heal his soul? Ruka... in his last days, he lost everything in 30 days, maybe 40... but either way, we both watched him lose everything... even himself."

"You have to lose yourself to find yourself. Just like Delux lost all of his things and he learned to let go... you need to learn as well, Doofus."

"My name's not Doofus anymore."

"I'm not calling you Rocco, you will always be my Doofus, Dog."

"If I could kill myself too, I would. Hang myself like Delux did. Life in here with you sucks, Ruka, or Tiga, whoever you are."

I started to cry thinking of Delux.

"You drive me nuts, Ruka, with how you explain things."

"You're driving your own self nuts, Doofus. You do this. You overthink stuff all the time instead of being present."

"You force me to think when you're vague all the time."

"Thinking for yourself is how you learn."

"If you knew something like Delux is gonna kill himself right after us, we are here to be his guide, teach him love and patience, and play fetch... tell me that shit from the beginning so I don't waste two and a half years fighting it."

"Like you're fighting me now?" Ruka asked me.

I was annoyed sitting in here all day and night with her with no real interaction with anyone else. No play, no walks, nothing.

"Doofus, I'll repeat it again. If I tell you what you told me not to tell you while we occupy these dog bodies, I will no longer be your guide, and you will lose our connection, starting over on your own. Remember what it's like to be alone?"

"Starting over from what? How can I tell you something I don't remember ever telling you," I said, frustrated with her.

Ruka laughed.

"Delux isn't dead, Doofus."

"You don't know that," I told her as I looked out towards the muddy road wishing I could see him one more time. Feel the energy of his touch holding my head.

"If you knew more of Delux's life, you would know something wants him alive".

"Something?" I asked.

"That's what his dad always said."

"He didn't even write to his dad," I cried some more.

"Doofus, as soon as Delux was born, he needed tubes in his ears and needed to be put in an incubator or something for a bit. Ok... not life threatening, Grandma had two other little Delux's before this Delux. The first two died young. Delux survived."

"You still paying attention or did you fall asleep?"

"I'm still here, Ruka, continue," I said, watching a guy go by us on a motorcycle.

"At eleven months old, Delux burned half his body with a pot of coffee. Delux's father had to clean dead skin off his arm for thirty days while he healed himself."

"Like Delux did with you after I pushed you out of the truck," I thought out loud, listening to her.

"Yeah, Doofus. Life… It has a cycle. Just over a year old, right after his arm healed from being burnt, Delux drowned in a swimming pool. Grandma pulled him out at the last second and got him breathing again."

"Delux hated coffee, and loved water…" I said again out loud, trying not to think about him.

"Just after he turned four years old, he drowned again, only this time in the Mississippi River. He sank to the bottom like you did when you learned to swim, only the Mississippi has a lot more current underneath. His uncle was there to swim down and find him in the murky water by his blonde hair and pull him up."

"This is why he was like a fish when he swam in the sea with me," I laughed thinking about us swimming together in the ocean.

"When he was 17, Delux and a friend ran into, then out of, a burning building completely engulfed in flames, holding a stranger's life in their hands. Something wants Delux alive," Ruka finished.

"He was so sad for so long. From Tess to Condo Lady to Jobe, three women in a row destroyed him."

"But Maria gave him hope. Remember?"

I thought back and remembered Maria and her kids. How much joy and happiness they all brought to him.

"I get it."

"What do you get?"

"As a dog, all we have to do is sniff a butt and nine times outta ten, dogs are down to play and have fun. Humans, they have to date and deceive each other to be liked."

"Sometimes some humans do that deceiving behavior yes, but not all," Ruka justified.

"Humans get to know each other, so they know how to fuck the other person over," I said like I had it all figured out.

"They meet each other's friends, and family, only to get cheated on and lied to. Fuck being human, loyalty is gone for them. Then they lock their dogs up on patios, chains, or in small metal garages like this one with no freedom," I said turning in a circle on the flat concrete floor.

"It's not that small. I mean, a truck fits inside here, and we still have room. It's a whole garage, no?" Ruka said positively.

"You and your optimism. Look out these bars, Ruka, what do you see?"

"Sometimes it's green I think, and other times it's brown maybe, I don't know, we're color blind. Half the time it's raining, I know that."

"That's freedom out there, Ruka. We've been here in this cage for years just living outside and not able to experience outside."

"Doofus, you're only in a cage if your mind allows you to be in a cage."

"What? Ruka, look around us in here. We're stuck in a cage. For this concrete box to be our life after we 'saved' Delux, something must have gone wrong somewhere."

"Everything is perfect, Dog," Ruka told me completely happy in our situation.

The truck that was usually parked in our cell, was gone at the moment so we had some space to move around, but we were stuck inside with our piles of poo spread around us on the concrete floor.

The seasons would come and go. Wet season, dry season, windy season, and fire season. That's what we had here, wherever here is. Born into a life stuck in a garage with Ruka, and no Delux. Why was I holding on to all my past memories? I'm supposed to forget everything, move on, and start again. I couldn't understand it, and I was tired of talking to Ruka.

People would come and go past us like the seasons. Some in cars, some in trucks, some on motorcycles, and some walking or on a bicycle. Nobody said hi to us, but we barked at all of them trying to get attention. Nobody waved or made eye contact, even with all of our barking and trying to say hello. A lot of people seemed to speak Spanish when they walked by this garage with Ruka and I.

We reincarnated together which is great, but with an owner who only spoke French when he spoke to us. We had no idea what he wanted when he spoke to us, and just left us out here in the garage.

Every now and then I heard English coming from a passing car or from two people having a conversation on a motorcycle, but it was never enough to figure out where we were, or what was going on with this chapter in our life.

Our French owner didn't spend any time with us to teach us anything. He just left us here in this metal box of a garage, day and night. We were pissing and shitting in our own space then the French guy would spray it all outside the gate with a hose. We were lucky if we got fed once a day as we sat to ourselves all day and night, barking at anyone who passed by.

"How did we go from Delux, to this?" I asked.

I looked outside, thinking the only reason I got myself into this situation is because I let Delux down. Ruka wasn't sharing anything new with me. What I could see is that I was stuck here with Ruka, in a metal garage in a place that got super dry and hot, or super humid and hot, with lots of rain.

"Let's do it again, Doofus," Ruka interrupted my sulking.

"Do what again?" I asked.

“What are some of your old memories you have?”

“I remember Delux in that treehouse,” I told her upset.

"Doofus, you have to let it go,” Ruka insisted.

“You know, if you knew he was going to die in that tree house, why didn’t you do anything to stop it?”

“If I knew the next lifetime was gonna be spent in this garage with you bitching for, what did you say, 1,809 days...? I would have told you everything while we were alive and separated us right then and there. Did you learn anything in that ten years?”

“What do you mean, you would have separated us right then?”

“You still don’t remember that part, do you, Dog?”

“What part, Ruka?”

“Your part, Doofus. Your part, Rocco. Your part, Dog. Dog... Don’t you get it? Dog?”

I didn’t get it and just laid there in silence. We’re in a new lifetime, but it’s the same old vague Ruka, unable to tell me a straight answer.

“Maybe you’re not asking the right questions.”

“What are the right questions, or is that too something you cannot tell me?”

“What do you think Delux wants now?” Ruka asked.

“Delux is dead,” I replied with my back to her.

“But if he was alive, what would he want?” Ruka asked again.

I laid there on the concrete ground looking outside like I always do thinking about her question. "Delux always wanted us to wait for him."

"Well, maybe that's what we're doing." Ruka said, walking up and sitting next to me putting her paw on my back.

"Delux always wanted hugs to answer your question."

I thought back to every time Delux came home. Ruka and I would both be fighting for his attention. Whichever one of us jumped up on him first, got a big hug, or a doggie sandwich, which is just like a hug only different.

"I have spent four years going over that day in the treehouse when Delux died. I don't understand why we faded away when we did. It feels so twisted that we're not able to know what happened to him."

"Do you think you really would have wanted to see it?"

I took a deep breath. I stood up again, turned in circles a few times, and laid back down.

"I guess I am happy to have faded away so I didn't have to see Delux hanging there. Why didn't we fade away sooner, like when Delux put us down? Why did you come back for me Ruka and make us do all this as ghosts?"

"Because without us as ghosts, Delux would have died before his time, and not effected the ones who needed it the most."

"Like Devin?"

"Like Devin, the guy in LA, and many others."

It was hard to accept, and I was living a life of anger because of it. I was a failure I thought. I got up, walked three steps and laid down after doing my circle.

"You know you still make the same 'doof' noise every time you lay down?"

"Fuck you, Ruka."

"Fuck me? I'm the one that always humped you your whole life, remember, Dog?" Ruka said jumping on top of me trying to play.

"Get off me," I said shoving her aside.

"I'm tired of all your complaints, Doofus. Didn't you learn anything in the last life, Dog?"

"Leave me alone, Ruka. I'm tired, I want to nap," I told her.

"You know..." Ruka said changing her tone and charging at my back leg, getting me from behind.

"Maybe you're right and we did fail. Delux is dead. The universe that you are, never picked up the connection YOU were supposed to have with HIM, because YOU were too busy living in the past, thinking about where YOU're from, instead of where YOU're at," Ruka said, frustrated with me.

"Jesus, Dog, all the work we did with Delux was pointless if this is your memory of it all. All the times we were the only ones there for him when the ones he trusted the most deceived him. Pointless, Dog! It only makes sense seeing I have to live with you, in this, 'poor little box', listening to Doofus and all of his problems from another lifetime ago," Ruka said like a whiny bitch mocking me.

I tried to shake her off my leg, but she just rolled me over.

"Let it go. Get out of your head, Doofus, and make new, good, lasting memories now, instead of living in the past. What's done is done," she said getting off of me.

"You told me to never trust anyone who says that," I told her.

"Says what?"

"What's done is done. You would say there was always a chance. There is always a way."

Before she could answer, a motorcycle came by, and the guy on the bike looked right at us. I imagined it was Delux for a second. The man looked at me like I was Doofus... What would be the chances I thought?
A loud explosion came from the house behind us.

"Ruka, that's the French guy's house," I alerted jumping up.

We were locked away separately from him so we couldn't tell what was going on, but there was some sort of fire after the explosion. The firemen came and put the fire out, but then the police came soon after and arrested our owner.

"Ruka, what do you think is going on?"

"I'm not sure, but I swear I just felt Delux go by not too long ago on a motorcycle."

"Really? That guy earlier looked at me like I was Doofus, but he kept going."

"Wow. Now that's a feeling I have not felt in a while, and now an explosion. See, Dog, these are what stories are made of!" Ruka said, excited barking out to the firemen.

The police came to our enclosure to see if we would bite them. Ruka and I were so confused as to what was going on all around us with that explosion, we stayed calm and let them come in and take us when they walked a body bag past with a person in it...

"Ruka, who's in the bag?"

"If the French guy is in handcuffs, that must be his son. Nobody else has come here today," Ruka said painfully.

"No. The boy Juan? No, he was such a happy kid all the time. What happened?"

The police grabbed Ruka and I and stuck us in two separate crates that shared a window together and drove us away.

"Is this destiny, Ruka?" I asked from my crate.

"I don't know what this is, but let's hope it'll be better than that garage we were stuck in."

"What are the chances that guy on the motorcycle was Delux?" I asked.

"Even if Delux was alive, Dog, it's a big world out here."

"I remember hearing people say that it's a small world out there," I told her, as we hit a few bumps in the road.

"Half of those people who say it's small, also say it's a big world out there depending on the point they are trying to support," she told me as we hit a few more bumps in the road.

"People are confusing, and this road sucks. I guess I'm glad we were in that metal garage. Traveling around on these roads here is tough."

"Speaking of confusing and tough, why are you my guide, Ruka?"

"What?" Ruka asked surprised.

"I can see now, Ruka."

"We're in boxes in the back of a police truck with a shared window, Doofus. What can you see?"

"All this time I've been in my head, here with you, I know you know me, more then I know me, so... who are you Ruka? Tell me who you really are. I want to know."

Ruka paused and became serious.

"You told me not to tell you, even if you made it this far, and remembered to even ask me that question of wanting to know," she said as the truck bounced back and forth on the road.

"I know if I ask you to say the words…?"

"If I say the words Doofus, you will lose me as your guide forever. Are you sure you want this, Dog"?

"I'm doing this for you, Ruka. I've discovered it's time. I need to let you go."

"Yob Doog", Ruka said the magic words and the story filled my mind's eye and then faded away.

"And…" I ask her, waiting for more.

"And if I tell you the rest, Dog, I'll have to kill you," Ruka told me from her crate, laughing.

"But I'm…" I started to say.

"I know who you are sir, but even when you were, Doofus, you weren't allowed in that building Delux went into for work all that time, remember?"

"I do remember. So Ruka… now that you told me, I guess this means good bye, my friend."

"Yes, God, it does. It has been an absolute pleasure serving you."

The entire time Ruka and I were talking, the police brought us into a room with some familiar equipment.

"I guess this is it, Ruka."

"This is it, God."

"Thanks again, Ruka. I couldn't have done it without you."

"Yes, you could've, you just like me."

"That I do."

"See you around, God," Ruka said, fading away

What will my next life bring me without the assistance of the one they call Ruka? I wondered as I faded away into life's dream or stream, or whatever this is, as everything faded away into white light.

I felt good. I felt whole. I felt complete. Then the beautiful light turned into darkness, and things got tight.

CHAPTER 24

CHOCOLATE TOES

Ah, that felt weird. Felt like I just walked through something. Where am I? It's dark now. I can't see. I'm inside a house. There's a lotta barking going on. I'm not alone from things moving around me. From the feel of it… I'm a dog again. Where's Ruka I wondered?

I tried calling out her name, but I still couldn't open my eyes or make much noise.

Puppy problems.

Ok… I need to remember… What do I need to remember?

Ruka, she's a friend.

She's my guide…

Fuck! Why do I know she's my guide? Shoot. I know I know this, but I also know I'm not supposed to know this. If I know this, something happened. Something went wrong.

She must have told me the secret.

Fuck, what have I done?

Quick, try to remember before your eyes open I told myself. I searched the darkness behind my eyes. Some of you call it the third eye. I know spirit lives there.

"Once again, Dog, as you will, the gift of life, shall be," a spirit voice said as its shaped, morphed into designs and fractals in the darkness of my consciousness.

A portal suddenly flashed in front of my eyes while two people sat in front of me in a car looking up at me.

Delux!

I remembered watching him watch a hole open up in the sky with a woman in the seat next to him.

Delux…What happened to Delux?

"Delux is in the hands of destiny, as are you now," Spirit guided me.

Yep. I fucked it up somewhere.

This is where you want to hit that reset button and try to remember all you can and live the previous life over again. Yet I felt my last life sucked. I was confused. What I think I realized is the more I try to control what's going on around me, the less control I have with what's going on inside of me. What's inside of me?

Ruka would ask me that.

Okay… Remember… Concrete garage, Ruka, portal, Delux, RV, skateboard, highway, lots of highways. The flash of the portal opened up in front of me in my head, pulling me straight into it.

"Oh my god!" Jobe screamed as I watched them like I was the portal. What the…

Bark!

My recollection of the past was interrupted.

Bark!

I lashed out at a man. I was running. I could not see the person behind me, but they were getting closer at as I bit a hand.

Bark!

I was leading a blind dog next to me.

Bark!

The light and images behind my new puppy eyes, was morphing from darkness to light. All these times I went to bed and saw the sun set and rise in previous lifetimes started to flash quickly through my mind.

I'm a puppy. Ruka. I'm in the military, I die. I'm a puppy, Ruka, I'm in training, I'm in the military, I die. Puppy... Big Man. Bite a kid. Ruka. Delux... die. What was this cycle I was on?

Still behind my sealed puppy eyes, the sunsets of my past turned into the RV parked by the beach. Tess was smiling, Delux was playing with Ruka all while the sun continued to rise and set around them.

The background of the three, changed to all the places we traveled to in an RV. Minnesota, Miami, New York. City, forest, beaches, towns...

Bark!

A flash in my mind and the images changed to a whole different setting. I had military handlers who were tough, no nonsense kinda people. I'm barking. I'm biting a man in a suit holding a stick to distract me and make me tougher. I'm taking orders as spit is coming out of my mouth and my claws are digging into the ground.

I'm being encouraged to attack more and more. I can feel the strength I have inside of me and the pain I can inflict. I could feel I liked being this savage beast.

Bark!

I was back with Delux again sitting on the floor of the treehouse. The three relationships Delux had flashed through my mind. His pain. His sorrow. His suicide.

Bark!

My eyes opened.

"Yep. I'm a puppy."

I have a tail. A long one. What's wrong with my ear? One wants to lay down while the other stands straight up.

A sibling punched and kicked me in the face. My eyes opened some more. I was gonna punch them back and when I did, they all learned real quick... I'm clumsy.

We're all clumsy in our puppy ways. My new brothers and sisters beat the crap outta me every day, but I also took part of the same pack that bit, punched, kicked, and scratched them as well.

"Move, bitch. You look like me, but you ain't me," one of my sisters said stepping on my face.

She was right, out of all us pups, she and I looked different than all the rest. The rest of my siblings were a light tan color, with dark faces. One of my brothers was already twice our size.

"Are you Ruka?" I asked my sister.

"Who motha fudda?" she said in a way Ruka would never talk with me, but I kinda thought would.

"Okay, it's not you, chill," I said.

"Damn right it ain't me."

"Are you fucking with me right now, Ruka?" I asked, trying to play with her.

"Get off me, kook. I'm not Duka, or whoever you're looking for. You're alone here on this one, kid. You only get assigned here if you fucked up somehow. Trust me, I know," my sister said.

Okay. I have a sister who's a bitch, but she calls me kid like Ruka did. She also said trust me, and for some reason I feel I shouldn't believe anyone who says that.

"Trust me"... What about "trust me" was I supposed to remember?

Delux's mom would call my sister a HAB if she were here. That stands for hard ass bitch. Yeah, that sister of mine is definitely a HAB. I laughed thinking of Delux's mom.

Grandma!
Wait, I don't have a grandma, how do I remember… that was…

Bark!

Flower beds, pool, grass, soft hands, treats. Delux! All these memories keep coming back to me. I must remember. What do they mean? I need to piece them together. Ruka. I thought again.
I shouted out her name amongst all my siblings, but again nothing.

"She's not here, bitch," my sister said to me, running past me kicking me in the side.

"Who you calling a bitch, you're the female here," I said to her.

"What'd you say to me?"

"You heard me. If you're not Ruka, leave me alone."

"Imma keep my eye on you, kid," she said walking away from me.

My sister and I looked alike but she was already a bit bigger than me, too. Three days would go by and all of us would be bigger. The one brother was gigantic already! He didn't say much. He was shy. I could tell he wanted to be left alone, so I moved around him without messing with him too much like the others would. I couldn't help it at times though, his tail was so long, fluffy and cute… It was way more fluffier then mine, or my sisters', so I had to bite his tail a few times to see where the tip was…
My sister was proud that she was already bigger than me. My other brothers and sisters who looked tanner, were smaller than both me and my sister, but we were all growing fast.
Momma had milk, and military training lady who was here with her son and two helpers, fed us some extra bits here and there every day while trying to figure out her new litter of maligators as she called us.

It was a scramble for food like anytime you are with other puppies just like you.

"Look at that one there with the floppy ear," military lady told her son.

"He seems like a scrapper for sure."

It was if they were talking about me, because my one ear was a bit floppy compared to the other one. Here, you had to be a scrapper in a cage full of tiny, furry alligators.

My biggest brother was the only calm one. My sister who looked like me was the killer of the group. She would bite and hold down the other siblings while she ate their food. If anyone walked by, even the military lady, she was in the front of the pack, barking ready to bite and take them down.

I could feel my puppy body getting stronger and stronger, every time we were let out to run around the facility. There was a ramp we could climb up and down outside when we got around the house we were kept at. One ramp was made for puppies, and one ramp next to it, was made for older, bigger dogs they said.

"Hey, our ramp is down here," my sister said to me.

"I'm already this far, I'm a keep going," I told her not looking back and jumping up onto the next step up, while all my siblings stayed on the kids ramp.

"Mom! look at him," the teenage boy of the military lady said, as I made it to the top.

"You're the feisty one, and look how handsome you are. I'm gonna keep you for me I think," she said holding me up in the air like I was Simba, Timba, or that little lion from lion king.

I accidentally just showed off, and now I think I'm stuck here. I think I'm supposed to feel some sort of bond or something. This lady wanted to keep me. But I didn't feel a connection with her like how I remembered I should with the people I help. I didn't know. There were so many distractions around me, it was hard to calm my puppy mind and feel the bond.

Delux flashed in my mind as the lady was putting me down. I remember not feeling the bond with Delux at first either... As soon as I touched the ground, a sibling ran into me at a good speed and knocked me over.

Bark! My mind flashed to something unfamiliar...

"Two years, Doofus! It took you two and a half years to finally accept us all," Ruka's voice said to me sharply.

Bark!

I think my memory is telling me I messed something up, but I can't remember how I messed it up. Or even when I messed it up.

Bark!

"You need to learn to let go. Just be." Ruka's voice came back into my head only softer this time.

Bark! I was back on my feet with my siblings again.

If I couldn't find Ruka, I know I made a mistake. What did I do?

"We're on our own here kid, toughen up already," my sister said to me.

Bark! I flashed back to an RV. I had to jump out to go to the bathroom my first morning.

Bark!

I came back to the present moment, and I ran and joined my siblings who were trying to climb on top of Mom. I felt life was going to be nice here. Mom loved us, and the military lady and her son treated us well. There was an obstacle course for us puppies around an even bigger obstacle course for the bigger dogs like my dad, outside the property where we were living. This looked like a true military training facility with all the structures you could climb on and rope bridges going from one platform to another.

I looked around and could see we were at the top of a mountain, deep in the jungle. I could see the ocean in one direction through a small opening of trees. The view didn't last long though. We were gathered up, put through training, and everything we did was assessed by military lady and her son.

I got extra attention from both of them because they wanted to keep me and my one floppy ear.

"Come on Viper, you got this," the lady said to me as she was directing me to climb the big ramp again.

Viper? They named me Viper. I liked to bite. It fit. Everything and anything was prey to my razor sharp teeth so I guess she thought of me as a venomous snake.

"With that tiny size of yours, you look like a snake all close to the ground," my sister said to me who was still noticeably taller than I was.

"Yeah? What'd they name you?" I asked.

"Onyx because I'm black and sexy, now move," she said pushing me out of the way.

One by one, day by day, we were trained, assessed, and allowed to eat and nap again. When we were awake, we all went from zero to 100 instantly except for the biggest brother. So he left first. Some couple came in and said they owned a hotel they wanted to keep safe, yet have a dog that could be social with their guests. Biggest brother was it the training lady said, and off he went, but he was back here and there for training with us later.

Then another, and another pup went to new homes. This selection process was normal for puppies, I guessed. Getting pawned off to strangers, hoping there was a bond.

You could see when some people showed up to look at the pups, there was an instant bond.

The puppy wanted that human so bad, it could not help itself. Jumping around, barking in excitement. Falling over because they could not control what was happening inside of them. Where do these people come from I wondered? We were deep in the jungle on a mountaintop.

I never was attracted to any energy of anyone who passed through. Even though I was already picked by the trainer lady to be hers, I tried to see if I could bond with anyone else who passed by.

Some pups were assigned to other training camps around the world somewhere based off of how well they went over the ramps, bridges, and biting the son, or one of the helper guys.

I remembered in that moment walking back to our cage, I spent a short lifetime in a box with Ruka discussing all the things I did wrong, and now, I was back in the military, ready to take orders all day to kill and destroy under the disguise of protection, but for who? And who was giving the orders?

I sat there looking out to the jungle waiting for Ruka's voice to come into my head and say something like "acceptance" or "let go" or something like that, but nothing. I could hear the breeze, the bugs, and the howler monkeys in the distance. I truly felt I was alone here.

Wait...

The concrete box with Ruka had the same monkey noises, I remembered. The more I tried to remember to piece something together, the more the thought faded away.

Military lady and the kid kept trying to bond with me. They would pick me up, hold me, try to snuggle me, but I didn't care. This life was gonna be intense and probably short, so I'd accept whatever, but don't expect me to be loving to humans. If I remembered anything from Delux, it was that love gets you nowhere.

My life was gonna be spent in a car with a police officer, sent off to bite the bad guy, or strapped to the chest of a military man jumping out of planes into areas that people want control over. I usually never came back from missions like those, but it doesn't matter when that's what you're trained for right. War defines what honor is, correct?

Sounds dumb if you ask me.

I felt used in that moment. As I looked around, this place is just that. A facility to train us maligators, for high-end police or military use in war. My name is Viper, and I'm the teacher's pick.

"You're the teacher's pet," my sister said.

"No, I'm not. She picked me, bitch, I didn't pick her."

"Yeah, whatever," she told me.

"I hear you got picked to protect a garage?"

"I've been picked to protect a little boy," my sister snapped back to me getting in my face but not doing anything.

Bark!

I had a flashback of a life where I bit a little boy after he forced himself into a little girl.
It then flashed to Ruka and I locked in a garage together with only one door to look out of.

Bark!

"Good luck with that gig. I'm sure I'll see you back here for training so you learn how to control your temper," I told my sister.

"Fuck you, teacher's pet," my sister said being carried away by a big man in cowboy boots and his son.

The guys who took my sister had good energy. I hope some rubs off on her, I thought as they walked away.
Military lady allocated all the puppies to someone, or somewhere. I was left with her and her son. It was fine. I learned to accept whatever came my way. No more hanging onto things. I let the memories that came up, fade away, and every day, I tried to bond with this lady or her son. They spent a lot of time with me, but I was ready for my task, whatever it was going to be. Just train me so I can figure it out, I thought.
I felt so accepting that I didn't care what was going to happen to me. All of my thoughts and memories were mixing around as I let them go and become cloudy dreams that were easy to let go of.

They called me a Malinois. A Pastor Belga. I'm here to work they said. So, I decided to take a nap. I learned to ignore people because I saw so many of them coming in and outta this place we trained in.

I ran around free a lot, minding my own business after following this lady wherever she went for a while. I could tell she enjoyed my company as she walked around her training facility with giant structures built out of trees, ropes, and used car tires.

"Dogs climb on this stuff?" I wondered, looking up at the giant world around me and the structures built here.

My lack of attention would pull me away to chase an insect or a breeze moving through the trees. I suddenly remembered I loved the outside. I was having a hard time remembering my past these days, and it didn't matter, but now all of a sudden, a few memories popped in as I felt the breeze go over my body.

I remembered a dog named Ruka. She and I were outside in a box for years. It felt like jail. I was mad at her... Why? Some guy... an RV that was my house... This guy would drive me around and take me outside every day... Everything faded away again.

I was back to the top of the mountain. I loved the outside I thought again as the breeze blew through the grass making me pounce on it before it could move again.

What was his name, I tried to remember the guy in my dream.

"Viper, let's go," trainer lady said, pulling me away from my thoughts and the wind in the grass.

Different people with different dogs would come and go for training here. Sometimes I could interact with the people or the dogs, but I'd rather be chasing grasshoppers, and jumping like they do into a large water bowl that was always full of cool water up here. It was hot up here on top of the mountain, and trainer lady kept me out here until noon.

Then it was in a cage outside with the rest of my siblings that were going away to special forces units around the world yet waiting in the process. I'd say how cool is that, but it sucks for them. I felt bad for some reason. I remember that life of taking orders and doing things that I wasn't sure I wanted to do. I didn't want that I felt.

This trainer lady was not just military, she was nice and helpful to people who had crazy dogs. Their owners would come for help, and she would help them. There were dogs coming in that were scared of their own shadow. Just two hours with trainer lady, the dogs would have a whole new perspective in life, making the owners have a new bond with their four-legged friends.

I looked at trainer lady, and her son was here as well. I didn't feel any kind of bond unfortunately. I just wanted to chase bugs and the breeze. Or climb on the ramps and teeter totter chasing down the son to bite him because he let me.

A guy on a motorcycle came up to the facility while I was outside. Trainer lady radioed to a helper and said something to them I didn't understand. Motorcycle guy came up to the training facility, and his dog was brought down from up at the house. He owned a bigger version of me. A strong male that could run this course with ease. I watched this dog climb a 30-foot vertical wall of tires and thorny bushes. The dog went across a bridge that moved from side to side. Up and down platforms that you had to jump to get onto them. He climbed walls, ladders, and cargo nets. This dog was the coolest thing I had ever seen.

I tried to mimic him, but I just sent myself headfirst into the bowl of water. I played it off like I meant to do it.

Another guy appeared wearing a big suit, and motorcycle guy's dog attacked the man in the suit and dragged him to the ground. It was terrifying and cool at the same time.

Every day here was outside in the open air. Training, outside. Playtime, outside. We even had a pool in the back yard, so a lot of my time was spent in there if I could be. I was clumsy on land, but a natural swimmer.

Another day, another motorcycle arriving. Moto's are the way to go here it seemed. All the workers used them, and this other guy with the Navy Seal dog that trainer lady was training used one. His dog even left with him one day sitting on the front of his lap... on the motorcycle! It was crazy. God, I hoped I'd get to do that stuff. Be that strong. Be that tough.

Another day, I took another trip into the big water bowl. I swear I meant to do that. "My one floppy ear isn't helping my image one bit," I said seeing my reflection in the water bowl.

Trainer lady met another motorcycle man while I was over to the side, minding my own business with the water bowl. I could overhear them talking about him wanting a dog. I thought he had a dog already, but before I could put any more thought into it, another grasshopper distracted me. I can get this one, I thought over hearing more of their conversation.

"I met Dave on the beach, with his big German Shepard looking puppy," he said. "It's a Belgian Malinois, and you are a breeder of them or something?"

"Yes, but at the moment I don't have any puppies left, they're all spoken for. Do you live here locally?"

"Yeah, I've been living here for about five years now," the guy said.

"What brought you to Costa Rica?" the lady asked him.

"Oh shoot, I'm in Costa Rica?" I thought like that meant something as I looked for the breeze in the water bowl.

"It's a long story," the guy laughed.

"Tell me, I like stories… Viper," the trainer lady said calling me over to them, but I ignored her.

I wasn't a fan of people's stories. They took too long, and people loved to tell them standing in the sun. Why do I remember that people do that? I shook it off and looked for the grasshopper. I took a breath, and let my thoughts go. Grasshopper! I pounced.

"I met a girl who I didn't know I was going to fall in love with, and she told me she wanted to drive an RV to Costa Rica. I only met her, because I was supposed to go DJ a party in Trinidad, but I didn't make it and was stuck in Miami for a few days with this girl. Fast forward some years when the girl and RV are no longer in the picture, when some random guy I helped at a job I had, told me to come to Playa *******. His name happened to be Trinidad. I thought that the Trinidad and Costa Rica connection was weird seeing it happened twice, so I took a trip here in 2011 with a homie to check it out. While we were here, I had déjà vu on the beach where it felt like I walked through an electrified screen of something you couldn't see, but I felt it like it was real but invisible. I instantly started crying on the beach like a little baby, and then I instantly felt like I remembered this place from a previous life or dream or something."

"Wow, that's wild."

"I was weeping on the beach that day. I never do that. It was so wild. Everything on the beach in that moment, was as clear as the night I first had the daydream of this place, that was causing the déjà vu, which I actually remember."

"Wait, so you remember having a day dream, that later came true as a déjà vu?"

"Yeah! After the beach déjà vu, my buddy and I went to the local restaurant in town. In the bathroom on the center to the mirror, was a big black and white sticker that said MINNESOTA, written graffiti style on it. Minnesota is where I'm from!" the guy said with excitement and emotion.

"What?" trainer lady said in disbelief. "What are the chances of that here?" she asked.

"When I left the bathroom to tell my homie, the day could not get any weirder. The local bartender offered me a job DJing there or in the big town close by. It's like destiny put me here, it's wild. I didn't surf, speak Spanish, or know anyone in this town, let alone country," the man talking to my trainer lady said.

I raised my head up from the grasshopper I had pinned under my paw and looked towards trainer lady and the guy who had his back to me.

"Someone graffitied that sticker and stuck it in the center of the mirror in the middle of nowhere Costa Rica. There was even a fat guy with no shirt on, drawn at the end of the word 'Minnesota', wearing overalls, holding a paint can and a paint brush that had a bit of red paint on the end. I swear I told myself this was my red pill moment, as I washed my hands."

"Wow. Crazy story."

"The sticker had so much detail, and you could still smell the sharpie smell from the sticker. So… here I am because of that day on vacation. I have a dog at home now that I rescued, so no worries if you don't have any more puppies," motorcycle guy said.

"Why are you looking for another dog?" trainer lady asked.

"My current dog is a great dog, but the worst companion, so I want to get her a friend and maybe she'll be happier, and I'll get a dog that might actually like me."

"Yeah I don't have any Malinois puppies at the moment, but I'm always coming across dogs that need good homes. I'm sure I can find you one."

"I was looking for a puppy like the one Dave has. I want to create that bond, you know. Like I saw in Chico at the beach with him. Plus, I need security. My motorcycle just got stolen not too long ago, and I'm a DJ so security would be nice," the guy said sounding like he had his hopes up for a dog.

"How much is a puppy usually?" the guy asked.

"Depending on training, but anywhere from five to ten grand usually."

I looked up again from the grasshopper I had pinned.
Trainer lady was now sitting on the ground with this motorcycle guy in the shade of the climbing structure where the tire swing was. I realized he was not the same guy with the other motorcycle and the Navy Seal dog we're housing here. I looked closer at him as every hair on the back of my neck rose with every step. I walked closer to them like I was stalking some prey. We didn't even have to make eye contact, I knew.

"Delux!" I shouted as I ran in my fastest puppy sprint, right into his chest at full speed.

"Holy shit, who is this little thing?" Delux said holding his arm to his chest and hand to his face to avoid my uncontrollable bites.

"Leave him be, don't touch him," trainer lady insisted.

"What? He's biting the shit outta me. Ow!" Delux said, pulling his hand out of my clenches.

"Delux! It's me! It's me! It's me, it's you! Oh my god, it's you! It's really you! I remember you. You're supposed to be dead! I thought you were dead!" I jumped up at his face mashing my face into a huge beard he now had hiding who he is.

"This little guy is fucking nuts! He's biting my face!" Delux let out.

"Don't touch him, let him bite you," trainer lady said with tears in her eyes.

Delux defended himself a little, but he let me push through his grip, and I was able to bite his big beard and lick his face. I wanted to rip the beard off and see the face I think I thought I remembered.

"Ha, I don't need to see it! I remember this energy," I screamed. I bit and licked him some more doing everything I could to push my way into his lap.

"I want this little guy's energy!" Delux said laughing.

I jumped and pounced some more and crawled all over his lap. I couldn't get enough of him. I rolled onto my back in his lap. I twisted around on my back rubbing his energy into mine. This is the bond I remembered we were supposed to feel when things are in alignment. I jumped up and bit at his face again and again. I was so fucking happy. I could feel he knew my bites were all my uncontrollable love I had for him.

"What do I do?" Delux asked trainer lady.

"Just let him do his thing with you. He is choosing you," she cried out.

"In the eight weeks we've had him, he's never done that with me or my son. That's your dog," trainer lady said full of tears and emotion. She wanted to keep me, I could tell… But this was Delux! Oh my god, this was Delux. I jumped and pounced some more on him, snuggling the shit outta every bite I could.

"Look lady, I have $400 in this pocket, and $100 in this one in case that wasn't enough. That's all I got. I'm not rich yet, and life is tough here in paradise. If you give me this dog, I'll ride back here and help pick up dog shit or whatever you need," Delux said.

"He's good at that, I swear," I told trainer lady, trying to help convince her as I snuggled Delux's lap.

"I'm handy, I can help build stuff. Whatever it takes. This little guy fucking loves me, holy shit, I have never experienced anything like this before," Delux said joyously as I still could not stop my body from rolling all over him.

"He chose you," she said again taking his $500.

"He's yours. We'll figure out the rest," she said.

"OH My Gosh!!!! Delux is back! Ba ba ba ba baaaaaa!!!" I shouted as I got my paws muddy in some mud.

"I think I'm gonna call you Chocolate Toes, look at your feet kid," Delux said to me.

Delux stuck me in his backpack that was placed against his chest, and off we went on his motorcycle, down the mountain. Back together again! I couldn't believe it looking up at him from inside a bag at eight weeks old with the bond of a lifetime.

"We gotta find Ruka!" I told him.

CHAPTER 25

ZARA

Delux and I went to the training facility late to drop off a dog Delux had picked up for trainer lady.

"Chako can't come out of the truck because Jose is here, but I can bring Zara down, and they can at least meet if you like."

"Sure, why not," Delux said sitting in his new 1988 truck he bought for me because I was getting too big for the motorcycle. I could see from the truck's side window, a short little pitbull pulled her way down from the main house dragging the helper guy.

"This is Zara," trainer lady said, introducing us.

"No fucking way! Ruka!" I shouted.

"Doofus!" she shouted at the same time.

"I can't believe it's you," I said, wagging my tail inside the jeep.

"I can't believe it's you," Ruka said, trying to climb into the truck and kiss my face.

"How can we tell Delux?" I asked.

"You mean you don't have that figured out yet? Doofus, what have you been doing all this time? How old are you, three?" Ruka asked, jumping her two front paws up on the truck again.

"I gotta fix some holes in the fence, and I will think about taking her. She seems a bit nuts. I'll let you know," Delux said to the trainer lady.

The following week, we went back to the training facility in the rain. Rain training is always fun because it's not as hot outside. With all the rain coming down, we went inside the main house to dry off.

"Hey, you wanna meet Zara again?" trainer lady asked just opening the door holding her back in a back room.

"Sure why not," Delux told her.

Zara came out and lay right next to Delux on her back. "Daddy, it's me," she told him.

"Wow she is like my old dog, Ruka, only super soft… holy crap, is she real?" Delux asked feeling under her neck.

"It's real." Ruka said.

I went over to join them and lay on my back licking her face. "It's her, Daddy," I told Delux.
We took Ruka, well Zara, and stuck her in the truck with us.

"Ok, remember. No kids. No cats. No animals smaller than her of any kind, and she will protect you and bite anyone who comes in the house," trainer lady reminded Delux.

"Holy shit, Ruka, what's wrong with you?" I asked her.

"Nothing. Just three years of trauma. Five different households could not handle me, and they were gonna put me down because of my anxiety. Nothing a little Delux love can't settle, right?"

"Right," I just agreed with her in fear she might attack me with her unsettled way of being.

"Ruka, how did we do?"

"It worked. We saved them both," Ruka said.

"Both?" I questioned.

"It's a long story, God."

"We have to get down a mountain, Ruka, we have some time."

"That day in the treehouse, Delux's phone made a noise it never had. That noise was enough to make him take the noose from around his neck and get down to answer the message."

"Wow, Good one…" I told her.

"On the other end of the call, was the restaurant guy in LA, he was crying while red-lining his engine, ready to drive off a cliff."

"What's up Jay, how you doing?" the man said over the phone.

"I'm good, how are you?"

"Oh, I'm fine."

"Are you sure, because it sounds like you're red-lining your engine there.

The man cried some more and composed himself while Delux sat on the floor of the tree house looking up at the noose he just took off his neck.

"Hey man, I got a message for your dad. Can you give your dad a message for me?"

"Yeah, sure man, what's up?"

"Can you tell your dad thank you for me?"

The engine in the background red-lined some more, making a loud noise on the phone.

"Hey, your engine is loud, can you shut it off and tell me that again?"

"Yeah sure, sorry man. Your dad, can you tell your dad thank you for me?"

"Sure, but thanks for what?" Delux asked, thinking about how he didn't write anyone a message.

"For everything he taught me back in the day when I worked at his restaurant. If it wasn't for him always shouting at us, and telling us to pay attention to detail, I never would have made it this far in life, and I just wanted to say thank you to him, that's all," he said.

"I can do that. Tell me, what's going on to spark this message and this call? It sounds like you're trying to blow up your motor, and you sound kinda sad."

"I'm having a real hard time right now, man. My girlfriend cheated on me with a guy I thought was my friend, and I just got fired from a restaurant that I started."

"Ah fucking women. They suck sometimes. What's going on with the restaurant. What happened?"

"They canceled my contract and stole all my ideas. This is the second restaurant I started as the head chef, and the owner steals my ideas and fires me after opening the restaurant and fucking my girlfriend."

The man on the other end of the phone cried some more, turned on his car, and revved the motor.

"Hey, hey, hey. Relax, man, don't do anything crazy," Delux said, looking up at the noose in the tree again.

"Look, if you can please just tell your dad thank you for me, I'd appreciate it."

"Hey, let's not do anything stupid now. I can hear your car in the background."

"I'm getting drunk, and I'm gonna to drive off the cliff here."

"No, you're not. Bro... Calm down. If you opened those two restaurants, Holy shit, what is your third restaurant gonna be? And forget about a chick for now man, if you open a restaurant, they will flock to you man, there are plenty of fish in sea, don't give up just yet."

The phone was silent except for the sound of the engine and the occasional suck-up of a runny nose.

"Dude, you're mad successful accomplishing what you've done. Who the fuck gets to say they opened a restaurant in a famous basketball stadium? It's seems crazy, but that's you! Who the fuck does that from our small little town?"

"Delux calmed the man down, they spoke a bit more, and Delux hung up the phone saving a man's life, as the man, unknowingly saved Delux's," Ruka tells me.

"Holy shit! What are the chances?" I asked.

"I still have a hard time believing it myself, but here we are. Broken bonds, yet we are all back together again.

"We did it, Ruka."

"No, you did it, Doofus. Can I call you that?"